## "YOU'VE BEEN CRYING,"

he said softly and reached into his pocket to withdraw a handkerchief. . . .

"I'm not crying!" she answered furiously, and waved away his attempt at aid. The last thing she wanted was to be seen as weak and chastened before this vividly alive man.

He looked at her skeptically but said only, "My mistake. Perhaps there's a cinder in your eye. Allow me to examine it for you."

"That won't be necessary," she answered, rapidly regaining her composure.

"But I insist." He moved to block her as she would have stepped past him. "I'm quite skilled and won't hurt you." He lightly lifted her chin with his forefinger. "Come, turn toward the light. A little more. Yes, that is better."

As he leaned toward her, Philadelphia forgot to resist. His bronze, absurdly handsome face was within inches of her own. Dark eyes fringed with long black lashes stared into hers, and she wondered if he could really look as deeply into another's soul as his gaze implied. "Ah yes, there is something painful here. . . ."

# BEGUILED

## LAURA PARKER

A DELL BOOK

Published by
Dell Publishing
a division of
Bantam Doubleday Dell Publishing Group, Inc.
1540 Broadway
New York, New York 10036

The trademark Dell® is registered in the U.S. Patent and Trademark Office.

ISBN: 0-440-21240-5

Printed in the United States of America

Published simultaneously in Canada

July 1993

10  9  8  7  6  5  4  3  2  1

OPM

# 1

## Chicago, April 1875

Senhor Eduardo Domingo Xavier Tavares had come to witness the final result of his revenge. Beneath the gilded and polychromed rococo tray ceiling of the Hunt mansion drawing room, the cream of Chicago society was gathered to participate in the auction of the late Wendell Hunt's bankrupt estate. Now that he had seen for himself the judgment on his enemy, he might have walked away and never looked back. Yet, he had stayed.

He had wanted victory over an old enemy. He had wanted justice served in a manner that no court of law would render to him. He had wanted an end to the years of planning and maneuvering and plotting. Three short weeks ago, with the front page headline announcing the failure of the First Bank of Chicago, that desire had been realized. Still, he had not counted on the one act he couldn't anticipate or prevent. One week later, Wendell Fletcher Hunt, founder and president of the First Bank of Chicago, had taken his own life.

It surprised Eduardo to realize that he was angered by the unnecessary loss of life. He had wanted Hunt to live, as he had, with the humiliation and uncertainty of life when all protection has been swept away. But Hunt had not had the courage to face that future, and instead chose suicide. For that, and that alone, Eduardo felt regret.

He knew Tyrone, his partner in revenge, would ridicule his remorse. Tyrone despised weakness of any kind. A man possessed of few words, a knife-edge temper, and a flare for attracting danger, Tyrone drew enemies like he drew women; both of whom came to him readily, a little sweaty yet eager to test his skill. He and Tyrone had met by chance and the only reason Tyrone had ever given for joining forces with him was that the three men Eduardo sought were his enemies also.

Eduardo cursed under his breath. He had learned the hard way that Tyrone had many enemies. Yet for seven long years no man could have been a more dependable ally, or more ruthless adversary. Preferring to remain in the background, Tyrone appeared like some spectral avenger only when needed. More than once each had saved the other's life and mutual respect had evolved into friendship, if one could call Tyrone a friend. For, if the pursuit of revenge had caused Eduardo's conscience to bend in unexpected ways, some secret rage had all but destroyed Tyrone's compassion long before they had met.

Eduardo's mind flinched away from an ugly memory of Tyrone interrogating a gunman who had been hired to ambush them. Unlike Tyrone, he had no stomach for cruelty. He never had. He didn't have the heart for mercilessness, though he'd learned to be merciless. He didn't belong in the role of avenger, yet it had been chosen for him years before by the strongest tie a man may know, the bonds of blood. He wasn't a vulture, he didn't need to pick his enemy's bones to be satisfied. He was a joyous man by nature, a lover of beauty and peace and harmony. So why was he here?

Eduardo glanced toward the French doors of the drawing room, which stood open to relieve the warmth of the afternoon. Through the doorway the garden looked inviting with its colorful rows of hollyhocks, gladiolus, and pansies. He ignored the first murmur of the crowd, for he wanted badly to retire to that garden to enjoy a cigar. But the murmuring grew, drawing his attention away from his own ruminations. And then he saw her.

She stood framed in the doorway, a tall slender silhouette swathed in midnight's hue. He didn't need to be told who she was. Without ever having seen her, he knew that she must be the reason he had come.

Though every feature and detail of her was veiled, she seemed more vibrant and alive than anyone he'd ever met. There was fury in her stance, a patrician's pride in the tilt of her head, and a singular calm that betrayed a gale of emotion held strictly in check. Amazed, he felt the power of her emotion wash over him. It tugged at him like the subtle but relentless pull of the moon upon the sea. When she began moving into the room he nearly stepped forward to intercept her. Then he heard one of the auctioneers call her by name and the connection was snapped by reality. *Miss Philadelphia Hunt.* Of course she was. Of course!

Intrigued, he moved back against the far wall, the better to observe the scene. He couldn't hear her words nor the auctioneer's response, but when she turned and walked down the aisle to take the last seat, he again felt a quickening within himself. He knew that he should leave now, but he felt the anticipation a theatergoer experiences moments before the curtain is to rise. Something was going to happen and nothing on earth would keep him from witnessing it.

Philadelphia Hunt paused in the doorway to the drawing room of her former home as the murmurings of the crowd swept over her.

"I can't believe that she's here."

". . . After all that's happened . . ."

"Suicide! A most unnatural business . . ."

"She might spare us the embarrassment . . ."

"What is one to expect, after all, when the father . . . ?"

"Evicted, that's what they told me. And here she is, bold as brass . . ."

Their words whipped her like frigid gusts from a wintery gale, yet she scarcely felt them. The relentless shocks and horrors of the past weeks had driven her into an emotional isolation that was far colder. Dressed in mourning, the symbol for her deepest and purest emotion, she felt invulnerable to their stares. There was only one reason why she was here. Until a week ago this mansion had been her home. Now it was lost to her, just as her security and her peace of mind were forever lost. So, let them look and know that she, the daughter of Wendell Fletcher Hunt, was among them.

Despite her resolve, molten anger began to seep through the fissures of her glacial calm as she moved across the parquet floor under their unfriendly stares. Once these people had counted themselves among her father's many friends and been glad for the association. Now they were only so many vultures come to fatten themselves on the remains of another's life.

Clenching her gloved hands into fists, she refused to look left or right as she passed familiar faces. She would show them the utter contempt in which she held them for their cowardly desertion of her father in his hour of need. She was a Hunt, representing three generations of Chicago Hunts. Let them look and whisper. Let them scoff, if they dared. She knew something that they did not. Someone in this room was responsible for her father's ruination. Someone in this room might even be a murderer.

"Miss Hunt!"

Philadelphia paused as a tall thin man hurried forth to intercept her. He was dressed in black as severe as her own. If not for the ruby stick pin in his cravat and the small scarlet figures in his silver cloth vest, he might have been mistaken for a mourner also. But he was not. He was another necessary evil with which she must deal. "Mr. Hoover."

The man smiled tentatively but his graying brows were lowered in disapproval. "Why, Miss Hunt, you shouldn't —that is, we didn't expect you."

Philadelphia felt her face form into the lines of civility despite her present anger as she said, "I'm quite amazed myself, Mr. Hoover, but as I'm here and you're now aware of it, shall we begin?"

Before Hoover could reply his partner hurried over, his too-large eyes bulging slightly in their sockets at the sight of the elegantly clad young woman. "Why, Miss Hunt, this is an unexpected pleasure." His smile wavered as he exchanged glances with his partner. Then, in a gesture meant to convey paternal concern, he reached for Philadelphia's elbow but she deliberately shifted to make his gesture impossible to complete.

Embarrassed, he cleared his throat as he lowered his arm. "Miss Hunt, we're delighted to see you, of course. However, I must warn you, you may find the events of the afternoon most distressing. It might prove wiser for you to wait in another room. Better yet, my carriage can take you to a place of your choice. I promise to report to you myself immediately following the—uh . . ."

"*Auction,* Mr. Sinclair. I can say the word. After all, it's your business and the sole reason for our dealings together. My household is being put up for public auction this afternoon. Everything! From the pots and pans in the scullery to my silk drawers in the Ruby Bedroom's armoire."

She found she enjoyed the shock that mottled the man's fair complexion. Surprise and initiative; she must remember to use them often in the future. A good weapon was rare enough to be prized.

She deliberately raised her voice a fraction to satisfy the curiosity of those nearby who were obviously straining to catch her words. "I'll stay, Mr. Sinclair, because I wish to make certain that you get top dollar for the things I've placed in your care. I see by your expression that you disapprove of my mention of money. Regrettably, I'm no longer able to abide by the dictates of the polite society in which I've been reared, for I'm both destitute and in great debt. It may also be poor form to mention debt, but then mine are notorious, wouldn't you say?"

Not waiting for his response, she turned and started down the aisle between the rows of dozens of gilt-back chairs that filled the room. Their royal blue velvet upholstery was familiar to her. They belonged in the ballroom. Before the day was done, they would belong to one of the people who sat upon them.

She had deliberately chosen this room for the auction because of its western exposure. Crystal, paintings, silks, silver, and jewels would be seen in their glory in the afternoon light. Her father had always been particular in his choice of setting for his art collection. He had been a passionate collector of objects both beautiful and rare. And he had shared his love of beautiful things with her, his only child. Left motherless at birth, her fondest memories of her often-absent father were on those evenings when he had returned from one of his frequent trips and would unveil for her his latest acquisition. How his eyes would light up in anticipation of her reaction. Because it pleased him, she had begun at a very early age to learn by heart the history of each piece, her accumulating knowledge a connection to the kind but sometimes remote man who was her father.

Philadelphia took a deep breath, her vision awash in tears. She mustn't think of her father now. It made her head ache and her chest tighten. She was among enemies. They had destroyed her father, and his reputation. She wouldn't give them the satisfaction of a single tear. She took the last seat in the last row. Only at the last instant did she realize that her knees were buckling and that, if not for the chair, she might have fallen.

Recovering quickly, she willed herself to sit perfectly still as the auction was called to order by Mr. Hoover. She knew which piece would be put up for sale first. It was her least favorite in her father's vast collection; a medieval German chandelier made of stags' horns and topped by a cast-silver siren's bust. He said he had bought it because he simply couldn't believe that anything so meticulously constructed could be so unredeemably ugly. And so it was. A smirk tugged at her mouth as the auctioneer brought it forward. It was a revolting piece and she hoped that it sold for a fortune.

Yet no offers were forthcoming when the auctioneer called for the first bid. Undaunted, he called a second time for an opening bid of fifty dollars but the audience remained silent.

"Now, ladies and gentlemen, we're here for an auction," Henry Hoover began with an encouraging smile. "Perhaps you, sir, will be kind enough to open the bidding at fifty dollars?" He gestured toward a gentleman in the front row.

"I'd not give you a half-dollar for that monstrosity!" the man replied.

"Fifty cents!" cried a man sitting in the second row.

"Fifty-one cents!" came a shout from farther back.

"Really, gentlemen!" Hoover chided with a tone of long-suffering patience. "The value of the silver alone exceeds a hundred dollars."

"Two dollars!" offered the man in the front row. "That'll put me ninety-eight to the good on the debts owed me by Hunt's bank!"

This drew laughter from a few of the bolder gentlemen, though others seemed constrained by Philadelphia's presence.

"May I have a bid of fifty dollars?" Hoover called again, his voice a little strained.

"You won't get it," the two-dollar bidder answered and rose to his feet. "You're holding this auction in order to settle Hunt's debts. You mustn't expect his victims to help you do it! Wendell Hunt stole from us! Don't expect us to give him much more!" As the speaker shook his fist at the auctioneer, his cry was taken up by several other gentlemen who rose in turn.

Philadelphia listened incredulously. She'd known most of these men all her life. They were men of banking and commerce, men of action and wealth who carried weight and demanded respect in the city of Chicago, but now they were threatening to become an unruly crowd.

As the auctioneer banged his gavel for order, the wives who had accompanied their spouses lay restraining hands on their husbands' arms and the noise subsided.

"May I have further bids on the item?" Hoover asked hoarsely.

"You've had the final bid!" said the man in the front row. "I bid two dollars and two dollars it is! Now bring out the good stuff. I've five or ten dollars left. That should buy me a handful of emeralds and a diamond tiara!" His guffaw was followed by demands from the others for the immediate auctioning of Wendell Hunt's famed jewel collection.

Philadelphia watched impassively as Mr. Hoover wiped his brow with his handkerchief and then signaled his partner, who brought forth half a dozen jewelry cases on a silver butler. But, when Hoover opened the first case to display an elaborate pearl collar with a paved diamond clasp, she caught her breath. She had forgotten about that piece. It shouldn't be for sale. It was her father's favorite and had been promised to her on her wedding day.

"That's more like it!" said one of the audience. "Now that's something I want! I open the bidding with one dollar!"

"Now be fair about it, Angus," said another of the

men. "You know it's worth at least—twice that! Two dollars!"

In dawning horror, Philadelphia realized that there was a conspiracy underfoot. As revenge against their bank losses, these men planned to purchase a fortune in art and jewelry for little more than change.

"No! Stop this auction! Stop it immediately!"

Philadelphia sprang to her feet and hurried toward the front of the room. She saw amazement register on the auctioneer's face but she was beyond self-consciousness. She caught up the lovely pearl choker from its velvet bed and, throwing back her veil, turned to face the bidders.

For a long moment she stood perfectly still, daring anyone to speak yet scarcely knowing where to begin herself. The sea of faces before her was suddenly blurred and unfamiliar. "You say you won't pay extravagantly for the belongings of a bankrupt debtor. That is your privilege. What is not your privilege is the right to insult this beautiful piece with your ignorance of its worth!"

She moved forward and held the pearls high so that they cascaded from between her fingers. "Look! Look at them. I hold before you three dozen perfectly matched pearls of exquisite size and color. But that isn't all."

For the first time she looked directly at a member of the audience and an old kindly face gazed back at her. She cast him a pleading look and her voice softened. "Dr. Richards! You must remember the story my father told you of these pearls. He'd just come back from a trip to San Francisco. I remember distinctly that he invited you to dinner especially to show you his latest purchase."

"Did your father use bank customers' funds to purchase them?" inquired a man's rough voice from the rear of the room.

Philadelphia looked up sharply. "Who said that?" When there was no reply she moved to the center aisle. "Are you, whoever you are, so much a coward that you would hurl insults yet dare not show your face?"

There was a momentary shuffling of feet before she saw a man in a brown plaid suit rise to his feet. "I don't know you, sir, and by the look of you, I don't care to. This is an auction. Do you have the value of these pearls in your purse or are you another of those spying reporters?"

It was a lucky guess, but when he began shouting at her about the rights of the press to seek the truth, she knew that she was right. Those nearby murmured in protest. The cream of Chicago society was no more fond of the press than she.

Sensing a victory, she pointed a finger at the man. "This is a private home; until this auction ends it is still *my* home, and you, sir, are not welcome in it." She turned to the auctioneer. "Mr. Hoover, I demand that you eject this man, immediately."

She turned away and shut her eyes to compose herself as the reporter was hustled from the room by two of the auctioneer's assistants. When the doors were firmly closed against him, she opened the diamond clasp of the pearl collar and placed the necklace about her own neck. As she walked forward she began to speak in a soft but clear voice.

"My father bought this necklace in Chinatown from a pearl merchant who told him the tale of its history. Long before they were formed into a collar, these pearls saved the life of an aristocratic lady. Her name was Mei Ling, favorite daughter of the Chinese emperor."

She hadn't meant to tell the story but she'd always loved it and the telling came naturally. "Many years ago, China was a country of many warlords with many loyalties, not all of them to the emperor. One day the most powerful of the warlords rode into the capital city with his army as an honored guest of the emperor. Like everyone else in the land the warlord had heard of Mei Ling, famed for her beauty. Each day, he asked the emperor to bring his daughter to court so that he might be dazzled by her perfection. Each time the emperor promised to consider it. But when after several days she didn't appear, the warlord decided to find out for himself if the rumors of her beauty were true.

"A man of great cunning and daring, he climbed the walls of the women's apartments one evening and saw Mei Ling with her handmaidens. Stricken not by love but by greed to possess the rare beauty of the lady, he instantly devised a plot to kidnap her.

"The emperor was inconsolable but unable to summon enough men in his army willing to do battle against the famous warlord. Yet the emperor was wise enough to know that greed, not love, had spurred the warlord to the theft of his daughter. And so, the emperor offered to the nobleman who could ransom the princess the reward of 'his heart's desire.' Many went forth to the warlord's fortress, bringing rare silks and perfumes and porcelains. The warlord put each of the men to death and kept their ransoms—and Mei Ling.

"Finally, in utter desperation the emperor offered 'his heart's desire' to any man in the country who could save his daughter. To his amazement, only one man came forth, a lowly pearl fisher, a man too unworthy to be allowed inside the walls of the capital city under ordinary circumstances. Once assured that the emperor would keep his promise even to him, the pearl fisher set out for the warlord's fortress. A month went by and when nothing was heard from the warlord or the pearl fisher, everyone, including the emperor, assumed that the man had been killed like all the rest.

"But, on the thirty-sixth day, to everyone's utter amazement, the pearl fisher came up the road to the capital city wearing only his loincloth and reed sandals, and leading a yak with Mei Ling on its back. When the story was told, it was more amazing than a fairy tale."

Philadelphia touched the necklace. "The ransom the pearl fisher offered the warlord was the first of these pearls. The warlord agreed that the pearl was indeed beautiful but said that Mei Ling was worth more than a single pearl. The pearl fisher replied that this pearl was the only one that had ever been brought up from its secret bed because he feared to dive there. There was a fierce dragon who guarded the pearls. The warlord asked how many pearls there were. Dozens, the pearl fisher assured him, and perhaps, if the warlord came to protect him, they could all be gathered up.

"Greed is a powerful lure," Philadelphia said with deceptive calm as her gaze searched the audience. "The pearl fisher saw the greed shining in the warlord's eyes and knew that he had chosen the right lure. So that no other would learn the location of the pearl bed, the pearl fisher slyly suggested that the warlord alone accompany him. The selfish warlord agreed.

"When they reached the diving place, they set up camp. Each day the pearl fisher made a single dive, bringing up an oyster that produced a perfect pearl. But, on the thirty-fifth day, the pearl fisher came up empty-handed. He said that the monster in the deep was angry and would no longer allow him to search for pearls. Even when threatened with the loss of his life, the pearl fisher refused to go into the water again.

"Next to greed and selfishness, pride was the warlord's greatest sin. He said that he was not afraid and would dive for the pearls himself. And so the warlord dived in and the sea closed over him. The pearl fisher waited a full day but the warlord was never seen again."

Philadelphia paused for breath but the woman nearest her was too anxious to hear the end of the tale to wait. "Well? What happened to the warlord?" she demanded impatiently.

Philadelphia lifted her eyes. "Why, the monster of the deep took him, a treacherous riptide that not even the warlord could defeat."

"And the pearl fisher?" another prompted.

"He achieved his heart's desire," Philadelphia an-

swered. "He'd known of that pearl bed all his life but had
been afraid to dive there because of the riptide. Love and
loyalty to his emperor gave him what he wanted, the
courage to dive for the most beautiful and perfect pearls
in all the world."

"Did he marry the emperor's daughter?" asked another.

Philadelphia shook her head. "He was already married
with half a dozen children. But he did become the emperor's personal pearl fisher, and his family became famous for producing the most beautiful and lovely pearls
ever found." She took off the necklace and held it up
once more. "These are from the pearl fisher's legendary
catch. Will you allow them to be sold for a mere pit-
tance?"

A howl of protest went up from the crowd.

"I demand that the bidding continue," said a woman in
the third row. "I bid five hundred dollars!"

The second and third bids were shouted out before the
auctioneer could reach his podium.

"Seven hundred and fifty dollars!"

"Eight!"

"Nine!"

"I bid a thousand!"

Philadelphia lowered the necklace as the sound of the
bidders' cries filled the air. The bidding concluded
quickly but not before a bidder offered five thousand dollars for the collar of pearls. She hadn't the heart to face
the man who had bought the pearls. It was enough that
they had drawn a respectable price. She handed them
over to the auctioneer without a backward glance and
headed for the door.

Suddenly she was exhausted, wanting only to be as far
away from the auction as possible. Her anger was gone,
her aloofness had melted away. She felt fragile and vulnerable, weakened by the memories of what could never
be again. She hadn't meant to share her intimate feelings

with the people at this auction. They didn't understand, couldn't appreciate the great and small joys she and her father had shared beneath this roof. Like the Chinese warlord, they were motivated by greed and covetousness. The realization made her feel ill, as though she'd taken part in some sordid transaction.

She picked up her pace, wanting only to be free of the noise and chatter and heat, yet as she reached the door she heard her name called.

"Miss Hunt!" Mr. Hoover hurried up behind her. "You aren't leaving, Miss Hunt? Not when you've been so successful."

She turned to him. "You were right. I shouldn't have come."

"Why, to the contrary. You've been a great success. Already people are inquiring about the other pieces of jewelry. Are there stories about any of them?"

Philadelphia sighed. "Yes. Everything my father bought was chosen for its uniqueness."

"Then won't you share with them a few of those reasons?" He added with a speculative look, "Anything you can do to increase sales will help alleviate your father's debt."

She looked away from him. Because she believed him to be innocent, she had publicly vowed to pay back every cent that her father had been accused of embezzling. That debt was shockingly large. She had been warned that the auction and sale of the house probably wouldn't cover it all. But, if she remained to encourage the bidding, perhaps she would owe that much less when it was over.

She slipped her hand into the pocket of her jacket and felt the folded packet of letters she had carried with her constantly since the moment she'd found her father's body. He'd been clutching the letters in his left hand, while a still-smoking pistol had been in his right. The police didn't know about the letters. No one knew of the letters. And no one would, until she'd learned the identity of the sender, or senders.

She gave her head a slight shake. "Very well, Mr. Hoover. I will stay if you think it will help."

Eduardo Tavares paced impatiently on the flagstones of the garden while waiting for the last bidders to claim their merchandise. The auction had become an excruciatingly long process. If not for the stamina of Philadelphia Hunt, he doubted that even the most avid buyers would have stayed once the afternoon sun rode low enough to slant its rays into the drawing room where the drapes weren't drawn. Yet, he couldn't leave. Nothing would have dragged him away as long as she continued to speak in her low, rhapsodic voice.

She was like Scheherazade, spinning her tales and weaving spells that wrapped the room in a timeless landscape where only her stories, told with intelligence and imagination, held sway. He'd been beguiled, transported beyond the past and future, into a single-minded desire to listen to her forever. Then she had brushed past him as she left the room, her veil thrown back, and everything he thought he knew about the moment altered.

Eduardo thought himself familiar with life in all its guises. He knew women of every sort and was certain he had experienced emotions to the limits of his ability to perceive them. Yet at the sight of Philadelphia Hunt's loveliness some new emotion had pierced him as cleanly as an arrow to the recesses of his being. Her eyes were a mosaic of bright amber and dark shadows, gleaming with unshed tears. Currents of rich honey-gold and deeper molasses-brown ran through her thick chestnut hair. She was more than pretty. She possessed that rare enigmatic beauty that makes women jealous and even the boldest men a little shy.

In that instant, he had also made a second disturbing

realization. In ruining Wendell Hunt's life, he had also ruined hers.

Until the anguished bewilderment that augmented her beauty touched a hidden chord within him, he had not allowed himself to consider the consequences of his actions. His need for vengeance had been a blinding rage directed toward the men who had stripped him of family, home, and nearly his life. If he were honest, he could not say he would have acted differently. Hunt deserved his fate. Yet, an innocent girl did not deserve the same.

Eduardo turned to gaze back at the house as expectation ran like new wine through him. Earlier Philadelphia Hunt had faced down a roomful of wrathful men and women who had come to buy her family's possessions. He admired her courage. Yet he doubted she understood the extent of the scorn and degradation a hostile world could heap upon a destitute and unprotected young woman.

Suddenly he knew what he must do. Circumstance had taught him to be brutal. Perhaps in helping Philadelphia Hunt he would learn once again how to be kind. He had no idea of what he would say to her to persuade her to allow him into her life. He only knew he must find a way.

The absurdity of his thoughts brought laughter from deep within him. Tyrone would think him mad. Perhaps he was, or perhaps he was thinking rationally again for the first time in many years.

Philadelphia waited until even the auctioneers were gone before she took a final walk through her home. Upstairs, the rooms were nearly bare, most of the furnishings gone in the auction. The house seemed even larger than its twenty-five-room size. As her heels resounded along the empty hallways, the echoes sent chills up her arms.

She paused before descending the main staircase, overwhelmed by the emptiness. It hung in the still air, the isolation of abandonment. It was as if not only her father but also her future had died. She was ineffably alone.

When a dark, upright figure emerged from the shadows of the entry hall below, she suppressed the instinct to cry out. After all, the house had been full of people throughout the day. This must be one of the workmen, she supposed.

Yet he didn't move like a servant. He moved with a fluid, long-legged grace unfamiliar to her. As he came forward to stand at the foot of the stairs, the late afternoon sunlight streaming in through the transom above the front door fell across his features.

She saw that the man's face was broad with high cheekbones, a wide brow, and a full, well-shaped mouth. His hair was coal-black, strongly waved, and brushed straight back from his brow. His skin was unusually dark, the color of polished cherry wood. Everything about him was strange, exotic, and strongly masculine. Even his clothing was unusual. He wore a short fitted jacket that ended at his waist, accenting broad shoulders and narrow hips encased in tapered trousers. This was no workman. Everything about him hinted at breeding, wealth, and, surprisingly, danger.

"Who are you?" she demanded with a confidence the day had worn thin.

He did not reply but she saw him smile as he ascended the steps slowly, and the charm in that smile caught her again by surprise. It was a strong smile, competent, confident, and oddly reassuring. When he was standing only two feet from her, he executed a formal bow, then offered her his hand.

"Permit me, Senhorita Hunt." His voice was slightly inflected by an accent she couldn't name. Yet she took the hand he extended to her, unable to think of a reason not to.

They descended the staircase in silence, and it never occurred to her that she should question the reason for his presence. When they reached the bottom, Philadelphia quickly withdrew her hand from his because, despite her glove, the warmth of his hand had reached her skin. Her palm tingled in a way that made her want to rub the sensation away. When she looked up to see his dark gaze regarding her with an intensity that was far from reassuring, an inkling of self-preservation made her move away.

He stepped quickly to reach the door ahead of her, and to her relief he opened it. As she walked past him, she saw the laugh lines about his dark eyes deepen with his smile as he said, "Go with God, *menina.*"

A private coach stood parked across the street from the Hunt residence. For nearly six hours the coachman had waited on his perch. Twice he had climbed down to water his horse but he had not spoken to his fare. The man who had hired him had given him a ten dollar bill, an address, and said he was not to be disturbed under any circumstances. The coachman suspected the gentleman had dozed off and forgotten the time.

Yet anyone who knew the passenger could have told the coachman that the man known simply as Tyrone never slept. He had the instincts of a jungle cat, could remain in apparent indolence for hours while in reality he watched and waited with concealed claws for the moment to strike.

It was dusk when the last two people exited the house. A curtain within the private coach moved a fraction to allow a better view. The woman passed through the gate and then turned to walk with quickened steps down the sidewalk. Following at a slower pace was Eduardo Tavares. He paused to watch the woman until she turned the corner and disappeared. Only then did he hail a passing cab and, entering it, ride away. A moment later the curtain of the private coach closed. A light flared in the dark interior. The brightness wavered briefly, the faint crackle of tobacco accompanying the action, and then dimmed.

Tyrone chewed thoughtfully on the end of his cigar. He had not wanted to intrude on Eduardo's moment of triumph and though he could not stay away, he had been content to remain apart from this final hour of revenge. Eduardo needed it, to look upon the vanquished and feel the sense of closure. Eduardo was an emotional, passionate man. That passionate nature made him a loyal ally, a fierce fighter, and the only human being Tyrone had ever allowed himself to think of as a friend. He envied Eduardo those emotions he denied himself. Together they had become wealthy men, gathering up the spoils of the enemies they had defeated and putting them to their own respective uses. But now that the need for revenge that had brought them together was gratified, he suspected Eduardo would want what he had so long denied himself: home, peace, and family. That meant breaking with the past and association with men like himself.

Tyrone's heart beat no swifter as he thought of losing Eduardo's friendship but his cigar trembled slightly in the hand holding it. The raw instinct for survival that had kept him alive many times when he should have died told him that they were not yet done with one another. He felt not a sense of closure, but the yawning of a new trap. While he trusted few other emotions, he never discounted fear. Yet, until he had discovered the reason behind his disquiet, he would leave Eduardo alone.

A sudden chuckle rumbled softly through the coach. That long look Eduardo had given the woman answered one question. He now knew where to look for Eduardo when the time came: between the soft thighs of a new love.

". . . and you see, of course, my situation is untenable."

Harry Collsworth ran a hand nervously through his golden hair, then thrust both hands into his trouser pockets as he paced the small parlor of Philadelphia's rented rooms.

"You're suggesting that we not end our engagement permanently?" Philadelphia asked calmly.

"No, no, of course not! What sort of a man would that make me if it were to get about that I'd dropped my fiancée in her hour of need?" He stopped before her, tossing her a grateful smile. "I knew you'd be sensible, Philly. You're always so very sensible about things."

"Yes. Sensible." She stripped off her left glove and removed from the third finger a small but decently mounted ruby. "You'll want your ring."

Harry gulped at the sight of the ring she held out to him. His father had told him not to come home without it, but now that he realized exactly what he was doing, he felt cheap and cowardly. "That really isn't necessary, Philly. It's only temporary. You keep it until I can put it back where it belongs."

"It belongs in your pocket, or in the rubbish bin!" She

was a little shocked by the tight anger that colored her words. She'd been expecting Harry to break off their engagement. In fact, it had been the one thing she hadn't been dreading. Yet now that it had come, she was quite thoroughly disgusted by the craven act. "Don't dissemble, Harry. Your affections were never engaged."

He looked as though she'd slapped him, and she was instantly sorry. It wasn't his fault that he'd found himself in the thick of a scandalous liaison. As for the rest, she was as much to blame as he for entering into an engagement whose suitability had more to do with family fortunes and connections than like-minded hearts.

She rose and held out the ring. "Don't look so stricken. I'm only saying what you're too kind and gentle to say." When he didn't move to take it, she tucked the ring into his breast pocket. "I don't expect you to saddle yourself with a wife whose father has been falsely accused of a terrible crime. You've your future to think of. You've expectations. Your father hopes to see you win a seat in Congress. I'd only be a burden, a hindrance, a millstone. Besides, I don't think I'd like politics."

She turned him by the shoulder and pushed him gently toward the door. "Now run along and tell your father that I wish you nothing but good."

Harry Collsworth faced her when he reached the door, and there was hurt and puzzlement in his fair, handsome face. His father had warned him that Philly might fight the breaking of the engagement. After all, she'd lost everything else. She would be desperate, might even threaten to sue him for breach of promise, and scandal was the last thing a promising young lawyer could afford. But Philly hadn't threatened anything of the sort. He had known she wouldn't and he was proud of her. Just wait till he told his father how she'd given him the ring without his even asking for it. He felt his cheeks begin to burn as he remembered the check he carried in his pocket. And to think he'd nearly been persuaded by his father into trying to buy her off.

"I do love you, Philly. I did and I do. I won't think of it as over between us. This'll pass. People will forget. In time. You'll see."

"Good-bye and good luck, Harry," she said with calm finality.

"Bye, Philly." Feeling in equal amounts chastened and relieved, Harry slipped out of the room and out of her life.

Only when he had gone did Philadelphia allow her shoulders to slump. How much more was she to endure?

A moment later a knock sounded on the door and she rose to open it reluctantly. If it were Harry, begging her to take back his ring, she thought she would slap his face. "Why, Sally, you're right on time."

A small woman in a black cotton dress and bonnet stepped inside, surveyed the tiny room, and sniffed. "Goodness gracious! I've seen closets bigger than this."

Philadelphia smiled. "Perhaps so, but they were probably less expensive. I never realized the potential in renting closet space until now."

The Hunts' housekeeper marched over to a cabinet and ran her hand along the surface. "Dust! Where's the maid who's seeing after you these days? She'll think twice about not leaving a room in order once I've finished with her."

"I'm afraid there isn't one." Philadelphia turned away. "Anyway, there's nothing left to see to, aside from my black drapery."

The small woman's face went white. "Oh, Miss Philly, I didn't think!"

Philadelphia turned back, forcing a bright smile to her lips. "Now, Sally, you mustn't depress me. I sent for you to give you your wages. I took care of the other servants before the house was vacated."

Sally sniffed, drew out a white handkerchief, and blew

into it. "Who'd ever have thought I'd live to see this day? It's terrible and wrong. I served your papa all your life. I'd work for you for free if I could."

Philadelphia resisted the desire to put her arms around the woman. One moment of weakness and she knew she'd dissolve into tears. Harry had been easier to deal with because there'd been her own anger to work against. She pulled a purse from her pocket. "Here's all but the last week of your wages, Sally. I promise to send you the difference within the month."

Sally stared at the purse as though it were a baited trap. "But if it's all you have, how will you live?"

"I've prospects, Sally."

The older woman brightened. "Then it's worked out. You're going to your cousins in St. Louis?"

Philadelphia's smile soured. "I'm afraid not. They don't relish the idea of housing the subject of gossip beneath their roof. There are the children to think of."

"Then what will you do?"

Philadelphia absently raised a hand to massage her throbbing temples. "Right now I'm going to have a cup of tea and then go to bed. It's been a difficult day."

Sally eyed the young woman closely and wasn't pleased by what she saw. "You look thin. Are you ailing?"

"Don't fuss, Sally. I just need rest. Now take this purse. Don't make me beg you."

Sally hesitated, but after all, there wasn't anything she could do. She took the money reluctantly. "The Lord keep you, Miss Philly. And if you need anything—"

"Just keep me in your prayers. I mean to clear my father's name and that won't make me any more popular in this city."

"You be careful, Miss Philly."

"I intend to do just that. Do you like your new job, Sally?"

"Yes, miss. I'm working for Dr. Ames. His wife's a bit of a chatterbox, but I know how to shut her up."

The two women exchanged knowing glances for, undoubtedly, Mrs. Ames's favorite conversation was the Hunt scandal.

When Sally was gone, Philadelphia leaned against the door and closed her eyes, waiting for the painful throbbing to subside. She hadn't cried in more than a week now. It didn't seem worthwhile to cry over each and every difficult task. Her tears would never stop. The day had been abominably long but now it was over.

The knock sounding against her ear made her jump. "Who is it?" she demanded.

"A friend," came the masculine reply.

Philadelphia put her hand on the lock to secure it even as she said, "My friends have names. What is yours?"

Again she heard a polite yet unfamiliar voice answer. "I phrase myself badly. I wish only to speak to you on a matter which could prove beneficial to us both."

She shook her head slowly. Would people never leave her alone? "I've had enough of reporters and journalists. Seek sensation somewhere else."

"I am not a reporter."

Something in his liquid tone, rich and deep as brandy, caught her attention. She had heard that voice before. After a moment's hesitation, she opened the door a crack. There under the gaslight was the handsome foreigner who had escorted her down the stairway of her home three days earlier. "You were at the auction."

He inclined his head, the hall light playfully slipping along the deep waves of his black hair. "I was there."

"Who are you and what do you want?"

He smiled and it increased his appeal. "I am Eduardo Domingo Xavier Tavares."

Philadelphia clutched the door tightly. "Your name means nothing to me."

Eduardo noticed that her knuckles were white where she held the door. He'd been impatient to see her, having waited on the landing for a very red-faced young gen-

tleman to leave her room and then a maid, who'd pushed
past him to reach her door first. Still he did not want to
frighten her. Her head was not held as high as it had been
throughout the afternoon of the auction. The realization
of her anxiety quelled his impatience. "You must be exhausted, senhorita, but won't you allow me to come in
and speak privately with you?"

Philadelphia closed the door a little. "No."

In a determinedly sensible tone he said, "I don't object
to conversing in the hallway but your neighbors seem the
curious sort and . . ." He glanced discreetly over his
shoulder.

Even as his voice trailed off she followed his glance and
noticed that the door opposite hers was ajar. Her mouth
tightened in anger. She was aware that her every action
was monitored. What did they expect her to do? What
outrageous act did they think she would commit?

"You're wondering if you should be talking to a
stranger, a foreigner," he said quietly. "I can assure you
your neighbors wouldn't approve."

"I'm beyond being distressed by the opinion of busy-
bodies," she answered tartly and swung open her door.
"You may come in, but only for a moment."

Eduardo entered the tiny room and looked about in
amazement. He knew that she was no longer wealthy but
somehow he had thought she would fare better than this.
The room was cramped, the ceiling low, the single window small and draped in velvet that looked rusty with
age. When he turned to her, he saw her blush and was
instantly sorry for the expression that must have been on
his face. But how to begin? Where to begin?

Embarrassed at being caught staring, Philadelphia
moved to a nearby chair and sat down. Yet she hadn't
been able to help herself. He was an extraordinarily
handsome man, though not in the conventional manner.
A little above average height, he was lean and broad-
shouldered and dressed completely in black. Everything

about him was dark; his crimped black hair, his deep black eyes. Even his skin was a deep bronze rather than the healthy ruddy complexion she'd been taught to value in a man. By his speech, he was a foreigner. He was not the sort of man she would ever have had traffic with under ordinary circumstances.

Still, she was too well-trained to allow her surprise to supersede her manners. "Please sit down. You wish to speak with me . . . ?"

"Senhor Tavares," he supplied, softly rolling the *r*'s as he sat in the only other chair in the room.

"You're Portuguese?"

He smiled, pleased that she knew something of languages. "Brazilian."

The fine hairs rose on the back of Philadelphia's neck as she stared at the handsome man. Brazil! One of the letters in her possession mentioned Brazil. "You've come to speak to me about my father?"

Eduardo took a seat opposite her. "Let's say I'm a person who's taken a special interest in you."

The reply put her further on guard. "You've heard the gossip, the reason for the auction, the reasons for—"

She broke off as he raised a finger to his lips, as though to admonish a child. "Senhorita, you need not speak of this to me. It has nothing to do with you."

She was struck by the plum-black eyes regarding her frankly. There was nothing disrespectful in his gaze yet it seemed to include everything at once. It was as if he were able to draw an object to himself for closer inspection simply by looking at it. She felt that pull very strongly yet refused to look away. "You're wrong, senhor. What happened to my father concerns me very much. He was not a thief. I knew him better than anyone and I know he was incapable of any wrong. His life was destroyed by lies. I am the only one left to prove his innocence." She thought she saw pity move across his face before being replaced by—what was it?

"Senhorita, can anyone know another completely?" he said quietly. "Strangers who've spent but five minutes together may know more about one another than people who've spent their entire lives beneath the same roof. To believe otherwise is to discount the secrets in every heart."

"I *know* my father was innocent."

He shrugged. "I only offer an observation. Sometimes we revere things that are the least worthy of our reverence."

"That's insulting!"

He regarded her solemnly. "No, senhorita, only honest. Honesty requires bravery and a willingness to seek, not our desire, but reality. Often, none of us is what we seem."

Philadelphia put a hand to her temples. He wasn't making sense, or was it only the inflection of his words that made them seem strange and nonsensical? "I'm very tired."

He glanced once more at the meager surroundings, then back at her. "Have you had your supper? I haven't. Perhaps you'd be kind enough to accompany me to a place where we might share a meal."

She shook her head. "No. I've had more than enough of whispers and stares for one day."

Eduardo saw her gaze move to the door and knew that she wanted him to leave. *A man of great passion must learn great patience.* His grandmother had told him that when, as a little boy, he had accidentally crushed a kitten to death by trying to hold on to it when it wanted its freedom. He wanted something very badly now, and he knew enough not to crush it.

"Very well. I'll be brief." He crossed his arms before his chest. "I wish to say first that I very much admire you, Senhorita Hunt. You have spirit and courage, and passion. You're proud, and not without cause. You're beautiful and yet I would not call you vain."

Philadelphia knew she was staring at him, but his arrogance and the utter confidence with which he spoke astounded her. "Do go on, senhor. I'm not yet certain whether I should be flattered or insulted,"

"Most certainly you should be flattered! What you did the other afternoon—the manner in which you handled those idiots who were predisposed to hold their purse strings tight—it was fascinating! You're a merchant of infinite skill."

Indignation dispelled for the moment her weariness. "I didn't enjoy selling my father's possessions! I did what I had to do to prevent the humiliation of losing them to people who wouldn't cherish them as my father did."

"And you were successful. I believed every word you spoke. That's why I'm here. I'm the owner of gem mines in Brazil. We mine mostly topazes, amethysts, a few rubies, and there is some gold. Like your father, I'm a collector. At present I'm in your country to sell a few very fine pieces of jewelry. The stones are beautiful but they need the proper setting in order to be best appreciated.

"Listening to you the other day, it suddenly came to me, the perfect way to insure that my jewels will bring the fortune they deserve. I have come to ask you to wear my pieces to the fashionable places in your fine city. I will pay you, of course. Once my jewels are seen about the neck of someone of your beauty and taste, I should have no trouble selling them."

Philadelphia continued to stare at him. He couldn't be serious? Gem mines and gold, indeed. His clothes were expensive and she hadn't missed the heavy gold ring on his right hand but he could hardly expect her to believe that he was some fabulously wealthy man who required her assistance to wear his gems. His story was more fantastic than the one she'd told about Mei Ling. He must think her a complete fool. "This is a poor joke, senhor."

"But I'm most serious."

"Then allow me to broaden your education with regard

to my countrymen," she said primly. "The accusations of embezzlement against my father, his subsequent bankruptcy and death have all made me infamous. Infamy is not a preferred situation for an American lady. My family has disowned me and my former friends will no longer associate with me. If I went about in public in the vulgar manner you suggest, I'd be snubbed or, worse, the jewels might well be confiscated in order to provide more revenue for my father's remaining debts. You've chosen the wrong merchant, senhor." She stood up, trembling. "Good-bye!"

In admiration mixed with consternation he rose to his feet. Every objection she made was a good one, and he hadn't thought of any of them himself. *"Peste!* I am a fool!"

She lifted an eyebrow. "I wouldn't presume to contradict you."

He cast her a look that made her draw a quick breath. "I am sorry to have disturbed you, senhorita. I shall go now but I shall return when I've sorted out these minor difficulties."

He left so quickly that she did not have a chance to tell him not to bother to return. When he was gone all that remained was the faint odor of . . . of . . . perfume.

Philadelphia put a hand to her mouth to forestall the laughter that moved within her. Well, it wasn't precisely perfume. Certainly no lady would have worn a scent that seemed a mixture of spice and wood. She supposed it was a masculine fragrance though American men didn't wear scents. Yet Senhor Tavares was imposingly masculine, with those wide-set black eyes that saw much more than was proper. Perhaps it was a trait of Brazilian men to wear perfume and address ridiculous proposals to destitute young women.

She shook her head as she locked her door. She'd been very foolish to allow him into her room, a mistake she wouldn't repeat. If he came back, and she doubted that he would, she wouldn't let him in. It had been a ridiculous finish to a disastrous day.

Only when she had turned out the light and climbed between the covers did she remember her surroundings. With sobering resolution, she tried unsuccessfully to put everything out of her mind. She was really and truly alone in the world now, with no home, no friends, no one to turn to.

"You might have been braver, Harry," she whispered sleepily as a tear slid out from beneath her closed lids.

"Pass the potatoes, dearie," said Mrs. Watson with a cheery smile at Philadelphia. "You should take another serving for yourself, too. A man likes a bit of a curve in his lady's cheek. Doesn't he, Mr. Miller?" she asked of the man on her left.

"Yes, ma'am!" Mr. Miller's large balding head bobbed up and down as he gave Philadelphia a speculative glance. "A man likes something to hold on to."

Philadelphia passed the mashed potatoes without comment. For three days now, she had shared her meals with the other boarding house guests. The experience was not improving with familiarity.

"Mr. Jones, I would so favor another slice of that most delicious ham," Mrs. Watson said to the man seated across from her and bestowed a smile on him. A rather plain woman with a plump figure and lively blue eyes, she was nonetheless a favorite among the male boarders because of her flirtatious manner. "Mr. Watson always said that he liked his ham to resemble a lady's lips, tender and moist with just a hint of pink!"

Philadelphia set her fork down as the woman's twittering encouraged the rough laughter of the two traveling salesmen sharing the table this night.

"You've a rare way with words, Mrs. Watson," the one named Jones said. "Wouldn't you agree, miss?"

Philadelphia looked across the table to see the mustachioed man grinning wickedly at her. Before she could stop herself she said, "It's a very vulgar way."

Mrs. Watson's gasp of outrage was echoed by that of Mr. Jones, "See here, young lady!"

Confronted by the disapproving stares of her three dinner companions, she rose to her feet with a flushed complexion. "I'm sorry but I don't care to have my meal compared to the female anatomy. It makes it quite indigestible. Excuse me." She dropped her napkin in her plate and turned away.

"Well, I must say!" Mrs. Watson said in her wake. "And to think she was somebody!"

"Was?" Mr. Miller echoed. "What do you mean by 'was'?"

As Philadelphia entered the vestibule of the boarding house, she heard Mrs. Watson begin the story of her father's scandal. Stung by anger, she swirled about to go back and face her detractor, but the sight of the two men leaning eagerly forward to catch the woman's every word stopped her. Creating a disturbance would only give the gossips more to say about her. The murmurs and stares had become like the hum of wasps in her ears, every comment a venomous sting.

Turning back, she reluctantly climbed the stairs to her quarters. The only thing she hated more than meals at the boarding house was her room. It was cold at night and too warm during the day. It smelled faintly of last winter's ashes, years of dust, ancient mildew. When she was feeling particularly low, she thought she detected the rancid odor of previous tenants. Even so, the room was her only refuge from the street.

The auction had brought more than three times what the auctioneers had hoped for but the courts had confiscated the entire sum, saying that she wasn't entitled to even a penny of it until all debts were paid. The hoped-for allowance, predicted by her lawyer, that would have allowed her to live modestly was not to be. And there was no recourse, for unlike her father who had been caught in the scandal, the other partners in the disastrous investment deals remained anonymous and therefore untouchable. According to her lawyer, the entire affair smacked of collusion to defraud the bank yet there was not a shred of proof that he could act on. He couldn't pursue his speculations, he had said, without knowing the identity of the secret partners.

Philadelphia recalled how anxious her father had been during those final days. He had looked—well, haunted was the word that came to mind. He'd even spoken once of old ghosts rising out of their graves to taunt him. When she had questioned him about it, he had smiled the smile she recognized from childhood as one that meant she was too young, too sheltered to understand. Yet the laughter never reached his eyes, and he had grown more reclusive with each day. She was accustomed to his habit of burying himself in his library after dinner. She knew nothing of the business that had always been paramount in his life. The love he had shown her had been doting but doled out during the quiet moments in his busy world. If only he had said something that last evening, anything that would have given her a chance to prove her belief in him. Maybe then she'd have been able to save him, and herself.

Philadelphia shivered and closed her eyes. She had dreamed the night before of being an item for auction. The pièce de résistance of Wendell Hunt's collection, the auctioneer had called her: a pretty pleasant distraction from the realities of life. Had she been of no more practical use to her father than his favorite objet d'art? The thought shamed her. Had she failed him, as she was now failing herself? In a week her rent would be due. Yet the scandal surrounding her made the possibility of finding employment in Chicago remote. With time and references she might find a teaching position elsewhere.

She caught back a sob. She did not want more time!

She did not want references! She did not want a job! And, most of all, she did not want to face another moment of the future! She wanted to be safe again and carefree, but that was never ever going to be. She had made a promise at her father's grave side to find the man or men responsible for his ruination. Some intuitive sense told her that the letters in her possession held the clues she needed, and that she should keep the secret of their existence until she knew more. Yet, unless some miracle appeared soon, she might wind up in a poorhouse.

Stung by frustrations and doubts, and unable to keep back a second sob, she hurried down the hall to her room and burst through her doorway.

"Senhorita Hunt!"

The sound of her name brought Philadelphia up short in astonishment. Standing by the small table that served as her desk and tea table was Senhor Tavares. On his face was a reflection of her own surprise as he said, "What's wrong?"

Even as he came toward her, she put hands to her cheeks to wipe away the telltale moisture. "No—nothing! I—I'm only surprised," she stammered out over the tears clogging her throat.

"But you've been crying," he protested and reached into his pocket to withdraw a handkerchief.

"I'm not crying!" she answered furiously and waved away his attempt at aid. The last thing she wanted was to be seen as weak and chastened before this vividly alive man.

He looked at her skeptically but said only, "My mistake. Perhaps there's a cinder in your eye. Allow me to examine it for you."

"That won't be necessary," she answered, rapidly regaining her composure.

"But I insist." He moved to block her as she would have stepped past him. "I'm quite skilled and won't hurt you." He lightly lifted her chin with his forefinger.

"Come, turn toward the light. A little more. Yes, that is better."

As he leaned toward her, Philadelphia forgot to resist. His bronze, absurdly handsome face was within inches of her own. Dark eyes fringed with long black lashes stared into hers, and she wondered if he could really look as deeply into another's soul as his gaze implied. "Ah yes, there is something painful here."

She could feel his strength as with the gentlest of touches he wiped the remaining tear tracks from her cheeks with his handkerchief. She felt his assurance as he smiled and those wide-set eyes narrowed in amusement. She felt his ease with himself as he nodded and moved away. "You must be careful in future, senhorita, to keep annoyances from your lovely topaz eyes."

"Thank you." Released, she moved away to the far side of the room, for in his vicinity the air seemed to be lacking. Belatedly, she remembered to ask the question she should have asked at once. "What are you doing here?"

"Waiting for you."

"You know what I mean."

"But certainly. I knocked. There was no answer. I entered. There was no one here. So I waited."

"I was below having my dinner. You shouldn't have entered my room without permission."

"You are right," he answered promptly. "I wouldn't have been able to do so had you locked your door." He frowned at her. "You're not accustomed to caring for yourself, senhorita, so I will warn you not to leave your door unlocked in future. Your next guest may not be as well meaning as I."

Small comfort, Philadelphia thought. He didn't seem the least bit safe to her with his arrogant manner and presumptions. He was dressed conventionally this time in an evening cutaway coat with velvet collar and silk lapels. Yet the careful tailoring that drew her eye to the superb lines of his body was distinctly un-American. And there were other traces of foreign influence. The studs of his white silk waistcoat and shirt were diamonds rather than the usual pearl. Instead of a stiff high round collar he wore a pristine soft white neck cloth in which was nestled an immense sapphire surrounded by diamonds. The contrast between the white linen and his deep skin tone was more remarkable because it drew the eye inevitably to his unusual profile and hypnotic eyes. Despite superficial appearances, he seemed as out of place in her parlor as a parrot in a sparrow's nest. To break the awkward silence she said, "You're a curious man."

He cocked his head to the side in puzzlement. "Curious?"

"Strange. Odd. Unusual."

He seemed to consider this before saying, "I would prefer that you found me attractive."

She looked away. He was flirting with her, she was almost certain of it. Harry had never flirted, he was too serious and earnest. But this man with a smile that transformed his whole being seemed to be constantly amused by life. Well, she wouldn't have it. She did not want to flirt, and certainly not with him. "I believe I asked you why you're here."

He gestured for her to sit. "I'm here to show you something, several things, which should relieve your mind concerning my intentions."

"I told you before that I'm not interested in any proposition you might have for me," she replied. "In fact, it isn't at all proper for you to be here. I'm not accustomed to entertaining strange men in my rooms."

He looked at her in disappointment. "Must we waste time with out-of-place modesty? I'm not interested in your virtue." Laughter flowed from him at her gasp of indignation. "So you're not immune to insult as you are to flattery. That is a curious trait."

Telling herself that the only way to be rid of him was to

hear him out, Philadelphia perched on the edge of a chair. "You may have five minutes, Senhor Tavares."

She hadn't noticed the stack of jewelry cases lying on her bed until he walked over to them and picked one up. Returning to where she sat, he opened the latch and then the lid.

Philadelphia gasped. She had seen many beautiful things in her life—her father had owned more than a few of them—but never had she seen a necklace as spectacular. It was a collar of gold; heavy barbaric medallions of gold hammered with designs that she recognized as pagan. In the center of each medallion was a topaz the size of her thumbnail. But that was not all. From each medallion there hung a gold lozenge. In the center of each gold lozenge was an amethyst the size of her thumbnail. Suspended from each lozenge was a conical drop of pierced gold. At the wide end of each drop a ruby had been set. Philadelphia looked up at him in mute wonder.

"Well?"

"It's incredibly beautiful." She looked up at him in amazement. "Is it yours?"

He didn't answer but smiled as he shut the case. "Perhaps something else." He went over to the bed and brought back a long flat case this time. When he opened it, Philadelphia thought she knew what to expect, but she didn't.

On a bed of white satin lay a choker of pierced gold in the Spanish style, an inch and a half wide. Studded along its length were a dozen faceted stones as bright as diamonds but the color of a robin's egg. "What are they?"

"Blue topazes," he answered, smiling as she reached out to lightly touch one. "They remind me of a summer day when the heat shimmers across the land and the sunshine hurts your eyes and the sky is a clear hard gemblue."

She glanced up into his face which always seemed too close for her comfort. "Are they from your mines?"

Again he didn't answer but withdrew the choker from its case and placed it about her throat. Nodding in approval he said, "Yes, you are meant to wear such a piece." Slipping his fingers behind and under her hair, he fastened the necklace, then reached for her hand mirror which lay nearby.

Philadelphia held up the mirror. Even in the poor lighting, the blue topazes winked cerulean fire. "The necklace is quite lovely. I can't imagine anything more exquisite."

"Certainly you can!" he answered. "You have the gift of making anything possible. All you need do is to imagine it."

Philadelphia turned to him, her eyes suddenly clouded. "I wish that were true."

His expression sobered but the light never left his eyes. "What you would imagine? New clothes? Money? More jewels?"

Philadelphia glanced away. "I'd imagine a way to prove my father's innocence," she said slowly. "But first, I'd find a way to pay back every cent he is accused of stealing so that when the truth is known, his debtors can choke on their recompense."

Eduardo saw the absolute conviction of her belief in her father's innocence in her face, and the barrier that lay like a mine field between them. "What about the truth? What if what you imagine is a lie?"

She looked up sharply. "You're strangely infatuated with the notion of the truth. I wonder if it's because you don't deal in it yourself?"

He shrugged and moved a little away from her, uncomfortable with his knowledge about her father and the hurt the truth would cause her. "The jewels are real."

Philadelphia reached up and released the choker. "Then I must return this to you and thank you for showing it to me." She offered it to him.

Instead of taking it from her, he closed his hand over

hers. "What if I could make real at least a part of your desire? What if I were to offer you enough money to pay off your father's debts in return for your services?"

Philadelphia paled. Money for her services? Was that the reason he had come here to dazzle her with jewels? Did he believe that she was so poor and despondent that she would sink to—to . . .

She tried to draw back her hand, but his held hers firmly and she began to struggle. "Let go of me. I'm no trollop!"

"Trollop?" He frowned and released her hand. Then his brow cleared. "Ah, you think I want to make you my mistress. No wonder you're insulted!" He sounded genuinely indignant. "I have told you, I want you to help me sell my jewels."

He sighed and took a few steps away from her to pick up the heavy gold collar he'd first shown her. "What if I told you that this piece is hundreds of years old, that it was made by the Amazon Indians for a Portuguese queen, and that it's for sale to any lady in Chicago who can afford it."

Uncertain whether or not she should believe him, she said stiffly, "I would answer that it's a stunning example of the jeweler's art but far too ostentatious for anyone less than royalty. No American lady would wear it."

He dismissed her words with a wave of his hand, for his newly formed scheme had taken that into account. "What if you weren't an American lady? What if you were someone else, an impoverished aristocrat, perhaps. You have come to America to forget past wrongs, to erase the memory of your lost family, your father's death at the hands of enemies. What if this necklace were the only thing left of your family's legendary cache of jewels? What if you were now forced to part with it? But not to just anyone, but someone who would cherish it as you do, if only the buyer understood what it represents!"

Philadelphia had closed her eyes before he finished

speaking, and she was reluctant to open them now. "You mock me."

"Never." He said the word softly but so persuasively that she opened her eyes.

He had moved to her side and, as he bent toward her to bring his face down on a level with her own, she had only one thought: *he's more beautiful than sin.*

She didn't know why she thought that or why she suddenly wanted so very much to believe him. But the thought came and remained as a shiver of fear and excitement. "What do you want from me?"

He smiled and the tremble of excitement in her deepened. "You possess the gift of dreams. You are able to make people imagine what they cannot see with their own eyes. I offer you a chance to use your very special talent. If you help me sell my jewelry, I'll give you half of whatever profit we make. What will it be, menina?"

His persuasive voice stroked her fears yet objections continued to sprout within her. "It's madness. I can't. If I went about with you, I'd be branded a whore. I'd be banned from polite society forever. I can't do it."

He straightened. "Can't or won't?"

"I won't take part in any scheme to defraud."

His smile widened until a dimple appeared in his left cheek and Philadelphia wondered if it had been there all along or if he were the possessor of the kind of magic he said he saw in her. "What jewel is more prized by a woman than the one she spies about the neck of another? Call it envy or mere greed. Because you are beautiful, every woman who sees you wearing my jewels will long to own them. By selling them, we will only be allowing these women to do what they've always wished they could do, which is to buy beauty from another."

Philadelphia was so astonished by his speech that she didn't know what to think. Oh, but yes she did. "That's outrageous! And illegal—I think."

He shrugged and dropped blue topazes back in the

box. "I beg your pardon for having disturbed you, senhorita. I misunderstood you entirely."

She knew she shouldn't provoke another word from him but she couldn't help herself. "What did you misunderstand?"

He shrugged, a habit she was beginning to associate with exasperation in his tone. "I thought you were adventurous. Brave. Willing to risk a great deal to prove your point."

Her eyes widened. Had he truly thought he'd found those qualities in her? Certainly her father had thought the exact opposite. She didn't feel adventurous. And yet there was a need, a great pressing need in her to be brave and adventurous. Perhaps Senhor Tavares was the savior she'd prayed for. She doubted it. With his outrageous masculine beauty, he seemed more like Lucifer than any guardian angel. "If I were to consider this—this offer, I would have to be assured that what we do is legal."

"But of course," he answered quickly.

"And, I must be free to leave your employ at any time."

He stared at her a moment. "You have a purpose for accepting my offer that goes beyond necessity, am I correct?"

She shrugged this time, a gesture she had never before made in her life. "I need my share of the profits, senhor. You can be certain I shan't leave it behind."

The look of triumph on his face was out of all proportion to the victory of her acceptance she decided with renewed suspicion, but then he was speaking.

"It is done! A bargain struck!" To her amazement, he put his hand out to her like one man would to another and when she extended hers to him, he heartily shook it. "Partners!"

"Partners," she echoed, feeling the heady winds of chance blowing hard against her back. Had she made this choice of her own free will, or had this gorgeous man

simply bedazzled her? Adventurous, he had called her.
Then why did she feel as reckless and foolhardy as a
schoolgirl? She knew the answer. It was in the allure of
his absurdly beautiful face.

# 3

The night was warm. Somewhere a woman was singing, her voice melancholy despite the tinny piano accompaniment. The fetid night wind came fitfully, teasing the curtains that he'd left open against his American landlord's advice, yet it didn't calm Eduardo's restlessness. The odors of baked pavement, dung, and the Chicago waterfront carried by the breeze were alien to his state of mind. He was far away from home, had been away far too long for his peace of mind.

At times such at this, he longed for the open veranda of his *estância,* where the air was scented with the bounty of his fields. He grew orchards of oranges, limes, mangoes, and bananas, as well as fields of cane, pineapple, and yams. At night the odor of jasmine and wild thyme and the smoky aroma of burning wood scented the air. There was peace there, a deep abiding peace that he'd never found anywhere else, not even in his dreams— especially not in his dreams.

Eduardo began to absently rub his left wrist. Hidden beneath his starched cuffs were knotted and smooth scars, tactile reminders of a past that had ruled his life these last fourteen years. The pain was long gone. Only memories brought it back occasionally when, like sharp-toothed ghosts, they still occasionally terrorized his nights.

After a moment he propped his booted feet up on the desk before him and picked up an unlit cigar. He had taken rooms along the Chicago waterfront because he was less likely to draw attention to himself and the comings and goings of the people he employed than if he were ensconced in the grand suite of a Michigan Avenue hotel. The rooms of the townhouse were much finer than the tiny dreary closet that had been Philadelphia Hunt's living quarters for the last few weeks, but the horsehair-stuffed seats, heavy velvet swags, and dark woods offended his eye. He much preferred the decor of Tyrone's New Orleans house, which was furnished in cherry wood, mahogany inlay, and the lightness of Louis XV chairs and a Directoire settee.

The reminder of Tyrone annoyed Eduardo. In his pocket was a letter containing the final accounting between them. For seven years they had worked in concert, but while Tyrone had proved a strong and resourceful ally, he was also unpredictable. Tyrone wouldn't understand what he was doing now. In fact, Tyrone might take exception to the fact that he was aiding the daughter of one of the men they'd schemed together to ruin. That's why it was better that Tyrone never know about it.

Eduardo patted his breast pocket. He was sorry to be severing their tie yet he was also relieved. He would mail the letter to Tyrone before he left Chicago. By the time Tyrone received it, if he were even in New Orleans to receive it, he and Philadelphia would be long gone and their trail quite cold.

He placed the cigar between his lips, bit off the end, and reached for a match, but he didn't strike it. Instead, his gaze went to the closed door of the guest bedroom. For more than three hours Philadelphia had been closeted there with the woman he'd hired to serve her.

The method of bringing her under his control had been

deceptively simple. She had been vulnerable to his proposition because she needed what he could most easily provide her with—money. Yet their association of a week had only deepened his fascination with her. He had expected that she would behave as other women of his acquaintance, offering him their company in return for his generosity. Yet she refused to move from her cramped quarters into his apartment and steadfastly refused his offers of dinner or the theater. Instead, she treated him with the polite respectful distance she would show an employer.

Eduardo smiled and shook his head. To his astonishment, she had accepted at face value his absurd excuse for hiring her. During what brief time they did spend together she talked of little else other than her desire to prove her father's innocence and pay off his debts. So, there was nothing to do but play out the first charade.

His offer of employment had been complicated by the realization that as Philadelphia Hunt, she was no longer accepted in "good" society. Therefore, it was necessary that she should become someone else. After years of altering his own identity in order to pursue his own purposes, choosing a new identity for her was easily accomplished. As of tomorrow morning, Philadelphia Hunt would no longer exist. In her place would be Mademoiselle Felise de Ronsard, aristocratic French orphan and heir to a lost fortune. It remained to be seen if the final ploy of the transformation would be a success.

Eduardo dropped the match back into its container and took the cigar out of his mouth. He should be pleased. He should be congratulating himself. He should not be feeling this twinge of doubt about what he was doing. Yet, he did feel it. His involvement with Philadelphia Hunt went against all reason.

Still, he couldn't simply walk away from her. From the moment he'd first seen her, he'd felt that they were fated to be together. He couldn't explain it nor the irony that bound him to the one woman who would be his mortal enemy if she found out the truth about his part in her father's ruination. For nearly as long as he could remember, he had been driven by an oath pledged over two shallow graves in the heart of a Brazilian rain forest. Now his fate was his own, and if necessary he would fight heaven and hell for the right to aid Philadelphia Hunt. He would be patient and gentle. He would make her trust him and then, perhaps, she wouldn't be able to turn away from him when the truth was revealed. That was his hope and his dread.

He murmured a Portuguese curse and sat back with a sigh. Suddenly the door he'd been watching opened, and he forgot about his doubts.

A young woman entered the room. Her brunette hair was caught back from her face to cascade in long dark curls over the slender shoulders revealed by her low-cut squared neckline. She was lovely, poised, and apparently a complete stranger.

Philadelphia entered the room reluctantly. She had balked at the idea of wearing clothing that Senhor Tavares had bought for her, preferring to remain in her own gowns, which reflected the strictest form of deep mourning. Yet, when she saw this formal black dress, she couldn't refrain from trying it on. About the rest of the changes in her person, she felt both foolish and a little anxious. When Senhor Tavares rose from his seat behind the desk, her trepidation didn't ease. He was watching her intently, and nothing in his lazy-lidded expression expressed approval.

Mrs. Collins, who'd helped Philadelphia dress, was quick to sense the gentleman's reservations and sought to ease the awkward moment. "Ain't she a picture? You must be pleased, sir."

Apparently he wasn't. His neutral expression became a frown as he came toward the elegantly dressed young woman.

Philadelphia held herself perfectly still under his dark-eyed stare, but her heart pounded in heavy strokes beneath her bodice as he reached out to touch the curl twining by her left ear. The touch of his finger, the merest brush of contact, sent a ripple of pleasure along her cheek. Instantly, she dropped her gaze, hoping he hadn't noticed her response.

When she glanced up again, he was still staring at her with that melting gaze that was deceptive. She sensed, for reasons she couldn't put into words, a frightening strength of will behind those almost too-tender eyes. The inspection made her angry. Why didn't he speak, even to say that he hated the way she looked? But no, he simply held her in his inscrutable black stare until she thought she'd either scream or faint. Finally, he made an impatient gesture with his hand to indicate that she should turn around.

Murmuring under her breath in protest, she made a sweeping turn about the room that showed to advantage the fan-shaped train of her skirts.

As she turned away, Eduardo smiled. The transformation was a success. No, an inspired idea! The dye that had turned her gold-highlighted chestnut hair into the darkest shade of brunette seemed to have transformed her features, as well. Her eyes appeared lighter now, amber without the dark honey, her complexion creamier. A bit of rouge cunningly applied to her lips and the subtlest of kohl darkening her brows and lashes made her features a little more prominent and piquant. Not even her best friend would recognize her at first glance, as he had not.

His smile widened as she walked about the room. The formal gown of black chambray gauze with gold-colored stripes accented the new contrast between her skin and hair while the trimming of embroidered scarlet, yellow, and black silk roses relieved the severity and accented her youth. His eyes lingered an instant on the low décolletage that revealed the generous swell of her breasts, then moved to where the sleeveless bodice exposed her softly rounded arms and dimpled elbows. The scarlet bow attached to her bustle accentuated the sway of her hips, and he felt a sudden quickening in his loins, but he resisted the pleasure. If she even suspected how she affected him, he knew she would be frightened away.

When she'd completed her modeling, Philadelphia turned to face him and folded her arms across her bosom. "Say something."

He smiled broadly to show the dimple in his left cheek. "What does a man say to a beautiful lady other than you are enchanting, menina, thoroughly enchanting and quite delectable."

Philadelphia blushed and glanced toward Mrs. Collins. "Thank you, though your compliments are more extravagant than is polite."

He, too, glanced at the woman. "You may leave us."

The woman nodded. "I'll be in the other room, in case you need me."

Eduardo withdrew his wallet and removed a bill. "That won't be necessary. You won't be needed again this night."

The sight of money brought a smile to the woman's face. "Why, that's most kind of you, sir!" The gentleman had hired her as a maid for his 'ward,' or so he said, but she hadn't missed the gleam in his eyes as they lingered on the girl just now. His mistress, was more like it. Still, it wasn't her business to sort out other folks' morals.

She gave Philadelphia an arch look as she passed her on the way to the door. "You have a nice evening, dear. Your gentleman's most generous when he's of a mind to be."

The woman's expression made the intent of her words unmistakable. Philadelphia gave her a chilly glance before looking away. "You shouldn't have done that," she said when the door closed. "That woman now thinks that I—that we—well, it's most improper."

He shrugged. "She knows less than she thinks." His attitude wasn't what she had hoped for and his next words didn't soothe her concerns. "In any case, we won't be here long enough for it to matter."

"If we are going to do business together then you must consider my feelings," she maintained. "You shouldn't have complimented me in such a manner. It isn't done in Chicago."

He looked amused, wanting to catch her against him and give her a thorough kissing that would erase her prudish expression, yet he held back. "A lady of my country would have pouted in response to so small a compliment as the one I made you and demanded more."

"I'm afraid I shall prove to be a disappointment then," she replied coolly. "I don't intend to make a goose of myself."

He shook his head slowly. "I begin to suspect this spinsterish attitude comes from too much starch in the many petticoats American women wear."

Insulted, she took a step toward him. "I may not be your ideal lady, but then you're hardly my idea of a perfect gentleman!"

His sudden laughter startled her. "Bravo, senhorita! This passion, I knew it was there!"

Philadelphia's cheeks burned as she realized that he'd deliberately roused her anger. "You baited me. That's unfair."

He shrugged. "Perhaps. But you refuse to flirt with me and I enjoy watching the roses bloom in your cheeks. I provoke them in the manner that you allow."

Feeling retreat was the better part in this case, she crossed her arms in silence.

"You are pleased with the dress?" he asked.

She saw his gaze lower to her neckline and remembered all the reasons she shouldn't be here. "It's a lovely dress," she answered formally, "but I feel I should mention that the style is dated." She caught up a handful of her skirts and twitched them so that the train swept forward. "The fan train is at least three years old. New formal gowns have court trains."

His black brows drew together over his dark eyes. "You were expecting the latest Parisian design?"

She blushed. "No, of course not. I wasn't expecting anything at all. I only mention it because you paid for the gown and I think you shouldn't be cheated by having outdated fashions foisted upon you."

"But this is exactly what I ordered. You are playing a role and must dress the part. Have we not agreed that you will present yourself in New York as a French aristocrat who was orphaned when the Prussians besieged Paris six years ago?"

"You agreed," she answered shortly. "I'm not at all certain that anyone would believe so ridiculous an assertion."

"They will believe it if you make them believe it," he answered. "Fortunately for us, your finishing school education included five years of the French language. Your accent is more than passably correct."

"Thank you, I think," she rejoined dryly.

"You think I'm not a good judge of this? Allow me to tell you that I have lived in Paris."

"You've a remarkable history."

Her sarcastic tone was not lost on him. "So, we are agreed about your role. You left Paris after the Second Empire fell and have been living abroad for the past three years. In the beginning you were dressed in the latest style, but now you are a little threadbare. This gown looks too new so you must age it. Sit down. I suggest that you spill something on the skirt during dinner. You might even tread on the hem once or twice. Nothing too difficult to mend. Then when it's laundered, it will be perfect."

She stared at him, appalled. "The gown clearly cost a

fortune and you want me to damage it? You really are mad."

"Not at all." He reached into his pocket and withdrew a slender leather book. "I have for you your papers. From now on you will be known as Mademoiselle Felise de Ronsard. Here is your ticket for the train to New York City. You will depart in three days' time."

She took the papers he offered her, but one glimpse of the unfamiliar name brought back all the misgivings she held about whether or not she should have agreed to this masquerade that bordered on deceit. She didn't trust him and yet if she hadn't agreed to work for him she wouldn't now have a roof over her head. "I'm not certain I can do this."

The dark eyes regarding her narrowed. "Why?"

She lifted her chin a notch. "I don't know if it's wise. How will I know what to say to people? What if I forget my new name?"

"Would you rather go about as Miss Philadelphia Hunt? You may do so if you wish." He turned away in annoyance at her repeated reluctance to join in the spirit of his game and began pacing the room. "I wonder what people will say when they hear that name? Gossip travels fast, much faster than you imagine. People who've never heard of you will have heard of your father's misfortunes. He was a man of business, of finance; his losses will have had repercussions, however slight, throughout American financial circles."

"I need not be reminded on every occasion of who and what I am," she answered in a husky voice.

He didn't expect what he saw when he turned back to her. Her regal elegance had vanished and in its place stood a lovely but vulnerable young woman with tears trembling on the end of her lashes.

He went to her and, reaching out instinctively to console her, brought her close against him. "Forgive me. I spoke without thinking."

He held her lightly but Philadelphia felt as if she couldn't breathe while his warm hands framed her bare upper arms. She was vividly aware of the masculine body only a breath away from hers. "Please let me go," she said softly.

He released her at once, but when he looked at her, expecting fresh anger, he saw that the icy look that was so often a part of her gaze had vanished. The gemlike amber, melted by sadness, was a liquid gold more heady than strong liquor.

Once more desire dragged at him, and it was only with the greatest effort that he took a backward step. "I'm afraid I must leave you for a while." The sooner the better, he added in his thoughts.

"Leave me? Why?"

"You must travel to New York on your own. You can't expect society to close ranks about you, the poor orphan, if there's a gentleman hanging about." He smiled. "They will think, as Mrs. Collins does, that you've taken me as your lover."

"Oh."

"Is that all? Only 'Oh'?"

Refusing to be baited once more, she said, "Well, what you say makes perfect sense."

"I always make perfect sense," he said carelessly, "but sense is not always to be preferred."

Philadelphia avoided his gaze. "Nothing about the last week has made the least sense. You can't expect me to go alone to a city where I know no one." She looked up. "Where will I go? What will I do?"

Eduardo returned to his pacing for standing near her was disturbing his train of thought. "You will be met at the station. Until you arrive, you needn't know anything more."

The stubbornness that was never far from the surface of her personality broke through once again. "I think I do. I need to know a great deal more before I set foot on the train."

"Very well." Eduardo paused and, turning to her, folded his arms. "What do you wish to know, *menina*?"

"I wish to trust you but how can I? I don't even know if the things you have told me are true."

Eduardo smiled. "Is it not a little late for second thoughts?"

Philadelphia tossed her head impatiently. "Oh, for heaven's sake! You say you are a wealthy man but how am I to know you did not steal the jewels in your possession?"

"If I were a thief I would not be offering to show stolen goods to the public. A jewel thief would break up an expensive piece and sell the gems separately because the original would be easily recognized. As for my wealth, I won my first gem mine in a card game in Santa Teresinha with a murderous *guaquero* who thought his luck could not run out. Would you like a listing of my other holdings?" He straightened and moved toward her. "I am *very* wealthy, *menina*." He reached out and brushed a curl from her brow. "Does that please you?"

"Just what exactly does the word *menina* mean?" she asked in hopes of distracting him.

"It's a Portuguese term of endearment." His smile deepened as devils danced in his black eyes. "Do you truly need a translation?"

Not to be intimidated, Philadelphia changed the subject. "How did you make your fortune, Senhor Tavares?"

As though he had not heard her, Eduardo pulled a jeweler's case from his breast pocket. "I nearly forgot this." He opened the box to reveal a stylized floral necklace in diamonds. "It's French, mid-eighteenth century. It's our good fortune that by that time French noblemen had stopped adorning themselves and instead decorated their wives. For the next few weeks, it will decorate your lovely neck. I call it *le collier de Ronsard,* the last of your inheritance. It's magnificent, is it not?"

As Philadelphia looked at the exquisite piece she forgot, for a moment, all her reservations. "It's more," she murmured. She bent closer to inspect the apparently flawless depth of each large diamond. "They're absolutely perfect! Why, each of the center stones must be three full carats."

"Four."

"And the faceting of the stones that form the leaves, I've never seen anything quite like them."

"They're unique," he agreed, pleased by her appreciation and knowledge of diamonds. He took the necklace from its box. "Let's see how they compliment your gown."

The necklace chilled her as he placed it about her neck yet his fingers were warm as they rested an instant along either side of her neck after he had fastened the latch. "Come, stand before the mirror over the mantel and tell me what you think."

Philadelphia allowed him to guide her by the elbow before the mirror. Yet, as she raised her eyes to the reflection it presented, she found herself looking at the man beside her rather than the necklace. He stood behind and a little to one side. She hadn't realized until that moment how much taller and broader he was than she. They stood as they might for a portrait. No, if they were being formally painted or photographed, he would have been seated while she stood behind him with her hand resting lightly on his shoulder.

Fleetingly, she wondered what it would be like to be part of such a portrait, the traditional pose of man and wife. Once she had thought Harry would be the man framing her world with the breadth of his body and the strength of his resolve. But Harry's resolve had been irresolute and his strength tempered by his father's mood. There was nothing of intemperate resolve about the man standing with her now. His easy grace and fluid movements held no trace of weakness or deference. She had watched him this past week move through rooms with a feline arrogance. His stride was one of strength controlled by a total belief in his competence to meet whatever he encountered. She suspected that if he loved he wouldn't be dissuaded by a father's disapproval or even by the lady's reluctance to return his desire. For, what woman would deny such a man if he loved her? Perhaps there already was a woman, even a wife, waiting for his return from the northern hemisphere.

Philadelphia looked away from him, for the thought of his loving another woman rankled—which was entirely ridiculous. He wasn't like her, they were from different worlds, different cultures. Why should she care who loved him and whom he loved? She didn't care. She was envious of the idea of any happy woman only because her own life was in shambles.

There could be no happily-ever-after in her life, not until she had found the answers to why her father had been ruined, and by whom, and how she might avenge him.

Eduardo watched her expression in the mirror from the corner of his eye while he appeared to be studying the necklace. It pleased him to be the subject of her perusal. Most often she behaved as though he weren't a virile man at all but some doddering old clerk or banker with whom she was forced to do business. There was a warm flesh and blood woman inside her cool exterior. Dressed as she was now there was no denying it. He was made excruciatingly aware of the fact by the manner in which his trousers began to bind him uncomfortably.

To relieve his discomfort, he directed his gaze fully on the necklace but, instead, he found himself looking down the front of her low-cut bodice at the swell of her breasts, and his discomfort increased.

"What if I should lose it, or if it should be stolen?"

Eduardo blinked once, then twice. She'd spoken to him, asked a question which he should answer, but for the life of him he didn't know what she'd said.

Philadelphia turned to look at him and mistook his frown as a reply to her question. "I don't intend to be careless, but if you don't trust me with your jewels you'd better take them back now."

As she reached up to unlatch the necklace he caught her fingertips in his hand. "I trust you implicitly, senhorita, and your cleverness. What would *you* do to protect such a piece?"

"Have it duplicated in paste," she answered quickly and slipped her fingers free of his disturbing touch. Was any other human being as warm as he? She didn't remember her father's touch being as heated, and Harry's hands were always cool.

"And so I have." He reached into his breast pocket to withdraw what appeared to be an identical necklace. The edge of it caught on the letter in his pocket as he withdrew it and the envelope slipped free and fell to the floor.

Philadelphia bent to pick it up. He was quicker and scooped it out from under her hand, but not before she saw the New Orleans address. He straightened up with a smile that for the first time didn't reach his eyes as he hastily shoved the letter back into his pocket. A chill shivered through her. He hadn't meant for her to see that letter.

One of her father's letters had a New Orleans address. Was it only coincidence that Senhor Tavares had written someone in that city or was he playing some deeper game? He had hired her to help him sell his jewels, and she in turn planned to use him for her own purposes. But in doing so she must never forget that he was a stranger and shouldn't be trusted.

Aware of her sudden distraction but not the reason for it, Eduardo watched her closely as he held out the second necklace. "This one's paste. I think the real one will be safer in my care until it's needed for display in New York."

Philadelphia stiffened. "I see. Which one do you intend that we shall sell, senhor?"

So, that was it. She still thought he might be a rogue, a charlatan. "You still don't trust me," he scolded gently.

"You give me little reason to," she answered. "I see you've written a friend. Do you know many people in New Orleans?"

Eduardo's smile straightened at the edges. She'd seen the address. She was smart and quick. He must remember that for he didn't want her to begin to dig into his past. "A few. Do you?"

"A few," she answered in the same noncommittal tone.

"Perhaps, at another time, we can compare acquaintances. We may discover that we have some in common."

He said it pleasantly, but Philadelphia felt more than heard irritation in his reply. She knew no one in New Orleans but she would allow him to think that she did. If he decided to go fishing for details from her, he might reveal something to her benefit.

"How have you left matters with your relatives?" he asked to distract her from the question of the letter.

"I wrote my mother's relatives in St. Louis and told them that I was going to visit distant cousins of my father's who live in New York City."

"Do you have relatives in New York City?"

"No, but they don't know that."

He nodded in approval. "And your lawyer, what have you said to him?"

"Much the same. I said that I'd be in touch regularly by mail."

"So you've good and truly cut yourself off from your life as Philadelphia Hunt."

She felt a tremor of disquiet at his phrasing. "Yes, I suppose I have."

"And do you yet feel like Mademoiselle Ronsard?"

"No, of course not." She looked down at the train ticket in her hand. "You will meet me in New York?"

"No, but don't worry. A very reliable and trustworthy fellow will be there to watch over you."

She looked up, startled. "Who is he? How will I know him?"

His dimple appeared. "You need not worry, Mademoiselle Ronsard. He will know you!"

Philadelphia snapped the lid of her portmanteau shut with a sigh and turned to look out the train window only to catch her breath in surprise at her own reflection. After nearly a week she still wasn't accustomed to the darkhaired young woman who gazed back at her. She leaned a little closer to study her reflection, suspicious that one eyebrow was darker than the other. She had yet to master the techniques of applying makeup. Too much rouge made her look like a cheap woman. Too little mascara on her light lashes betrayed the fact that her hair was dyed. After a squinting search of her face, she sat back with a second sigh.

"You're excited about your arrival, aren't you, dear?" said the matronly woman who sat on the seat opposite her.

"Yes . . . *oui*," Philadelphia added the French word as a delayed afterthought. Lord, how was she going to make people believe she was French if English came out of her mouth every time?

"Your first time in New York, is it?"

Philadelphia gave the woman a smile and nodded.

"You're sure to enjoy yourself. Are you being met by relatives?"

Philadelphia shook her head. *"Non."*

"Really?" the woman looked askance.

"I am being met," Philadelphia quickly added in French-accented English but her chest felt suddenly tight. Eduardo Tavares had instructed her to tell people that she had spent a good deal of the last few years in India with an English cousin and, as a consequence, had grown comfortable with the language. Yet, she lacked the absolute confidence with which he spun stories so quickly and cleverly. Anything she said on the spur of the moment was certain to trip her up sooner or later. She'd been mad to agree to this game of make-believe. The knot in her chest tightened. She didn't have the nerve or temperament for it.

"Have you been in the country long?"

Philadelphia jumped as though the woman had stuck her with one of the knitting needles she'd been plying with such dexterity since she sat down. "What? In this country?" She quickly gathered her thoughts. What had he told her to say? *"Mais non,* only a month. I came to San Francisco by ship."

The woman's graying brows peaked over her short nose but her needles continued to click and lock into place the threads of her red wool. "That's an odd way round from France, I'd say."

"Not France. India." Philadelphia blushed at the sound of her voice. She sounded quite backward.

"India? That's quite a trip for a young lady." The woman smiled. "I should know. Went sailing many a year in my younger days for my father was a whaling captain and my mother often shipped out as his first mate. My eldest boy, Jamie, makes the rubber run from Brazil to Boston. Have you been to Brazil?"

Philadelphia's wandering gaze swung back to the woman in alarm. "What about Brazil?"

Taking the young woman's startled question as desire for conversation, the woman said, "Never been there myself, if that's what you mean. Jamie says it's as wild a place as God ever set his hand to. There's jungles full of heathens and rivers full of man-eating fishes, and snakes, and I don't know what all. Not the sort of company for an upstanding Christian boy like my Jamie, and I told him so. Didn't want to think he could come sailing into harbor with one of them skinny brown gals like Tom Foster done ten years back." She leaned forward in confidence. "Tom said he bought her! Imagine that! Bought himself a wife!"

"It sounds very interesting." Philadelphia enunciated the words very carefully. "We will be arriving in New York soon, yes?"

"Not precisely New York. The Pennsylvania Railroad ends at Exchange Place in New Jersey."

"New Jersey?" Philadelphia echoed in surprise. "It does not go on?"

"You can go on, dear, by boarding the ferry to Manhattan."

"Oh." Philadelphia was nonplussed. Eduardo Tavares had said she'd be met at the railroad station in New York. Was he unaware of the ferry ride?

The woman gave Philadelphia a long hard look and realized that the girl was dressed in black. "You're in mourning, aren't you child?" Philadelphia nodded. "Your parents?" Again she nodded. "Poor thing, and you've come this way in a foreign land to be met by strangers?" Philadelphia nodded once more because she couldn't think of anything else to do.

"Well, don't you worry your pretty little head about it. I'll see you get there." She set aside her knitting and offered Philadelphia her hand. "My name's Sarah Crabb, of New Bedford, Massachusetts."

Philadelphia took the extended hand. "I am Felise de Ronsard, of Paris."

Within the hour Philadelphia was glad she had decided to accept Mrs. Crabb's aid. The enormous terminal called Exchange Place was a calliope of locomotive smoke and steam and noise and baggage and crowds. From the moment she set foot on the platform beneath the iron-girded canopy of the station, she felt both lost and a little afraid.

"You wait here, dear, while I get a porter for our bags,"

Mrs. Crabb instructed before setting off and being swallowed up in the crowd.

Philadelphia didn't notice at first the man striding toward her, though he caught the attention of every other member of the throng lining the platform. He was tall and soldierly erect, a posture exaggerated by the snug fit of his white jacket trimmed in military braid and buttoned with gold buttons from the neck, past the fitted waist, to the flared skirts that reached his knees. His black trousers were full but gathered at the bottom and tucked into polished boots. People stared as he passed them for his head was covered by a white silk turban, and at its center, above his forehead, an enormous blue stone was set.

He stopped before Philadelphia, his graying mustache and whiskers bristling with his smile. "Mademoiselle de Ronsard, at your service."

Philadelphia blinked at him, her eyes taking in every detail of his weathered face, lined by age. "Who are you?"

"Your faithful servant, *memsahib*. Sent ahead to make the proper arrangements for your stay in New York."

"Your name?" she questioned, too astonished to think to ask about Eduardo Tavares.

He brought his right hand up to touch his forehead then dropped it in a graceful arch to touch his chin and then his chest as he bent in a bow and said, "I have the honor to be called Akbar, memsahib."

He straightened, looked down at the pile of luggage about her feet, and then correctly picked from the pile only those things that belonged to her. "Follow me, memsahib."

Philadelphia stood for a moment in indecision. Realizing that he had no intention of looking back to see if she were following, she caught up the skirt of her traveling gown and hurried after him. Passing the gape-jawed Mrs.

Crabb just as she was returning with a Negro porter she cried, "I've been met! *Merci! Au revoir!*"

"Well! Did you ever see the like?" Mrs. Crabb murmured when she'd regained her voice.

"Naw, ma'am, I ain't," answered the porter with a grin.

# 4

*New York City, May 1875*

"You wretch! You scoundrel! You—you cheat!"

Eduardo Tavares easily dodged each of the oriental silk pillows Philadelphia threw at him but his amusement was his undoing. As a gust of laughter escaped him, he tripped over the corner of the settee behind which he was seeking marginal cover. As he went sprawling, he heard her say smugly, "Serves you right, you charlatan!"

Rising to his knees, he peeked over the top of the settee. "Is memsahib's tantrum over?"

"Oh no!" She reached for another pillow only to discover that her supply was depleted. She reached, instead, for the porcelain vase on a nearby table and raised it menacingly. "How dare you present yourself to me in a disguise that your own mother would not see through. You might have revealed yourself yesterday at the station. But no, you hid behind that horrid costume and let me go about on cat's paws in fear of you! If you hadn't just now addressed me as senhorita, I wouldn't yet know! You deserve to be stoned!"

Eduardo got a foot under himself but didn't immediately rise for his turban had been knocked askew and covered one eye. As he righted it, he said, "If you'd disarm, I'd be more than happy to explain to you why this" —he gestured to his false whiskers and turban—"was not only a useful disguise but also a very necessary one."

"Not likely!" She drew back her arm. "If you don't leave my rooms this instant, I'll have you forcibly ejected by the hotel detective!"

Eduardo smiled at her flushed face. It might almost be worth the price of his ejection to see the reaction of the concierge and hotel detective when she summoned them. Gowned in lavender which accented her dark tresses and golden eyes full of righteous indignation, she made a picture they wouldn't soon forget. The incident might even be recorded in one of the gossip columns. But, of course, he wasn't ready for her name to be bandied about in that manner just yet. She needed to get her bearings. He'd been quite busy with the three days' head start he had had before she reached New York, and if his work proved fruitful, she'd be thrust soon enough into the public eye.

"You're magnificent in your anger, memsahib, but I must beg you to hear me out before you destroy what appears to be a quite expensive piece of chinaware."

Philadelphia glanced at the vase in her hand, and recognizing the design as Ming, she lowered it. "You're right." She put the vase back on the table and reached for the bell pull.

Eduardo rose to his feet. "Why did you do that? I can get for you anything you desire."

"Then get out!"

He crossed his arms. "You're being very difficult. While I am willing to indulge you as often as is possible, senhorita, I won't be dismissed from rooms for which I am paying."

He had dropped the servile flatterer's voice he had used with her for the past twenty-four hours, and the sound of his own forceful tone reminded her that she was, indeed, in his debt. Following his lead, she crossed her arms before her. "Very well, explain yourself."

He smiled, at least she thought he must be smiling because the detestable false whiskers he wore bristled. "You are in character and I, too, need one in order to be near you. I chose the role of East Indian servant because it is one with which I am familiar. My character is drawn from life, so to speak. Some years ago, I obtained a Delhi servant by the name of Akbar. He resides at present in—well, that's not important. A few instructions to a clever and quick seamstress, a visit to a theatrical establishment and"—he indicated his person with a flourish of his hand—"voilà, Akbar lives. Now," he continued in a good-humored tone, "would you care for a cup of the hot chocolate which I brought in with your breakfast?"

"No!" She said the word emphatically yet the fragrant aroma of cocoa which filled the air was almost irresistible.

"You won't mind if I have a cup?" he asked, moving to serve himself. "I find being a servant most demanding. I was unable to eat my own breakfast before you rang. Perhaps that explains my slip."

Philadelphia's expression suddenly brightened, but she looked away before he looked up from the cup he poured. "Is that the part you are playing in our little drama? You're my servant?"

"At your service, memsahib." He made the gesture with his hand that she'd seen him make many times since he had met her at the New Jersey station the day before.

"What sort of servant are you, exactly?"

"A gift, you might say, from your dear aunt Agnes who resides in Delhi, India."

Philadelphia eyed him suspiciously. "People don't give people as gifts."

He offered her the cup of chocolate which she took without comment. "Your country recently fought a war on that point, did it not? I fear mine will soon be forced to a similar fate."

"Your country has slaves?" she asked, subsiding in a chair despite her desire to maintain a defiant stance.

He poured a second cup and sat down opposite her on the settee. "My country has any number of slaves; Indian slaves, African slaves, mulattoes, caboclas, and many other mixtures whose divergent ancestry is forgotten."

Philadelphia's cup paused midway between her saucer and lips. She was reminded of his boasts of vast wealth and expansive enterprises. "Are you a slave owner?"

He saw her expression and decided to have a little more fun at her expense. "Why do you ask? Does the idea fascinate you?"

"It horrifies me!" She put her cup down. "Are you a slave owner?"

He laughed. "You're a Yankee blue-belly, *sim*?"

"And you're a Simon Legree!"

*"Simon?"* He said the name in his own liquid accent that took away the sting. "This Simon, he is the bad slave master of Senhora Stowe's novel, *Uncle Tim*?"

*"Uncle Tom,"* she corrected. "You're evading my question."

"You're undeniably lovely when you blush. You must do it often in public, then even these stiff *norteamericanos* will fall at your feet like leaves in autumn."

He was flirting and the knowledge that he considered her reaction simply a distraction made her furious. She stood up abruptly. "You can't expect me to countenance your practice of that odious institution."

He sighed. "Why don't you just say what you mean? This formality, this stiffness, it isn't necessary between us. If you wish, say, 'I hate slavery and slave owners, and I refuse to do business with you if you are one!' "

Philadelphia drew herself up. "I detest slavery and slave owners and I refuse to have anything to do with a man who believes that enslaving his fellow creatures is acceptable!"

"Well said." He clapped his hands, then gave her a

rueful glance. "Unfortunately, I'm not a slave owner and so your speech loses something of its intended bite. But I will keep in mind that you are an opinionated woman and a formidable force to cross."

Philadelphia's cheeks caught fire. Furious with him and with herself for allowing him to use her gullibility against her, she glanced once more at the oriental vase. If a knock hadn't sounded on her door just then a lovely piece of antiquity might have met it's demise at her hand.

She moved to open it, but Eduardo was there ahead of her, waving her back with one hand while he opened the door with the other. Only then did she remember that he was supposed to be a servant. *Her* servant. A smile of absolute guile eased into her expression, replacing her frown.

A man of middle age entered the room, dressed in the morning dress of the hotel concierge. "You rang, madame?"

Eduardo reached out and siezed the man by his collar. "No one addresses the memsahib unless she gives her permission!"

The effect of Eduardo's thunderous voice on the man would have been laughable had Philadelphia not been too angry with him to concede him the satisfaction of her amusement. "Unhand the gentleman, Akbar," she said abruptly.

He released the man instantly. "As memsahib wishes." His tone was almost worshipful as he backed away to stand before the door.

Philadelphia came forward with a brilliant smile for the frightened man. "I do apologize for my servant. He forgets that we are no longer in the wilds of India." She saw Eduardo gesticulating over the man's shoulder and realized that she'd forgotten to use a French accent. "You will forgive *moi*? *Oui*?"

"That's all right, madame," the man replied, regaining his dignity under the warmth of the lovely young woman's smile. "India, did you say? We here at the Windsor Hotel are accustomed to dealing with all sorts. We had an East India Company man through here not long ago. He's a regular."

"That is most interesting," she said, ignoring Eduardo, for he was still making suggestions by his expressions and it was unnerving her. "Now how may I help you, monsieur?"

The man looked startled. "It was you who rang me, madame."

*"Moi?"* Philadelphia looked about as if for confirmation until her eyes came to rest on Eduardo. "Akbar!" she said in a reproachful tone. "You know you aren't to disturb the hotel staff. Shame, shame, shame!"

She turned back abruptly to the concierge. "You will forgive this mistake. My servant is, how you say?" She made the circular sign for crazy with her finger. "Sometimes he forgets that we are no longer in a house with a hundred servants for him to order about. Here in America, he must do the fetching and carrying. You do understand, *n'est-ce pas?*"

The man nodded but his Adam's apple was working up and down so quickly she wondered how he could breathe. "You had a hundred servants, ma'am?"

Philadelphia shrugged, wondering why she'd chosen so outlandish a number. "It's not as convenient as it sounds, monsieur. Think of the washing and the feeding and the sleeping arrangements. Akbar is quite sufficient for my present needs. Now, you may leave—after Akbar apologizes to you."

The man glanced at the bearded turbaned man, standing with arms folded and glaring at him, and shook his head. "That won't be necessary, madame. No harm done."

*"Mais oui!* I insist." She took the man's arm and said in a confidential tone, "Akbar must learn proper conduct. He has this terrible temper, but terrible! In India he wore

a huge sword at his side. A servant disobeyed?" She drew a finger across her throat. *"Voilà!* No more servant!"

The man's Adam's apple dove down into his collar. "You mean . . . ?"

"I mean he will—he must apologize! We are in America. We will behave as Americans, *oui*? Akbar?"

Acting on her cue Eduardo made his gesture of servitude and said gravely, "As memsahib wishes. A thousand apologies, you insignificant flea!"

The poor man jerked with surprise at the barb but catching Philadelphia's eye and seeing the quick shake of her head, he decided not to press the issue. "Apology accepted. Now I'll just be going." He put out his hand which Philadelphia stared at blankly. He turned to the turbaned man but the servant merely placed his arms akimbo, a position made more threatening by his flat dark stare. The man dropped his hand and made Philadelphia the sketchiest of bows. "If there's anything you should require, madame—"

"Mademoiselle," Philadelphia corrected. *"Je le regrette,* I am unmarried."

"Unmarried," he repeated, filing that bit of information away in his mind beside the note about her hundred servants. "Very well, miss. I am entirely at your disposal. Good day." He turned, relieved to see that the "clothheaded savage," as he would describe the foreign servant to his desk clerk, had opened the door for him.

When the door was firmly closed behind the concierge, Eduardo turned to Philadelphia, his black brows riding low over his dark eyes and his hands on his hips. "Do you know what you've just done?"

Philadelphia took a step back. "You deserved it!" She saw him take a step toward her and took another hurried step backward. "You said that you're my servant." He moved another step closer and she made another retreat. "How am I to be believed if you go about giving all the orders?" Two steps. Double retreat.

She glanced back to judge the distance between herself and her bedroom door. "If, if you don't like what I've done, then leave me. I don't expect you to—what are you doing?"

He was in full stride toward her. She made two desperate backpedaling steps before whirling about to flee. The doorway didn't seem that far but even as her hand reached the knob she was siezed from behind, turned about, and lifted off her feet.

Eduardo caught her high against his chest and spun the two of them about twice before setting her back on her feet.

Philadelphia leaned back dizzily against the door, not knowing what to expect next but the sound of full-throated laughter surprised her.

"You—you, wondrous creature!" he cried when he caught his breath. *"Mãe de Deus!* Do you know what you've done?"

She shook her head slowly, wondering if, whatever it was, it had been her last act.

"You've done in a single stroke what it might have taken me weeks to achieve. You've made an impression on the concierge that he isn't likely ever to forget. By afternoon this incident will be the talk of the hotel. It will be the topic of half the guests at dinner. By noon tomorrow, much of Fifth Avenue will know you are in the city. It was brilliant! A stroke of genius, that business about my having murdered recalcitrant servants. How did you happen to think of it?"

"I don't precisely know," Philadelphia said, gathering her wits now that she realized that she wasn't about to be strangled herself. "If you're pleased, you might have said so in the first place rather than chasing me around the room."

He leaned toward her. "But I most enjoyed chasing you!" He moved even closer, until she could see that while his irises were dark, they weren't clearly so black as the pupils which were engulfing them. She moved back a little only to meet the barrier of her bedroom door. "If you were a Brazilian lady and had behaved so wonderfully, I would kiss you."

She stopped breathing. His face was only inches away from hers, that beautiful, sinfully gorgeous face shrouded now in hoary whiskers and some sort of makeup that made him appear older. He was teasing her, and she didn't like it, not one bit. So why was she hoping against hope that he would carry out his threat to kiss her?

Eduardo watched the play of emotion on her face and wondered how anyone so strong-willed and resourceful could, at the same time, be so completely unguarded at a moment like this. He saw her trepidation and her anxiousness, and her desire for his kiss. His gaze moved to her lips. They were parted to draw the breath she was holding. The pink rouge made them seem even fuller and more tempting than necessary. It would be so easy. Only an inch or two separated them. He wanted to kiss her.

As he bent to her, Philadelphia shut her eyes and lifted her chin. She waited. One heartbeat. Two. Three. Nothing happened.

When she opened her eyes in confusion she saw that he'd moved away from her, half a room away. He was headed toward the door and he didn't pause until he reached it.

He turned but didn't look directly at her. "You should eat your breakfast before it becomes cold. I will return in an hour. You must be seen in public. For that, we will go shopping." He reached for the door, opened it, and walked through, shutting it very carefully behind him.

Philadelphia bit her lip. What had she done, or not done? Why had he backed away? Humiliation crept up her neck like a stinging rash. He'd been teasing her again! She turned abruptly to hide her face against the door. "He's hateful! Hateful!"

*   *   *

"If I may say so, you'd look lovely in that shade, miss."

Philadelphia idly fingered a length of mandarin yellow silk cloth at one of the millinery counters of A. T. Stewart and Company. "It's pretty," she replied to the saleslady, her tone wistful. "So many lovely things. Perhaps, one day I shall wear them, if I'm ever happy again."

"Oh, miss, I do apologize," the salesgirl gushed, belatedly realizing that the young Frenchwoman's dove gray was a sign of a mourning not yet complete. "My sympathy, miss, over your loss."

Philadelphia turned a stricken face to the girl. *"Merci."* With that, she turned and walked hurriedly away.

Not until she reached the street outside the imposing iron facade of the five-story establishment, did she trust herself to speak to the man who followed her about like a shadow, seen but not heard from. "This is disgusting!" she whispered in fury. "Lying to rouse the sympathy of strangers! I detest it!"

"Memsahib does not lie when she says she is in mourning. There is her father," he reminded her in a low voice behind her.

She turned about to face him. "That is my business. I don't enjoy soliciting pity from others."

"Memsahib would do well to remember her surroundings," Eduardo replied in French this time, aware that his unusual appearance had snared the attention of the drivers of the many private carriages lined up on Broadway to wait while their owners shopped.

She squared her shoulders and, looking him straight in the eye, said in English, "If you don't approve of my conduct, you can well find yourself another partner!"

He checked the impulse to shake her until her teeth rattled. Patience, that was what he always seemed in need of and what was most in short supply. Ever since he'd made the slip of revealing a desire to kiss her, neither of them had been able to speak two civil words to one another. It had been a stupid, needless thing to do, and he was very sorry about it; but he couldn't allow one small mistake to ruin what had begun so well a short time earlier. If only she would stop staring at him with those enormous gold eyes, taunting him, daring him to behave as more than a simple obedient servant. "Memsahib is feeling tired. Is she desirous of her lunch, perhaps?"

Philadelphia turned a cold shoulder to him. "I am hungry but it needn't concern you. I see a confectionery shop just across the street. You may go home." She angled her head so as to slant a withering glance his way. "In fact, I order you to leave me this instant!"

"I would cut off my right arm if memsahib commanded," he said in a dramatic voice, but as he bowed before her he added in a low growl, "but she'd find that an arm without a purse is of little use to her."

"Must you remind me at every turn!" she cried in French, then murmured, "You're no better than my father's creditors, forever plaguing me about debts."

She was insulted, he could see it in every rigid line of her posture, and he was immediately sorry that he'd stooped to the demeaning retort. He reached into the red satin sash tied about his waist and handed her a small purse. "Memsahib will find that she has all she needs and more. She has only to ask her humble servant."

She refused the purse. "Oh no. You'd better carry it. I shouldn't want to be accused of overspending my allowance." She turned and walked to the curb but found she couldn't immediately cross. Before her the thoroughfare was choked with vehicles; hack-drivers, truckmen, omnibus drivers, and myriad private carriages and conveyances. In the middle of the intersection she spied a blue-coated traffic policeman with his baton raised, blowing shrilly on the whistle he held between his teeth.

The din and confusion were unlike anything she'd ever experienced in Chicago. Her father had always been very careful in choosing the times and places when she went out in public. On those occasions when she had been allowed to go out on her own, she had ridden in the family carriage and only between the morning hours of ten and noon. Nothing had prepared her for the crush of people on foot at midday on Broadway.

As the traffic before her halted and the cross traffic began to move, Philadelphia was thrust forward into the onslaught of noise and voices and dust. A gasp of surprise turned into fright as she realized that she was being swept along against her will into the street. Growing more alarmed with each second, she swung her head from side to side, hoping to find Eduardo but he was nowhere to be seen in the press of the crowd.

Suddenly, out of nowhere it seemed to Philadelphia, she heard new rough voices added to the crowd and the pedestrians about her began to scatter, shoving hard past her. Then she heard the bells and knew what was happening. A fire engine had been dispatched. The men roaring out orders to vacate the street were the firemen who ran ahead on foot to clear a path for their company's engine. The din became a cacophony as frightened horses whinnied and reared, cabbies swore, and drivers shouted and cracked their whips above the heads of their horses as they began the laborious task of clearing the intersection.

She swung around, trying desperately to return to the curb, but others were pushing past her in the opposite direction. All of a sudden she felt the heel of her shoe catch in a crack in the cobblestone paving. A hard shove from behind made the heel snap. Losing her footing, and with a scream of genuine terror, she fell before the approaching hooves of a carriage horse.

Eduardo's heart contracted at her cry. From the moment they'd been separated, he'd been trying to reach her. She'd been nearly within arm's reach when she suddenly pitched forward and was lost from sight just as a pair of matched bays drawing a crested carriage lurched forward.

Like a madman, he shoved and roared at the people in

a free mixture of Portuguese and English, and they scattered before him more quickly than they had the passing fire engine. Uncaring for his own safety, he lunged at the horse who reared up before him as he reached Philadelphia's crumpled form. Sidestepping the flash of iron hooves, he caught the bay by the bit to bring its head down.

"Curb your damned animals!" he cried at the driver. The moment the horses were forced into a backward step, he was on his knees beside Philadelphia. She lay so still a sudden sharp pain squeezed his heart.

"Menina!" he cried desperately as he bent over her and gently touched her throat in search of a pulse. It beat strongly and regularly. "Philadelphia," he whispered softly as he gathered her up against his chest. Her face was ghostly pale except for the bloody bruise on her right cheek, but as he tenderly brushed a strand of hair from her cheek he was rewarded with the flicker of her lashes.

"What's happened here?"

Eduardo looked up into the beet-red face of the traffic policeman. "Ask him!" he answered with a gesture toward the driver of the expensive carriage. "He nearly killed her!" Then he dropped his gaze back to Philadelphia, who was now staring up at him.

"What happened?" she asked weakly, clutching his arm in the hope that it would stop her world from spinning.

At her touch, he felt himself tremble. "You fell. Are you hurt, menina?"

She started to shake her head but thought better of it. "I fell. My heel broke."

Heartened by her lucid reply, Eduardo felt his fear for her slipping away. "I'll take you home." Wrapping one arm about her shoulders and sliding the other under her knees, he picked her up as he stood.

"Just one minute!" the policeman cried as Eduardo

moved toward the curb. "The driver says the girl stepped in front of his horse and there was nothing he could do."

Eduardo glanced contemptuously at the driver who held a smug expression and then back at the burly policeman. "The man's a liar and a coward. He should be arrested for having less skill than a heavy-handed ox driver!"

"That won't be necessary," said a voice from the interior of the coach. As the crested carriage door swung open a footman sprang down from his rear perch to assist the person stepping down. A silver-haired woman gowned in mulberry crepe stepped out onto the pavement. She was tiny, inches short of five feet, but every spare inch was girded in regal self-respect and importance. She inclined her head to look the great distance up into the six-foot policeman's face and said, "I saw the entire incident and my driver was to blame for it."

Raising a silver lorgnette to her eyes, she inspected her driver. "Jack, you're fired. I've always said you were heavy-handed with my animals. Even a wretched foreigner can see it. Get down. Get down at once, man! I don't intend to wait about all day while you rehinge your jaw. Scat!"

She turned to Eduardo, giving him, too, a thorough going-over with the aid of her lorgnette. "Who is that creature you're carrying about like a sack of meal?"

Eduardo glanced down at Philadelphia, who was actually smiling at him, and a sudden queer feeling moved in his chest. "This is my mistress, Memsahib Felise de Ronsard." He'd noted the crest on the carriage and the jewels that adorned the woman's ears and fingers. She was obviously a Fifth Avenue matron. In other circumstances, he'd have been tempted to capitalize on the moment but now all he cared about was getting Philadelphia to safety where he could reassure himself that she wasn't more hurt than she seemed. "If you will excuse us, I must take her home and fetch a doctor."

"I won't excuse you," the tiny woman answered and when Eduardo moved to ignore her, he found his path blocked by the policeman. "Best hear the lady out, laddie," he said.

The lady's expression was neutral. "Does your mistress reside in the city?"

Eduardo ground his teeth but said civilly. "Memsahib resides at present at the Windsor Hotel."

"And your mistress knows a good physician, does she?"

He gave the lady a considering glance of his own before saying, "No, memsahib."

"Well, I do. Put the girl in my carriage. I presume you know how to handle a carriage and pair?"

Eduardo nearly smiled as the import of her words sank in. A woman of quality was offering them her hospitality. Misfortune had a golden lining. "You presume correctly, memsahib."

"What does it mean when you call me *meem sad*?"

"Memsahib means 'mistress.' It is a sign of respect in my homeland, India."

The woman made a sound suspiciously like a grunt of satisfaction. "Well, heathen, I am Mrs. Sutterwhite Ormstead. You may drive me home. I'll send for my physician once we arrive. It's the least I can do, considering my horses nearly made suet of your memsahib."

"And so, you say you're looking for the remaining members of your family?" Mrs. Ormstead mused as she stood beside the bed that Philadelphia occupied. "Why don't you go home to France? I suspect they're most likely to be found there."

"Perhaps I should." Philadelphia clutched the comforter that lay over her, wincing as the physician continued his examination of her foot. She was in pain, confused and uneasy in the company of this kind stranger, and not at all up to the task of lying vividly and imaginatively. "Where is Akbar?"

"Akbar? Is that the name of the heathen in the head cloth? Well, I never! Akbar. Sounds like the sort of noise one makes when a bone's caught in the throat." Her perfectly winged white brows rose speculatively. "Who exactly is this Akbar person?"

"My guardian—ouch!"

The physician looked up with a contrite, "Sorry, miss." He straightened from his examination and turned to Mrs. Ormstead. There doesn't appear to be a break, only a severe sprain. The young lady will need to remain in bed for a few days, until the swelling goes down."

Mrs. Ormstead glanced at her guest. "You do have a maid?"

Philadelphia held her eagle-eyed stare. "I have Akbar."

"Indeed, and quite an improper arrangement that is. Oh, I can see that he's devoted to you. It took my butler and three footmen to persuade him to remain below stairs while the doctor came up to examine you. He's a remarkably fit person for one of his years."

Picturing in her mind the scene that must have taken place, Philadelphia didn't meet the older woman's gaze but used the excuse of the pain in her foot to shift her attention to the physician who had begun wrapping her ankle in gauze. "Akbar is an extraordinary person."

"No doubt. But he isn't a fit nursemaid for a young lady, and that's what you need. Dr. McNeill says you should remain in bed for a few days. You'll do so under my roof. Tut, child, I will brook no resistance in the matter. I am old and rich enough to have become quite accustomed to having my way."

Alarmed, Philadelphia shook her head. "That won't do! I mean," she paused, seeking desperately to regain the treacherous French accent that deserted her every time some new emotion surged to the fore. "What I mean, madame, is that I do not wish to disrupt your life.

You have been *très gentille* to me. *Merci,* a thousand thanks, Madame Ormstead. But I must go home."

"You have no home. You have *rooms,*" Mrs. Ormstead said the word with distaste, "at a local hostelry. No young lady of breeding should be found on the premises of such a place without the accompaniment of a male relative. This dark-visaged Akbar does not qualify. I've already sent my housekeeper for your things. You will stay here." She smiled suddenly, and it transformed her arrogant features. "You see, I do get my way."

Philadelphia subsided against the pillows propping her up. Mrs. Ormstead reminded her of her father's aunt Harriet, who'd died when she was twelve. A kind and busy woman, she too allowed no barriers when she wanted something. "You are most kind, but most difficult to say no to."

"Mr. Ormstead used to say the same." For a moment the older woman's ice-blue eyes softened but then she gave her head a tiny shake. "He's been gone these last three years. Seems like thirty. Told him he should forego those extra helpings of trifle with cream. But he was a most stubborn man. Never could abide the trait. Can't think why I married him."

Impulsively, Philadelphia reached out to touch the woman's hand. "You must have loved him very much."

Mrs. Ormstead looked down at Philadelphia as though seeing her clearly for the first time. "I do believe you're right, dear. So I'll tell you a secret. Never marry a man with traits you can't abide. Just about the time you've grown accustomed to them, he'll die and then you'll have spent all those years of cultivating accommodation for naught." She turned briskly to the doctor. "Aren't you finished yet? The girl looks all in."

The doctor had finished and, after handing Philadelphia a draft for the pain, left the two women alone.

"I want to see Akbar," Philadelphia said at once.

"No doubt you do," Mrs. Ormstead replied, "but I

think you should rest. A nice nap is what you need and afterward a bit of supper. Then we shall see."

"He will be most unhappy," she said petulantly. "And I, too."

"Good. There's nothing like a little unhappiness to make a young girl's day. I was often unhappy at your age and never so pleased as when I was." With that cheerfully spoken bit of nonsense, she turned and walked out of the room.

Philadelphia lay a long time watching the closed door and straining for the sound of footfalls that would announce that someone was coming to her door. As the minutes accumulated she finally conceded that Mrs. Ormstead was having her way again, and that Eduardo wouldn't be visiting her anytime soon.

Annoyed, she turned her attention to the room in which she lay. It was furnished in the latest fashion for simplicity and airiness. A simple blue-and-white-striped paper covered the walls. There were several small skirted tables covered in pictures, porcelains, and trinkets. White lace curtains veiled the windows and a matching blue-and-white half-canopy draped her bed. Near the window stood a bamboo chaise lounge with a blue and white silk patterned cushion. An oriental screen stood before the fireplace, closed for the summer months. India matting covered the floor. Behind a large Japanese lacquer screen standing in one corner she spied a toilet service, a stack of fluffy towels, and the edge of a bath pan. It was a lovely room, a peaceful room, and one in keeping with Mrs. Ormstead's claim to wealth.

Finally her thoughts returned to her ankle. The doctor had packed it in ice but the dull pulsating pain had not completely subsided. Her hip was sore and her cheek burned from the scrape. All in all, she was miserable and tired and hungry.

Hunger was the last thought she had before her eyes

slid shut. There was a bowl of fruit on the table near the
doorway. The pieces looked ripe, sweet, and bursting with
juice. Yet they might as well have been a thousand miles
away. Where was Akbar when she really needed him?

# 5

"Feeling better?" Eduardo stood with his arms folded, scowling down at Philadelphia as she lay on the bamboo chaise lounge.

Philadelphia shook her head, aware of the maid who hovered nearby. "My ankle, it throbs horribly. And my stomach feels hollow."

Eduardo scowled at the maid. "Memsahib wishes to have her breakfast. You will fetch it at once!"

"V-v-very well, sir!" The maid, fascinated by but also frightened of the turbaned man, dropped a curtsy and fled.

"Ouch! You're hurting me!" Philadelphia said as he bent a knee and took her bandaged ankle in his hands.

"Serves you right," he muttered as he began unwrapping the gauze. "Anyone foolish enough to trip and frighten a horse deserves what she gets."

"You're just jealous," she replied, dropping the fake accent now that the maid was gone. "You've spent the night in the servant's quarters while I've been here."

He glanced about the blue and white bedroom of the Ormstead mansion. "It's quite nice. Still, even the servants' quarters have their charm. For instance, the maid who just left shares the room next to mine. She and her roommate were quite solicitous of my welfare last evening."

Philadelphia shot him a hostile look, then realized that he was taking great liberties with her ankle. "What do you think you're doing?"

"Making certain that idiot who calls himself a physician knows what he's talking about."

He hadn't had a moment alone with Philadelphia since they had entered the Ormstead house the afternoon before. In fact, the only time he'd been allowed to see her had been after she'd had her dinner. Even then, Mrs. Ormstead had stood by his side, her bright eyes taking in every nuance of movement and gesture between them. He'd not been free to touch Philadelphia or even question her about how she was faring in her guise as Mademoiselle Ronsard. Now he was determined to examine her himself.

He rotated her foot first to the right and then to the left, pushed her toes forward, then pointed them.

Watching him, Philadelphia forgot how pleased she had been to see him when he entered the room moments before. She had slept badly, awakening again and again with the uneasy sensation of being watched. But, of course, there had been no one there but her conscience, which plagued her with remorse for taking advantage of the kindness of a stranger. How upset Mrs. Ormstead would be if she knew that she housed an imposter under her roof. They simply had to leave and go back to the Windsor Hotel. Thoughts such as these had contributed to the throbbing in her temples. "Well?" she demanded irritably. "Are you satisfied that my foot is still attached?"

"I am satisfied that it's not broken," he answered, not glancing up. "I do think he might at least have left you with liniment. I treat my horses better than this."

"By all means, I should be treated better than you're treating me. You've managed to make my ankle throb worse than ever."

"Have I?" He looked up at her in blank surprise. "Then I must make amends." With slow deliberate strokes he began to massage her ankle, his touch at first light, then deepening in pressure as he worked to remove the soreness from the muscles of her ankle and calf. All the time he held her heel in the firm embrace of his left hand.

Philadelphia sipped in a breath against the first pangs of discomfort as he began to knead her aching muscles. But, gradually the ache departed under the soothing heat of his hands. After a minute, the hypnotic motions of his fingers relaxed even the pain in her head, and she eased back against the pillows of the chaise lounge and closed her eyes.

She'd spent the night in fitful sleep, keenly aware of being in unfamiliar surroundings and plagued by pain. The effort to be both a civil guest and remain in disguise had been almost more than she could bear. Now, she was so relaxed that she didn't even realize when she began to sigh contentedly. In his hands she felt both safe and at ease.

Eduardo heard her soft sighs of pleasure with mingled feelings of pride and annoyance. He was aware of what her response meant even if she wasn't. Had she been another woman, he would have assumed that she was encouraging him to take more liberties with her. But he didn't assume that. He simply understood that she was too untutored in the ways of men to realize the implication of her total submission to his touch. Why, she didn't even react when his hand moved from her ankle up under the skirt of her dressing gown to the full curve of her shapely calf. She seemed totally oblivious to the impropriety of his caress.

To confirm the fact, he slowly slid his hand up farther, to her knee. He felt her involuntary start as he touched the ticklish place behind her knee but she didn't rise up indignantly to demand that he cease. Instead he heard her murmur drowsily, "No fair tickling."

Annoyed that his caress was taken as a tease, he eased his fingers up to cup her kneecap. What would she say to that? Nothing.

His hand slipped down her leg then moved up once more, and he admitted to himself that his pleasure in touching her was far from one-sided. His self-imposed celibacy was beginning to strain at its bonds. A dizzying kind of heat spiraled down through him with every stroke. As he began to knead the soft and silky skin of her calf, with its warm play of tendon and well-formed muscle beneath, a deep sigh of sensual longing escaped her.

He held his breath, willing himself not to move, not to dare venture his touch beyond the boundary of her knee to what he knew would be the even softer, more compelling flesh of her thigh. He looked up at her, hoping that her expression would forbid him to move. What he saw was not what he sought, but what he dared not seek.

She lay with her head thrown back, her lips softly parted, her cheeks and neck pink with the telltale flush of desire. Her eyes were closed, as if she couldn't look at him and admit what she felt. He opened his hand and laid it against the tender swelling of her ankle. Through his palm he recorded the quickening throb of her pulse, and it echoed in the throb of his arousal.

Never looking away from her face, he directed his hand once more up under the edge of her skirts, past the delicate column of her lower leg, under the swelling curve of her calf, up to the narrowing joint of her knee and then beyond.

Philadelphia didn't know when she stopped relaxing and began instead to feel a subtle but insidious coiling inside her. She had been drifting halfway between consciousness and sleep, riding the pleasant ripples of sensation caused by the passage of his hands over her skin, when the shadings of the impressions gradually altered.

The soothing, calming strokes became more powerful than the achy threads of pain. Strong fingers smoothed over the jagged twinges, replacing them with a sweet heavy somnolence. Splinters of discomfort dissolved under his caresses, blending and spinning out again to become silky threads of pleasure winding and binding her in a gossamer of delicious shivery feeling.

Her breathing deepened. Her pulse tripped up its even tempo to find a faster beat. All at once she knew that he was no longer easing her pain but deliberately stirring very different sensations, inexplicable but troubling sensations she'd never before experienced. Even so, she wasn't at all certain she wanted them to end.

The knock at the door jarred her awake, snapping the threads of secret pleasure. Her eyes flew wide open, and she met Akbar's gaze. So intense was his black stare that, for an instant, she thought she saw in his eyes a match of the secret pleasure that made her body pulse. In shame, her gaze skittered away from his. When she felt his hand slip from beneath her skirts, she realized as shame deepened into disgrace what she had done. She'd lain like a wanton under his touch, enjoying his caress, and he knew it!

She shrank back into the pillow, wishing that she could creep away and hide from his all-seeing gaze. Even as she drew her legs up and away from him, the inside of her thigh still tingling with the memory of his fingertips, her fiery blush moved lower to sting her breasts and stomach.

"Breakfast, miss!" came the cry from beyond the doorway after a second sharper rap on the door.

"A moment!" Eduardo quickly rewound the bandage, cursing the circumstances that had forced Philadelphia's sudden withdrawal from him, and then rose to cross the room to the door. He hadn't known what he would do next—no, that was wrong. He had known exactly what he *wanted* to do next. He had felt her tremble as he caressed her and known the rare pleasure of being nearly out of control himself. He, Eduardo Domingo Xavier Tavares, master of his own emotions and actions, had known an elusive moment of indecision. For him the moment was rarer than yellow diamonds, more precious than gold, and far more dangerous than the bite of the piranha.

"I was about to call Mr. Hobbs, the butler," the maid said when Eduardo swung open the door. "Thought your mistress had fallen asleep."

"Memsahib does not raise her voice to answer servants," he replied censoriously and took the tray from her. "You may go."

"No one but I gives orders in my house." Eduardo looked up to find Mrs. Ormstead standing in the open doorway. "Your manners are atrocious, Akbar. You will apologize to me."

Bowing low to hide his smile of amusement, he saluted the old woman. "A thousand pardons, Memsahib Ormstead. May the sting of a thousand bees stab my eyes should I offend you again."

Hedda Ormstead turned to her maid. "Did you hear that? A trifle overstated, perhaps, but I like the spirit of it. You may pass this incident on to those below and say that I wholeheartedly approve of the groveling tone of this apology. Hereafter, I should like it to be emulated. Well, girl, have you nothing to do?"

"Yes, ma'am." The maid bowed and hurried out.

Hedda watched the girl's flight in amusement. "I do so wish I had her vigor. I'd keep her hopping then, I can tell you." She turned to her injured guest, whom Akbar was bending over with her breakfast tray.

When she'd followed her maid up the stairs, Hedda had expected her guest would be alone. Finding Akbar with her was a rude shock. Her gaze sharpened as she saw the young woman refuse to meet her servant's eye as he spoke to her in whispered French. Her face was averted from him, as though she were embarrassed or felt put upon by the man.

A fine figure of a man he was, too, Hedda mused. With his broad-shouldered silhouette and narrow waist he recalled to her mind the young gallants who'd come calling on her when she was forty years younger. The thought surprised her. Indeed, Akbar possessed the physique of a man much younger than his graying whiskers would suggest.

Hedda smiled at her own wayward thoughts. Folly. So much folly. In the last twelve hours she'd found herself thinking of things that she hadn't thought of, or allowed herself to think of, in years. It was having youth under her roof, she decided. Youth troubled the tranquility, disturbed the peace, and maddened the reason of maturity. She was well rid of her own youth but, oh, something was afoot here. Curiosity was a feeling long absent from her, but here, surely, was a puzzle worth exploring.

Suddenly she changed her mind about what she'd come to say. "Good morning, Mam'zelle Ronsard," she said crisply as she came forward to stand before Philadelphia. "Goodness, child, you look as flat as three-day-old ale. You didn't sleep a wink, did you?"

Philadelphia smiled at the lady. "*Bonjour,* Madame Ormstead. I am sorry I cannot rise to greet you properly."

"If you could do that, you'd not be here," she answered in a severe voice. "Why didn't you ring for a sleeping draft? You wasted a perfectly lovely night. I slept like the dead, which is no small matter to a woman of my advanced years."

Philadelphia didn't mean to laugh but the conflicting pent-up frustrations of pain and acute embarrassment suddenly sought release and she found herself erupting in peals of laughter, long and loud and unstoppable.

Hedda Ormstead's lips twitched as she watched the girl's pretty face turn scarlet with mirth and her eyes fill with tears of embarrassment. "You're a naughty child, mam'zelle. I should toss you out but I've developed a rather sudden and wholly illogical desire for your company. Oh, do subside, dear, so that you may agree to be my houseguest for a while."

Philadelphia sputtered to a stop, her gaze darting to Akbar in a silent plea for advice.

Eduardo turned to the woman. "Memsahib Ronsard is most humbly flattered by your gracious invitation, Memsahib Ormstead, but does not wish to overburden you with her person."

Hedda's winged brows took flight up her forehead. "Remarkable! You read all that in a glance? Can you tell the future as well?" She looked at Philadelphia. "I thought it was your ankle that was sprained, not your tongue."

Philadelphia smiled. "Akbar cares for me so well that he sometimes forgets that I can speak for myself. I am most flattered by your invitation—"

"And so you accept it," Hedda finished for her. "Please don't protest, I do so hate mealymouthed protestations. I am determined to have you. Have I not as good as kidnapped you? You are here. Your things are here. The bill for your hotel rooms has been settled."

"My bills are paid?" Philadelphia said in wonder. "But why? You don't know me. I am a stranger. I could be anyone."

"But you happen to be a pretty young thing who fell under the hooves of my horses in an hour when—oh, never mind that. Do mend quickly. There's a play, the final one of the season, to which I have tickets on Thursday. You will accompany me. And, of course, the redoubtable Akbar."

Her eyes twinkled as she looked him over. "I most especially wish society to view your heathen. It will give them something to chew over during their Sunday visiting. Now eat your breakfast before it's spoilt. You may come with me, Akbar. I'm interviewing a new carriage driver this morning and want your opinion in the matter.

After that, you may review my stable. I'm not at all pleased with the look of one bay's mouth. That hamhanded fool, Jack, may have ruined him."

"As you wish," Eduardo answered but he didn't immediately follow Mrs. Ormstead as she left the room. He waited until Philadelphia was forced by his silent presence to look up at him. "Is the pain better, menina?" he said in a low and husky voice.

Philadelphia thought that holding his gaze was the most difficult thing she had ever done. "Yes. The pain is better."

"Good. That was my only purpose," he replied and turned and left the room.

Philadelphia caught her lower lip between her teeth when he was gone. A relief of her pain, that was all he sought in touching her. It was she who had allowed her emotions free rein and so had needlessly embarrassed them both. The thought that she had been such a ninny shamed her all over again. She groaned and sank lower in the lounge, feeling very young and very green and very confused.

"The gown will do," Mrs. Ormstead said with a single nod of her head.

Philadelphia stood before the free-standing mirror as Amy, the maid, fluffed her train. When Senhor Tavares had provided her with the black silk gown she couldn't imagine when she'd have an opportunity to wear it, but she had to admit that it seemed the perfect item for the theater. Of course, had she been going about under her rightful name, she wouldn't have dared wear so frivolous a gown a scant two months after her father's death.

Her father was dead. The sorrow cut sharply and instantly through her pleasure. How could she forget? How could she be happy even for a moment when her father lay in his cold dark grave while infamous lies still went abroad to haunt his memory?

Remorse poisoned her thoughts. She'd joined in this mummery for a noble purpose but had she accomplished anything? No, she had allowed herself to be caught up in a set of useless circumstances.

"Whatever is the matter, dear?"

At Mrs. Ormstead's distressed tone, Philadelphia looked round, blinking back the brine of tears. "Nothing, madame."

"I doubt that. You look as though you've suffered a sudden attack. Does your ankle still trouble you?"

"*Oui.* That is it," she answered, using the ready excuse. "But it will pass, I am certain." Hedda regarded the young woman sympathetically. "Perhaps I've pushed you from your sickbed too soon."

Philadelphia turned about, her train sweeping a graceful arc on the floor. "Oh no, madame, you haven't pushed me. I leaped from it gratefully. The monotony of my days had become a burden."

"Very well. You make a pretty picture, Mademoiselle Felise." She noted in approval the way Philadelphia's hair had been swept back from her face and held in place by a corsage of red silk roses. "Amy managed a credible job with your coiffure. I particularly like the way that single curl trails down your back. What did you say, Amy?"

The maid blushed. "I said, ma'am, that I didn't do the mam'zelle's hair. She did it herself."

Hedda's eyes widened. "Why ever did you do that?"

"I have not always had the services of a maid," Philadelphia replied with a simple shrug. She couldn't very well say she didn't want the girl to see and question the telltale stains her dyed hair left in the washbasin. "Akbar is many things. A hairdresser, alas, he's not."

Mrs. Ormstead looked about. "Ah yes, Akbar. Where is that wretched heathen?"

Eduardo detached himself from the shadows of a nearby alcove. "I await the memsahib's pleasure."

The older woman's eyes widened again. He was

dressed in much the same manner as usual but the color and fabric of his attire were more elaborate. His coat of heavy scarlet silk brocade reached just below his knees. A sash of gold belted his waist. A matching piece of gold silk was wrapped about his head and held in place by the now familiar sapphire brooch. In place of black trousers and boots he wore white silk trousers which narrowed at the ankles to reveal black patent slippers. But the item which caught and held her attention was the heavy gold chain which he wore around his neck like a chamberlain's collar of rank.

Eduardo came forward slowly to meet Philadelphia. She looked beautiful and, if possible, more desirable than she had the first time he'd seen her in that gown. "Salutations, memsahib. I have brought your jewels." He reached into his coat and withdrew a necklace. "Allow me," he intoned solemnly and reached up to clasp it about her neck.

"Good heavens!" Hedda Ormstead exclaimed when the full glory of the diamond necklace was revealed.

Philadelphia reached up to touch it shyly. "It is all that is left of my family's treasures."

*"Le collier de Ronsard,"* Akbar announced. "No doubt, it is honored to bask in the light of your beauty, memsahib."

The older woman's gaze shifted briefly between the pair. Odd talk that, from a servant to his mistress. He spoke more like a lover than an underling. As for the look in his eyes, if he were not instantly obedient to the girl's every wish, she doubted the girl's aunt would ever have allowed him to accompany her halfway around the world.

Philadelphia, too, felt the weight of his heated gaze on her naked shoulders. The breathless sensation that often came over her when he was near turned quickly into the constriction of shame. She'd made the mistake of misreading his intentions before. Never again. "Please help me with my stole, Akbar," she said in a husky voice.

Only when his warm hands brushed her skin as he enfolded her into the garment did she realize that asking for his help was a mistake. He stood so close behind her so that the fragrance of his cologne enveloped her. For an instant she drowned under the twin sensations of his touch and smell.

"Shall we go, children?"

Hedda smiled as the pair started guiltily. Good, she thought. Let them be ashamed to gaze at one another like sick calves. A mistress and her servant; it had all the makings of a deplorable, treacle-sweet—and disastrous! —romance. It must be nipped in the bud.

She had not been blessed with children of her own but retained the thwarted motherly instincts of forty years keeping. She knew exactly what to do. Felise de Ronsard needed a proper suitor, a young man of breeding and a little money, someone who would show her that Akbar, handsome though the scoundrel was, was not at all what she needed and should have.

The frown lifted from Hedda's expression. She had a nephew, really a nephew's son, from a branch of her family whose company she usually avoided as being too tedious to be endured more than once a year on their New Year's Day visits. The boy must be about twenty-one, graduating from Harvard soon, if memory served. His name was Harry or Herbert, or was it Delbert? It didn't matter. She recalled him as a pleasant-faced child with soft brown curls and bright gray eyes. If his mother hadn't ruined him with smothering or his father with a too-generous allowance, he might be a suitable match for Felise. She'd arrange a meeting quite soon.

The Booth Theater blazed with gas lights as the Ormstead carriage drew up before the arched doorway. As she was handed down by the footman, Philadelphia decided that the granite facade of Italianate Renaissance styling made it one of the handsomest buildings she had ever seen.

With Mrs. Ormstead leading, they made their way through the elegantly dressed patrons thronging the lobby. What she lacked in stature Hedda Ormstead more than made up for in presence and character, to which the crowd responded by parting neatly before her passage. The movement was rather like that of the Red Sea before Moses, Philadelphia observed with a smile.

In fact, the stir created by the arrival of the silver-haired matron eclipsed for a moment the presence of those who had come with her. It wasn't until the theater-goers realized that the bearded, turbaned man and beautiful girl in black were with Mrs. Ormstead that they began to turn their stares on Philadelphia. Yet Mrs. Ormstead didn't give anyone a chance to address her. She led her party up the staircase, past the lovely frescoes lining the walls, and into the narrow hallway that backed the tier of box seats.

Only when she was seated in one of the first chairs of her box did Hedda Ormstead permit herself a tiny smile as she looked at Philadelphia. "That went well. Of course, we shouldn't have arrived before the end of the first act, but then one would have remained in ignorance of the point of the story, and I do so enjoy a good rousing tale."

Philadelphia smiled. "What is the play this evening, Madame Ormstead?"

"I haven't the slightest idea," Hedda answered and raised her lorgnette. "Do sit forward in your chair, mademoiselle. You can't be seen properly by those in the orchestra seats. That's right, now remove your wrap. Akbar? The mademoiselle is warm. Take her wrap." The order given, she turned her lorgnette and attention to the galleries. "I only hope those present are worth our efforts," she added, half under her breath.

Philadelphia had avoided looking at Akbar as he moved from his place by the door so she was greatly surprised when he gently but firmly squeezed her shoulder under the guise of removing her cashmere shawl. It was a gesture meant to hearten her spirit but it annoyed her instead. "Madame is pleased to show off her houseguest?"

The young lady's cool tone brought Hedda's attention back to her. "Have I offended you, mademoiselle?" She reached out and laid a small smooth hand over one of Philadelphia's. "I mean you no harm, dear. I'm only an old lady with too little to occupy my time and mind."

Philadelphia turned her hand under the older woman's to give hers a squeeze. "Forgive me, too, madame. I am only a little—how do you say—skittish?"

"I would never say that," Hedda remarked in amazement. "That's a racing term, is it not? Where would you learn it?"

Philadelphia flushed. She didn't know where she'd heard it.

"Memsahib's uncle was a cavalry officer and now maintains private stables near Delhi," Akbar supplied smoothly from the darkness behind them. "The conversation at his dinner meals is often full of talk of bloodlines and racing."

"Really!" Hedda shuddered. "How positively horrid for you. The English may think themselves the peak of society but I say the talk of hounds and horses has no place at a dinner table where ladies are present. Now, turn your head to the stage, mademoiselle. I perceive that the curtain is going up. Once the lights dim, you'll not be nearly so noticeable."

She need not have worried, Philadelphia thought, as for the next hour she sat with hands folded calmly in her lap while enduring the attentive gazes of what seemed to be half the audience. Had the patrons given as much attention to the play as they did her, the players would have thought themselves a smashing success.

The vulgar ogling was all that any jewel merchant could have hoped for, Philadelphia noted in growing irritation as she reached up to touch the diamond necklace. Was Senhor Tavares already contemplating a hefty price for his jewels? More and more she felt his eyes on her back as he remained at the back of the box. When she could endure it no longer, she stole a glance at him.

He stood ramrod straight before the curtains with his arms folded high across his chest and his eyes closed. She had mulled over the incident a thousand times until she was no longer certain who was to blame for the intimate moments of luxuriating pleasure that had left her shaken and awkward in his presence. Her only consolation was that he seemed unaware of the difference in her. She would remember that in future. He was playing the part of her servant, no more, no less. His feelings were of no personal interest to her.

Though she couldn't guess it, Eduardo's thoughts were far from serene. He was weary of his disguise. His cheeks under the false beard itched from a rash caused by the sticking plaster. The makeup and lines drawn on his brow to age his appearance were easily smudged. He wished he'd chosen a less demanding disguise, like the one he'd given Philadelphia.

He opened his eyes and was surprised to find her gazing at him. It was a fleeting glance that scarcely met his before slipping away. At once, her expression stiffened. She set her mouth, pressing her lips slightly to keep them from appearing as full and soft as they were. The thought that he was to blame for the change pricked his conscience. Even in the semidarkness the translucent quality of her beauty shone through. Did she know how truly beautiful she was? He doubted it. There was nothing haughty or vain about her.

She was predisposed to take life a little too seriously.

He had recognized that the instant he first saw her. He admired her reserve, though he suspected that the tight control she exerted over her emotions might easily turn into bitterness if she didn't learn to release them. She was young, warm, and full of life. She lacked only joy.

He'd been unforgivably abrupt with her in a moment when she'd been most vulnerable. He'd been forced to back away from her just as she'd become aware of the passion he'd inadvertently aroused. No wonder she wouldn't meet his gaze. The gaucherie of the mistake nettled his masculine pride. He liked women and they he. It was the fault of this ridiculous costume. He should never have made himself subservient to her. It was a mistake he wouldn't repeat.

When the lights came up for the first intermission, Philadelphia felt headachy and thoroughly picked over by the stares of strangers. She rose from her seat. "I am in need of fresh air, Madame Ormstead. If you will excuse me."

"I won't. Absolutely not. If you should set foot in the hall now, you'd be trampled by your admirers. We'll wait here and allow Akbar to show in a few select visitors for an introduction. Sit down, dear. You mustn't seem eager."

Philadelphia subsided into her seat with a sidelong look of recrimination at Akbar. It was his fault that she was in this situation. How, precisely, she wasn't certain, but she felt an overwhelming certainty of his responsibility.

There was a knock at the box door and the corners of Hedda's mouth curved up. "You may request the identity of our caller, Akbar."

He nodded and disappeared behind the curtain only to return within seconds. "The gentleman gives the name Henry Wharton, memsahib."

Hedda's smile softened. "My nephew? Show him in. Herbert, my boy! Do come in." She motioned impatiently to the tall young man in evening clothes who entered the box. "Where is your silly mother, Herbert?"

"It's Henry, Aunt Hedda," the young man answered, his well-featured face flushing slightly beneath a thatch of soft brown curls. "Mama's fine." His gaze moved eagerly to the beautiful young lady by his aunt's side as he added, "But she's not present tonight."

"Thank goodness!" Hedda declared in frank pleasure. "I do so detest chatting with your mother. She's quite stupid, really. I know one shouldn't speak unkindly of the infirm, and I do not generally, but your dear mother refuses to acknowledge her disadvantage and will go on interminably in a most unenlightened manner about every subject. Well, don't just gape, Delbert, speak up."

"It's Henry, aunt," the young man repeated with a rueful smile at Philadelphia. "I'm most pleased to find you here. The family had quite despaired of ever seeing you in public again."

Hedda lifted her lorgnette. "And why is that? May a lady not keep her own company when society has nothing half so interesting to offer in its place? I daresay you spend a great deal of time being bored or boring your associates. By remaining in my own residence, I save myself the onus of one and the sin of the other." She turned suddenly toward the door. "Akbar? I'm in need of refreshment. Three glasses will do nicely if Harold will stop lounging about like a drugstore dandy and take a seat."

Akbar bowed. "As memsahib commands, so will I do."

Hedda's smile was smug as she turned to her nephew. "What do you think of him?"

Henry's mouth fell open in astonishment. "He's yours? I mean, he's your servant, Aunt?"

"What else?"

"Well, though he opened your box door, I thought he was some sort of costumed usher."

"In fact, he belongs to my houseguest." Hedda acknowledged Philadelphia for the first time since her nephew entered the box. "Mademoiselle de Ronsard, I would like to introduce my least disliked relative, Horace Wharton. Horace, my guest, Mademoiselle de Ronsard."

The young man drew up to his full height, then executed a very formal bow. "Pleased to meet you, mam'zelle. I'm Henry Wharton."

"Didn't I say as much?" Hedda demanded impatiently, then glanced at the door. "Where's Akbar? The man's amazingly slow unless he's running an errand for you, mademoiselle."

"I'm certain he's doing his best," Philadelphia answered and quickly turned her full attention to Henry. "I, too, am delighted to make your acquaintance, Monsieur Henri Wharton." She gave his name the French pronunciation which omitted the *H* and softened the *y* to an *i*.

The effect of her voice on the young man was startling. His jaw went slack and his eyes widened. "I've always hated my name but after hearing you say it, mam'zelle, I'll never feel the same way about it again."

Had he not been so earnest, Philadelphia thought she might have laughed. "*Merci,* Monsieur Wharton, you are but too kind to me. I fear my English is sometimes incorrect."

He took the seat beside her, leaning slightly toward her. "You can pronounce my name as much and as often as you wish, mam'zelle."

Eduardo returned just in time to find Henry Wharton leaning toward Philadelphia; and though he hadn't heard the exchange, he recognized the results of a feminine conquest. Philadelphia had completely charmed the boy within just moments.

Inexplicably piqued, he came forward and thrust his tray between the pair. "Refreshment, memsahib?" His tone was civil but the glare he gave the young American made Henry sit back.

"Serve Madame Ormstead first, Akbar," Philadelphia said reprovingly.

"As memsahib requests." He bowed and withdrew the barrier of the tray, but not before subjecting the hapless young man to a second more penetrating stare. "Would memsahib like me to remove this male person from her presence?"

"To the contrary," she answered. "This is Madame Ormstead's nephew, Akbar. Monsieur Wharton, Akbar is my faithful servant."

Henry looked at the forbiddingly dark, bearded face and murmured something like an acknowledgment.

Only when Akbar had served them all and retired to the back of the box, did Henry lean forward and say in a low tone to his aunt, "Are you certain that it's safe to have such a fellow under your roof, Aunt?"

"Never felt safer," she declared with a chuckle. "The man's a wonder. He's unfailingly courteous but not a toady. He's equally adept at driving my carriage and preparing tea. In Delhi he ran a household with more than a hundred servants. One mistake among them and chop!" She made an appropriate motion with her small ladylike hands.

Henry Wharton wasn't the only one with his mouth agape. Philadelphia, too, sat stunned by Mrs. Ormstead's statement. Had any of them bothered to turn toward the back of the box, they would have noted Eduardo's pleased smile.

Hedda's smile was as impish as a child's. "Gossip is one thing this town has in abundance, dear. Did you think my servants wouldn't discover all when I sent them to collect your things?"

"But, of course, madame," Philadelphia said as she cast an uncertain eye at Henry. "But I am afraid that even the best people will exaggerate the truth a tiny little bit, *mais non*?"

"Yes, of course," Henry answered but he cast a suspicious glance in Akbar's direction and received a penetrating stare in return. "But if the fellow's not familiar with our customs, I mean, being a heathen and—"

"He's a foreigner and a heathen, neither of which makes him a savage, Derwood," Hedda said censoriously. "You should get about in the world more, nephew. Mademoiselle de Ronsard is French by birth yet in her short life she has nearly circumnavigated the globe."

Philadelphia smiled sympathetically at Henry, whose guileless face was registering more awe than before. "I didn't accomplish this feat myself, monsieur. Akbar did the rowing."

For a moment there was complete silence while Hedda wondered in vexation if her nephew had inherited his mother's stupidity, and Philadelphia regretted her failed joke. Then, Henry's face split with a boyish grin of understanding. "I got it! You're a great tease, mam'zelle."

Philadelphia shrugged, without a thought as to where she'd picked up the gesture. "A small tease, monsieur. A lady must never be a great tease, *non*?"

Henry turned the most fascinating shade of pink. "No, of course not! Didn't mean to imply."

"Saints above!" Hedda murmured faintly and lifted her lorgnette to eye the other boxes. Henry wouldn't do at all. He had made a fool of himself in less than two minutes. While the de Ronsard girl was doing her best to help him along, it was like watching a lame horse pull a heavy cart; the progress was slow and painful to witness.

Philadelphia maintained her part in light inconsequential chatter with Henry until, to her relief, the house lights dimmed and the curtains rose for the third act. She was surprised when the young man winced, then jumped to his feet. If she hadn't thought it impossible, she'd have suspected his aunt pinched him.

"Well, I must be going. People waiting for me and all." He looked longingly at Philadelphia, then turned to his aunt. "May I visit you on Sunday afternoon, Aunt Hedda?"

"Why? You never have before."

"Perhaps he would like to see your horses, Madame Ormstead," Philadelphia prompted, feeling sorry for him. "Until Sunday, monsieur?" She extended her gloved hand to him.

He took it, shook it for lack of another idea, and then fled the box.

"Henry hates horses," Hedda pronounced. "That ninny of a mother of his put him on a pony before he could sit. She said it was a family tradition that the children ride early. He fell off onto his head." She paused with a tiny frown. "I suppose that tradition might explain a great deal."

Philadelphia abruptly turned her face away. Mrs. Ormstead was really too naughty.

# 6

"It's quite thoroughly off-putting," Hedda declared as she gazed with distaste upon the stack of invitations piled on the silver salver by her right elbow. "One can't attend a single public performance without being inundated by requests for additional appearances."

"You have many friends who were pleased to see you out in society again, Aunt Hedda," Henry Wharton answered as he sat on one of the yellow silk chairs in his aunt's drawing room.

"Rubbish! Half these people thought that I was buried in Woodlawn with my husband until Mademoiselle de Ronsard appeared beside me at the theater last week." Philadelphia made a sound of protest. "There's no need to deny it. It's *your* society these invitations demand."

"I am most entirely in disagreement, madame," Philadelphia said with a small smile of embarrassment. "I am but certain these invitations come for the express purpose of your entertainment. I am, after all, but a poor orphan without rank or reputation in your exalted world."

"I protest that assessment," Henry said quickly and turned an earnest look on her. "You're wellborn, and certainly without fault or blemish." His cheeks pinkened.

"What I mean to say is, you're beyond reproach. Why, you're related to royalty."

Hedda's silver brows registered surprise. "Royalty? Why should you imagine such a thing?"

"Akbar told me," Henry answered, using the opportunity to speak to continue to address Philadelphia. "Well, he didn't say you were royalty, he said that your family was very intimately connected to the Bourbons and that with the end of the Second Empire you lost a great deal more than your home and wealth. 'Generations of breeding trod asunder,' is how he put it."

"Did he?" Hedda murmured darkly. "Akbar sought you out to say this to you?"

Henry cleared his throat as his aunt's shrewd gaze pinned him, and as usual he felt at a disadvantage. "Actually, we happened to meet in the hallway when I came calling the other day." His coloring rose as he continued. "I believe that he was waiting for me. He seemed most anxious that I be made aware that were she to regain her proper place in Paris, Mam'zelle de Ronsard would be courted by noblemen."

Philadelphia's laughter was light and pleasing. Akbar was going too far in his desire to impress. "I doubt that very much, monsieur. The nobility of France are no more different than men of rank in any country. They perceive marriage as the necessity that binds together position, land, and wealth. *Enfin,* I lack the requirements for a *mariage de convenance.* As for the other, I am too proud to align myself in a *mariage de la main gauche. Voilà,* I shall remain *une vieille fille."* She looked to Mrs. Ormstead. "How do you say it in English, please?"

"A spinster," Hedda supplied dryly.

"A spinster! Yes, that is me!"

Henry's expression turned comical. He leaned forward, on the edge of his chair now, with eyes rounded in avid protest. "A spinster? My dear Miss Ronsard, nothing could be further from the truth."

"Nor from your wishes, nephew?" Hedda offered dampeningly. Really, the boy was a noodle-noggin! "Do unpop your eyes and relieve the strain upon my upholstery. Mademoiselle Ronsard need not concern herself about becoming a spinster. Shame on you, mademoiselle, for provoking the poor boy." She stood up abruptly. "Good morning to you, nephew. The mademoiselle and I have a fatiguing number of things to attend to. If you must, you may accompany us to the Montagues on Saturday, but only if I don't catch a single sight of you in the meanwhile. Do I make myself clear?"

Henry had never before objected to the fact that his aunt always addressed him as though he were a boy of eight. But now it rankled that she spoke so peremptorily to him before the mam'zelle, whom he was determined to win by means as yet unconceived. "Really, Aunt Hedda. I've scarcely the time to linger about. I've only been doing my part as a member of the family to see that your guest feels at home."

"You usually visit me three times a year. You've been here that many times this week," she replied irrepressibly. "Surely something needs your attention, Horace."

"My name is Henry, Aunt. Henry," he said in exasperation. "A simple name."

"Simple is as simple does," she answered. "Until Saturday evening."

Defeated, Henry made a bow to the ladies and left.

"Well, now," Hedda began when he had departed. "We must go through these invitations together. We won't accept most of them. If one appears in society too frequently, the element of novelty will fade."

She picked up the first of the gold-edged invitations in the pile and lifted her lorgnette to examine it. "We'll accept the Montagues' invitation. They're Newly Rich, and as such what you might expect. Yet, I hear they give some of the most costly and handsome entertainments on the street. The husband made a series of fortunate speculations on Wall Street and so speedily came into possession of great wealth. The gothic mansion on the corner opposite mine is theirs. A vulgar display of piled stones, don't you think? I'll accept in both our names. That should boost their stature on the street considerably."

"Madame," Philadelphia began in smiling protest. "You're most kind to include me in your plans but I cannot accept."

Hedda turned a sharp eye on her. "Why? You don't care to consort with inferiors?"

*"Mais non.* I would never feel that way about people gracious enough to invite me, a stranger, into their home. I am only—how do I say it?—not equipped with the means to do you justice."

"Do me justice?"

"As your companion." Philadelphia looked away from the gray-blue eyes that regarded her steadily and removed an imaginary speck of dust from the skirt of her blue serge gown.

"Oh, I see."

She glanced up and saw that Mrs. Ormstead was still looking at her but with less scrutiny in her gaze. "Poverty is always a misfortune, child. In this city, it's branded a crime. You were frank with my nephew just now though I doubt he understood you. I've been aware of your circumstances since the day you entered my house. Your luggage was slight: only two cases and a small trunk, they spoke for themselves. A fashionable woman must have as many dresses as she has places to wear them. You're not prepared."

"No, madame."

"At least you don't attempt to hide anything from me. Have you come to New York in the hope of marrying well?"

"No."

"Then why are you here?"

It was a question Philadelphia had been expecting for

days but one which she hadn't been able to answer to her own satisfaction. Mrs. Ormstead said that she wasn't hiding anything from her but the truth was she was hiding nearly everything. Her name, her disguise, even Akbar, were all lies. Yet, the scheme with Senhor Tavares to sell his jewelry had nothing to do with her association with Mrs. Ormstead. Certainly she wouldn't repay the woman's generosity by stooping to the ploy of offering her the necklace for cash. Still, that didn't answer the question being put to her.

"I'm here," she began reluctantly, "because I have nowhere else to go."

Hedda considered a dozen observations she might make under the circumstances but chose to say only, "You say you aren't in New York to find a husband, yet you'll be courted if you choose to go about with me, constantly and with a great deal of persistence precisely because you seem impervious to blandishments. Young men are foolishly struck with the idea of pursuing the impossible. Such a waste of energies, but I suppose it keeps them from worse folly. Then, too, you may change your mind." She picked up another envelope. "Now, let's proceed, shall we?"

When, at last, Philadelphia escaped the drawing room, the morning was nearly over. Throughout the interview, she'd repeatedly refused Mrs. Ormstead's offers of assistance in enlarging her wardrobe. In the last moments, the conversation had become so heated that Hedda had ended the discussion by calling Philadelphia "an unfeeling, ungracious guest with a perverse ambition to thwart the wishes of your hostess!" She then thrust the half dozen invitations she had deemed acceptable into Philadelphia's hands and dismissed her in order that Philadelphia compare their requirements to her wardrobe.

As she walked along the hallway toward the conservatory, Philadelphia made a mental list of her gowns. She possessed a traveling dress, two day dresses, the ball gown that she had worn to the theater, a white linen visiting dress, and a green silk reception gown that she had purchased just days before her father's unexpected death. It was the one item she had cheated the creditors of.

The memory made her heart painfully skip a beat. Too late she realized that there had been a dozen other things she might have saved from the greedy grasp of those unscrupulous men had she not been too shocked by her father's death to think properly. Most of all, she wished she had saved the pearls that were to have been her wedding present. Instead, to increase their profitability, she had participated in their sale. Strangely, she didn't regret her broken engagement. She had not loved Harry Collsworth. He had been her father's choice and to please her father she would have done anything.

She shook her head, unwilling to be drawn in by the pain that lurked always at the edge of consciousness, and glanced down at the envelopes in her hand. The invitations were for dinner parties and receptions. She could wear her black ball gown once more. The green silk would serve twice, worn first for a dinner and then with an overskirt of lace for a soiree, but she didn't possess gowns for the other occasions. How would she manage?

Looking up from her contemplation as she entered the conservatory, she saw that the room was occupied. "Akbar" sat on a wrought-iron bench near a bank of ferns, his chin propped on his fist, lost in thought. For a fleeting instant she wondered what matter held his rapt attention. When the mood suited him he was as secretive as a mole and as changeable as an April sky. In rare moments when he thought himself alone, she sensed a melancholy solitude about him that was at odds with the vigor and energy he displayed to others. He was an enigma.

Eduardo sat in uneasy alliance with his distracted thoughts. This was not the first morning he'd spent in idleness while Philadelphia enjoyed the company of Mrs.

Ormstead and her nephew, but today's wait had been more frustrating than most because he had disturbing news to keep him company.

He should have known that Tyrone wouldn't be mollified by a parting letter, but he hadn't expected to be contacted so quickly. Tyrone's letter had arrived for him in care of the hotel where he usually stayed while in New York. It was one of several methods they had established over the years in order to stay in contact while traveling. No doubt there were duplicate letters waiting for him in San Francisco, Chicago, Boston, London, and São Paulo. The letter was brief and to the point. Tyrone wanted him to return to New Orleans but didn't say why. That left only one conclusion. There was trouble.

Tyrone had never sought him out unless it had to do with his own quest for revenge. Yet that was at an end. If Tyrone was seeking him for another reason, he must be desperate. "The devil ever rides at your heels, amigo," Eduardo murmured in his native tongue. He would have to act quickly for it was imperative that Tyrone never learn of Philadelphia's existence.

Distracted by the sensation of another presence, he looked up sharply to find Philadelphia standing in the doorway. He rose to his feet. "Memsahib wishes something?"

"Yes. I need your advice." She marched over and presented the invitations to him.

Alert to every subtlety of her expression, he didn't even glance at the envelopes she held out to him. "What is it that puts a frown upon the face of memsahib?"

"Invitations which Mrs. Ormstead intends to accept in my name."

"Is that all?" The deep frown lines eased out of his expression as he slipped from English into French. "But that is marvelous! Your first foray into New York society was a success. You will, of course, accept them all. The de Ronsard diamonds should have a number of outings before they're sold. After all, the more admirers they garner, the more valuable they become."

"You miss one salient fact," she said, following his lead in speaking French. "My wardrobe isn't equal to these occasions."

He shrugged. "You're here to draw the attention of prospective buyers to the jewels. You must contrive something."

His preoccupation with the price the jewels might bring annoyed her. "Is the money so very important to you?"

He raised one black brow. "Isn't that the reason you agreed to accompany me to New York?"

"Money was never my goal."

For a moment he merely gazed at her, noting a dozen small things about her, like how her beauty was composed of firm bones beneath the velvet skin, how the purplish tinge of her lids gave a haunting background to her clear golden eyes, how her darkened lashes lay against her plush-peach complexion, how even in the simplest lavender morning dress she appeared both drawing-room correct and yet possessed of the grace of a wild wood creature. She was young and impossibly lovely, and quite without his reasoning it out, he allowed jealousy to invent a new and irritating possibility for her interest in being appropriately dressed. "What is your goal, memsahib? Is it the *norteamericano*?"

For a moment Philadelphia was at a loss to follow his reasoning. "Do you mean Henry Wharton?"

Eduardo frowned in annoyance. "Henry, is it? Have things advanced that far?"

"What things?" Her expression of amazement turned quickly to amusement. "You don't seriously believe that Hen—Mister Wharton is interested in me?"

"I do. He is. An ass could recognize the symptoms."

Caught between the impulse to laugh at what seemed to be his jealous tone and yet not quite able to credit it, she said, "Why did you tell him that the de Ronsards are nobility?"

Again his shrug that managed to be both elegant and masculine. "I saw no reason to encourage his infatuation. You will soon grow bored."

"That's insulting. You can't presume to know what sort of man I prefer. And I don't find Henry boring!"

She'd deliberately used the name again but he didn't snap at the bait. "Then perhaps you will explain to me your interest in this Henry."

"I certainly will not. It's none of your business."

"You won't because you can't!" he said triumphantly. "You care nothing for him."

She didn't like one bit the feeling of being cornered, even by the truth. She had no serious interest in Henry Wharton but this display of jealous temper by a man whom she'd begun to think of as a friend smarted. "Mrs. Ormstead approves the association. She acknowledges Henry as her favorite relative."

"She also acknowledges that he was dropped on his head as a child," he responded with obvious delight. "Is it his childish awkwardness that you find endearing?"

Philadelphia folded her arms across her bosom. "I refuse to say another word to you on the subject. We're business partners and this is not your business."

"I could so easily make it my business," he murmured in Portuguese. In French he said, "Very well, mademoiselle partner. I bow to your wishes. I must absent myself from you for a few days. This will give you time to complete your conquest, if that is what you truly desire."

She heard nothing beyond his mention of leaving. "You are leaving? Where are you going?"

The alarm in her voice was balm for his ego. "Does it matter so much to you?"

"Of course it matters!" she answered before she could stop herself. To temper her confession, she added, "What will I say to Mrs. Ormstead? You're *my* servant, after all.

I should be sending you on some errand if you're about to disappear."

His voice was flat. "How well you've accustomed yourself to the role of lady and her servant. You may tell her anything you wish. I will be absent a week, ten days at the most."

"Ten days?" Dismay rapidly replaced her annoyance. "Ten days? I can't remain under this roof another ten days."

"Why not? Mrs. Ormstead is a generous hostess and quite fond of you." He reached into the sash about his waist and withdrew a purse. "This should cover the cost of a new gown, perhaps two if you choose wisely. You've a handful of invitations to a fortnight's worth of entertainment. What else could you wish for?"

She refused the purse. "I can't afford to be more indebted to you."

"It is a gift."

She was about to deny him again but instead she found herself staring up into his eyes, those great dark eyes that were at once imposing and yet vulnerable. She tried to remember what he looked like without the aging makeup and the false beard. She recalled the blue-black shade of his wavy hair hidden now beneath his turban, and the generous shape of his wide firm mouth lost beneath the bristle of beard. Then there was his dark copper coloring aged by rice powder and greasepaint.

There was no mistaking the look of passion when it came into his face. The potent strength and vitality of it was there in the bright shimmer of his bittersweet chocolate gaze. A ripple of apprehension washed through her. This was like standing before a blazing fire; in taking in the heat she took the risk of being burnt.

Against his will but not against his need, Eduardo reached out to lightly cup her cheek. She trembled beneath his caressing fingers. They were playing a dangerous game, he more so than she, and he didn't want her to be hurt when, and if, certain revelations came to light. That was the reason he was leaving her, to protect her from his past, and her father's.

But his body wasn't listening to reason. Except in rare moments, she seemed unaware of him as a man. In becoming her servant, he had become a eunuch in her eyes. She discounted his feelings and treated him with the friendly companionship of a brother. Well, he wasn't her brother nor was he without the drives and passions of a whole man. He ached to draw her closer. Or was it she leaning toward him that presented the irresistible lure?

*Patience.* The word his grandmother had spoken with no other direction when he was about to lose his temper, or refuse a parental judgment, or balk at the inevitable. *Patience.* The word tolled in his mind. Philadelphia Hunt was a rare and beautiful being whom he had no wish to frighten with a precipitous display of his intense desire for her. She was worth patience and frustration. It wasn't her fault that when she gazed at him with those honey-colored eyes he felt the heat of that gaze curling deep in his loins. She wasn't to blame for the fact that when he looked away from those eyes he saw her lips, full and softly parted, and begging for a kiss. He mustn't touch, shouldn't touch. *Patience.*

Misinterpreting the strain on his face for distress because of her refusal to accept the money, Philadelphia took the purse from his hand free hand. "Thank you, Akbar. I promise that I will put the money to use in a good cause." On impulse, she leaned forward to place a kitten-whisker kiss on his bearded cheek.

A hard shudder passed through Eduardo as she touched her lips to his cheek, and he reached up to capture her face between his hands. Turning his head, he placed his lips against hers for a moment. Only that. No more.

Philadelphia felt with surprising shock the touch of his

mouth on hers. His lips were firm and dry and warm—and instantly gone.

As he drew back, she stared up at him wordlessly, unable to comprehend what had just occurred. And then she did, and the unfairness of the too-brief moment moved her to speak. Drawing a breath to protest, she was taken by a sudden seizure that ended in an enormous sneeze.

The inelegant timing of the percussive sound was what Eduardo needed to break the fragility of the moment. "The beard," he murmured as he offered her the handkerchief he quickly withdrew from his pocket.

Mortified, she grabbed the linen square and sneezed into it twice more before she could regain control of herself. As she looked up, eyes brimming, she saw that the upper edge of his crescent-shaped dimple showed above his beard.

"I am most sorry to hear that memsahib suffers from the hay fever," she heard him say in English as he reached out to turn her by the elbow toward the conservatory door. "Memsahib must remember to maintain a respectful distance from the flowers in the future," he said in a resounding voice.

Several things registered in her thoughts at the same moment as she looked toward the entrance. One: they were not alone. Mrs. Ormstead had paused in the hallway, in full view of the conservatory entrance. Two: his talk of hay fever was a ruse to cover the intimate scene the woman must have witnessed as she passed. And three: his warning about keeping a respectful distance had nothing whatsoever to do with flowers.

"Thank you for the suggestion," she answered in a clipped tone she would never have used with a real servant. "As I've said, you must leave at once, as soon as you are packed."

"As memsahib wishes," he answered with a respectful bow. "When I have accomplished all that you command,

I shall return to you with the swiftness of the wind." He walked out of the conservatory, pausing only long enough to give Mrs. Ormstead a nod of his head before he disappeared down the hallway toward the servants' stairs.

"What's this about Akbar leaving?" Hedda demanded when Philadelphia reached her, not at all abashed to admit that she was eavesdropping.

"There are affairs, madame, private matters which only Akbar may attend to for me. If you don't mind, I wish to intrude upon your hospitality a little longer. A week, perhaps?"

"He'll be away a full week?"

"Perhaps a little more."

"Remarkable," Hedda murmured. "When I was a girl no proper chaperon would abandon his charge for even a hour."

"Akbar isn't at all a proper chaperon," Philadelphia answered with gentle laughter as she moved toward the stairway. "He is a most singular individual."

"So he is," Hedda said, but her gaze lingered on the young lady as she climbed the steps, for unless her hearing was at fault, Felise de Ronsard had spoken to her in English free of a French accent.

Unaware of her mistake, Philadelphia suddenly smiled to herself as she reached the second floor. She hadn't been burnt beyond recovery by braving the flame of Eduardo Tavares's kiss, but the distinct smoky aroma of smoldering passion seemed to cling to her as she made her way down the hall to her room.

"Here he is again, the odious man!" declared Julieanna Wharton, Henry's sister and Philadelphia's companion for the evening. "I don't know how you bear his company, even if he is one of your countrymen."

Philadelphia looked up in vexation at Julieanna's words. It was true, the bane of her existence this last week had entered the Ferguson's ballroom: the Marquis d'Edas.

Even as he lifted one long-fingered hand in an intimate gesture of greeting that set her teeth on edge, she looked away, pretending not to notice him.

"I could just swoon in mortification when he looks at me," Julieanna confided. "Mama says his way with ladies isn't quite decent."

"Your mama is quite right," Philadelphia replied, and looked around for Henry only to discover that he had disappeared. With resignation she pulled her wits together, knowing that she'd need every bit of them to match words with the marquis. From the moment she'd been introduced to him at the opera a week ago, she'd sensed a quickening interest in him that had nothing to do with masculine appreciation of her beauty. He'd plied her with questions about her family and history, questions she couldn't answer with the facile lies that came so easily to Eduardo Tavares.

In the succeeding days, each time they met, he pressed her for details about her life in Paris, and her family and friends, until she began to feel the sinister touch of foreboding whenever he entered a room. Lies were difficult enough to tell when the dupe was ignorant of the subject. But how could she hope to hold off for long a man who was Parisian by birth?

For the dozenth time that day she wondered what had become of Eduardo Tavares. He'd said he'd be gone only a week yet more than two had passed, and still he hadn't returned. He'd not sent a message, or letter, or even a telegram. Sometimes at night she lay awake wondering if he were ill or injured or, God forbid, dead. No, she mustn't think that way, not when she had to face the marquis yet again.

"Oh, here he comes!" Julieanna whispered. "What can we do, Mam'zelle Ronsard?"

"Nothing, *je regrette.*" Philadelphia watched him move

closer after having paused to greet another of the guests. He was dressed as always in a tailcoat with a French ribbon of rank slanted across his narrow chest. It was his thinness that gave him the illusion of height when seen from a distance. In fact, he was only an inch taller than she, and scarcely broader in the shoulders. His hair was parted in the middle above his lean face and plastered to the sides of his head with a too generous application of macassar oil so that it gleamed in the gaslight. Everything about him was calculated to arrest the eye, from his hair to his curled mustaches to the fastidious details of his dress which made him a favorite among many of the ladies. He possessed the figure of a young man but his eyes were old, she thought with a shiver of distaste.

"Mademoiselle de Ronsard," the Marquis d'Edas said with exaggerated pleasure as he bowed before her. "Again we meet, and again and again, and yet never is it enough."

Philadelphia didn't offer her hand as was customary. Though his expression was meant to convey ardent interest, she was aware that his eyes had strayed to the magnificent diamond necklace she wore whenever the occasion permitted. "You flatter me too greatly, Monsieur d'Edas. The other ladies present will begin to think you find their considerable charms less to your taste."

The man's pale blue eyes narrowed but his smile didn't falter. "You tease me, but unmercifully, Mademoiselle de Ronsard, to say such a thing before the ladies. Ah, but I forgive you, I must forgive you anything!"

"Then you must prove your sincerity." She gently took Julieanna by the upper arm and urged her to the edge of her chair. "Mademoiselle Wharton is dying to waltz. Only she is too shy to admit it."

"Well, I—that is!" Julieanna's fair complexion flooded scarlet with embarrassment.

"But of course I will dance with the fair Mademoiselle Wharton," d'Edas said as he reached for the younger

girl's hand. "Mademoiselle de Ronsard will save a dance
for me also?"

Philadelphia pretended to survey her dance card. "Oh,
but I'm—how you say—filled up. *Je le regrette,* monsieur."

The marquis bowed. "I, too, regret it," he said with
little pleasure for he had plainly glimpsed her card and
seen that most of the spaces were empty. "Perhaps you
will reconsider me at a later time?"

"Perhaps," she murmured and looked away only to spy
Henry striding toward her with a scowl on his handsome
face. She rose quickly and thrust out both hands to him as
he neared her. "Ah, but here is my partner. This is our
dance, Henri, is it not?"

Henry didn't know, nor did he care. Whenever Mademoiselle de Ronsard looked at him, he nearly forgot to
breathe. Now she had said his Christian name in public,
for all to hear, and the realization made him giddy. He
caught her hands and led her out onto the floor to sweep
her along into the graceful circle of waltzers.

Round and round they went, her lovely green silk skirts
swirling out about her like a storm-tossed sea. The sheer
pleasure of holding her nearly erased his anger of moments before. It was as though nothing had been whispered in his ear moments earlier. Breathing in the faint
lavender scent rising from her skin, he could scarcely recall the accusations.

"How absurd," he said, as though he'd spoken all
rather than only the last of his thoughts aloud.

Philadelphia tilted her head back to look up at him.
"What is absurd?"

He smiled down at her. "The very idea, saying that you
couldn't possibly be who you most certainly are. Oh, my
dear! I do apologize for my clumsiness. Did I hurt you?"

"No. My fault," Philadelphia replied, straining to recover from her misstep. But she could no longer feel the
rhythm of the waltz flowing through her for the awkward
pounding of her heart. "Who says I am not who I am?"

He shook his head. He was humming in tune to the music, something he had never before done, and enjoying it immensely.

She paused in the middle of a turn. "Who says I am not who I say I am?"

Confused, he frowned at her. "Who said? My dear mam'zelle, I do apologize for even mentioning it. The piker isn't worth a thought."

She held his gaze as she said carefully, *"Who* spoke so of me?"

He colored to the roots of his fair hair. "Oh, very well. This d'Edas made a comment to Mrs. Rutledge this morning while they shared a carriage ride through Central Park. He let slip the fact that he'd never heard of your family. Of course, he said he didn't know every hanger-on at court but he knew nearly everyone of consequence in Paris."

"And?" she demanded, uncaring that the other dancers had to pivot about them as they remained at a standstill in the middle of the floor.

"And," he said impatiently, faintly embarrassed to have opened the subject, "when Mrs. Rutledge pressed him on the point, he suggested that, perhaps, you aren't quite all that you seem."

"What is it I seem, Henri?"

He smiled at her now, certain of what he would say. "You seem the very embodiment of dreams come true." He hadn't meant to say it with such eloquence but her beauty affected him far more than any other influence in his life. It moved him to strive for poetry, for a semblance of words that would convey this incredible feeling welling up inside him. "The man's a fool."

Philadelphia nodded once and resumed the steps of the waltz. "I must remember to send your sister a very large bouquet of flowers."

"Whatever for?"

"Condolences," she answered with a quick glance in

d'Edas's direction. He held the scarlet-faced girl more closely than was strictly proper, and the fact wasn't going unnoticed by the matrons seated on the gilded chairs lining the ballroom. Poor Julieanna, she thought in sympathy. Yet the girl would survive. It was her own reputation that was in real danger.

When the waltz ended, she caught Henry's sleeve. "Would you accompany me for a breath of air? The room is so crowded."

"Delighted!" he said, his chest swelling until the buttons on his waistcoat were strained.

But the escape was not to be. She didn't notice his approach, or that he had deliberately steered his partner in their path but suddenly she was facing d'Edas's slyly smiling face. "Mademoiselle de Ronsard, does the orchestra not remind you of the orchestras of the Tuileries?"

She smiled stiffly. "I don't recall but then I was merely a child, and in my family children were not permitted to run freely about the city."

"But of course. Your family." Once more his avid gaze lingered on the diamonds encircling her throat. "The *collier de Ronsard*. Mademoiselle Wharton has just been telling me that it's quite famous." He looked up into her eyes. *"Il est magnifique! Enfin,* it is most amazing I have never before heard of it. Where, exactly, did you say your family resides?"

"I didn't." Philadelphia heard Henry suck in a breath of surprise at her abrupt reply but the marquis had been rude in asking for her address in the first place. "They are dead, monsieur. They reside in their graves."

"But I am too forward. Forgive me, mademoiselle. *Adieu."* The Frenchman smiled cunningly but said under his breath in French as he brushed by her, "You little cheat!"

She turned away as though his words had failed to reach her but her hands were clenched into fists by her sides as she walked toward the doors which opened onto the balcony. Dimly, she was aware that Henry followed her but the desire to breathe air untainted by the marquis's presence made her unable to consider the young man's feelings.

D'Edas had called her a cheat, his hissing voice sounding as dangerous as that of a snake. He would find her out. It wasn't the threat that frightened her, it was the realization that he *could* find her out to be a cheat because she was. The knowledge appalled her. How had she come so far from what she knew to be right and good and just?

"What's wrong, dearest?" Henry stood irresolutely by her side in the darkness where she'd paused by the balustrade.

She turned to him, and in the illumination from the room behind him, he saw that she was close to tears. "Monsieur Wharton, I must tell you something, something that will make you like me less."

All the tender feelings a man can possess for a woman in distress came rushing to the fore as he reached out to bring her into the circle of his arms. "Don't say anything yet," he whispered against her hair as he held her in a gentle embrace.

Grateful for his blind comfort, she rested her head against his shoulder a moment. But it was folly, and in the end she knew he would only be hurt when he learned of her duplicity in the face of his honest innocence. She leaned away from him and though he didn't restrain her he didn't release her.

"It's that devil of a fellow d'Edas, isn't it?" he said quickly. "He frightens you. Well, I don't care if you're not royalty. Don't know that royalty has a place on Fifth Avenue." He flushed at his own temerity. He was moving much faster than he'd expected to but events were forcing his hand and he wasn't a coward. "I don't care who your people were. It's apparent that you're a product of good breeding. Why, your table manners are impeccable and you light up a drawing room as no one else of my acquaintance. Then there's your family jewels. If that isn't proof of ancient lines, I don't know what is."

He knew he was probably saying too much but she was staring up at him mutely, and so he felt free to babble to his heart's content. "Aunt Hedda likes you, too. Says you're worth any dozen of the season's debutantes and though she doesn't often approve of what I do and say, she'd clearly approve of having you in the family. 'New bloodlines, that's all that will save the Wharton line,' is how she put it."

Caught between amusement and faint horror at this declaration of—of, well, she supposed it was affection with intent to wed, Philadelphia changed her mind about what she had been about to say. "Henri, you're a dear, dear man and I'm afraid that if you don't release me this moment I'll fall in the most deplorable state of love with you."

Deplorable. Love. The words collided in his rioting thoughts as he released her. "Are you saying—"

"I'm saying the situation is impossible," she supplied with a gentle smile. "You're a young lion of society. I'm but a poor exile. Without a home or family or even the wherewithal to protect myself from the slander of strangers, I will always be the target of speculation—and rumor," she added in a rising tone that forestalled his protest. "It is my destiny. And so you must allow me to leave your life as much a stranger as I came into it. Only know that your concern for me has made this parting a little easier to bear."

"Parting? But I wish to marry you!" he declared, casting away twenty-one years of training in appropriate conduct.

Philadelphia sighed. "Marriage is impossible. No, don't say more." Acting on impulse, she rose up on tiptoe and

briefly pressed her mouth to his. "Adieu, *mon cher.*
Adieu."

She moved back from him with a smile but it never
fully formed. Instead she blanched, staring across his
shoulder as though a ghost had suddenly appeared on the
balcony beside them.

Henry whipped about but saw nothing unusual, only
the familiar shape of her East Indian servant Akbar, who
stood with his back to the open balcony doors. He turned
back to her. "What is it? What's wrong?"

"Nothing."

Too caught up in the moment to question her more
closely, Henry saw only a reflection of his own misery in
her stricken gaze as it came to rest on him once more.
She had refused his proposal before he'd properly made
it.

Philadelphia stared at Henry Wharton as though he
were a stranger. She was no longer capable of being with
him. Akbar had returned! And she'd just kissed another
man! Even though Akbar's back was turned when she
spied him over Henry's shoulder, she wondered if he'd
seen her in Henry's arms. The thought sent a shiver
through her, though she couldn't say why.

Ashamed and annoyed at the same time, she backed
away from Henry. "Good-bye, Henry," she said in English as she moved away from him.

As if on cue, Akbar moved away from the open doorway and entered the house where he walked swiftly onto
the ballroom floor, and right into the crowd of dancers.

Philadelphia tried to follow him, heedless of the surprised glances that followed her across the floor, but the
dancers seemed to block her path even as they had parted
for him. She was a lady seeking her servant. Surely they
were aware of that and saw nothing untoward in it. Or
was there? Was it there on her face for all of them to
read, the heady excitement, the flush of embarrassment,

the high hope and shameful secret of the joy she felt in
knowing that he had returned?

When she finally reached the opposite side of the room
she could no longer find him. She moved into the foyer
only to be told by the liveried butler that her servant had
left the house. "Call a cab for me at once!" she demanded in agitation.

"That won't be necessary if Mademoiselle de Ronsard
will allow me the privilege of providing her with the service of my carriage."

Philadelphia knew who addressed her before she
turned. "Monsieur le marquis. *Merci,* but that won't be
necessary."

He was smiling, a small cold smile that managed to dim
a little of her excitement. "*Enfin,* mademoiselle, I must
insist," he said as he came closer. "You and I have never
been properly acquainted and now is the perfect time for
a little private chat, *n'est-ce pas?*"

"That's totally out of the question," she answered
firmly and turned again at the butler, "A cab, *s'il vous
plaît?*"

"There's one waiting just outside, miss," the man answered smartly. "At your convenience."

"My convenience is now," she answered without even a
backward glance at the marquis.

# 7

The plodding ride up Fifth Avenue did nothing to calm Philadelphia's agitation. The pace of the late-evening traffic seemed deliberately designed to stretch her patience to the breaking point.

"Can't we have speed?" she cried as she thumped the hansom roof with her gloved fist.

"We're just about there, miss," came the cabbie's startled reply.

"Hurry!" she countered and sat back, crossing her arms tightly across her bosom.

In her rush, she'd left behind her shawl. The night air puckered her arms with gooseflesh but her body's reaction made little impression on her. She gazed out at the gaslights lining Fifth Avenue, their golden nimbi shining brightly through the black shroud of night, and in each she saw a reflection of Eduardo Tavares's face.

Why had he reentered her life without warning and then left again without so much as a word? Couldn't she guess how much she'd missed him and been afraid that something was wrong? Well, when she caught up with him, she'd have more than a word to say to him, and he would listen until his ears blistered from the tirade!

When the hansom pulled up before the Ormstead residence she climbed down unaided and marched up the steps to ring the bell.

The butler appeared at once, surprise showing on his face when he realized that she was alone.

"Pay the cabbie, please," she said peremptorily.

"Certainly, miss," he answered as she brushed past him on the scent of violets and youth. Belatedly, he called after her, "Your servant has returned, miss. Came in just now."

*"Merci."* She didn't pause but a smile of joy replaced the determined look on her face. Heart pounding in time to her quickened steps, she climbed the stairs to her floor, traversed the hall, and flung open the door to her bedroom, half-expecting that Eduardo had sneaked into her rooms to wait for her return.

He wasn't there.

Disappointment jagged down through her, leaving her torn between hurt and annoyance. She closed the door and marched across the floral carpet while stripping off her white kid gloves. When she reached the dressing table she dropped them there and then pulled the pins from the garland of violets which decorated her hair and flung it down beside the gloves.

When she glanced up at her reflection in the mirror she was amazed by her expression. Her cheeks were deeply flushed and her eyes shone with the inner light of fine topazes, but there familiarity ended. Her hair was a strange dark shade and her lips had been cunningly rouged to mimic the deep natural rose of a brunet. In her eyes she looked cheap and theatrical. Everything about her was a sham. She seemed to be drowning in the sea of deception and duplicity which she had helped fashion but could not control. She needed a harbor, an anchor, protection from uncertainty and doubt. In Eduardo Tavares, she thought she had found a savior, someone on whom she could depend. Perhaps she had been mistaken.

A slow flush crept up over the low neckline of her ball

gown. Perhaps Senhor Tavares had seen her kiss Henry Wharton. It was brazen and unlike her to do such a thing. Yet if he had seen the gesture, it might answer the question of why he had simply walked away. Perhaps her kissing Henry had offended him.

Resentment pricked through her embarrassment. He had no right to be insulted, to judge her actions when he knew nothing of the anxiety in which she had lived these last days. He didn't know about Monsieur d'Edas and his innuendos, nor the fear that she would trip herself on her own lies.

She glanced at the millefleur needlepoint bell pull that hung beside the fireplace. She would send for him. She reached for the bell only to be interrupted by a knock at her door. Startled, she whipped around. "Yes? *Oui.* Come in!"

The maid appeared from behind the opening door. "Do you require help in undressing, mam'zelle?"

"Yes. No! I require nothing!" Philadelphia snapped.

"Very well. Good night, mam'zelle."

"Wait!" She forced a smile to her lips. "I'm told my servant Akbar has returned. Where is he?"

"Can't say for certain, mam'zelle, but I expect he's retired. Anyways he ain't below stairs."

"Thank you. You may go."

She felt stifled by the burden of the clothing she wore. She reached up and removed the diamond necklace and earrings, pausing to look at them. The lamplight caught fire in the center of each stone, sending riotous rainbows of pure colors dancing among the shadows of the ceiling. No wonder the Marquis d'Edas was fascinated by the jewels. The stones were perfect and exquisite.

Unaccountably angered by their beauty, she placed them in their box and closed the lid. The diamonds would go back to Senhor Tavares and he could then dispose of them in any manner he wished. It was time to leave New

York, before d'Edas publicly declared her a fraud. The pretense was over.

She undressed quickly, replacing her dress and corset and petticoats with a full-flowing night dress and cambric dressing gown. In the distance she heard the chimes of the huge mantel clock that stood in the library below. Nine . . . ten . . . eleven . . . twelve. Midnight.

She refused to stop and think about what she planned to do, or she knew she would lose her nerve. She turned down the lamp by her bed until it was no more than an ember's glow, then crossed to her door and opened it a crack.

The gloom of the empty hall made her brave. She moved through the darkness like one long familiar with nighttime treks. In truth, she wasn't feeling very brave but her fear of d'Edas was greater than that of black shadows and moon-pale slats of light. At the end of the hall she found the stairway that led up to the servants' quarters, which were under the attic eaves, and began climbing into the impenetrable darkness of the stairwell. Using sensitive fingertips and toes she felt her way.

When she neared the top, she spied a faint glow from beneath the door of the room nearest the stairs. From a room further along the hall, she heard a feminine giggle, muffled footfalls, a whispered call for silence, and then nothing more. For the space of a dozen heartbeats she waited in the stairwell, wishing that she had paid more attention when he told her about his quarters. She remembered that he didn't share it with other servants and that it was next to one shared by the two maids. Perhaps if she listened at each door she would hear something that would give her a clue.

She mounted the final steps slowly until she stood in the narrow, low-ceilinged hall. If she should be caught here, in her robe and slippers, there could be no proper explanation. She reached for the door handle of the nearest one, as if by touch she could learn the name of the room's occupant. Even as she touched it the handle moved beneath her hand, and frozen by horror she watched helplessly as the door swung open.

Quick as lightning illuminates the black-mantled night, her eyes saw instantly what her thumping heart took longer to realize, that the room was occupied.

A man bent over a basin of water. Handfuls of water dripped from between his fingers while other droplets cascaded down his beardless face and bare chest. His black hair steamed like ink. A little foam of soap bubbles clung to one ear. The light gave his skin a dull copper gleam that seemed to have an almost inhuman beauty to it. The long sleek lines of his stretched torso were taut, the contours of hard muscle strongly delineated beneath his skin.

This was not the turbaned and bearded Akbar she had become accustomed to dealing with nor was it the superbly tailored Brazilian gentleman named Senhor Tavares with whom she had first done business. This dark, half-naked, well-muscled man seemed a stranger, and wholly different from anyone in her experience.

Eduardo allowed the shock of the opening door to wash over and beyond him when he saw who stood there. Philadelphia Hunt was on his threshold! He saw to his astonishment that despite her dressing gown, the soft womanly shape of her breasts and hips was discernible beneath the layers of sheer fabric. For a moment he discounted his own eyes for the image of her in dishabille had become one of his favorite idle speculations.

Then he felt, like a touch, her gaze as it roamed over him and the curiosity in her expression both warmed and disconcerted him. He'd been so eager upon his return to New York to see her that he'd dared the impropriety of going to the Fergusons in search of her. Then he'd found her, rising up on tiptoe to kiss Henry Wharton. If she'd suddenly jumped from hiding and knocked the breath out of him with a two-by-four he couldn't have been more surprised and angry . . . and hurt. It had taken every ounce of self-possession and pride to make him turn his back. Even then, several heartbeats had galloped past before he was able to feel that his legs would carry him out of the room.

She'd kissed another man freely! The memory fueled the not-quite-dead anger that remained in the backwash of his mood. He straightened up. "Why are you here?" he whispered, but in his deep voice the stinging ire was unmistakable.

Philadelphia didn't reply. She knew she should say something, anything, explain her presence but she couldn't. Finally she glanced down at her hand which still held the door handle.

He followed her gaze and then came forward quickly to gesture her inside and close the door.

She held her breath as he turned back to her, amazed to find him standing so close. She remembered Eduardo Tavares as thoroughly handsome but not possessing this flagrant male beauty that made her faintly ashamed to even look at him. She lowered her eyes until her vision was blocked by the broad expanse of his chest. The rich-toned skin was smooth satin, undulated by the shift of muscle over bone as he breathed, and punctuated by two flat chocolate-brown nipples. She'd never before seen a shirtless man and the anatomy lesson cost her more of her poise than she would ever have admitted.

She took a step backward but there was no more space for her to occupy between the wall and the narrow bed and his washstand. "I shouldn't be here."

She spoke so softly he was forced to watch her lips to catch the full meaning of her words, and he found himself remembering the kiss she'd given Wharton. No, she shouldn't be here. In his present state of mind she shouldn't even be beneath the same roof as he.

She clutched the front of her gown self-consciously. "I came to warn you of danger." She said each word slowly, hoping single sounds would not carry through the walls as clearly as regular speech.

He didn't respond. He had forgotten how beautiful she was, the warm golden depths of her wide eyes, how her mouth could be both aesthetically correct and yet beg a very human kiss. He had forgotten how the fragile bones of her face merged into a strength of character that made her vividly real. The pulse beating at the base of her throat moved hot blood through her. The breath rising and falling within her chest would be warm upon his face if he leaned nearer to catch it. The tremors shaking her shoulders were not altogether the trembling of fright. She was aware of him as a man, at last, and he meant to capitalize on the moment.

He reached for her, one hand rising to cup her chin and lift it, the other to embrace the back of her head and draw her close.

As their bodies met from waist to shoulder, her cambric gown drank in the dampness on his skin until she could feel the heat of his nakedness against her breasts. The shock of it was like the touch of a hot iron to tender skin. She took an instinctive step back but there was nowhere to go as his arms slid about her in an embrace, nowhere to look but into the black eyes of his handsome face. And so she looked into them, hoping that she might hide in that deep welcoming darkness as he bent to her.

"You kissed a boy tonight," he whispered as he lay his damp cheek against hers. "Now kiss a man."

She shut her eyes to block out the knowledge of what was about to happen but it didn't help. The instant his lips touched hers, her eyes opened wide in surprise.

For a moment there was only the warm persuasive pleasure of smooth firm lips covering hers. Then his lips parted, the heat of his mouth engulfing her, and her lids again fell shut.

Yet it was only the beginning. With the tip of his tongue he stroked her lips, then lightly licked at her tongue to draw it from between the shelter of her teeth. Acting on instinct, she followed his example, pressing the tip of her tongue to his, then darting away. She heard his moan of pleasure and felt his shiver of delight as he gathered her closer. Greatly daring, she embraced his waist, marveling at the smooth solid feel of his naked body, so much broader and harder than her own. Her arms rose. Her hands spread up and across his back to hold him and the moment, while behind her closed lids a shower of falling stars shot through the enraptured darkness.

He felt her melting surrender as his own need became painfully acute. So easily, so naturally he could press her back against his narrow cot and make love to her. But he mustn't. He was angry and jealous. He'd meant to shame and embarrass her for having the temerity to kiss Wharton while she treated him as something less than a flesh and blood man. He hadn't counted on her passionate return of his kiss. It was as if she sought to seduce *him*.

Drawing on a strength of will that caused near physical pain, he lifted his head. He'd been snared by a fool's trick. He should have known that he could no more draw passion from her without igniting his own than he could slit his wrists and not bleed.

He groped behind himself for the door latch and lifted it. "Go." He said the word like a sigh as he gently pushed her past him into the hallway.

Philadelphia gasped in disbelief as he closed the door on her. The feeling of unreality was so strong that she nearly gave into the impulse to throw herself upon the barrier of his plank-board door and cry out against his action, yet she didn't even dare draw a deep breath.

Dizzy with amazement and warmth and a deep stirring that had shaken her to her toes, she sagged weakly against the opposite wall and closed her eyes. She felt hot and cold in a dozen different places. Her body tingled and ached with unnameable needs. One moment she had been caught in an embrace she hoped would never end.

The next she stood in the blanketing silence of the dark hall, listening to the roar of her own heart fill her ears.

After a long moment, when the pounding in her chest was no more than a dull thudding, she turned and groped her way blindly down the stairwell back to her floor.

Only when she was under the covers of her own bed did she try to think. And what she thought both exhilarated and shocked her. She had kissed Eduardo Tavares and liked it! She had touched his naked back and shoulders, had felt the pulse and power and heat of his body. Even now her breasts still ached with the remembrance of being pressed against the muscular wall of his chest. She should be ashamed, mortified, outraged, appalled. In a rational moment she would be all of those things. Yet now, still caught up in the outrageous emotion of the present, she was excited beyond any experience of her life. She felt alive from her fingertips to her toes, quiveringly, tinglingly alive.

When she shut her eyes every instant of the kiss came back to her and she found herself pressing her fingers to her lips in a vain attempt to emulate the feel of his mouth on hers.

She hadn't told him any of the things she'd risked impropriety to say. Yet it didn't seem to matter at the moment. There would be time enough in the morning for conversation, and regret. Only one thing remained clearly in her thoughts, that she had been kissed twice this night and that the second had erased the impression of the first from her mind forever.

Philadelphia sat up straighter as a rap sounded gently on the library door. "Come in."

The maid opened the door, as always just enough so that she could poke her head through. "Akbar is on his way, mam'zelle."

"*Très bien,*" she replied with a calm she didn't feel.

She had dressed carefully for the meeting. The lines of

her lavender dress were plain, the bodice closed by a row of tiny pearl buttons that ended just under her chin. She felt prim and reserved, a perfect antidote to her appearance the night before. She would offer him no distractions, and she hoped he would offer her none.

The library door opened quietly, admitting the familiar figure in East Indian costume. His false beard was once more in place and the makeup applied. In disguise, he seemed very different from the man she'd intruded upon the night before, and for that she was grateful. There was so much she had wanted to say to him and felt now that she couldn't. Only a short day ago she would have said how glad she was for his safe return, how she'd begun to be afraid for him and herself. But, to say those things after what had occurred in his room seemed too forward and, perhaps, foolhardy. He was as far removed from the passionate man she'd embraced hours ago in the small of the night as Bombay was from New York.

He bowed low as he made the Indian gesture of greeting. "Memsahib calls her servant and he is here."

The strange intonation and phrasing further removed him from the images that had tantalized her dreams. "Akbar," it seemed, was another man. He was her friend, her confidant, her servant. The other? He did not bear thinking about just now.

"So you have returned," she said, mimicking his formality. "Why didn't you present yourself immediately to me?"

"I did."

He had switched from English to French, a sign she had come to recognize as meaning he wished to speak more intimately than was proper between servant and mistress, but she wasn't about to be maneuvered into a discussion of the night before. "You should have made yourself known in a proper manner," she answered in English.

Black eyes regarded her steadily over the brush of

beard. "I would have but I did not wish to disturb memsahib's enjoyment of the evening's entertainment."

Philadelphia fumed as he neatly sidestepped her barrier and went straight to the heart of the matter. "Yet you came," she persisted, wishing to make him as uncomfortable as she was.

"I came to see you." He used the French familiar instead of the formal "you," imbuing the ordinary sentence with intimacy.

Talking with him was like playing lawn tennis. Each time she made a proper serve he returned an answer to which she had to scramble. "What kept you away so long?"

"Business."

It was plain that she'd learn nothing more. "Very well, I am pleased by your safe return." Then, because she couldn't wait any longer to broach the subject, she spoke in French. "There's a man in the city who knows that I am a sham."

She thought at least his expression would alter but it didn't. "What man?"

"The Marquis d'Edas. He's something of a favorite among the Fifth Avenue set. From the moment I saw him I knew he would be trouble. Why, just yesterday, he told one of Mrs. Ormstead's friends that he's never heard of the de Ronsards."

"I have never heard of him."

The arrogance of his comment provoked her. "Of course you've never heard of him! How many French aristocrats would you know, in any case?"

"More than a few," he answered and for the first time there was a hint of good humor in his tone, as if her anxiety amused him. "Tell me what you know of this man."

"I met him a week ago at a soiree. I think he's been deliberately following me ever since."

"You seem to have collected an alarming number of admirers in my absence," he said dryly.

"That is my business, not yours," she snapped too quickly.

"Isn't it?" he asked softly.

She looked away from him, her mouth thinning in indignation. "I don't wish to discuss last night."

"Then, perhaps, we can return to the matter of the marquis. You say he thinks you are a fake. How can you be certain?"

Her gaze swung back to him. "He called me a cheat under his breath only last night."

"Was that before or after your dalliance on the balcony?" She saw his brows lower ominously. "A man smitten by a woman will often consider her his long before he's made claim to her."

Philadelphia stood up. "I can see I made a mistake in trying to warn you of the disaster which looms before us. You would rather make odious comments about a private moment in which you had no part or interest. Snoops aren't well liked in America, Senhor Tavares."

He made no protest, only the widening of his eyes alerted her to the blunder she'd made in calling him by his name, and in English.

"I don't care," she said defiantly, falling back into French. "The lie can't stand when one man knows the truth."

He moved toward her, and though she held her ground her legs began to tremble. If she moved away he'd know, damn him, just how much he affected her and how vulnerable he made her feel.

Eduardo stopped a few scant inches from her, looking her over with insulting intensity. "You're flustered. And you don't appear to have slept well. Does Henry Wharton make so ardent a suitor? It was *his* kiss that kept you awake, wasn't it?"

He dared her to deny it and because she would have

died before admitting anything else she said, "Henry is a charming and gallant suitor. He wants to marry me."

She hadn't meant to say the last but his lips were curved in mocking derision. She wanted to slap his face. The effect of her last remark was nearly as good. The smirk straightened and the twinkle died in his dark eyes.

"He wants to marry you." He said it like one might say, "The sun rose today." "And your answer?"

"My answer?" She looked at him in disbelief. "What answer could there be? I'm here under false pretenses."

Nothing changed in his face. "Then tell him the truth. If he loves you, he will understand."

"Will he?" Her voice was suddenly bitter. "Will he understand that I was driven to this sham of playacting by desperation because my father's life and reputation had been villainously ruined?"

For the first time since they'd left Chicago, Eduardo saw the shadows of confused hurt and loss in her expression. "If he loves you, it won't matter."

"You're wrong!" she flung at him and turned away, biting down hard on her lower lip. After a moment she continued. "I've seen the look of lost confidence in the face of one man who promised to marry me. I won't risk that again."

She turned back to him, the unshed tears locked behind her fierce gaze. "I won't marry Henry Wharton. I can't."

Eduardo resisted the urge to gently and quietly embrace her. He denied his need to soothe her pain and hurt. He stifled the longing to tell her that he'd do anything for her, that if she stayed with him she'd never be alone again, that nothing would ever hurt her again. He crushed the inclination to return to Chicago to do murderous harm to the young *norteamericano* fiancé who'd deserted her. He thought and felt and ached to do everything, but he did nothing.

From the moment he had first seen her he had been

beguiled by an innocent girl's beauty and courage. Guilt had prompted him to help her. But now it was the woman who fascinated him and the charade they played was only an invention to keep her near him. Yet how could he tell her the truth, that his act of revenge had driven her father to suicide. He was locked in inaction by his own duplicity, and the knowledge was slowly tearing him apart. "Do you love him?"

It was a chance to lie to him again, and the lie would hurt him. Philadelphia recognized that fact in frank surprise. Why should he care whether or not she married, or even whom she loved? What was the cause of this new vulnerability in his eyes?

She looked away, not wanting to see his face as the words came reluctantly from her. "No. I don't love Henry Wharton."

He was glad that she bowed her head with her final words. He couldn't have remained silent had she looked up and seen the relief and sympathy and joy on his face. Yet he had to do something or go mad. He turned abruptly away and with purposeful strides headed for the door.

Philadelphia looked up at the sound of his footsteps. "Where are you going?"

He turned as he reached for the door handle. "To visit this Marquis d'Edas."

"What will you do? What will you say?"

He smiled broadly. "Enough."

Philadelphia stared at the unopened letters on her dressing table. She was dressing for an evening out but she knew that she couldn't put the moment off any longer. Eduardo had not found the marquis at home when he went calling but had seconded Mrs. Ormstead's insistence that Philadelphia go out tonight.

She bit the inside of her lip. Going out meant that she would probably run into the marquis. If he publicly denounced her as a fraud, she would be disgraced and forced to leave New York immediately. Going back to Chicago would be futile, yet staying with Senhor Tavares would be equally impossible. The moment had come for her to read her father's letters carefully and from the clues she gathered to decide what action she would take next.

She hadn't been able to bring herself to read them in over two months, not since the night of her father's death. For the first time she noted that one was postmarked New York, and wondered why she hadn't realized that before. She glanced down at the others. One was postmarked New Orleans. The other was unmarked. Had it been delivered by hand? She picked up the New York letter, slipped the single sheet of paper out of its envelope, and unfolded it. She scanned it quickly, feeling with repugnance its link with her father's death and yet compelled to know the contents.

The tone of the letter was one of fear. It spoke of old alliances and warned of the dishonor that would follow discovery. It hinted at a divine retribution for past sins and damned the day they'd met. Yet the writer didn't mention the sins by name nor the suspected source of the retribution he feared. It was as though those things were already known to the person for whom the letter was intended. It was signed: John Lancaster.

She laid it quickly aside. She'd never heard her father speak of a John Lancaster, therefore he must have been a business partner rather than a personal friend. Her heart began to pound. Could he have been one of the secret partners in her father's banking investments? If Lancaster were an investor, then he might be wealthy enough to be known in New York society circles. But who could she ask about him? And where would she start when she didn't know anything about him at all?

As she lowered her gaze to the letter once more the

hair lifted on the back of her neck. Was this letter a warning about the impending failure of her father's bank?

The knock at her door brought Philadelphia to her feet with a start. "Your carriage is come, miss," the maid said from the other side of the door.

"Thank you. I'll be down in a moment." She looked at the other unopened letters. There wasn't time to read them. With regret she swept them up and put them away. Finally, she picked up her gloves and purse, dreading the evening's ordeal.

"I just love chocolate, don't you, Miss Ronsard?"

Philadelphia turned her head toward the woman who spoke to her, but she hadn't really heard what she said. "Pardon?"

"The dessert," Prudence Booker prompted. "Don't you just love chocolate desserts?"

*"Oui.* It is most delicious." Philadelphia absently added a chocolate bonbon to her plate of goodies but the buffet table, laden with assorted delicacies, held little fascination for her. The heat of the June evening weighed her down in spite of the icy glass of lemonade she had just consumed.

She glanced at Prudence as she tucked a mouthful of chocolate into her mouth. She was soft and pretty with a round forehead and chin that made her appear nearly half her twenty-six years. As the youngest matron of Hedda Ormstead's acquaintance, Prudence had been recruited to accompany Philadelphia to this soiree that Hedda had decided not to attend.

"I'm no longer able to stuff scrimped shrimps and myself into a corset on a regular basis," is how Hedda had explained her decision to remain at home on this particular evening. "Go along. Prudence is a goose—then, most women are, so I don't hold that against her, and neither should you."

Philadelphia smiled to herself. She had always thought

of her father as a man of strong opinion and will, but she believed he would have met his match in Hedda Ormstead.

Prudence's constant chatter about her two young daughters and the rewards of married life were agreeable but Philadelphia couldn't enjoy a single moment of the outing while waiting for the arrival of the Marquis d'Edas. Akbar had accompanied her and stood in the hallway just outside the salon but his presence didn't embolden her. Be brave, he'd said with maddening high spirit. It was all very well for him to treat the outing as a diversion, he wasn't locked in a struggle with doubts and the anxiety of not knowing what to expect next.

Her gaze kept wandering back to the salon entrance. Every masculine profile that crossed the threshold gave her an unhappy jolt until she saw that it wasn't the marquis's.

"I know I said so before but I will say it again," Prudence remarked, "that yellow silk gown looks quite splendid on you, Miss de Ronsard. You've an eye for colors. I would never have attempted the shade myself." With a sweep of her small hand, she dismissed several thousand dollars' worth of monthly shopping with the words, "I never know what to buy, so I buy everything!"

Reluctantly, Philadelphia turned away from her surveillance of the door. "You would look exquisite in blue, Mrs. Booker. And sea green, and rose."

"Now I told you, you're to call me Prudence. Everyone does, excepting, of course, a—a certain someone who still calls me Prue."

Philadelphia smiled and in an attempt to better hold up her end of the conversation asked, "But who is this certain someone?"

Flustered, Prudence blushed as her lids drooped over her china-blue eyes. "Oh, only a companion from my childhood years. I can't think why I even mentioned it."

Preoccupied, Philadelphia nodded as her gaze again

strayed toward the entry. This time she saw someone enter whom she knew. With relief she recognized Henry Wharton. He was with another gentleman. She lifted her hand to draw his attention, but he had already spied her and the warmth of his smile was all she could have hoped for in a friendly face.

"Good evening, ladies," Henry said, but his smile was for Philadelphia. "Aunt Hedda said you were out for the evening but she didn't say with whom." The slight vexation in his voice hinted that he thought his aunt had deliberately chosen to withhold the information in order to needle him.

"Aren't you going to introduce me, Henry, old man?" his companion said impatiently.

"Yes, of course." Henry's manner was faultlessly polite but Philadelphia sensed beneath it a vague unhappiness. "Mam'zelle de Ronsard, may I present Mr. Edward Gregory."

"Call me Teddy," the handsome young man answered. "Henry and I go back to nappers, don't we, old man? Best of friends always. Harvard, class of '75. Roommates all four years. Of course, we don't share everything. For instance, he hasn't said a word about you."

"You just returned to town yesterday," Henry said quietly.

"That's true enough. Been abroad. Paris. London. Rome. The lot." He eyed Philadelphia a little more closely than was strictly proper. "De Ronsard. French, by any chance?"

"*Oui.* I am French by all chance," she returned politely, but her smile was reserved.

"Imagine that. Me fresh off the boat from your country and you newly arrived in mine. You're new to the city?"

"*Oui.*"

Unabashed by her single-syllable reply, he went on. "That's swell. There must be a dozen things you haven't seen. Henry's something of a dull stick when it comes to showing a lady a rare good time." He winked at Henry and received a pained smile in reply. "But now that I'm back, you'll see everything. How about a ride in Central Park tomorrow afternoon? No—better! Roller skating. Do you skate, mademoiselle?"

"No." Philadelphia smiled to take the sting from her reply for, after all, he was an old friend of Henry's but, really, the man was too forward. His cocky smile made a strong counterpoint to Henry's quiet seriousness, making her wonder if Teddy often outmaneuvered his best friend when he wanted something Henry had.

"I skate."

The peevish sound of Prudence Booker's tone brought Edward's attention to her. She looked at him and said, "Hello, Teddy. You might have informed your friends of your return."

"Now, Prue, you heard it yourself. I only returned yesterday. Went round first thing this morning to collect Henry. We were going to pay our respects tomorrow, weren't we, Henry?"

Prudence felt Philadelphia's speculative gaze on her and said, "Teddy and Henry and I grew up together, Miss de Ronsard. Don't allow our familiar ways to embarrass you."

"I understand," Philadelphia replied. Yet, as the two fell into easy conversation about mutual friends, she saw Prudence's rapt attention to Teddy's every word, and the thought struck her that Prudence Booker was a little in love with Teddy Gregory, and probably had been since childhood. Did he know? She doubted it.

"Will you be attending the soiree at the Riverstons' tomorrow evening?"

She turned to find Henry bending close so that he might not be overheard. "Perhaps."

He smiled at her and the passion in his clear bright gaze made her heart sink. She didn't want him to love her. She'd only taunted Eduardo with the idea because, well, for reasons she didn't have time to sort out just now. To distract him from mooning over her she suddenly asked, "Do you know a banker by the name of Lancaster?"

He frowned thoughtfully. "Can't say that I do. But if you're looking for a reputable bank, I suggest you try mine."

"No, it is the man I wish to find." She gave him an appealing glance. "I met a friend of his daughter's during my travels, and she asked me to look up her friend while I was in town but I lost the full name and the address and . . ." She made a helpless gesture with her hands. "All I remember is the name Lancaster, and that her father is in banking."

Henry stroked his chin. "That presents a puzzle, doesn't it? I imagine a conversation with my banker might turn up a clue or two. He knows just about everybody in New York worth knowing, or so he says. Would you like me to question him for you?"

"I would so much appreciate it. Yet, you will be discreet?"

As Henry pledged to do his best to help her find Lancaster, from the corner of her eye Philadelphia saw Akbar enter the salon. General conversation ceased as the exotic stranger made his way through the room, but she didn't care. Without a word to Henry, she moved to intercept him. When she reached him, she rested a hand lightly on his arm. "Is everything all right?"

Eduardo looked past her to where Henry Wharton stood, before allowing his gaze to come back to her with distinct censure. "I see memsahib has not been idle."

Philadelphia threw an impatient look over her shoulder. "I do as you instructed," she murmured, "I'm modeling your jewels." He glanced at the brilliant wreath of diamonds circling her neck. He was both a miner and collector of jewels but the mad lust that drove some men to lie, steal, and even murder for the icy fire trapped within the depths of perfect stones had never infected him. What did stir his blood was the woman standing before him. He found himself mesmerized by the pulse beating at the base of her throat just above her jewels. Had they been alone, he might have placed a kiss on that pulse point.

"Why are you here?" she prompted, aware that all eyes remained inquisitively upon them.

Eduardo lifted his gaze to hers. "Your countryman arrived more than an hour ago. Why have you said nothing about it to me?"

"The marquis is here?" she whispered as her heart began to thud painfully. "I've not seen him."

His black eyes held her steadily. "Perhaps if you were less attentive to nephew Henry . . ."

She drew herself up and stepped back from him. "I want to return home," she said loudly. "I am tired and will make my excuses."

Eduardo bowed and said equally loudly, "Memsahib commands and Akbar obeys." Only as she turned away did he add under his breath, "But she had better stay away from nephew Henry if she hopes for a pleasant journey home!"

A scream, sudden and piercing, interrupted Philadelphia as she was about to reply. Even before she could react the cry came again. All heads swung toward the front hall and the source of the cry as a woman burst through the entrance into the salon, clutching her bosom and sobbing. She was dressed in the height of fashion, but that didn't stop her from staggering through the group of elegantly dressed guests to accost their host. "Mister Dogget!" she cried. "You must do something! It's gone! Stolen, I tell you! He took it!"

She swung about, her wild-eyed gaze searching the assembly until she spied the foreigner in white. She pointed at Akbar. "That's him! That's the thief who stole my pearls!"

Then, to the astonishment of the entire assembly, she swooned at her host's feet.

Everything seemed to happen at once. Several of the female guests rushed to the aid of the lady who lay sprawled on the carpet while several of the male guests turned to confront Akbar with the intention of detaining him.

Eduardo didn't move but he tensed in anticipation of a struggle. In fact, he almost hoped it would come to that. He'd been cooped up in drawing rooms for far too long to suit his temperament.

After a moment of hesitation, one of the men stepped forward. He was a big man with a large head and thick brown mustache, who carried the solid bulk of well-to-do middle age well. He stuck his fingers in the pockets of his waistcoat and reared back his head to look at Akbar through half-closed lids. "You have been accused of stealing, I say, stealing a lady's pearls," he boomed. "What do you have to say for yourself?"

"He has nothing to say," Philadelphia answered and stepped between Eduardo and the man accosting him. "My servant would no more steal than I would. How dare you accuse him!"

"Mrs. Oliphant accused him, not us," the man answered in the full volume of the hard-of-hearing, "And I say she should know!"

"Fiddle-faddle!" Philadelphia rejoined, her French accent forsaking her as it often did in moments of stress. Instantly she felt the prod of Eduardo's finger in her back. *"C'est incroyable!* Impossible!"

The spokesman took Akbar's measure in a long searching glance. "Your employer is, of course, within her rights to expect sound morals from the man she employs but I will have a look at the contents of your pockets just the same."

Eduardo smiled as he moved his feet farther apart for better balance. "With memsahib's permission, you may make the attempt."

"I'd be careful, Mr. Broughton," Henry Wharton advised from the edge of the semicircle of men. "There are rumors that this fellow committed murder in his own country."

"Thanks to memsahib," Eduardo murmured so softly only Philadelphia heard him. Until that moment she'd forgotten about her wild fabrications for the concierge at the Fifth Avenue hotel about how her Indian servant had executed recalcitrant servants.

She tossed Henry a dark look. "You, sir, I supposed to be my friend. I regret to learn I am mistaken in my confidence."

She almost felt sorry for him as he reddened to his ears. "I have every confidence in you, Miss de Ronsard." It was Akbar he didn't trust, but he could scarcely say that to her. He looked sheepishly about, weighing lifelong associations against taking the side of a near stranger, even if he was in love with her. "The lady says her servant is innocent of the crime and I, for one, believe her."

A gleam of humorous sympathy for the young man's plight brightened Mr. Broughton's eyes. "Well I regret, I say, regret having to say, young Henry Wharton, that when a clear cut identification's been made, the matter must be taken up by the authorities. We'll send for the police and allow them to proceed."

"Send a servant for the police," one of the men called.

"Yes, that's it," agreed another. "The police!"

Philadelphia blanched. She didn't need to hear Eduardo's muttered invective to realize that the last thing either of them could afford was to be interrogated by the police. Why, if they peered closely at him, they might discover his disguise and if that happened . . .

". . . one can never be too careful. Strangers. Unknown to society. I, myself, have never heard . . ."

As the nearby voice continued its litany of innuendo, Philadelphia turned her head until the sly features of the Marquis d'Edas came into her line of vision. He stood in the midst of a circle of ladies, one arm folded across his chest with the hand propping the elbow of the other arm, while he waved his free hand about to punctuate his speech. When had he entered the room? And why was he so pleased by her predicament? If he mentioned to the authorities his suspicions about her, she as well as Eduardo might wind up in jail.

"A moment!" she cried, desperate to forestall the action. "Am I to submit myself to this indignity? *Non,* I say! And *non,* again!" She swung to face Henry, feeling pangs of conscience at once more trading on his feeling for her but determined to save Eduardo and herself, whatever the cost. "Can you do nothing to prevent this, monsieur? Your aunt, what will she say when she learns what has happened to me?"

Henry moved to her side and took both her hands in his. "My dear mam'zelle, you may rest assured that I will protect you."

"And Akbar?"

He glanced at the bearded heathen and wondered again why the man seemed to find him particularly distasteful. "He's been accused of theft which is a matter for the police," he said helplessly.

She snatched back her hands. "Very well, monsieur. I see where your loyalties lie. I will handle this myself."

With a gesture of dismissal, she moved beyond him and crossed over to where the distraught lady who'd lost her pearls sat sobbing on her hostess's sofa.

"Madame Oliphant, you will give me your attention for a moment, *s'il vous plaît.*"

The authority in her voice roused the weeping lady and she looked up at Philadelphia in bewildered hurt.

"Madame, you have falsely accused my servant of theft, and I request most urgently that you will recant your statement."

"I won't!" the lady said in injured affront. "My pearls are gone and I want them back!"

"Of course you do. I, myself, would despair if the de Ronsard diamonds were taken." In afterthought, she raised her hand to verify that the brilliant collar still hung about her neck. "But I wouldn't accuse you, madame, of taking them because you stood next to me when I discovered the loss."

The lady's eyes widened. "Why, I should think not!"

"Exactly. So, you will unaccuse my servant of theft."

The lady gave her a resentful glance. "He's been lurking in the hallway the entire evening. One has been forced to pass by him each time one leaves the salon." She flicked a glance at Akbar and the sight of him made her shudder. "Look at him. He reminds one of the bearded Saracen infidels. I'm certain we should be protected from him."

"He's my protection, madame, and I trust him with my life as you would your husband." Even as she said it, Philadelphia glanced about in the realization that Mrs. Oliphant's husband had been curiously absent from the fray. "But where is Monsieur Oliphant?"

The lady's gaze fell before the younger woman's. "He isn't here. He didn't feel well this evening."

"You are alone?"

She shot Philadelphia a hostile look. "Certainly not! I've been escorted by the Marquis d'Edas."

"Ah." Because she had no other weapon, Philadelphia imbued the word with all the significance she could muster. "The marquis witnessed the theft?"

Caught off guard, the woman stuttered, "Well, I—I, couldn't say, exactly."

"Then say approximately," Philadelphia snapped, her nerves fraying under the strain. "Was the marquis with you when the theft occurred?"

"No, that is, I don't know the precise moment when the pearls were taken. The marquis was the first to realize that they were missing." She grew agitated. "The raspberry ice I'd eaten did not agree with me, and the marquis had gallantly offered to accompany me to the library where it was less crowded so that I might recover." She looked vaguely about for the marquis and saw that he was staring at her with obvious distaste.

"Madame Oliphant is correct," the marquis said as all eyes turned on him. "I, too, had been made uneasy by the presence of this turbaned savage. He deliberately stepped into our path as I escorted Madame Oliphant from the salon. It was after we'd entered the library that I noticed that the pearls were gone from Madame Oliphant's neck. Then I remembered the jostling in the hallway by this man. My jeweled snuffbox was recently stolen by a thief who picked my pocket as he bumped into me on the street." He fixed Philadelphia with a frosty, half-lidded gaze. "I've been told a light-fingered thief may secretly remove a ring from the finger while merely shaking hands." He turned to his host. "I beg you, do not be offended by the comparison I have drawn, Monsieur Dogget. One does not expect such occurrences in our present surroundings, of course."

Philadelphia also turned her attention to their host. "Tell me, Monsieur Dogget, these robberies in salons, they are rare occurrences in New York, *n'est-ce pas*?"

"Dear me, far from it," Gerald Dogget answered. "Theft has become the plague of the New York social season."

"It has?" Philadelphia struggled to hide a smile of grateful surprise at this piece of news. "But what has been done about it?"

"Often little can be done, if the gathering is small and those in attendance are well known to the hosts."

"And you, monsieur, you have lost items to these thieves?"

"A gold pocket watch, an onyx ring, and some cash during the New Year's Day festivities," he said testily.

Eduardo had kept silent but now he chuckled as he saw where Philadelphia was directing the conversation.

"This thieving goes on in the best homes?" Philadelphia demanded of her host.

"Yes," he answered begrudgingly.

"I lost my favorite watch at the Oliphants' after the Easter parade," Henry volunteered in a surprisingly cheerful tone for he had just realized what was dawning on the whole assembly; that Mademoiselle de Ronsard and her servant had been part of society only a few weeks while society thefts had been going on for months.

"So. I begin to understand," she said triumphantly. As she looked slowly about the room, an embarrassed silence fell. "Theft is nothing new to you and yet, tonight, you choose to turn on the stranger in your midst because it's easier to accuse me and mine than to search among yourselves for the real thief."

When she'd stared down every eye, she turned with deliberate calculation to the marquis. "I must declare a truth to you good people. There is a thief among you! And it isn't my servant!"

As her words sounded in the stunned silence, she turned quickly and walked over to Akbar and presented her hand that he might offer her his arm. "You will escort me home, Akbar. I am most thoroughly fatigued by the evening's events."

"A most interesting evening," Eduardo observed in a bemused voice as the carriage they'd engaged pulled away from the curb.

Philadelphia sank back against the seat beside him, her voice trembling like her hands. "It was vile! Horrid! Humiliating! I've never been so frightened in my life!"

"You were magnificent."

"I don't feel magnificent! I feel like I've eaten spoiled meat!"

"It will pass. It is only nerves."

"Oh! And for that I should be grateful?" She rounded on him in the narrow confines of the cab which forced her shoulder to be wedged tightly against his arm. "And you, you wanted a fight!"

"Perhaps," he murmured, more interested in their touching than their conversation. How pleasant, he thought, were these moments when she forgot to be afraid and careful and proper.

"Are you mad? Your disguise might have been discovered."

He grinned at her. "Why shouldn't I defend myself? We have done nothing wrong."

"Of course we have. I was there as a guest solely because the Doggets believe I am someone I'm not."

He shifted his body slightly so that his shoulder rubbed hers. "Haven't you noticed? Half of Fifth Avenue is passing itself off as what it isn't. They are common people who struck it rich in some trade or another. Now they've sloughed off their old lives and are hard at work to manufacture new ones. It's done in my country as well." He shifted again, lifting one arm to stretch it along the seat behind her. "I made my fortune by scratching around in the dirt and finding pretty pebbles like the ones you wear around your neck." He flicked the necklace with a finger.

"Did you ever ask your father where and how he began his fortune?"

"He was a banker," Philadelphia answered.

"Before that what was he?" His fingers brushed the side of her neck. "Or were you always rich?"

She knit her brow in thought. "I don't know."

"Yet you never asked. Interesting." He said the words with an impartiality that made them sound faintly damning. "You might not have liked the answer."

Before she could switch moods to match his, he lightly dragged his fingertips up the nape of her neck and said, "At least we haven't harmed anyone with our little deception."

"Haven't we?" she rejoined, faintly alarmed by the feel of his fingers tracing her nape. "What about Mrs. Ormstead?"

He considered this. "I believe she might second our little enterprise. She possesses spirit and the rare talent of finding amusement in the simplest experience."

She stared at him, trying to fathom the reason for his amused tone. The reckless expression she glimpsed as they passed under a streetlight made her keenly aware of the pressure of his knee against hers. He looked like Akbar though the soft-voweled speech of Senhor Tavares addressed her, yet his gaze belonged to the half-naked stranger whose kiss had made her wonder if she knew him at all. She pressed herself into the corner of the carriage saying, "You're the strangest man I ever met."

He reached out and lightly drew a circle on her cheek with his forefinger. "I told you once before, menina, that I would rather you found me intriguing."

She brushed his hand away from her cheek. "I don't understand you."

He gently took her face between his hands. "You understand everything, menina. Only you are afraid to admit it. For instance, you have this most amazing need to protect me, even when I am not in serious danger. Why do you suppose that is?"

"But I—"

He halted her words by brushing his thumb over her lips. "Hush, menina. You have already said a great many things this night. Now it's my turn. I am not criticizing this protective spirit of yours. It is most endearing. But who, menina, will protect you from me?"

"Do I need protection?" she whispered, rapidly falling under the mesmerizing spell of the thumb that continued to stroke her lower lip.

"But certainly. You are alone with a man who isn't your relative, or your servant. Foolish girl. Have you not been warned about such things as ravishment?"

"Yes," she answered a little breathlessly and unconsciously licked her lower lip to relieve the tingling sensation his teasing touch provoked. "But I believed that you wouldn't take advantage of me."

"Ah. Menina, you wound me." He watched, fascinated, as her tongue again darted out, this time accidentally grazing the tip of his thumb. "Am I not a man? May I not be moved to indiscretion by your nearness?"

He reached down and lifted one of her hands to slip it inside his brocade jacket where he held it palm-flat over his heart. "Do you not feel my blood pumping there? Am I not warm to touch? Does my body not tremble under the pressure of your hand?"

"Well," she began evasively, "if you would allow me to remove my hand—"

"I believe I might die," he answered with a chuckle. "I would show you just how warmly and strongly my blood runs elsewhere but we are not, I think, ready for that lesson."

Philadelphia opened her mouth to finish her sentence but, remarkably, she found she couldn't think of a single word. In fact, she couldn't think at all. There was only an awareness of the slow hard pounding under her hand that communicated itself up her arm through tremulous muscle until her own heart caught the exaggerated rhythm.

"Don't kiss me." She didn't know if the thought had crossed his mind but it had crossed hers—and the anticipation was unbearable.

"I could more easily stop breathing," he said as he bent to her.

As their lips met he felt her flinch, and he drew back a little to look at her. Her eyes were screwed shut and she had compressed her lips as if in expectation of a mouthful of castor oil. "What's this, menina? Am I so distasteful to you?"

She opened her eyes a fraction. "The beard. It scratches."

With a Portuguese curse, he yanked off the offending bush. "Now then, menina, for your comfort and mine."

Philadelphia shut her eyes again as he bent toward her, but for a very different reason this time. In the last instant she'd seen shining in his gaze a blend of amusement, affection, and—if her bewildered senses didn't mislead her—something akin to the besotted adoration that afflicted Henry Wharton.

He'd kissed her before, a brief exchange in the Ormstead conservatory which had ended in a sneezing fit, and again in his attic room when anger had held equal sway with passion. But, from the moment their lips met, she knew this was an utterly new experience.

For a long moment the smooth warmth of his lips overlay hers like a seal of perfect peace, and the urge to draw back from him melted away under his gentle persuasion. Then his hands framed her cheeks, and he lifted her chin higher as he turned his head to one side to slant his mouth across hers. He moved his head slowly back and forth, teasing her with his lips as he had done earlier with his thumb.

Some instinct of feminine intuition whispered in a waspish but wise voice that this was the caress of an experienced lover, a sweet torment designed to embolden a shy partner, and that she should put an end to this at once. The voice went unheeded as he continued the subtle and yet inexorable abrasion. Soon he would stop himself as he had done before, she thought, and she would be free. Instead, her lips became so sensitive that each brush made her moan softly. When her moans turned to sighs through parted lips, he licked the newly exposed softness with long slow sweeps of his tongue.

Once, at a state fair, she'd been induced to touch an electromagnetic device said to imitate the production of lightning and had felt the current run like a live thing up through her fingertips. She'd snatched her hand away, horribly embarrassed by the intimate tingling that had flowed through her body and lifted the hair on her head and arms and . . . well. She'd never told a single soul of the sensation that had made her hurry home to inspect herself for evidence of the violation. Now the moist heat of his tongue pushed a pulsing current of delicious sensation every bit as strong along her skin and beneath where it invaded with equal intensity her lungs, her breasts, and her loins.

Finally his lips left her mouth, tracing the curve of her cheek to its crest, which he sucked gently, and then moved on until the icy touch of diamonds met his lips. With his teeth, he pulled the earring from her lobe and released it into her lap. Then he claimed his prize, the velvet shell of her ear. He pressed a kiss into it and then the tip of his tongue.

She gasped at the shock of it, but he moved away so quickly that he caught the last of her cry in his mouth.

There followed kiss after heavy drugging kiss that seemed to dissolve her muscle and melt every bone. When he finally lifted his head, there was no more strength left in her to think or imagine or even support her own weight, and she nodded forward to lean weakly against his chest.

"You should have told me," he whispered beside her ear.

"Told you what?" she murmured.

"That you needed a thorough kissing."

"But—I didn't."

"Oh, but you did, menina, and you should always have what you need."

Philadelphia closed her eyes. She felt as though she were hanging over the edge of an abyss, her fingernails raking flinty granite in a desperate bid for purchase. His kisses left her exhilarated, yet with such marginal control that she had to set her teeth in her lower lip to keep from begging him for more.

"I don't understand anything anymore," she complained as an unforgivable tear bloomed from up under the sealed edges of her lashes. "Least of all myself."

Eduardo lifted her head and smiled at the great perplexed misery on her face. "The answer is so simple, menina, that I believe I must demonstrate it for you very soon or go mad. But first I must, as you *norteamericanos* say, see a man about a dog."

"I never say that," she protested as he shifted on the seat and gently pressed her back into the corner.

"Mrs. Ormstead will wish to know all about the Doggets' evening," he said in a voice remarkably free of the sweet agony under which his body labored. "You can entertain her with stories of our misadventures while I am gone."

"What will you do?" she asked, half-distracted by the discovery of a sticky substance clinging to her cheeks.

"Nothing that should concern you, menina."

"Oh, very well, be mysterious. But don't expect me to wait up for you. I shall be in bed."

"Then when I return I will most certainly go straight to bed."

The tone of his voice made her look up into his dark eyes which gleamed like dewy sloe plums. Afraid and unwilling to learn if, in reading between the lines of his declaration, there was a reference to his coming to *her* bed, she looked away in silence.

Eduardo longed to embrace her, to hold her close and make her believe what he sensed she was beginning to doubt—the sincerity of the passion he felt for her—even though the wet imprint of his kisses remained on her mouth. But he didn't. The carriage was drawing up before the Ormstead mansion. If he touched her again, he knew he wouldn't be able to stop and then the cabby would be treated to a sight that would be the talk of the Fifth Avenue hackney trade by morning.

He snatched up his discarded whiskers, pressing them into place with the hope that there was enough plaster still remaining on his cheeks to hold them for the time it took for him to deliver her to the door.

It was only after he'd helped her down and escorted her to safety inside the front door that it dawned on Eduardo that he'd scarcely touched her at all. He'd not brushed a single caress over the fullness of her breasts or sought to learn the shape of her hips. The sweet hot scalding passage of desire through his veins fired the conviction that she regretted the oversight as much as he. Was that part of the reason for the accusation he saw in her wide eyes before she turned and fled up the stairs? Did she feel as he did, that they'd only begun what must now, somehow, be finished?

Half an hour later, Eduardo left the Ormstead mansion by the back entrance and hailed a cab. The cabby saw nothing remarkable about his elegantly dressed fare, but was surprised when the man called out the name of a hotel on Twenty-sixth Street before climbing in.

Eduardo was not surprised to find that the marquis's lodgings were in one of the more modest hotels of the city. Emigrés were welcomed into American society not for their wealth but for the one thing money couldn't buy the New Rich: a proud lineage and title.

He smiled as he entered the hotel lobby and adjusted his evening coat. It had been weeks since he'd worn any of his own clothing. In purely sensuous pleasure, he admired the tight but elegant fit of the fine fabric as he flexed his shoulders. A warm bath and close shave had rid him of the vestiges of sticking plaster and face paint. He'd traded the scent of sandalwood for ambergris. All in all, he was quite pleased with his transformation from Akbar to Senhor Tavares.

When he reached the third floor, Eduardo strode confidently down the dimly lit hall to number 305 and knocked. After a second rap roused no answer, he withdrew a long thin piece of metal from his pocket, jiggled it in the keyhole until the lock turned, opened the door, and stepped inside.

He'd barely finished his brief but enlightening search of the room when the first reedy notes of whistling preceded the sound of footsteps moving along the hall. Quickly and silently, he moved behind the door and waited, more anxious than he'd been upon entering the room for the confrontation which was about to take place.

The marquis was more than a little drunk, which more than a little pleased him. He preferred drunkenness from good brandy to any other form of intoxication. Its attendant warmth, rushing in his veins, reminded him of the liquid gem fire of fine rubies. As he inserted his key in his door, he picked up the thread of the tune he'd been whistling, enjoying the exhaled heat of his breath which brushed like dragon's fire against his face. *Sacrebleu!* He was pleased with himself.

With exaggerated care, he walked over to the table where a lamp burned low and emptied his pockets. Two rings, his wallet, a jeweled cigarette case, and last of all, a three-strand necklace of pearls. He picked it up and held it in an unsteady grasp before the light.

It was a good catch but not the prize he'd sought. If not for the amorous demands of the Oliphant bitch, he might have collected the prize of his career this night. Still, when she flung her arm about his neck, he could not resist slipping off her pearls while in her ardent embrace.

He smirked and laid the pearls carefully on the table. It was due payment for having had to suffer her embraces these last weeks. He would have preferred the de Ronsard girl's embrace. To have successfully removed that heavy collar of diamonds from her neck while she lifted her beautiful face for his kiss would have been the crowning achievement of his life. Just thinking about it made him run his hand strongly over the placket of his trousers. He'd have been set for life with that one theft.

"Forgive me if I interrupt this—intimacy."

Eduardo almost felt sorry for the man who whipped around so quickly he nearly fell.

The marquis's eyes widened as he saw the immaculately dressed stranger who stood in the shadowy corner beside his door. "Who are you? What do you want?" A quick flicker of his pale gaze toward the pearls lying nearby betrayed his first suspicion.

"I didn't come for the pearls, marquis, but I'll take them all the same," the stranger said in a pleasant lightly accented voice. "But first you will chat with me, I think."

The marquis squinted, his hand moving casually toward his jacket pocket. "Do I know you?"

"No, you don't." The stranger revealed the derringer he palmed. "And, if you so much as reach for whatever it is in your pocket, you never will."

The marquis dropped his hand to his side and straightened up, remembering suddenly who he was. "I am the Marquis d'Edas, and I demand to know who you are and what you're doing here!"

"Who I am is of no value to you. *Why* I am here is." He

reached into his pocket and took out a coin and tossed it to the Frenchman.

Despite his drunken state, the marquis recognized the glimmer of gold as the metal disk arced toward him and with surprising agility snatched it from the air. But when he looked down at the Spanish doubloon with the bullet hole in its center, his expression fell. "Where did you get this?"

"From the same source as you, unless the one in your bureau drawer is stolen."

"No!" He shook his head violently. "I would not dare steal such a thing."

"Then explain to me why you are so highly valued by the man who gave you his token."

The marquis licked his lips several times as if fear were being spoon-fed to him. "I have nothing to say to you."

"It seems that you are at a disadvantage."

"How so?"

"You give me no reason not to simply kill you."

"You wouldn't dare!" he cried, dropping all attempts to maintain his dignity. "If Tyrone learned of it—"

"Tyrone," the stranger repeated thoughtfully. "Now you begin to interest me. Are you on such terms with Tyrone that you feel free to use his name as talisman against your enemies? I think not. In any case, a coward of your stripe must have many enemies. Who's to say which one found you first?"

"But I've done nothing!"

"To begin with, you are a liar. Your French accent belongs on a bayou back of New Orleans, not the Île de la Cité. Second, you are a thief. Third, you have distressed a lady of my acquaintance. That reason alone would suffice for me to murder."

"What lady? Some mistress of yours?"

"The *lady* to whom I refer is a Mademoiselle de Ronsard. Ah, I see you do know her. Why does that frighten you?"

"I haven't so much as danced with her!" the man flung at him.

"No, but you would like to do so much more than dance with her, yes? She responds to the threat she feels whenever you are near. So, I must kill you—or remove you from the city."

Now that an alternative to murder had been introduced into the conversation, the marquis felt certain that the man didn't intend to carry out his threat, and the knowledge emboldened him. "I swear never to approach the lady again."

"Yet, you were inordinately interested in her. Why?"

Before he could stop himself, the marquis's eyes shifted again to the pearls.

"Ah, I see. The diamonds. You are a fool. You'd never have lived to enjoy the theft. You may return my property." He beckoned with his hand for the coin the man clutched. Without hesitation, the marquis tossed it to him. "I'll take your coin as well."

The marquis paled. "You can't have it. It's my protection."

"Which I am withdrawing. The coin. Now."

For the space of a few heartbeats, the marquis silently debated what he should do. He feared many things but he dreaded the man called Tyrone. He had never met Tyrone, but the name was potent enough to strike disquiet in every port from New Orleans to St. Louis. Years earlier, when New Orleans had been his milieu, he'd been offered a job, a minor bit of thievery. When the job was done, the coin had been placed in his hand by a man who had said it was good for one favor from Tyrone. It was priceless. "Who sent you to do this?"

"No man gives me orders," he answered.

"Tyrone?" the marquis breathed incredulously.

There was no reply. The marquis suddenly felt as sober as a judge. "I had no idea, about the lady, I mean. Didn't intend her any harm." He spread his arms wide in a Gallic shrug. "It was the diamonds, mon ami. They are worth a king's fortune. But, of course, they are safe from me now."

"Yes, they are. Now the coin."

The marquis went and fished it reluctantly from the drawer. When he turned back he saw that the man had moved from the door over to the table and was scooping up the pearls. An instant before the lamp was snuffed, its light illuminated the stranger and the marquis glimpsed the man's profile and realized that there was something familiar about his black hair and bronze skin. As the dark descended, the marquis tensed with the impulse to flee but then the stranger's voice, sounding deeper and more weighty in the darkness said, "It is well known that Tyrone can see in the dark like a cat. One step, marquis, and I will kill you."

The marquis froze, his hand closed painfully over the gold lucky piece in his palm. "I saw nothing, not enough to identify you. I swear it!"

"How can I believe you?"

The marquis felt his knees begin to buckle as a wave of nausea rolled through his middle. He wasn't a brave man nor was he strong or daring. He had nothing but his life to which he clung with the unreasoned desire of any living speck. "The possessor of a coin is promised a favor," he whispered.

"You've had it. You're not dead."

The marquis nodded in understanding though it was now too dark for the other man to see the motion. "I wish to go back to New Orleans."

"No."

The marquis caught his breath in an attempt to ride out another tidal wave in his stomach. "Farther? Texas? Colorado? California? Leave the country?"

"The first ship outward-bound," the stranger suggested. "Now the coin."

"I can't see you."

"Ah, but I can see you."

The marquis held out his hand, fingers spread, and was unnerved by the rake of fingers lightly over his palm as the coin was removed. The man could see in the dark. It was Tyrone!

"The next ship!" he whispered as the man shoved him aside and went out through the door.

# 9

"You can't leave. I won't have it! And do stop staring at me with those golden eyes awash in limpid tears," Hedda Ormstead scolded as she reached for another slice of toast to butter. "I'm immune to hysterics but I detest them all the same!"

"I'm not weeping, madame," Philadelphia answered across the length of the breakfast table. "I'm only sad to be put to the necessity of saying farewell."

Hedda eyed her young companion of the past month with great disfavor. "Does your leaving have anything to do with Akbar's return? What, precisely, is the man to you?"

Philadelphia frowned at the invective in Mrs. Ormstead's tone. She had expected that her hostess would regret losing her, but this scorching anger was not expected. "He is my servant."

"Hogwash! I heard about your imprudent defense of him at the Doggets." She lifted a brow. "Is that what has upset you? Put the matter from your mind. I'm certain the Oliphant woman did the moment her pearls were returned. Though the thief wasn't apprehended, you needn't play hide and seek with your lives as though *you* were wanted by the police."

Philadelphia felt the full power of the woman's inquisitive gaze on her. "Other circumstances dictate the course of my life."

"That sounds vaguely distasteful. Am I to suppose, then, that you mean financial circumstances?" Hedda took a bite of her toast and chewed it thoroughly before continuing. "I've told you before that I enjoy having you as my guest. If I've not provided adequately for you, all you need do is say so. I'll pay you a salary." Her gaze swung away from Philadelphia. "I'm a very lonely old woman and can be generous when the need arises."

Abruptly as a thunderclap, the meaning of Mrs. Ormstead's offer roared through Philadelphia's thoughts. She was being offered carte blanche to remain, even if it meant the older woman would have to pay for her continued presence. Hurt and humiliation swept over her, only to be caught in a swift crosscurrent of sympathy. How lonely the woman must be to open herself up willingly to what amounted to little more than blackmail. And how mercenary she must seem for the woman to believe that she would accept.

She rose and rounded the dining table to stand before the older woman. Reaching out, she took one of her parchmentlike hands between hers. "I've come to care for you very much, madame. If I could, I would remain."

Hedda tilted her head back to look down the length of her nose at the young lady standing before her and wondered if she'd been half as beautiful at the same age. "If you cared for me, you would remain."

"I do care, madame, that is why I must go."

Hedda's chin trembled a moment before she caught herself. Straightening up, she snatched her hand back. "Willful! Spoiled! Contrary! Ungrateful! Wait, I've not finished. Foolish! Reckless! Indiscreet! You might remain with me, or if you prefer you could marry. That twit of a nephew, Horace, would build a castle for you if you directed it."

"His name is Henry, madame."

"Hah! You have been paying attention. Poor boy. I don't suppose he's much in the way of eliciting flame and fever. You French do place a great deal of emphasis on that sort of thing. Still, if I remember correctly from his diapering days, his parts are in order. Perhaps, you'll inspire him. In any case, he has other qualities. He'll be a doting husband and an equally doting father. And there's money, lots of it. With your elegance and charm, he'll think himself more lucky than he deserves—and he'll be right."

"I don't love your nephew, madame."

Hedda looked at Philadelphia as though she had spilled tea all over the floor. "Of course you don't! You love that turbaned savage. I have eyes in my head, and the pair of you are as transparent as panes of glass."

"Madame is mistaken," Philadelphia said carefully and moved away in order to shield herself from the woman's too-keen gaze.

"If the man were any less self-contained, I'd have had him thrown out of here the first day," Hedda retorted. "His feelings were appallingly apparent from the first. I haven't forgotten the look on his face after you fell before my horse. If he could have, he'd have lifted my carriage, driver, horses and all, and tossed us into the nearest gutter."

"Surely you are mistaken, madame." Philadelphia forced a light tone. "I'm convinced Akbar thinks of me as a mere child."

"Really?" Hedda's voice tone was icy enough to lower the thermometer several degrees. "That was no peck on the cheek I observed in my conservatory a few weeks ago. Well, you should blush! Osculating in the full light of day like any foolish maid with her randy footman! I should have thrown the pair of you out then and there!"

Philadelphia hung her head in acute embarrassment, thinking that chaste kiss was the least of the indiscretions she'd committed while under this roof. "I'm sorry, madame, for having offended you."

"Don't speak to me in that presumptuous manner. I didn't say I disapprove—but I do! He's too old for you, and a heathen in the bargain. If you married, you'd be cast out of good society and remain a curiosity to those who would accept you. Think, my girl! What is love compared to comfort and security?"

Philadelphia looked up and smiled. "Since I have neither love nor comfort nor security in any great degree, madame, I'm at a loss to make comparisons."

"Minx!" Hedda sighed deeply. "I should throw you out, but I won't. I should throw *him* out, but I won't."

Philadelphia eyed the woman with great admiration and bemusement. They were engaged in what could certainly be termed the most eccentric conversation of her life. Yet she sensed beneath Mrs. Ormstead's brusque disapproval genuine feelings of affection. She longed to tell her who she was and why she was in New York. Was Eduardo right to think that Mrs. Ormstead would understand if she explained how she and he were business associates, that in reality Akbar was Senhor Tavares, a handsome and wealthy Brazilian not many years her senior? The urge was strong yet she didn't say a single word because she wasn't convinced herself of what was the complete truth.

She reached into her pocket. As doubtful as she was about the necessity of it, she had promised Eduardo that she would go through with their plan. "Madame Ormstead, you have been most kind to me and I do appreciate your advice. That is why, if I may, I would ask one thing more of you."

"Very well," Hedda said coolly.

She lifted the diamond collar and earrings from her pocket and laid them on the table. "I must find a buyer for these."

Hedda gasped in spite of herself. "The de Ronsard diamonds! Sell them? Absolutely not!"

"Yes, I must. I have debts."

"How many debts? Of what nature? To whom?"

The rapid-fire questions startled Philadelphia though
she was quickly coming to the conclusion that nothing she
said or did would ever catch Mrs. Ormstead completely
off guard. Feeling a chasm of guilt yawn wider at her feet,
she looked away. "Debts, madame, are private."

She was surprised by the strength in the hands that
suddenly closed on her arms. The grip tightened until she
felt the distinct impression of each and every one of
Hedda's nails through the fabric of her gown.

"What is this mystery?" Hedda demanded in an urgent
whisper as she studied the misery in the young face so
close to hers. "Whatever it is, I can help you. I've influence."

Philadelphia gazed down upon the elegant elderly face
with wonder. "Why are you willing to do this for me? You
know nothing about me."

"Nor do I care to," Hedda snapped. "I believe I should
be greatly put out with you if I knew the entire truth. So
allow me to keep my ignorance. Is it Akbar? Is he black-
mailing you?"

"Akbar isn't my enemy, madame. Believe me."

Hedda sighed and subsided into her chair. She picked
up her teacup to inspect the contents. A quick sip
brought a look of distaste to her features, and she placed
it back in its saucer. "So, you do love him. I was afraid so.
A pity."

Philadelphia's embarrassed gaze wandered to where
her diamonds lay in the sunlight like a brilliant pool of
pure spring water. "Will you recommend a pawnbroker to
me, madame?"

Hedda stopped pouring a fresh cup of tea. "Are you
determined to part with the gems?"

"I must."

"Family pride notwithstanding?"

Philadelphia gave her a distracted smile. "What is pride when one is poor, madame?"

With great restraint, Hedda withheld the caustic remark that Philadelphia need have no fear of poverty if she remained beneath this roof. "Very well. I will buy the diamonds."

"No!" Philadelphia didn't realize how emphatically she'd spoken until she saw the amazed look on the woman's face. "That is, I couldn't allow you to, madame, after all you've done."

Hedda reached for the necklace and held it up to the light with one hand while she lifted her lorgnette from its ribbon about her neck and closely inspected each diamond. "They're real," she declared finally. "Five thousand dollars."

"But, madame—"

"Eight thousand!"

"Madame, please, you—"

"Ten thousand. That's my final offer. Take it," she urged in annoyance. "You won't get a better offer elsewhere, certainly not from a pawnbroker. I ask only one thing in return."

Philadelphia swallowed carefully over the lump of emotion lodged in her throat. "Anything, madame."

Hedda turned very deliberately to her. "I will permit you to leave on the condition that when you've sorted things out—and I recommend that you do so quickly—you will again present yourself at my door with a full and thorough explanation of what has really been going on these last weeks. That French accent of yours is more unreliable than my new plumbing!"

Philadelphia smiled her chagrin. "There's nothing I'd rather do, madame. Believe me."

"Another thing, and I say this in the full knowledge that no one else of your acquaintance would ever advise you thus: if you are in love with that man, then tell him so. He's not getting any younger and heathen or not, a man is in his prime when he can still think of himself as young."

To Hedda's surprise, Philadelphia's face fell and her golden eyes took on the distinct sheen of unshed tears for a second time. "You're mistaken, madame. I don't love him."

Hedda didn't say another word as Philadelphia turned and left the room. If she didn't yet realize what her feelings were, no good would be served by pressing the matter. Still, she regretted the necessity of losing the girl before the little drama had been played to its conclusion.

Hedda picked up the diamonds and held them to her bosom over her heart. Yes, she regretted that, and the size of this enormous old house with only one small old woman to fill it.

Eduardo shifted into a more comfortable position on the leather seat of the private carriage as it rolled out of the coach yard of an inn half a day's journey north of the city. Instead of reentering the major thoroughfare, the driver directed his horses onto a wooded lane that ran close to the shore.

Beyond the narrow trunks of trees on his left, Eduardo spied the broad back of the Hudson River gleaming in the early afternoon sunshine. Fifty yards from the shore a sailboat left a snail-track wake on the calm surface, its white sail arched proudly before a gentle breeze. The sight cheered him. It was a perfect traveling day, warm yet breezy, sunny but not blindingly so. It was the sort of day that offered endless possibilities of simple pleasures, the kind of day that made a man glad to be alive and not alone.

"Where are we going?"

The sound of Philadelphia's voice dragged him from his musing, and he turned to smile at her. "Saratoga's gambling season doesn't open until August. Meanwhile, I thought you'd enjoy a holiday in the Hudson River Valley while we plan our next masquerade. I've rented a house for us on the river."

"You mean for us to stay there by ourselves?"

He pursed his lips to hold back amusement until he could easily say, "Who do you suggest we invite, senhorita?"

Her gaze fell before his. "Oh."

After a few moments of nervous silence, she darted a look at him and was glad to see that he'd gone back to his contemplation of the view. It gave her a chance to try to re-adjust to the changes in his appearance. Her gaze lingered curiously over the blue-black sheen of his hair and the rich caramel of his whiskerless chin. He smiled at some distraction in the distance, drawing her eyes to the sensually shaped lips that had pressed themselves to hers more than once.

She had left the Ormstead residence four hours earlier and traveled alone until noon in the rented carriage as per his instructions, when the driver had paused for luncheon at a traveling inn. It was when she reentered the carriage after her meal that she discovered she would no longer travel alone. But it wasn't "Akbar" who occupied the opposite seat. It was Senhor Tavares, dressed for traveling in the latest European fashion.

The abrupt transition, without warning, was unnerving. She knew Akbar, trusted him. Did that mean she knew and trusted Eduardo Tavares? She wasn't at all certain that that was so. He seemed as much a stranger to her as if he were an altogether different person. As he turned his head to smile at her, she looked away.

Something was wrong. Eduardo had noticed it the moment she climbed into the carriage, but he couldn't fathom the reason for it. Unless it was the fact that he'd intercepted Henry Wharton before the man could say good-bye to her. Was that it? Was she sitting there grieving over the loss of that pale, dim-witted *norteamericano*?

The idea that her distress owed itself to another man rankled. What sort of man allowed a servant to prevent him from saying good-bye to the lady he loved? Yet Wharton had given up his attempt to see her without even a heated word. Had he been in Wharton's place, he'd have braved half a dozen servants to see her. The coward shouldn't even have been allowed the grace to leave a note.

She was well rid of Wharton, and if she didn't soon realize it he'd put the matter to rest in his own way. After all, he had time and success on his side. Their first venture together had been quite profitable. Which reminded him.

"Here's your share of our sale. It comes to something just over four thousand dollars."

Philadelphia looked down at the banker's note he placed in her lap. "I don't want it."

"Senhorita, you always say that when I offer you money."

The sound of his voice, soft-voweled and unaltered now by the necessity of disguise, sent a shiver of disquiet along her spine. He was like quicksilver; liquid, bright, uncontainable, flowing naturally and effortlessly into whatever shape and need the moment required. There were moments, like now, when she wondered why she had ever trusted him at all. "I can't accept Mrs. Ormstead's money. It'd be like stealing from relatives."

"She has a beautiful necklace in place of her cash," he reminded her.

"Still." She paused to reach for as reasonable a tone as she could muster. "If we hadn't left the city so quickly I might have sold the diamonds elsewhere. A few days would have been all it would have taken to place them."

"We didn't have a few days."

"Why not?" She tensed herself as the silence drew out. "I demand that you tell me why we left the city so precipitously. Is it because of the marquis?" Her voice quavered as she added, "Did he threaten to expose us?"

"You need not concern yourself with thoughts of the marquis," he said shortly.

"Why not? What happened? I know you went to see him. What did you do? You didn't—?"

He leaned forward. "Didn't what?"

The challenge in his gaze gave her pause even in her thoughts. "Well . . . I don't know precisely *what*."

"Something like murder, perhaps?" he suggested softly.

"Murder?" she whispered, hoarse with shock. "You . . . ?" She knew she couldn't have finished the thought if her life had depended on it.

He sat back, his bold mouth flattened into a straight line. "Do you see me as a bloodthirsty *bandoleiro,* senhorita? Do I remind you of every dark-skinned savage who ever threatened you in your schoolgirl nightmares?"

"Certainly not!" she snapped as his barb stuck closer to her thoughts than was comfortable. He did haunt her dreams, his kisses and those gorgeous eyes that saw more than was proper, but the fear she felt was only for her own sanity. How could she desire in her dreams a man she scarcely knew in her waking hours? "I'm quite capable of levelheaded thinking, senhor. I simply wished to know what had become of the marquis. It was you who suggested murder."

"Did I? I apologize. The marquis is quite alive. He has decided, however, that America does not agree with his health and is at this very moment sailing for Europe."

"I see." But she didn't. Did he possess such power that people did as he ordered, even if it meant leaving the country?

As every turn of the carriage wheels carried her farther from New York, she regretted more and more not throwing herself on Mrs. Ormstead's mercy and confessing everything. She regretted so many things that she didn't even realize that her thoughts had translated themselves into tears.

Annoyed with her for her foolish thoughts and his own jealous ones, Eduardo tried but failed to keep his gaze from straying toward her. He was amazed to see her weeping in absolute silence. At least, he supposed, crying was the correct expression. Two crystal tears slipped down her cheek, but neither by shortened breath nor movement did she betray any awareness of the event. It was as though her body were making a secret attempt to dislodge its overburdened senses without the consent of her mind.

The women he'd known in his life would never have let a display of tears go unnoticed. Nurtured on centuries of the stormy intercomingling of Portuguese and Spanish drama, native Indian passions, and African spirituality, all communicated in physical dimensions, a Brazilian woman could wring more emotion from a single tear than he'd seen Philadelphia Hunt reveal in all the weeks of their association.

He shifted his gaze away from her proud, if slightly damp, profile. She wasn't unfeeling. She wasn't cold. *Deus!* Just sitting beside her was warming him so thoroughly his skin seemed to simmer beneath his clothing. How long had he been without a woman? The realization registered with mild shock. That long? He nearly qualified for sainthood.

He reached into his coat pocket and withdrew the note Wharton had quickly scribbled. If her tears were for him then she'd better read it now and have it over. Before they left the Hudson shore, he intended to completely wipe the man from her thoughts.

"Wharton asked me to pass this on to you." He held the note between two fingers as he offered it. "I suggested that he forgo maudlin and trivial good-byes but . . ." He shrugged.

Philadelphia snatched the note, half-expecting him to withdraw it. "Did you read it?"

"I've never been driven to reading the scribbling of a lovesick schoolboy."

"Then how to do you know it's a love letter?" she challenged.

"The drool on the envelope," he pronounced with glee.

She looked down at the note. "I should have said good-bye."

"And given him the chance to spout whatever passes in his mind for passionate pleading? You'd have been subjected to a dozen awkward moments, perhaps even a threat of suicide. I don't think you'd have liked it one bit."

"I know one thing," she answered with a cold unfriendly look. "I don't like you one bit!"

"Fire from the ice maiden at last!" His rich laughter purled through the carriage, filling it with eddies of deep masculine good humor. She ignored him and opened the note.

Eduardo expected any of several reactions; sadness, a repetition of silent tears, guilt, regret, poignant loss. The stricken look that dilated her eyes was one he didn't expect. "What is it?"

Philadelphia looked up at him, but in her mind's eye she saw only the wording on the page she'd just read. Lancaster was dead.

Eduardo leaned forward and reached out. "Let me see what the idiot's written that disturbs you so."

"No!" She snatched the paper out from under his grasp. "No," she repeated in a more reasonable voice. "It —it's nothing. I was only reminded of something else." She quickly stuffed the note in her purse and closed it.

"You're trembling, senhorita."

"Am I?" She laced her fingers together in her lap, not looking at him. "It must be fatigue. I didn't sleep well."

"That's unfortunate," he said mildly, but he was aware

of every shade of expression that slipped across her face like clouds shadow the sun. "I, myself, always sleep the sleep of the innocent. I'm told, however, that there's nothing like the breath of country air to calm a troubled spirit. Our hiatus on the Hudson would seem the perfect remedy for your problem."

She didn't answer him. She scarcely heard what he said. She wanted only silence.

*Lancaster was dead.* What were Henry's exact words? She couldn't remember. Anger threaded through the chill that had enveloped her. She didn't dare retrieve the note. Tavares would try to take it from her and the last thing she wanted was for him to see it. Yet she couldn't resist a fishing expedition. "Tell me, senhor, do you have business dealings in the United States?"

"Of course."

"Then you can advise me. I would like to open an account with my newfound riches. I had asked Mr. Wharton to recommend a bank to me and he named the Manhattan Metropolitan Security Bank as a favorable choice." She slowly lifted her eyes to his, hoping that her expression was unreadable. "Do you know of it?"

Years of experience kept his expression from altering but inside Eduardo recoiled as if from a striking snake. What had Wharton to do with Manhattan Metropolitan Security Bank, and why was she asking him about it? "If memory serves, senhorita, that bank closed more than a year ago."

"Did it? Why?"

He shrugged. "Bad investments? Cash flow problems? Shortages? Embezzlement?"

"So many problems for one bank?"

"I only suggest possibilities, senhorita."

She looked away. "Don't you find it odd that so many banks fail? I'm reminded of my father's case. The circumstances were so unexpected and brutal in their consequences."

"Banking is a risky business," he said, his gaze never leaving her. "Why does the fate of this bank interest you?"

"Henry Wharton is a friend of the banker," she lied.

"Then why does he recommend to you a bank that he must know has been closed for more than a year?"

She could have bitten off her tongue. She wasn't any good at lying. Why did she try? She looked back at him, hoping a direct gaze would help her weak defense. "I meant to say they were acquainted. I suppose they lost touch through the years."

"The scandal was quite well known," he said carefully. "It made every major paper east of St. Louis. Strange nephew Henry missed reading about it when even I heard of it."

"Did you have business dealings with the bank?" She held her breath.

*Softly, kitten, you tread on a panther's tail,* Eduardo mused. "I am very particular in my choice of business associates, menina. I don't deal with thieves or imbeciles, or fools."

"I will accept that as a compliment," she replied in a curiously husky voice.

"It was meant to be. In future, I would prefer that you come directly to me with your questions. I will be as frank with you as reason allows."

"Your reason," she returned with particular emphasis.

"My reason, of course. Now look there, menina, and you'll see our new home."

Philadelphia followed the line of his pointing finger to the top of a hill overlooking the river where a many-gabled house stood on the crest of a wooded cliff. The sight gave her a chill. It might have come directly from the pages of one of Mr. Edgar Allan Poe's stories. Was Eduardo Tavares toying with her or had his words only provoked her because she knew something he did not?

She didn't know the answer to that question nor, at present, a way to find it.

She sat back, subdued and chastened. There were two other letters in her purse. In a private moment, she would look to them for direction.

The terrace of the house overlooked a sunken garden streaked with the vivid and abstract shades of a painter's palette. Nearby, the fragrant honeysuckle wreathed the balustrade and scattered its scent on the breeze. The last rays of the late-June sunset cast long purple shadows across the expansive green yard, which dipped brown fingers into the shallows of the Hudson.

Philadelphia stood with her back to the house, absorbing the joy of her first day at Belle Mont. How foolish she'd been in ascribing any hint of darkness and disaster to the house. It was large and airy with many windows facing the river and many more looking toward the distant mountains. There wasn't anything in the least foreboding about the tranquil scene stretching out before her. Even Eduardo Tavares had seemed subdued upon his entrance into the house. He had elected to remain inside for an afternoon nap while she walked as far as the river to clear her head of old worries and new fears.

The exercise had done wonders for her mood. At this very moment, she would have welcomed his companionship. The thought surprised her as much as the realization that it was true. She missed Akbar. Though she discounted Mrs. Ormstead's assertion that she had fallen a little in love with him, she had felt a genuine companionship in his presence. Perhaps she could make her peace with Tavares equally well. After all, Akbar and he were one and the same. At least she would try, beginning at dinner.

Eduardo watched her from a window in one curving wing of the house. He had deliberately chosen to place

her in the bedroom wing opposite his, for her peace o
mind and his. One thing had emerged very clearly an
sharply from his afternoon musings. Before they move
from here, he would plumb the depths of her feelings fo
him and see if they could withstand the shock of what sh
might learn about him at some future date.

He looked down at the note crumpled in his hand
He'd read it half a dozen times, marveling at how, ami
the clumsy sentiment, Henry Wharton had delivered a
innocent but deadly sword thrust to his peace of mind.

Miss de Ronsard, darling

I cannot account for the grief that your swift depar
ture leaves within me. It is my finest and fondest hop
that you will shortly return to the city and your friend
I, most of all, shall await that day.

As per your request, I made inquiries about th
banker, Lancaster. I regret to inform you of his death
last year, following business difficulties that ruined hin
and the Manhattan Metropolitan Securities Bank. If
can be of further service . . .

Ever faithfully yours,<br>Henry Wharton

Eduardo very carefully smoothed out the note an
placed it back in her purse. What was she up to? Ho
could she know of Lancaster? And, if she knew of him
what else did she know?

He turned back to the window. She had moved to si
on the edge of the balustrade, the curves of her slende
body gracefully outlined as she turned toward the river
Suffused in the rosy glow of sunset, she seemed a woo
nymph come lately to rest at the edge of her domain.

"You have secrets, menina, which I must and will learn
But, first, the game of love will be ours."

# 10

Philadelphia held a hand visorlike over her eyes as she peered anxiously up into the face of the man who stood over her in his shirtsleeves. "Are you certain this is necessary? It seems a drastic measure."

Eduardo gave her an interrogatory glance. "We went over this matter last evening at dinner. Saratoga will be filled with New Yorkers and though you met only a few, we can't afford for you to be recognized. Therefore you must have a new look, a new disguise. Now lie down and we will begin."

"I'm sure this isn't the least bit proper," she murmured as she knelt down on the blanket he had spread in a sunny area of grass beyond sight of the house.

After several companionable evenings and surprisingly good nights' sleep, she had thought to spend her days at Belle Mont walking by the river and planning her future. But she should have known that Eduardo Tavares would have his own plans. Mumbling invectives against tyrants, she lay back upon the quilt. "Now what?"

"Nothing more is required of you," He assured her,

and bent on one knee beside her. "Put yourself in my hands and let me do what has to be done."

He reached into the basket he had brought with him, retrieved a lady's hairbrush, and tentatively stroked it through the tumble of waist-length waves nearest his knee.

Thanks to several hard scrubbings with lye soap followed by applications of equal parts of olive oil and castor oil, her hair was once more its natural honey brown shade. The strands crackled with russet highlights while threads of sun-gold shimmered through the darker waves near her hairline. The lushness pleased him, and he ran his fingers through the length, luxuriating in the tactile pleasure. The waves corked and curled about his fingers, tangling in a playful tease of reluctance to escape. It was a shame to alter the color again. Yet at dinner the night before, she had begun talking about leaving him, saying that her share of the money from the diamonds was enough to repay her father's debts and therefore she wanted to return to Chicago. She had lied but he could not say so without betraying that he was aware of the true amount of those debts. That, he suspected, would frighten her more than she already was. He knew the real reason she wanted to get away from him. It was to escape her attraction to him that she could no longer successfully hide.

Poor frightened menina. How cautious she had grown in his company, afraid to look him in the eye when they spoke, shunning his offer of a hand in assistance as they walked the grounds. Yet he had mentioned none of this to her. Instead he had reminded her gently but firmly that she had agreed to help him sell three sets of jewelry and that she was honor-bound to see their contract through. Her reluctant agreement had satisfied him for the moment. What she did not yet know was that he had no intention of allowing her leave him for any reason.

Philadelphia had shut her eyes to keep the midmorning

sunlight from her eyes, but when his fingers delved into her hair, they flew wide in surprise. "What are you doing?"

"Testing for tangles, menina. What else?"

She didn't know what else he might be doing, but she was certain that whatever it was, there was some hidden reason behind it. "I'm perfectly capable of brushing my own hair. If you'd just give me—"

"And deprive myself of the pleasure?" he broke in softly. "What man doesn't dream of brushing a beautiful woman's hair?"

"Oh, and have you brushed many?"

"Thousands! I'm quite an accomplished ladies' maid."

Philadelphia stiffened. "That doesn't recommend you highly to me. It sounds quite ungentlemanly and, well, vulgar."

He paused in mid-stroke, and she looked up to find a slight frown furrowing his wide brow. "This fear you have of me, is there any reason for it? What have I done to deserve it? You didn't fear Akbar, not after the first day. Why then, senhorita, do you thrust double-edged words at me at every opportunity?"

Gazing up at him from a prone position was definitely a disadvantage she decided as new emotions squirmed inside her. She knew that if he bent over and kissed her now she wouldn't say another word against him. The very idea that his nearness evoked the yearning further disconcerted her. "I don't know what you mean. Just hurry and finish before I'm baked by the sun."

He reached behind himself and picked up a small Japanese parasol made of bamboo and oiled paper. "I try always to provide your comfort. Trust me."

As he returned to his brushing, she opened the parasol and slanted it at an angle that shaded her face. Only then did she peek at him again and the sight was less than reassuring. Trust him? She did not even trust herself when he was about. And with very good cause.

How could she say to him that her distrust was borne
of the way sunlight and shadow played shamelessly over
the surfaces of his gorgeous face? Just watching the light
lick to a copper sheen his broad cheekbones while shadows slid down into the hollows beneath made her feel as
giddy as did two glasses of champagne. Then there were
those great dark eyes which obliterated sunlight, making
midnight of noon. How could she explain the threat of
intimacy that darkness brought forth? And his hair, soft,
black, curtaining the temples of his face in waves as he
bent over her, how dare it make her fingers itch to stroke
it back behind his ears?

Oh, there were a thousand other little distractions.
Though he had recently shaved, the shadow of his beard
still darkened the plane of his upper lip and lightly sooted
his cheek and jaw. The natural tint of his lips seemed
stained by rich red wine. Fine black brows, heavily drawn,
were arched as gracefully as a woman's. The radiance of
his white shirt front made one draw favorable conclusions
from the contrast it made with his skin. Even before she
of thought it, the scent of his cologne had made her measure her breath in shallow intakes. The sun warmed his
face and neck and she knew that the scent rising off his
skin was what she breathed in. Even without touching
her, he shared himself with her. Everything about him
seemed a calculation in disturbance, disruption, and distraction. Had he planned this full-scale assault on her
senses? She shut her eyes in defense of the sensation that
she was saturated with the presence of Eduardo Tavares.

Not unaware of her observation, Eduardo continued
his administrations. This was only the first of several gentle assaults he planned to make upon her defenses. *Patience.* That was the key. Soon she would become as comfortable with him as she had the subservient character he
had played before. Then he would teach her about love
and she would offer her mouth for his kiss as she had
Henry—damn him!—Wharton. In the meantime, he

didn't dare register even in his thoughts his pleasure at the simple victory of being so close to her.

Having tamed her hair to his satisfaction, he carefully stretched it out to its full length on the quilt behind her head. Then, with a comb he pulled from the basket, he parted off another length of hair and applied the brush to it.

In the quiet peace of the summer morning, he repeated the action again and again until, finally, she lay with her waist-length hair spread out around her head like a sunburst halo. Though her face was hidden by the small parasol, the deep even breaths she drew told him that she was at ease, perhaps even dozing to the accompaniment of droning insects who inhabited the nearby shrubs.

He sat back on his heels and withdrew from the basket a jar, the contents of which were known only to an elite class of Rio de Janeiro prostitutes. He had once made a bet with Tyrone as to whether or not a certain new and extravagantly priced girl was, indeed, a natural blonde. When the usual means had been tried, and their purses both a good deal lighter, Tyrone proclaimed himself the winner, having bet in favor of her authenticity. Eduardo smiled, remembering one of the few times he'd bested Tyrone. It had taken him a week and cost him several times the amount of the bet involved to win the woman's confidence and learn her secret. In the end, he'd coaxed her into allowing him to help her apply the mixture to the more delicate places required. Later, he'd demonstrated the results of the mixture in Tyrone's presence using a cutting from a wig.

He opened the jar and gently stirred the mixture. The air filled with citron tangs, sharp hints of hydrogen peroxide, malty textures from the brewery, and faint eggy sulfur fumes. Had he not seen its results firsthand, he would never have dared apply the noisome concoction to her hair. Even so, he'd watered the portions down by fifty percent. He quickly dipped the bristles of the brush into it and began stroking it through her hair before he changed his mind.

The first inclination that something unexpected was taking place came as a rough pungent odor cut through Philadelphia's drowsing. She wrinkled her nose in defense and lowered the parasol. "What is that noxious smell?"

"Magic," he answered. "Be patient, and you'll be pleased with the results."

"It smells like boiled renderings after lye has been added to make soap."

"It's only 'Eye of newt and toe of frog, wool of bat and tongue of dog,'" he quoted with a laugh.

"Don't prose at me," she answered sharply, laying the parasol aside. "Your humor always precedes some mischief of which I am usually the victim."

"I swear to you, menina, that I mean you no harm."

"That isn't very reassuring." Then, "Must we have that odor about us? You're *not* putting it on my hair?"

Eduardo dropped the brush and caught her by the shoulders just as she started to get up from the quilt. "Don't move, menina, or you will spoil my work."

"You have put it in my hair!" she cried indignantly. "I want it out. Now!"

"Fifteen minutes, menina, that's all it takes." He came to his knees beside her, pressing her firmly back with a hand on each shoulder. He looked down at her, laughter shaping his long mouth into a wicked scythe. "Think of it this way, we won't be bothered by river flies while it works."

She stared back at him with murderous intent. "Release me this instant, senhor!"

His grin softened under the heat of her gaze. "When you look at me like that I can't imagine anything but holding you even more closely." He saw apprehension snap her eyes wide and released her slowly, his hands hovering in case she tried to rise again. He had applied

the mixture to only some sections of her hair but he suspected that a tactical retreat was in order. It would take
several applications to complete the process, in any case.
"I'll make a bargain with you. If you remain lying so, still
as a mouse for fifteen minutes, I'll leave you in peace."

She reached up to touch her damp hair. "You swear
you haven't ruined me?"

Eduardo looked up quickly. Please, please, he thought,
don't let me say it. Double entendres offered doubtful
results at the best of times. And this was definitely not
one of them.

He rose to his feet, careful to avoid her gaze. "Fifteen
minutes, menina, then you may go and wash your hair."

Philadelphia watched him collect his things and then
walk away without giving him her promise. When he was
out of sight, she adjusted her parasol to shade her eyes
from the advancing sun. Fifteen minutes didn't seem like
a very long time, and besides, she did feel a bit drowsy. If
she remained it was because she wanted to, not because
he commanded it.

She awakened to the whispery sensation of a char-
treuse butterfly climbing her nose. Wiggling her nose
didn't dislodge the creature, so she very gently flicked
him with a finger, and he took light as though caught on a
gust of wind.

She sat up to watch his progress toward the flowers of
the garden and then smiled at the beauty of the day. A
yawn reminded her that she had fallen asleep. She
reached back to catch her flowing tresses which the
breeze was teasing into somersaults about her shoulders
and realized that they were dry. Without thinking about
it, she twisted her hair into a knot and secured it at her
nape. The medicinal odor had abated somewhat but the
faint scent still offended her. She had no idea what he
had applied to her hair but she would have no more of it.
In fact, as soon as she washed the odor out of her hair,

she would tell him so. She rose for the quilt and gathered it into her arms, surprised to notice faded streaks on the cloth that she didn't remember being there before. Oh well, she supposed the sun had done it. She was vaguely aware that more than fifteen minutes had passed. Precisely how many more she wasn't certain of, but if the rumbling in her middle was any indication, it was nearly lunchtime. She would have to hurry and wash her hair if she didn't want to miss the meal altogether.

She crossed the lawn in quick lithe strides, thinking that the pleasure of summer in the country was that fresh sunshine and air made every sense sharper and more sensitive. For instance, her scalp tingled in response to the sun and her spirit was as light as the butterfly that swooped past. She was actually looking forward to sharing a lunch with Eduardo Tavares. She increased her pace in order not to be later than strictly necessary.

Eduardo waited patiently at the head of the table for his luncheon companion. She'd sent word that she would join him, if tardily. He hoped that she was pleased by the morning's work. A few more applications and he was certain she would look born to her blondness.

He had even settled on the roles they would play in Saratoga, but he wasn't ready to tell her just yet. While mothers and children streamed up to Saratoga from the first of June through the end of July, August was the month he had tapped for their visit. That was the month in which the resort city was vacated by thousands of wholesome families and reinvaded by the flashier set, racing and gambling people flush with money and excited by the idea of spending it.

He drummed his fingers impatiently on the white linen tablecloth, wondering if the trip to Saratoga would be necessary, after all. He hoped not. He was determined that Philadelphia would learn to love him during the days they would spend here in this idyll by the river. If she did, there would be no need for future masquerades between them. Honor had kept him from actively pursuing her before, but now that hesitation was gone. The inquiries she had made about Lancaster were proof enough that she wouldn't give up her false belief in her father's innocence unless forced to. He wanted her, must have her. He was aware of her tentative response to him. With every seductive charm at his disposal, he would turn that attraction into passion, before they both went mad—or the truth drove them apart.

The first pitiful cry from the hallway outside the dining room launched him to his feet. The next instant Philadelphia lurched into the room. She was staggering, her hair streaming wildly over her shoulders and down her back while she moaned as if in mortal pain. She held a brush in one hand, a mirror in the other. She flew at him, hands lifted in attack. "Look at me! Look at what you've done to me!"

Eduardo swallowed his astonishment. Sections of her waist-length hair were bleached nearly white while the rest remained a rich golden brown. He swallowed again, this time to curtail the amusement he knew was deplorably out of place. "You—you didn't heed my instructions, senhorita. I distinctly remember telling you to you wait only fifteen minutes before washing your hair. No more."

Philadelphia bared her teeth in a very unladylike grimace. "You didn't warn me that disaster would strike if I didn't! You have ruined me!"

"How so?" He looked away as the lashings on his amusement burst thread by thread. "I see a little damage, but it is temporary. I think you look—unusual. The effect is most—Ah yes! I'm reminded of—of—of . . ."

"Stripes!" she cried. "Stripes! I look like a jaundiced zebra!"

Eduardo lost the battle. His laughter burst free at an immodest volume that shook the china.

Philadelphia stared at him as though he were the embodiment of all the gates of Hell. He was laughing, laughing at her humiliation and shocked hurt.

Eduardo had turned away, as embarrassed as she by his schoolboy sense of humor. It was unforgivable. She must be furious. He was furious, too, with himself. When his mirth passed, he turned back to beg her pardon.

He didn't at first credit her trembling as the expression of tears hidden behind the latticework curtain of her hair. But then she was sobbing as loudly and freely as a child. She'd shed exactly two tears over the loss of Henry Wharton and none the day she helped auction off her home and its contents. *Mãe de Deus!* Women took this business of their hair much more seriously than he'd ever realized.

He moved toward her slowly, half-expecting her to lash out with her mirror when he got within range. But she didn't and when he slid one arm tentatively about her waist, she sagged against him as though his embrace had come at the last moment of her strength.

He curled one arm tightly about her, gathering as much of her weight onto himself as he could, and reached for a dining chair with his free hand. When he had brought it within range, he sat down and pulled her onto his lap. All the while she sobbed like her heart was in too many pieces even to count.

He caught the soft shape of her cheek with his hand and bent to lean his chin against her forehead. "Menina, don't cry. You break my heart with your tears. My sad little one. Please." English failing, he resorted to more virtuoso endearments in Portuguese, feeling free to say any number of intimate things to her as he pressed consoling kisses into her afflicted hair.

Once begun, Philadelphia realized she didn't know how to stop her tears. She'd been so angry when she realized what had happened. Now she felt deflated by the tempest of her tears. Helplessly, she moved her head back and forth as hiccuping sounds replaced the sobs.

When a hand wedged her chin and lifted it, she was grateful for the interruption.

Eduardo brushed his lips across her brow, savoring the pleasure of touching. "Hush, menina. It is only a temporary problem. I can solve it. Tomorrow." He lifted her chin higher until he was staring into her fretful gaze. "Another application or two and no one will ever know of this present misfortune."

Philadelphia bit her lip several times before she could capture it and bring the trembling under control. "I—I look like an alley cat!"

Eduardo bit his own lip. She reminded him more of a stoat at its mid-seasonal change but he didn't think she'd appreciate that comparison either. "I like cats," he said, gently stroking the striped tresses trailing over his arm.

"I—wish—you—would—" She didn't finish what she was about to say and Eduardo thought it was just as well. Ladies of her ilk never expressed themselves in that manner, and he had the distinct impression that whatever she had been about to say would have been a first for her—coined in the mint of extremity.

"It is a small thing, really," he murmured, fascinated by the deliciously warm soft woman in his arms. "Now, won't you have your lunch?"

She shook her head. She was discovering that while losing one's self-possession is a terrible thing, regaining it can be an even more humbling experience. "I think I should go and lie down for a while."

"But not in the sun, I trust." It was a calculated risk and, when her head snapped up, he wondered at the thinking that had made him believe it would work.

She rose from his lap with as much dignity as she could and sent her hair flying back behind her with a toss of her head. "I suppose I am to be fair-haired for our next adventure?"

He nodded, not trusting his voice.

"And I suppose you had some method in mind when you began this experiment."

Again a safe nod.

"Then I suggest that you give more specific instructions next time, though I'm at a loss to imagine—no, that's not true. I could be bald." She turned and marched from the room.

Eduardo studied his lap for a long moment. She'd sat there, a full and very real womanly weight pressed against him. Sad to say, he wished now that she'd cried longer. Then he might have moved his kisses from her forehead and hair to her lips, and tasted a measure of that tempestuous spirit he longed to stir to passionate response.

*Mãe de Deus!* Women!

Already dressed for bed, Philadelphia stared beyond the remains on her dinner tray to where the sun had set, its fiery splendor still bleeding into the blue-gray clouds at twilight. After the scene she'd made at luncheon, she didn't have the nerve to face Eduardo Tavares again. By morning she would feel differently. At least she hoped she would. Besides, she didn't want anyone else to see her hair as it was, not even the three servants he had hired to look after them. If he succeeded in turning disaster into victory, then she would eat in the dining hall. Until then, she preferred twilight and shadow.

The hours alone in her room had also given her time to think and make plans of her own. Though she had not again broached the subject with Eduardo Tavares, she had decided not to go to Saratoga with him. One adventure with him was enough to convince her that she didn't have the disposition for fakery. Now that she had money of her own, she was free to set about tracing the authors of the two other letters in her possession. Of course, half of the four thousand dollars she had received from Senhor Tavares was already earmarked. She intended to wire it to her lawyer in Chicago to go against her father's outstanding debts. Then, too, she would pay Senhor Tavares for her wardrobe. It was the least she could do, since she was leaving him so abruptly. Whatever remained would keep her for a good while if she managed it carefully.

Yet she had waited until now to act on the most important matter on her mind. She had told herself that she needed the privacy that only the night could provide, but in reality, she dreaded the ordeal before her.

Before she lost her nerve again, she rose and went to turn the key in her door and then retrieved her portmanteau from the corner. After opening it, she removed the letters from the hole she'd snipped in the lining and then went to turn up the light on the desk.

Opening each one, she lay the letters out side by side on the desk. She knew the contents of the first by heart but she felt somehow that the three together might turn out to be more than their separate parts.

She scanned Lancaster's letter quickly and set it aside. More cautiously she opened the second letter and inspected the contents. It had a bullying tone, ordering the reader to remember an oath of silence. It spoke of "damned Brazilians" and "nervous Nellies." It closed with the suggestion that the reader ride out the present misfortune without "spading over old graves." Scrawled in a bold hand was the signature: MacCloud.

Philadelphia put it down in distaste. The name MacCloud was slightly familiar. She frowned. Why was it familiar? Had MacCloud been one of her father's business associates? From the tone of his letter, MacCloud didn't seem the kind of man her father would have done business with. Yet, she thought the same about Lancaster. What was the connection between these letters?

She looked at the letter's date, June 7, 1874. It was written more than a year ago. She looked again at the Lancaster letter. It was dated April 14, 1874. Lancaster was alive in April of the previous year. MacCloud's letter

was dated in June of the same year. Henry Wharton said
Lancaster died a year ago. That would place his death
between mid-April and June of last year. Was Lancaster's
death the "present misfortune" to which MacCloud re-
ferred? A chill brushed lightly against her spine.

If only she had spoken to Henry Wharton before leaving New York she might have learned when and how Lancaster had died. Men died every day of natural causes,
disease, accident, fire—a dozen different but ordinary
ways. There was no reason to assume that Lancaster had
been murdered. Eduardo Tavares had said that he had
read of the scandal that surrounded Lancaster's death.
Did she dare ask him about it when MacCloud's letter
mentioned "damned Brazilians"? Was there a connection
between MacCloud and Tavares?

She shook her head to dispel the notion. No, of course
not. Fancy was taking over. If she were not careful, she
would soon be starting at shadows and dodging phan-
toms. She mustn't begin to suspect conspiracy in every
person she met. And yet, why the mention of Brazil? She
didn't recall her father ever mentioning the country. In
fact, he had once refused a piece of stone that had come
to him from Rio de Janeiro.

Her heart lurched into a quick, painful rhythm that
sent blood surging through her veins. That was it! She
had been a little girl, no more than five, the one and only
time she had ever seen MacCloud. He had come to see
her father at Christmas. She remembered his boisterous
laughter in a quiet dignified house that had never before
heard such raucous tones. She remembered that he had
brought her hard candies and peppermint, and a doll
dressed in tartan. And, most of all, she suddenly remembered how her father had reacted to the gift MacCloud
had brought him. She had scarcely caught sight of it, a
deep sky-blue stone large enough to fill a man's palm.
Her father had started away from it as though it were
about to explode, and then cursing, which she had never

before heard on his lips, he sent her from the room. The next morning, MacCloud was gone, as were his gifts to her. How could she have forgotten that? She had cried for days over the loss of the doll in tartan.

She looked down again and gingerly picked up the third letter. It had no postmark but it was dated the day of her father's death. The most cryptic of all, it was little more than an unfamiliar quote.

*"This is the first of punishments, that no guilty man is acquitted if judged by himself."* The rain forest shelters two graves and a desecrated altar. The Judgment is rendered. You will find no rest until you are but ashes and dust.

Philadelphia crumbled the letter in her fist, stunned and cold as ice. She had forgotten this letter, blocked it from her mind, but now the pain and shock of it were as fresh and bitter as before. Her father had taken his own life, clutching these letters in his hand. Was this unsigned challenge what drove him to suicide? He had meant for the letters to be found, she was certain of it. But who did he expect to find them? Were they for her? Was it his way of offering her clues to the men who had ruined him, or of some great transgression that he could not face? It had been the latter fear that lay behind her decision to take and hide the letter before the police arrived.

"No!" She rose. To think that way meant considering the possibility that her father had done something wrong, something so terrible that he had taken his own life rather than continue to face it. She couldn't believe that. There was another explanation. There had to be.

Perhaps if she went to New Orleans and found Mac-Cloud she would learn the answers. Yet, what could she say to a man who had warned her father not to "turn over old graves"?

If only she felt she could trust Eduardo Tavares with

the truth. But how could she when the word Brazil also appeared in the third letter? Was it a coincidence? It was possible. Nothing he'd done or said indicated anything else. And yet.

The strains of a guitar came slowly into her consciousness. The notes wafted sweetly through her open window from the terrace below. She moved toward the window as sounds strung themselves together into a melody. Who was playing? Was it one of the servants hired to keep house for them?

As she reached the window the player launched into full song. The music was quick and lively with sharp rises and falls. The melody swung wide and loud only to fall soft again. It was a song of joy unfettered, an expression of defiance against all that was staid and grim and proper.

As she leaned out to look down, a voice was added to the melody. The language was foreign but the baritone was full and strong and slightly colored by a vibrato on the sustained notes. Even at dusk there was no mistaking him.

Eduardo Tavares sat below her window on the balustrade of the terrace, one foot braced against the ground while his guitar rested on his other drawn-up leg. As she watched, his fingers touched the strings with a careless ease that spoke of long-practiced skill.

Fascinated, Philadelphia crossed her arms and braced them on the window sill to remain and watch. When the song was done she heard him catch his breath in sharply and then expel it in laughter that moved her as much as a caress upon her skin.

The music began again. This time it was a slow piece with lingering notes that reached out through the half-dark evening to snare her with the most beautiful sound she had ever heard.

The melody drew the night into itself and she felt drawn toward the source, as if he knew she stood in her window listening and directed his energies at flushing her out. The vibrations of the strings reached inside her, replacing the shock and sorrow of the last moments with their own compelling emotion until she forgot everything else but their sound. The music altered her breathing to make it ebb and flow in time to the melody filling the night with sweet song. The pleading notes were sustained until they seemed to embody all the yearning of his soul. Her body swayed forward on her elbows but her toes curled inside her shoes in resistance until she stood transfixed and taut while his music strummed this new inexplicable tension within her.

When the piece ended, she held her breath, afraid that she might not be able to breathe again without the direction of his music. For an instant longer she remained immobile, waiting for him to begin another tune while the strange wild aching inside her grew unbearable. Afraid that he had stopped for good, she turned and hurried across her room, headed for her door and the terrace below.

# 11

As Philadelphia reached the first floor, she realized that the strummed chords of the guitar could only be faintly heard in the dark interior of the house, but it was enough. Like a treasure hunter following clues, she followed the drifting music into the lighted library. Beyond the library, she saw the French doors standing open. On river-freshened air came such beautiful sounds that she felt a strange burning in the back of her throat. She didn't want to disturb him, but she couldn't keep herself from moving quietly forward until she stood within a foot of the doorway.

He sat on the balustrade, just beyond the reach of the light, a sharp silhouette in a white shirt that glowed faintly as if it had absorbed the last of the sunset. The shirt was open at the collar revealing the strong dark column of his throat. She remembered how, the first time she saw him, she had thought he possessed an unusual, exotic, and strongly compelling masculine beauty that would have left its impression on her had she never seen him again.

From the moment he had entered her life, she had cast aside reason and propriety and common sense, yet she hadn't allowed herself to wonder why. It had nothing to do with jewels or her father's debts, or the masquerade that allowed her to forget for a little while that she was all alone in the world. She'd not come with him out of idle curiosity or because she had nothing better to do. She knew that she had come for the same reason she was here now. She'd come in answer to his serenade, because she wanted to be with him.

"Is that you, menina? Come out and join me."

The sound of his voice surprised her, and then she realized that while she'd not been bold enough to cross the threshold her shadow had. Her silhouette was smudged inside the sharp-angled wedge of candlelight slanted across the terrace bricks. Gathering her courage, she stepped out into the night.

Without interrupting his playing he said, "I thought you abed, menina. Did I awaken you with my clumsy attempts to make music, and have you come to throw old shoes at me?"

She smiled in spite of herself. He knew he played wonderfully, but like a small boy he wanted her to say so. "You play remarkably well, senhor."

"Do you really think so?" His smile was a brilliant flash in his dark face. "I studied in Lisbon."

"Lisbon? You studied music?"

His fingers paused over the strings. "Why are you so shocked?"

"I'm not shocked," she hedged, though in truth she was amazed. "Musical study is usually the prerogative of ladies, that is all."

"Ah yes. In America women learn to play the harp or the violin or the piano while men learn to shoot and ride and gamble. In my country a man is expected to learn both things. But then, we are a backward people, yes?"

"I meant no disrespect."

"I accept your comment as ignorance, senhorita."

The rebuff hurt but she held her tongue. She had obviously insulted him. Reluctantly, she turned to leave.

"But where are you going? The night is sweet and your company would be also."

She looked back at him. "I didn't mean to disturb you. I only wanted to say that I enjoyed your music."

"Then stay with me and I will play for you. Would you like that?"

Like a child offered a sweet after a scolding, she smiled with joy. "I would, very much."

He indicated that she sit beside him on the balustrade. She found a place several feet away from him and lifted herself up onto the painted wood.

The first tune he played he said was a Brazilian folk tune. She enjoyed its toe-tapping rhythm behind the simple line of the melody. After he played through she asked, "Are there words?"

He nodded and began to sing.

He was not ashamed of his voice, that much she realized from the moment he began. He sang full and strong. Not one note was chastened or softened because she sat beside him. In fact, as he stared at her with those intense dark eyes which gleamed in the semidarkness, she had the distinct impression that the words he sang in Portuguese would have made her blush had she understood them.

When the song ended, he slipped down from the balustrade and turned to her. "Come and dance for me, senhorita."

Embarrassed, Philadelphia shook her head. "I don't know how."

"But of course you do. Every woman knows how. When I was a child, the women of my village loved to dance. Never were they too young or too old, or too fat or too ugly to dance. Each and everyone of them was beautiful when she danced, and she knew it. Come, I will show you."

He began another tune, moving his feet in time to the rhythm. "It is easy. Just do as I do."

She watched him, shyness holding her back long after the rhythm had caught her. Suddenly the guitar fell silent as he flattened the strings with his palm.

"Oh no, don't stop!"

"If there is music there must be dancing!" he answered, stern as any schoolmaster.

"Oh, very well," she said without heat, and slipped down from her perch. "But I warn you, I'm not very clever at this sort of thing. I think one thing while my feet do another."

"Then don't think, senhorita, only feel." He began a ballad, its slow tempo seductively sweet. "Feel the music in your feet and in your heart and in your soul."

He moved closer and Philadelphia knew he would not allow her to escape the challenge in his eyes nor the laughter in his smile, nor did she want to. There was something irresistible about the thought of dancing with this man to the music he made.

Yet, shyness kept her from moving as he showed her. It was his eyes watching her, those enormous eyes that saw everything and more. How could she move gracefully when he looked at her with such expectancy?

Eduardo guessed the source of her hesitation and turned to stride slowly away from her into the darkest corner of the terrace. "Close your eyes, menina. Close them and listen. Listen until your feet begin to feel the need to move."

Philadelphia obediently closed her eyes, embarrassed yet excited by the idea of only feeling the music.

As he continued to play, she listened acutely for the feeling he described but it didn't come. Instead, thoughts continued to rule her. She thought of the fact that she was standing in her nightclothes on a dark terrace with a man. She thought that she should be in bed, safely tucked beneath the covers. She thought, if only his playing had not been so persuasive she wouldn't be standing here feeling foolish and awkward. Yet, it compelled her even now when she felt shackled by embarrassment and hesitation.

As his fingers lightly teased the strings they seemed, also, to tug at her skirts like the breeze lifting off the lake. The eddying currents on which the music drifted made her long to move, to sway before it like a delicate flower on a slender stem. Suddenly in the darkness behind her lids she felt safe, and with that safety came confidence. Shyly, she made a few tentative steps in time to the rhythm of the piece he strummed.

Eduardo watched her first steps with the sweet sense of victory. *Yes!* he thought. *That's right. Move as you will, menina. Your feet understand the music. You need not watch them to know that they are right.* "Now feel the music in your in arms," he said softly from the darkness as the pace of the tune picked up. "Don't be afraid to lift them. Feel the music with your body, menina."

Philadelphia smiled, her eyes sealed with the pleasure of this new experience. She began to sway in time, her arms and legs flowing independently of one another yet joined by the tempo of the music, his music, filling the air about her. It swept her up, lifted her beyond herself into the realm where there was only feeling and freedom. Yet she was not free. She followed the beckoning, alluring notes of his guitar.

Eduardo moved toward her as he strummed the final chords of the song, hoping that he wouldn't frighten her but compelled to do this one thing. She spun to a halt before him as the music died, eyes still closed but with a soft secret smile on her face. Quickly and deftly he reached out and pulled the tortoise shell pins from her hair and shook loose the ugly knot.

Startled, Philadelphia opened her eyes and met yet again his soft and brilliant black-licorice gaze. For a moment she thought he would kiss her, hoped that he would, but his lips offered merely a devastating smile that brought his dimple to prominence. Then he said in Portuguese, "You are woman. You do know how to dance."

Though she didn't understand his words, she heard in them his pleasure at her dancing and the quiet praise emboldened her.

Determined not to force the pace with her, Eduardo backed away and casually plucked a new melody. "Shall we dance, senhorita?" he asked with a slight bow.

He stepped out a simple pattern and nodded for her to repeat them, which she did, faltering only once. When he smiled his approval she felt as though he'd given her a gift more precious than pearls. As he continued to dance, she matched her moves to his, turning as he turned, swirling and dipping when he did, marking the cadence with her silent slippers as the heels of his boots tapped loudly.

When he turned away from her she slanted a curious glance at his body. She'd never seen a man move as he did, with such supple grace. From hip to shoulder with seamless ease, every sensual line of his lower body flexed repeatedly in taut display. Tailored trousers rode the tightly drawn curve of his buttocks as the firm supple muscles of his thighs shifted sinuously.

Unable to shift her gaze a single degree, she watched, fascinated, as he rocked his pelvis lightly against the guitar which he held like a woman in his arms. As he brushed it again and again, riding his rhythm into the wood, an incandescent spark burst to life deep in her loins, seared her in a heat as fierce as it was unexpected. Unconsciously, she began to move her own hips in time to his, as if her body understood that his intimate rhythm was not merely part of the dance but meant explicitly for her and demanded her response.

He turned then, catching her look of astonished admiration, and it dissolved instantly into embarrassment. Her face flushed with the heat of it, making her suddenly too warm and dry-mouthed.

But he laughed the moment aside saying, "How quickly you grow accustomed to the rhythms of my homeland, menina. Perhaps I'll take you there one day. But, for now, we will content ourselves with the music and the dance. Do not falter now, menina. Regret is a bitter potion."

As he played on, Philadelphia again shut her eyes, allowing herself to feel in the rhythm what she did not now dare witness. Behind her closed lids she felt the brush of his pelvis, not upon wood but upon the sensitive skin of her hips, and the accompanying diffusion of warmth through the nerve endings of her body was a revelation.

Shocked with this new knowledge of herself, she opened her eyes. He was smiling at her, the sensual line of his lips more potent than any words he might have uttered. At any other time, in any other place, she would have been ashamed of this feeling of wild abandon he evoked. But it was nighttime and they were alone and the purple ether held them in its protective embrace with none to see or blame or even envy. Once more she began to dance to his tune.

On and on he played, one melody flowed into the next and then yet another, and with each he offered her an enticement not to be denied. Swaying and dipping and swirling, she danced until perspiration gathered on her brow, in the valley between her breasts, and flowed along the cleft between her thighs, and still he would not release her. Increasing the tempo to the fast-paced *sapateado,* he tapped out the rhythm with his fingers against the wood of the guitar. The heels of his boots answered in staccato fashion as they rang against the bricks.

Without thinking she shrugged out of her dressing gown and let it trail onto the bricks. She sighed with pleasure as the night breeze rushed forth to soothe the feverish skin of her arms and shoulders and bosom exposed by the scoop neck of her nightgown. Then she caught handfuls of her nightgown and held the skirts high so that they wouldn't be trampled or bind about her ankles as she spun around and around.

*"Muito bonito,"* he murmured in approval of the flashes of trim ankle and curvaceous calf.

When he slowed the tempo to a tango, she no longer watched his fingers play over the strings. Instead, she seemed to feel them on her body. They strummed lightly over her breasts and stomach and hips, and where they touched her skin grew taut and vibrant. She moved as he willed, his tempo dangerous and seductive and impelling her onward. When he sang she felt possessed of a high fever that fed on its own heat, offering no relief except in the desire to become one with him and the sensual power he wielded with such devastating ease.

Eduardo watched, the fever of desire riding him as he saw that she was lost in the music of his making. Her eyes were overbright, her lips parted by quickened breath. Her skin was flushed beneath its sheen of moisture. Hair trailed over her back and shoulders in wild tangled slats of moonlight and midnight shadow. She was no longer Miss Philadelphia Hunt, the young socialite who wore lovely gowns and garlands of violets in her hair. She was only a young woman dancing beneath the stars in her slippers and nightgown, and she had never been more beautiful in his eyes.

He knew then that he loved her, had loved her from the very instant of first seeing her, and that he could no longer deny it. The knowledge frightened him. For, he thought, what man ever looks at one he loves desperately and does not feel the frail breath of mortality whisper past his ear? In admitting his need he admitted the possibility of never having that need met.

*Seize the moment,* every instinct told him. Tomorrow was not promised.

The final vibrations of the strings faded and he lay the guitar aside. As she swirled to a stop, he caught her against him. "You are beautiful and your man knows it," he whispered huskily in his native tongue. "He loves to watch you dance."

"What are you saying?" she asked breathlessly, her heart still throbbing in time to the music's last chords.

He laughed softly, a little embarrassed to have retreated to Portuguese when he might have told her straight away his feelings. "That I love to watch you dance. Does it please you to know this?"

She saw the truth of what he said in his eyes and the recklessness of it, and she could be no less brave. "Yes."

"Then dance with me, menina, and we will make our own music."

In a sinuous motion, his hip caught lightly against hers as it had his guitar. But now it was she who was in his arms. Those clever hands that had strummed the taut strings and brought forth achingly beautiful music were now curved over the indentations of her waist, her skin separated from his fingers only by the thin damp weave of her nightgown. She tried to follow his steps but he held her so close that every movement brought her legs against his, the hard jut of his hip impressed upon the slim curve of her stomach. She hesitated once too often and stepped on his toe.

He paused, his gaze resting on hers like a caress. "Are you still afraid of me, menina?"

There was a rapt moment of silence as they stood staring at one another and she knew what question he really asked. "Yes. No. A little."

"It is good for innocence to be cautious. But you know that I will not hurt you?"

Even though he held her in his arms, the strength and power of his body commanding the compliance of her softer self, she knew he would not hurt her. She thought of Mrs. Ormstead's judgment that she was in love with him. Was it possible? Was it possible to love a stranger, to feel impelled by forces greater than herself, and be joyous in that surrender?

"Yes."

He began again, reaching up briefly to pull her head into the cradle formed by the juncture of his neck and shoulder and then his hands were on her waist again, holding her close and moving her to his own slow rhythm of desire.

She closed her eyes once more, not to block, but to better capture the dozen different sensations pressing in on her. His skin was warm and damp beneath her cheek, his scent a combination of fine exotic oils and his own essence. She heard the hard rhythm of his heart under her ear and it frightened her a little. She'd never since childhood been this close to anyone and heard the mortal drum of another's existence. His breath came clean and light upon her face. Wherever they touched she felt the tightening of her body, in her breasts, her stomach, her hips, her thighs. His body became the center of her world.

She reached to embrace his shoulders, feeling a drifting away of everything else finite. *Let it go,* she thought, *if only he remains with me.*

He moved backward suddenly, pulling her close, and pressed his knee strongly between hers. She caught her breath as her legs were parted and then the surge of his hip pressed close to the center of her own desire. He turned her quickly and efficiently, bringing her back up against the balustrade and then he lifted her face and brought his mouth down on hers.

She tasted the music on his lips, embraced the whole of the rhythm in her arms about him. The sultry dance he'd taught her was there, too, along with fleeting images of a place there the jungle grows so thickly a man cannot pass and rivers wash in floods as strong as his passion. He fed her old Brazilian legends, let her taste of trade winds and spice, dazzled her with jeweled kisses more brilliant than diamonds.

Beneath her hands his neck muscles became rigid. This time when his knee parted hers, his hands ran in a heavy molding caress down her back over the flare of her hips to gather her buttocks in his hands so as to lift her onto his thigh. He held her there while she rode the long slow strokes that surged into her, teasing, demanding, begging a response. And, in the secret darkness, she yielded to his rhythm and it sent sweet waves of sensation, urgently flowing, thick as honey, through her body.

She didn't realize that he had lifted her gown until she felt the hot strength of his hands settle on her naked waist. She shivered, knowing and yet not knowing what he intended to do. The fall from grace. She was catapulting headfirst. And yet, the tiniest hesitation whispered over her passion-warmed skin like a chill breeze.

Aware of her every shuddered breath, Eduardo knew the instant she reached that invisible but very real barrier that every woman raises before the moment of her first surrender.

He lifted his mouth from hers. It was her right to accept or refuse, and he would respect that right. But he ached with a need of her so strong that his hands flexed on her waist to hold her high on his thigh where her slightest move eased and teased his arousal.

When he broke their kiss, Philadelphia used her hands against his cheeks to steady her enraptured world as she looked up at him. His hair was in wild disarray, falling across his brow and over his ears. She saw in wonder that his handsome mouth, usually firm and shapely defined, was blurred and moist from her kisses. But it was his expression that made her suddenly cold. "What's wrong?"

He stared at her without humor or joy or pleasure. "Do you trust me?"

Instinct warned her against the eager reply that came to her lips, for he asked so much more. "Should I?"

He smiled, feeling old as sin and twice as randy. If she but knew it, she had more reason than most to distrust him. It was a cowardly thing to ask her to betray herself.

"What woman trusts a man at a moment like this, menina? You must ask if you trust yourself."

She understood but she didn't want to. He wanted her to take responsibility for what would happen between them. Yet, how could she? Confusion eddied into the whirlpool of her desire, the cooling currents steering it off course. Why didn't he, the stronger of the two, either pull her back to safety or lure her to disaster? The power to beguile was his. She had no words courageous enough to ask him to make love to her.

He saw her struggle, longed to lead her across the barrier of uncertainty but he did nothing, only looked at her with the gentlest of expressions. He'd felt her urgent need of his lovemaking in her deep shudders. He'd caught in his mouth the soft explosions of breath that he had forced from her as he'd made love to her through the barrier of their clothing. Yet, he'd not deliberately set out to seduce her. It was the music and the night and the ready passion lying in wait between them that had nearly seduced them both.

A breeze whispered past her ear and she stiffened, hearing in it the ghostly echo of his guitar. Then she realized that the wind had risen, and it stroked the strings of the guitar that lay a little distance away. She looked back at him, saw the passion so strongly etched there, and the coward in her recoiled.

Eduardo released her slowly. The power to free her seemed to take a force of will never before exerted.

She slipped off his thigh, defeated desire whipping the blood through her most tender parts. With stiff fingers she tugged her gown down, too shamed by his desertion to even look at him. Confused and stunned by the sudden backlash of unfulfilled yearnings overwhelming her, she turned away and weakly hid her face in her hands.

When she felt his hand lightly touch her shoulder, she whimpered, wanting more than anything to turn and hide herself in his arms. To prevent the shameful gesture, she snatched up her dressing gown and ran into the house.

Eduardo cursed himself thoroughly when she was gone. He was caught neatly in a trap of his own devising. He knew what she needed to hear from him, but how could he speak when he had ruined her father and felt justified in doing so? He knew things about the man that she might be better off never learning. Yet, if he did not tell her the truth, was there any hope of a future for them?

Oh, but she'd felt perfect in his arms, all warmth and soft yielding and filled with sweet womanly desire. She would not come regretfully to lovemaking. She burned for it, as he did. She burned for him, and he wanted it to always be so. He had nearly won her with his music, then lost her in a moment of doubtful honor.

He swore and picked up his guitar. Swiftly, he swung it up and then brought it smashing down upon the top of the balustrade where it splintered into dozens of irreparable pieces. It would be a long time before he played again, a very long time.

Eduardo turned onto his back in his bed, an arm flung above his head. Perhaps it was better that he remained awake, for he knew what waited in his sleep. Some nights, like this one, he couldn't deter the dream. He knew why it crowded in on him this particular night. He had wanted Philadelphia and yet allowed her to escape, and he knew that he might regret it the rest of his life. Yet, gradually, the weariness of his body won out over the regrets and he drifted out and away and back of present cares.

"Not my child!" his father cried. "You mustn't harm my son!"

Pain radiated down his arms to his shoulders as Eduardo hung suspended by his wrists from the stout limb of a tree. The rope had bitten into the skin of his wrists until his forearms were damp with his own blood. But worse, much worse, was the hard merciless crack of the *bandeirante's* whip that tore the flesh of his back. In shame he heard his cries keening out under the canopy of the dense jungle foliage as he failed to find the courage to be silent.

His father had said he must be brave, must die if necessary to prevent the desecration of the Blue Madonna's shrine. At twelve years of age he had thought that he was brave enough to withstand any torture, but no imagining had prepared him for this searing, blackening pain that made all resistance, all bravery impossible. Through it all he heard his father's pleading voice followed by the bite of the lash and the bandit's demand.

"Tell us, *caboclo*!" came the gruff command. "Where have you hidden the Blue Madonna's treasure?"

"I cannot! I've sworn an oath!"

"Then watch your son die."

Eduardo choked on his tears. His mother was dead! These men, these *bandeirantes* with their fancy silver buckles and spurs, they had killed her!

"Please! Torture me! The child is innocent!"

"Then save him! Tell us where to find the jewels! It is said that the Madonna's rubies are the color of your son's blood. That her emeralds are as big as hens' eggs. And the blue topaz, the one said to be formed in her image, it is as large as a melon. Show it to us!"

"I can't. I've sworn to the Blessed Mother to protect her shrine."

"Then watch, believer, as your son dies and know that you could have bought his life for a handful of the jewels which your Blessed Mother is too selfish to spare!"

Eduardo awoke with a start, automatically rubbing the aching in his wrists. When the phantom pain subsided, he lay with his arms by his sides and very deliberately sought out the remainder of the dream. Yet, he didn't dream it this time. He stared at the dark ceiling until the memory

came stealing back, knowing that only when all was recalled would he be able to sleep untroubled.

Amid the ashes of his family's burned-out home, he lay
on his stomach on a straw mat beneath the stars. His
head was cradled in the lap of his aunt Mehia. His
breaths came fast and shallow because it hurt too much
to breathe deeply. His aunt said he would live but he had
seen the dark fright behind her kind eyes. The *curandeira*
had come and smeared his back and wrists with noxious
herbs but then gone away quickly, less she, too, suc-
cumbed to the devils who infested the Tavares's home.

The whole village was whispering about it. They knew
what his father had done. The *bandeirantes* had gone,
taking the sacred jewel of the Blue Madonna, which his
father had given them. In return they'd spared Eduardo's
life—but taken his father's.

Some said his family's downfall was the work of a
*quebranto,* that someone jealous of the Tavares's wealth
and position in the village had cursed them. Others said it
was pride that brought about Joao Tavares's downfall,
that he whom the villagers had entrusted with the care of
the wealth of the sacred Blue Madonna was, after all,
only a selfish old man who could not bear to part with his
only son.

But Eduardo knew they were wrong. The blame was
not his father's. If he'd been braver, his father's courage
would not have faltered. And so he wept, ashamed to be
alive when his parents were dead.

Through the next few weeks of fever and pain, when all
despaired of his life, Eduardo knew he would not die. He
knew that the reason he had been left alive was to be the
instrument of retribution upon those who had stolen the
Blue Madonna and her treasure, and murdered his parents. He would live to see the act of vengeance done. This
time he would not fail, no matter how awful the torture
he must endure, no matter how painful the price. He

would not turn back or look back until he had avenged them all.

Eduardo sighed in resignation as the memory receded. He had kept the pledge made fourteen years ago. He had hunted down the *bandeirantes,* though it had taken more than three years, and killed each of them. Before the last man died, he had learned from him that the theft of the Blue Madonna was no random act. Adventurers, American men of some wealth and influence, had paid handsomely for anyone willing to bring them the sacred treasure. It was they who had been to blame for the desecration and the deaths. From that moment on, he had amended his oath to include their destruction. Rage drove him another eleven years, crowding out every other consideration and human emotion.

But now the rage was gone. He was empty, and weary, and sick to death of loneliness. His wealth, accumulated through the years by luck and shrewd calculation to usurp the gains of his enemies, meant little to him. Wealth had been a means to an end, a means to gain power, nothing more. What had been missing from his life all these years was what he ached for now. Love.

He sat up, his face tight with the agony of his physical need. The comfort he so desperately needed waited for him in the far wing of the house; comfort, and love, and an end to his loneliness. He had lied to her earlier and to himself. He could no more keep away from her than he could stop his beating heart. Only she could end this deep abiding ache. The pain would give him no peace until he saw her again, touched her again.

Philadelphia awakened to the sensation of uneasiness. It wasn't a totally new experience. Sleeping in strange beds in unfamiliar surroundings, she had awakened often in the weeks since she had left her home in Chicago, not knowing precisely where she was or why. Then gradually, memory would assert itself and she would remember with a pang of regret. Yet this time, the feeling of unease didn't recede. It sharpened into the pricking sensation of not being alone.

She sat up, a spurt of panic injecting its toxin into her veins. "Who is there?"

She didn't know if he moved or if her eyes only adjusted in that moment but suddenly she was aware of a man's silhouette in her room, standing by the open window. He was braced by a hand along either side of the window frame. His shirt had been pulled out of his trousers and hung open. The moon had risen during the night and she saw clearly the sensually modeled profile of Eduardo Tavares.

The passion that she thought had been drowned in the watershed of tears she had spilled before falling asleep sprung instantly back to life. But she was wary now of the pain that lurked in that wanting.

He turned from the window, as though he had known she would awaken sooner or later. "I couldn't stay away."

She clutched at the muslin sheet fallen to her waist but she didn't lift it to shield herself. "You should be in bed."

"I should be in *your* bed."

Too raw and achy with need, she didn't answer that.

He turned fully toward her and came slowly forward. There was nothing predatory in his stride, nothing urgent or eager. He came gently to the edge of her bed and stood a moment staring down at her. In the moonlight her face was like a porcelain mask, the only color in her bluish-red lips and the delicate purplish sockets about her eyes. He reached out to stroke her cheek with the back of his hand and felt the stiffness of dried tears. He had wanted to make her happy. He had made her cry.

"Let me sit here beside you, just a little while," he said quietly. He bent a knee on the bed and, framing her shoulders, pressed her back onto her pillows. "Do not be afraid, menina. I only want to be with you. I need you near me tonight."

He released her at once and sat back on his bent knee. Then he spread the wrinkles from her sheet, careful not to touch her.

He looked older in the moonlight, she thought. The joyous man of a few hours earlier had disappeared. There were never-before-seen lines in his handsome face and a sharp set to his sensual mouth. It struck her with force. He was in pain.

She reached out to where his hand lay dark and sinewy upon the pale sheet and touched his thumb with her forefinger. "What troubles you?"

"Old dreams."

"Will you tell them to me?"

He jerked his hand an inch away from her touch. "You're the one who tells stories, menina. Tell me a story that will give me peace and then, perhaps, I will be able to sleep."

When she didn't immediately answer, he turned an angry face to her. "I heard you the day of the auction. That day you spent your passion for stories freely on strangers. Why do you deny me?" His voice was harsh and accusatory.

Deny him? What she had done on the terrace, is that what he meant?

Not knowing how else to comfort him, she stretched out her hand again and with the smallest of touches stroked the back of his. "If I have no stories for you, perhaps it's because there is nothing of which I need to convince you."

He turned his head slightly, looked down at where her hand moved lightly on his. "Because I already love you."

He said it simply yet the words did not fall simply on her ears. They struck like the collapse of the walls about her head. It came before she was ready. Feelings often came too quickly whenever he was near. They rushed at her like blasts from an angry wind. How was she to know those feelings by name?

"Love takes time," she said slowly, turning to craven retreat in the face of overawed sensation. "It's fragile and cannot be rushed or mistreated."

"Lies!" His voice was low but cutting. "Love is not timid and fragile. Love burns and lays waste to its victims. It's rude and presumptuous. It will betray your most preciously held secrets in search of itself. Love takes you hostage and if you're strong enough to recognize it, you'll gladly throw away the key to your soul for it!"

He lunged forward, bracing himself with a hand on either side of her head. "Do I frighten you? I frighten myself. And still there is this . . . wanting."

The last word was choked out of him, and she saw him shut his eyes against it. He was in torment and she was the cause. The thought appalled her. He was the joyous free spirit, the gorgeous man with the sinfully beautiful smile. He was desire itself when he sang and played the guitar and danced. He dropped jewels in her lap with careless ease. Suddenly she was ashamed of her cowardice. She had thought she only hurt herself, but now she knew that she had hurt him as well.

She reached up and slipped a hand behind his neck where his skin was scalding hot. With her other she touched his cheek, smoothing away the tense lines of pain. "Love me, Eduardo."

She thought he would never reply. The silence seemed to stretch until even the sound of their breathing was an intrusion. She felt her heartbeat as a hollow achy pulse and wondered if she'd waited too late to be brave.

When at last he did speak, she started because his voice was so different from what she dreaded. It was tender and persuasive, and enigmatic. "I do love you, *menina*. That may not be enough, but it's what I have to offer."

He leaned forward and with the gentlest of kisses

touched his lips to her brow, her eyes, her cheeks, and finally her mouth.

Tears of relief sprang into her eyes but she held them, giving him back kiss for kiss, and trembling as he eased his upper body down on top of hers and the reality of him enveloped her in sharply etched desire.

Eduardo buried his head in the hollow of her neck and shoulder and brushed his lips against the fragrant skin there. He was supremely confident in his ability to please her, but was humble and as grateful as he'd ever been in his life for the opportunity to so do. He wanted more than to please her, he wanted to absorb a little of her into himself so that he would never again be without her.

Philadelphia caressed the firm column of his neck as he rested quietly against her, and waited. When he lifted his head, she found the courage to look up into his face and hold the weight of his passionate gaze. When he kissed her she held her breath. There was a question in his kiss. Fear, delicious and sharp as cat claws lightly raked her spine. But this time, she answered it honestly. She pushed her fingers through the heavy silk of his hair and brought his head down hard to meet her kiss.

She heard him moan as his kiss deepened, and then she tasted the dark jungle and ferocious, wild, untamed land that had given birth to him. He was still a stranger in many ways, but he would be less so by morning, and she wanted very badly for it to be so.

His kisses bore revelations of delight. Wherever he touched her, she learned new things about herself. How firm were the bones of her face into which he pressed hard kisses. How splendid was the curve of her collarbone which he licked from end to end. How cool was the skin of her thighs when his warm hand reached down to skim up her nightgown. And how marvelously sensitive were her breasts. At first he scarcely touched them yet the brush of his lips over each soft nipple sent rippling shivers down over her stomach into the juncture between her thighs.

Then his fingers followed his lips, those clever learned fingers that had brought forth such beautiful music. Now they stroked so lightly up and down her breasts and stomach. She moved to the rhythm of his touch, wanting it, needing the fiercely gentle glory of it and hoping it would never stop. He strummed desire through her, and deep inside where the vibrations gathered she hummed with pleasure.

When he opened his lips over a breast and drew her into his hot mouth, she softly crooned this pleasure too great to hold. She cradled his head to hold him there, but he turned and laved the other nipple until she arched against the thready aching there that only his hands or mouth could soothe. He seemed to understand for his hands came up to cup each fullness and hold them for his kisses and the lap of his tongue and the graze of his teeth.

When she was near weeping he moved lower to scatter hot open kisses on the plane of her stomach, in the hollows beside the jut of her hipbones and lastly to push his tongue into the apex of her thighs. She couldn't explain the utterly new sensation of the sweet honey running inside her but she writhed under his mouth with little whimpers of helpless need. When he suddenly lifted himself from her she caught him by the wrist in panic. "Please!"

"Gently, menina," he said in the tender voice she was growing accustomed to. "I wouldn't leave you now for God or devil." He bent and offered her a slow tongue-stroking kiss that left her in acquiescence.

He stripped off his shirt, and she knew then why he'd risen. His chest was sleek in the moonlight and, just as she remembered, strongly muscled. He pulled off his boots and then unbuckled his belt, his eyes never leaving her face. And then he stepped out of his trousers and stood before her. Nothing she had ever known before quite prepared her for this moment. His thighs gleamed hard as marble in the moonlight, the turn of muscle and striation of sinews clearly marked in the silver light. And then she saw the place where his passion bloomed full, proudly arched and magnificent. She remembered riding the hard pressure of his thigh and understood a little more. And then he was moving toward her.

She pressed both hands against his chest, the virginal instinct for preservation resurfacing to override the heavy opiate of desire. But he dipped his head and kissed her mouth and then each breast and then cupped her face in his hands. "Trust me."

And she knew then how simple it was. "I do."

He stretched out on her, his warm hard longer length completely covering her, protecting her from the night, and the moonlight, and every other thing in the world. He came into her slowly, murmuring tender words of encouragement and hushing every fear with the warm liquid flavor of Portuguese spoken into her mouth until she relaxed under him. He flowed into her, higher and deeper with each surge of his body. He found and fitted into very contour of hers until she scarcely knew where she ended and he began.

Then came the moment when there was no longer any separation at all, when the tempo of blood guided their bodies in the primal dance of desire. Together they rode the undulations of pleasure until she wept at the summit of joy, and he gasped in rough convulsions of ecstasy.

# 12

Eduardo stood watching the pale streaks of sunrise infuse the sky, but the beauty of dawn was lost on him as he gazed unseeingly out the window. He shut his eyes. Not now! Not after this night. *Mãe de Deus!* How was he to leave Philadelphia after this night and what had passed between them?

Awakened by the insistent call of nature, he'd slipped from Philadelphia's bed to relieve himself. Upon his return, the first rays of the dawn were pinkening the sky. Whim had made him glance at her desk as he moved back to the bed, yet why had he moved closer to look at the letters lying there? Jealousy! He was afraid that she had been writing to Wharton. Had he been wiser, he would have gone back to where she lay naked beneath the sheets and made love to her to convince himself that Wharton was no threat. Instead, he'd scanned the first letter and, amazed, had read all three.

MacCloud! MacCloud lived!

Somewhere in the unseen distance a cowbell rang dully as a herd moved out to pasture in the river-misted grass. In the amethyst sky above a swallow sailed by. The river, dark as oil in the dawn, slipped silently past in this gentle American setting. The morning was new but old debts

and old vows were stirring again inside him. Three men.
Three acts of vengeance. Lancaster. Hunt. MacCloud.
Only MacCloud had gotten away, thought to have died
during the Civil War. But just now he'd seen proof that
MacCloud lived, in a letter written only a year ago. Post-
marked New Orleans. Right under Tyrone's nose!

Eduardo smiled grimly. Tyrone would be the first to
appreciate the irony of it. And the last to forgive if
Eduardo did not inform him of the fact. He would tell
Tyrone. There was no question of doing anything else.
They were bound by a blood oath older than his love for
a woman.

And what of this woman whose bed he'd shared? How
did she come into the possession of these letters? Did she
know about the association of these men? No, more
likely she had stumbled upon those letters, not knowing
that they contained in them the power to destroy her. If
MacCloud were to learn of the existence of the letters,
proving that he still lived, her life would be in danger.
From the beginning he had wanted to spare her the pain
in learning the truth about her father. Now it was essen-
tial.

He loved her! And she, even if she hadn't yet said the
words, loved him back. He had felt it in her kiss and the
willing way she'd given of herself. She had been shy yet
touchingly eager to please him. Long after she had fallen
asleep in his arms, exhausted by their lovemaking, he had
lain awake and savored his newfound contentment. No
moment in his life had ever seemed so full of promise, of
purpose, of peace and harmony.

How fragile are dreams, he now thought. How easily
they shred when rasped by chance and reality.

"Eduardo?"

He turned back from the window to see that she had
awakened. She sat up in bed, the half-light of dawn falling light as mist upon her naked shoulders and breasts,
and the slatted waves of her hair. Her face held the

blurred softness of one just awakened from deep sleep, the expression inquisitive yet uncertain. She needed to be kissed.

He moved slowly toward her, wanting to remember the moment forever. If he could, he would turn back the clock, giving them another night of darkness. He did not want the dawn and the reality that came with it. He wanted the night and the music and the passion, and most of all he wanted her, forever.

He bent to her and kissed her slowly. He felt her response as her lips softened under his, but as he brushed a caress over one breast, she, suddenly shy, reached for the sheet. "Don't, menina. Let me love you." Her hands fell away.

He made love to her slowly and completely with a fierce passionate need to stretch out each moment to its fullest, to hold her, and hold back the dawn. And when it was done, he pulled her so tightly against him that she wiggled unconsciously to ease his embrace but he didn't yield. Later, perhaps, he would yield, but not until then.

Philadelphia lay awake with the astonished joy of being in Eduardo's arms. He moved slightly as he lay on his stomach beside her, his hand curling tightly down on her waist to hold her even in exhaustion against the next rise of passion. His thigh was slanted over hers. Feeling his knee lying arrogantly between hers, the imprint of possession lingering in the wake of the deed, she trembled at the glory of its weight and scalding hot strength. It was unlike anything in her experience, this flesh-and-blood clamoring inside her to touch and hold and stroke and kiss every inch of him.

There were no words for her feelings, no clear comparisons in her experience for the precious hours of the past night. He had made love to her twice, first while the rapturous fever-fed yearning of his music still flowed in her veins, and now at dawn. The amazement of her own passion was still fresh to her senses.

The first time had been too bright, too feverish to recall in detail. In his arms she'd been all joy and shock, snared by the last latent strains of maidenly modesty and utterly awed by the power and muscular warmth of his body that had covered hers and gently but inexorably opened her to his pleasure.

The second time she felt the inadequacy of her new knowledge and the lack embarrassed her though he didn't seem to notice. She knew that she didn't truly know how to make love to him, didn't know how to hold him as expertly as he held her, didn't understand how to return his subtle musician's caresses which left her body humming and near-weeping in joy. She didn't know how to beguile as he did with his kisses. And so, she simply imitated him, caressing and kissing whatever part of him which came like an offering under her lips and hands; the hard scallops of his shoulder blades, the shallows behind his collarbones, the heated moist skin of his neck where the pulse beat more strongly than her own, and the sweat-sheened expanse of his chest. She found the slope of his spine, running her fingers lightly down it until he had gasped and arched under her touch.

And then, he was inside her again, filling her with his body and his spirit and his life, and she gave up to his throbbing heat and her uncalculated joy of being a part of him.

The night had shielded him from her sight but now the sun had risen above the distant hills and the room was awash in a golden haze. She turned her head to look at his face on the pillow beside her, more daunted by his beauty than ever before. He faced her, one long almond-shaped lid with heavy straight lashes shielding his eye in sleep. The bold wedge of his nose pressed into her pillow and his gorgeous mouth, that had offered such luscious kisses, curved tender as a child's in his contentment.

She stared in amazement at the blue-black stubble of his beard that had appeared as if by magic overnight. Heavy as a peppering, it defined his cheek and jaw and chin. She reached out and drew her thumbnail across the wiry hair, pleased by the texture so different from any womanly counterpart.

Strangely exultant and yet embarrassed by the raw desire curling once more through her, she lifted her head to see more of him. She saw first his muscled forearm with its dark copper skin lying in vivid relief against the fairer mounds of her naked breasts. A deep blush raced down over her bosom, but she didn't look away. She followed the black hair furring his arm, fine as silk thread, from elbow to wrist, and frowned.

His wrist, powerfully shaped, was a mass of braided scars, some smooth and naturally colored, others puckered and hard and pale. The wounds were old but they had been deep and brutal. Empathy, sharp and painful as his injuries must have been, jolted her as she ran a finger over the tortured surface and wondered how it had happened.

His arm was heavy with sleep, and she needed both hands to lift his wrist to her lips for a kiss. He murmured but didn't open his eyes as she cupped his palm against her cheek for a moment. There was so much she didn't know about him, and she wanted to know everything. Were his parents alive? Did he have brothers and sisters? Had other women felt about him as she did? No, she didn't want to know that. Once she had wondered how any woman would resist this man if he wanted her. Now she knew the answer, no woman would. She fingered the heavy gold band on the third finger of his right hand, wondering who had given it to him. So many unanswered questions.

A few short hours ago, she had wondered if he were somehow connected with her father's ruination. Now she lay like a wanton beside him, without a stitch of clothing, so astonished by how far she'd strayed from what she thought herself to be that she had no room left for shame or regret or even fear for the future. He was not her enemy, the feeling was so strong that it blocked every other consideration.

Rising up on her elbow, she half-turned to him to gently stroke his shoulder but her hand never touched his skin.

The faint morning light revealed a dozen long silvery ribbons of scar tissue which crisscrossed his back, and she knew with a shudder of rage and revulsion that he'd once been whipped.

Accustomed to a much more dangerous and unpredictable life than the one he'd lived these last few months, Eduardo sensed even in sleep the shudder passing through Philadelphia. He lifted his head sharply and looked at her and her expression made his blood run cold. He saw fear and abhorrence on her face. For an instant he didn't react, wondering if she'd just realized exactly what she'd done in allowing him into her bed. And then the precise angle of her gaze registered in his mind and he knew that she had seen his scarred back.

He hadn't forgotten it, he had simply forgotten to prepare her for the sight. The realization embarrassed him. In the wild jaded world where he had lived much of his life, women were sometimes strangely moved by those scars but none of them were ever horrified. A few even wanted to know the details of his ordeal, their gazes quickening with desire. He never shared their beds, for he'd learned that cruelty wasn't reserved to those with the courage to act on it. There were those who sought doses of cruelty vicariously, sucking from the misfortune of others the tainted sweetness of forbidden and twisted desires.

He sat up. "You saw the scars."

Stricken, she nodded and looked away. "I—I didn't mean to stare, only—"

"You are disgusted by the ugliness."

"No, not that!" She turned to look at him fully, searching for the words to explain her feelings, and absorbed the mixture of emotions on his face. There was reproof against pity, a flare of old anger and an older pain that would not soon leave him, and a vulnerability she had seen there only once before, when he'd asked her if she loved Henry Wharton. Did he care so very much about what she thought that she had the power to wound him?

She reached out her hand and rested it against his cheek. "I hate what was done to you, but I am not disgusted by your scars."

She saw a softening in his gaze that didn't reach his mouth but he didn't answer her in the way she expected. "Menina, if you could have but one wish, what would it be?"

She answered promptly. "I would have my father's name cleared and his enemies destroyed."

His smile was bitter. "At least you are honest."

Philadelphia saw pain reappear in his eyes, and guessing that it was because she had not mentioned him in her wish, she put her arms about his neck and lightly kissed him. "You didn't ask me what my second wish would be. I would wish that the pain I see in your eyes would heal and be gone forever."

"One cancels out the other, that is the rule." He framed her face in his hands, feeling both a protective tenderness and the bleak realization that they were headed on a collision course that no amount of wishing would avert. "I once told you that what we often want to believe is what comforts us. Would you settle for the truth?"

"Of course."

"How easily you say that. It must be a wonderful feeling to have someone who believes so completely in you. Your father was a lucky man."

The question came to Philadelphia without thought or reservation. "Will you help me find the truth?"

Time, he desperately needed time to think and plan. Yet as he looked at her, he knew that he would lose her if he gave any other answer. "I know how to help you find out the truth about your father, but before I agree to do that I want a promise from you."

Her heart thudded violently, and she found she could no longer bear the intensity of his black gaze. "You know something about my father? Tell me!"

He smoothed a hand through her hair then cupped the back of her head in one broad hand. "Look at me." She lifted her head and her golden eyes were wide with trepidation and doubt and something new, fear of him. This was not a good beginning. He should never have brought up the subject of her father. "I want you to promise to spend the summer with me. Then I will help you find out the answers you seek, I swear it. But the summer, let it be ours alone."

"Why?"

He moved his hands strongly down over her shoulders, and along her flanks to her hips, which he gripped tightly. "Don't you know, menina? For this! And because I love you!" He lifted her toward him as he bent his head for her kiss.

She felt both exhilarated and fearful of the strong current of desire for him that ran like a flash flood just beneath her skin even now when the hunger of her body was sated. He had spoken of love but she wasn't as certain of her own feelings. Perhaps he was right, that they needed time to sort out the emotions flaring quick-set as kindling between them.

He murmured in Portuguese against her mouth, and she withdrew a little from his kiss. "What did you say?"

He lifted his head, his black eyes searing her in their hunger and raw need. "I said you make me hot, menina.

So hot my skin burns and my blood boils. Cool me with your soft skin, take me into you and love the heat away!"

His deliberately outrageous words shocked her as she glimpsed for the first time the hard, primitive, dark forces he'd always hidden from her. The strange sense of mystery about him that had affected her so strongly the first time they met surfaced. She knew so little about him.

His hands drew her hips in to his. Unmistakable, his need. Fear quaked through her but he didn't retreat from his ruthless acknowledgment of his lust for her. She braced her hands on his chest and leaned a little away. "Please."

Eduardo held her firmly with his gaze, not allowing her to look away. "Don't be afraid, menina. Feel how it is between us," he said softly in his dark-toned voice. "You, too, are warm for me. It is good, natural, this need. Nothing to fear."

Philadelphia choked back a sob. Moments before he had calmed and reassured her against other fears. Now he made blatant what she would rather not face directly. He wanted her and demanded that she be honest in return, admitting that she desired him. There was no retreat from his clear black burning gaze that refused dissemblance.

"I love you." He said it quietly but not with the deep persuasive voice that he could wield with such devastating affect. It was a statement. Flat. Unadorned. A challenge.

She remembered how much he admired courage and suddenly she wanted to be courageous for him. Her hands softened. No longer repelling him, the fingers curled naturally onto his skin. She was capable of meeting him equally, of defending this moment for both of them, of providing whatever he should need in order to make him happy. "I love you."

When he turned her onto her back, following her down onto the bedding, she welcomed him with a warm embrace and suspension of any thought but pleasing him.

*Saratoga, August 1875*

"Everything is in order, sir, just as you requested," said the manager of the Grand Union Hotel to the aristocratic young couple before him. "Your trunks arrived three days ago and were unpacked in anticipation of your arrival. I trust you will find everything to your satisfaction."

"That remains to be seen," the handsome young husband answered with a casual glance about the lobby of the most famous hotel in Saratoga Springs. "I am unaccustomed to this wild American frontier, but I suppose compromises must be expected when one travels beyond the more civilized cities."

"Oh, and did you enjoy your stay in New York?"

The young man turned to rake the manager with an indifferent stare. "I speak of civilization. I speak of Naples. Paris. London when it is not raining. I found your New York hot, foul-smelling, and crude. Filth oozes from the streets and one may mistake half its humanity for dogs sporting men's clothing. It quite fatigued my bride. She is delicate and suffers with a weak chest." He glanced with indifference at his bride who stood beside him. She was swathed in the yards of white veiling that cascaded from her hat and disguised every feature. "That is why we are here, to recover from your New York."

"I see," the manager said politely, but sized up the arrogant young man in expensively cut clothing as trouble. Wealthy foreigners were always his most difficult guests. Nothing they saw or did or experienced ever compared favorably with what they had left at home. He would put Polly, the head chambermaid, on to them first thing. She was good with foreigners, put them at ease and treated them in the manner they thought they deserved. And, just in case the young lady was seriously ill, he'd put a word in Dr. Clary's ear so that he might call on them and leave his card.

"If you're ready to be taken to your rooms, sir?"

"My wife is. I don't suppose there's a place nearby where a gentleman might indulge in a few of the more refined pleasures? The train ride has put me out of sorts."

"There are the springs—"

"Mineral water?" The young man's handsome features expressed distaste. "I'd as soon drink turpentine. The racing season does not open for a few days. Is there no compensatory diversion offered until then?"

The manager lowered his voice discreetly. "Would you by any chance be interested in certain diversions involving cards?"

His smile surprised the manager with its attractiveness. "Exactly!"

The manager nodded. "I can, of course, direct you in that matter, sir. Would be glad to."

"Vittorio, *caro,* no!"

Struck by the lovely modulated voice that spoke from behind the veiling, the manager looked at the young wife and saw her lay a white-gloved hand on her husband's arm. The young man's face instantly became a study in icy fury. He turned to whisper something to her and the manager saw her visibly recoil. Her husband caught her by the wrist, his voice menacingly low as he spoke to her in a foreign tongue. The manager did not understand him but he saw clearly the results of the speech on the young lady. With each invective phrase her husband hissed at her, she bowed her head lower until she was hiding her face in the arm she'd raised in defense of his barrage. The voices of those guests nearby ceased abruptly to watch the drama going on in their midst.

When her husband finally released her, she staggered a little, gripped her bruised wrist protectively to her breast, and burst into pitiful little sobs.

The transformation in her husband was nothing less than miraculous. He looked stunned and then stricken by guilt. Emitting a low groan of distress, he reached out and

quickly gathered her shaking, weeping form into his arms.
Crooning words of comfort, he held her until the sobbing
lessened. Then, he turn to the manager and said, "Where
are our rooms? What kind of place is this that you keep
ailing ladies waiting about in your lobby until they weep
from weariness?"

"Very well, sir," the manager answered shortly, aware
of the necessity of keeping his opinion to himself about
what caused the lady's distress. "Follow the bellboy to the
elevator." He pumped the bell at his fingertips. "Peter,
show the"—he glanced down at the signature—"the Milazzos to their suite."

As he watched the young man shepherd his new wife
with great solicitude across the lobby he was reminded of
the hotel's code, that the guest was always right unless he
refused to pay his bills or began a public brawl. Spats
between husbands and wives did not fall into that cate-
gory, no matter how much he wished at the moment that
they did.

Besides, he'd seen the look in the young man's hot
dark eyes and knew him for what he was. He was a gambler of the most reckless sort. Looks and money. A bit
dark for convention, perhaps, but already certain ladies
were casting glances his way, in spite of the fact that there
was a bride attached. He'd be a good customer, expend-
ing his looks on the light and frail, and spilling his money
at the gaming tables. "I must inform Mr. Morrissey at
once," he murmured to himself. "Perhaps he'll set up a
private game for our guest." A good tip was always worth
a bill or two. He looked down at the name again. Milazzo. Neapolitan.

Vittorio Milazzo carried his bride across the threshold
of the elegantly appointed suite of the hotel and directly
into the bedroom on his left. Waiting patiently by the
door, the bellboy heard several short exchanges between
the couple. The lady seemed in distress while the man
sounded impatient and peeved. Finally, the rakishly

good-looking young man strode back into the parlor, one hand clapped to his brow, the other riding his hip.

Seeing the bellboy, he stopped short. "You!" he cried accusingly. "Why are you still spying on me?"

The boy swallowed hard. "I ain't spying, sir. I was waiting in case you wanted something. Anything you need, the Grand Union Hotel can supply."

"Peace!" the enraged man shot back. "How much will that cost me?"

"Compliments of the house," the boy said quickly, realizing that the tip he had been waiting for was irretrievably lost. He bowed jerkily and started to back out.

"Stop!" The man held up a hand while delving into his pocket with the other. He came forward and thrust cash into the bellboy's hand. "My wife needs a lemonade to revive her. I will make it myself. We must have fresh lemons, water, sugar, and ice. Send them at once." He looked down at the money he'd given the boy. "That is for you. This other, put it on my bill."

The bellboy looked at the dollar bill lying on his palm and a grin split his freckled face. "Thank you, sir! I'll get what you need lickety-split!"

When the door closed behind the bellboy, the man went over and turned the key in the lock, then leaned his shoulders against the door for a moment.

"Vittorio?"

"We're alone," he answered, and began to laugh as he saw a blond head poke through the bedroom doorway.

Philadelphia looked questioningly at Eduardo, and when he opened his arms to her, she flew across the room into them. Feeling them close warmly about her was the best feeling in the world, she decided as she nuzzled his shirtfront. This whole consuming desire to be with him was different from any need she'd ever known. "I thought surely we'd be thrown out just now!"

"You poor innocent!" He kissed the top of her hair, still amazed by the golden luster of it. "Do you think a quarrel between a man and his wife is grounds for an ouster from this hotel? In a place such as this, marital quarrels must be as common as leaves on trees."

Philadelphia slipped her arms under his coat and about his waist. "I was so embarrassed! I nearly ran out on you."

"Instead you cried, which was so much better." He propped his chin on the top of her head. "A nice touch. I wish I had thought of it when we rehearsed."

Philadelphia jerked up her head, clipping him on the chin as she did so. "Give me some credit for imagination."

"Oi g've 'oo kra'dit!"

"What did you say?"

Eduardo grimaced. "'Oo made me bihe my 'ongue."

"Oh! I'm so sorry."

He grinned down at her. "'Hen kiss ih an' make ih behher."

Smiling, Philadelphia reached up and very carefully brought his head down to within an inch of hers. With her fingers she parted his lips and said, "Open wide," giggling at her own temerity. He obeyed and stuck out his tongue but his eyes were wickedly amused.

Three short weeks ago, she would never have dared to tease him so but after spending twenty-one wondrous nights by his side, she was no longer afraid of the passion he roused so quickly in her. She parted her lips, moistened them, and then very gently closed them over the pink tip of his tongue and delicately sucked it.

She felt the jolt of pleasure that went through him with a surge of triumph. Most often she was lost in the sensual world of desire that they created together but this moment gave her a new knowledge of relationships between men and women. In controlling her actions she could give him pleasure rather than simply return it. As she continued to suck the sweet tip, she added the soft abrasion of her own tongue, running it along the sensitive edge of his.

She heard him moan softly in answer and his arms tight-ened suddenly on her.

When at last she released him from her torment, desire had misted her eyes and quickened her breath. "Better?"

Eduardo grinned down at her. "No. I need more kisses."

She pressed both hands to his chest. "Well, you won't get them! You've been an unkind husband, and you must now run along and play errant spouse to some other audi-ence. Besides, it's the middle of the afternoon."

He caught a fingerful of blond hair which lay scattered across her brow and twined it about his finger. "I haven't yet shown you the absolutely wicked delight of making love in the middle of the afternoon. It is most pleasant, under the shade of a tree or with the warm sunshine on your skin."

Her arms fell away from his chest. "You sound as though you've much enjoyed the activity."

The change in her expression made him ridiculously pleased, and he hugged her tight. "You're jealous! Of me? Menina, there's no cause."

She turned within his embrace, giving him her back to hold to his chest. "Why should I believe you? You are handsome. You are wealthy. You need not work for a living. You have no callouses on your hands, even if you did scar your poor wrists." Distracted by the thought of those scars, she added, "You never said who hurt you so badly."

"Didn't I?" he answered faintly. "But don't change the subject, menina. You were blackening my character. Con-tinue."

She shrugged within his embrace. "I'm not completely ignorant of life. I know wealthy young unmarried men like you have mistresses, many mistresses because you can afford them."

"Many?" he asked in amusement. "Would your jeal-ousy cede me a harem, menina?"

"No," she answered in a voice constricted by the sudden realization of what she was thinking. "For the moment it appears that you have only one." The moment the words were out she could have strangled herself. She hadn't mean to think that, let alone say it. Her need for him ran far deeper than carnal desire, it was an ever-present and exhausting yearning to be wanted and protected and loved by him always, yet they hadn't spoken of the future beyond this summer of loving.

Eduardo quickly turned her about and forced her to look up at him. "You are not my mistress! You are my love."

Wanting to go back three steps to when she had been kissing him, yet knowing she couldn't, she said, "What's the difference?"

The knock at his back made Eduardo bite out a curse but he kissed her, quickly, roughly, and thoroughly, before letting her go. "Later, menina, we will finish this discussion. For now you are Signora Milazzo."

Philadelphia went and seated herself on one of the two yellow-and-cream roman-stripe settees that framed a lovely maple wood fireplace while he let in the bellboy with the makings for lemonade.

"Just as you ordered," the bellboy announced as he carried in the tray.

Being a third year veteran of the summer trade at the Grand Union Hotel, the boy had seen many pretty and wealthy young women within these walls, but the sight of Mrs. Milazzo, a vision of golden curls in a white summer lawn dress seated on a yellow-and-white settee, was one he would carry with him for years.

When he had placed the tray on the table beside her, he snatched his cap from his head and bowed respectfully. "I hope you get to feeling better real soon, ma'am." Encouraged by her dazzling smile, he went on. "Saratoga's climate is known to do wonders for those of delicate health. And your presence sure perks up the scenery.

If there's anything, *anything at all* you need, you just ring for me."

Philadelphia lifted a hand to her mouth to hide her laughter. "You are much too kind, sir. I hope the hotel appreciates the sensibilities of a man of your charm."

Eduardo leaned against the door, watching this interplay with wry amusement. Few men were immune to Philadelphia's beauty. He would have to keep a close eye on her or she would be inundated by admirers. The thought seared his humor, shriveling in an instant. As the bellboy approached the door with a silly grin on his face, Eduardo subjected him to a glance so blighting he turned bright red as he quickened his step out the door.

"That was not every kind of you," Philadelphia said when the door closed behind the bellboy. "You frightened him."

"Did I? Good. He should know better than to stare at another man's wife."

"He meant no harm. He's only a boy."

"There are whiskers on his chin," Eduardo said darkly as he came toward her. "He's old enough."

Philadelphia looked at him in surprise. "Why, you sound jealous."

Eduardo shrugged. Did she not yet understand how deep his feelings were for her? Perhaps he should remind her that he was born and bred of the jungle, that his air of sophistication was a mere veneer for the primitive feelings that ran hotly in his blood. He did not want any man to look at her with admiration and lust. Part of him, the savage possessive side, wanted to shut her away from their lewd glances and lascivious thoughts.

Philadelphia watched the play of strong emotions in his face, marveling at how open he had become since their stay on the Hudson. Before that, she would have sworn she could not discern a single emotion in his expression that he did not wish her to read. But jealousy? He did not seem the kind of man to be concerned about losing anything that belonged to him.

She did not belong to him. Philadelphia's spirits sank at the thought. She was his mistress, a less than permanent arrangement. He often said he loved her. Yet, moments before, he had not had a ready answer to the question about the difference between being a lover and a mistress.

She looked at him, her heart in her eyes. "I suppose real husbands are less jealous because they are pledged to their wives."

"Exactly." Eduardo turned abruptly away from her on the pretext of retrieving his hat and cane, but the arrow of her accusation quivered in the wood of his soul.

He knew the idea of being his mistress distressed her. She must wonder why, if he said he loved her, he did not mention marriage. Yet, how could he explain to her his convoluted sense of honor which allowed him to keep her with him but did not allow him to deceive her into marriage with the man who had ruined her father? His dilemma had become acute those last days on the Hudson as he wrestled with the knowledge that one of his enemies remained alive. Just when his life was beginning to move forward the past had risen as if from the grave, and with it the blood oath he had sworn to Tyrone.

He had written Tyrone. His sense of honor would allow him to do nothing less. But he had decided to let Tyrone fight this last battle alone. He had at last found peace after years of turmoil. He would not jeopardize Philadelphia, not after all he had learned from her in the last weeks about the quality of love.

That is why they were in Saratoga. He could not have cared less about selling jewelry, yet in suggesting that they resume the scheme he found an excuse to leave the Hudson. Tyrone might come after him, and he did not want to be found.

He straightened abruptly. "Well, if you have everything

you need, *cara minha,* I will take the air. A stroll of an hour or two should set up my appetite for lunch."

"Very well," Philadelphia answered, longing to say more but aware of the strain between them which she had caused. "Until lunch."

When he was gone, she went back into her bedroom and opened the first closet door to hang up her shawl. The sight that met her eyes brought her up short. The closet was crammed with clothing, dresses of every kind and description, enough to fill an enormous cabin trunk. Where had they all come from? She lifted out one of the dresses with a billowy skirt of a white lawn and held it up to herself. It seemed it would be a perfect fit.

Eduardo! She knew instantly that he had once again outfitted her for their scheme but this time he had spent far more than was necessary. There were easily two dozen outfits in the closet.

"Do they fit?"

She spun about. "Eduardo! I thought you'd gone."

He smiled as he came into the room. "I forgot to tell you about the clothes. If anything isn't to your taste, I'll send it back."

"They're beautiful but you spent far too much. And how did you know what size to order?"

He stopped before her and took the dress from her hands and threw it on the nearby chair. "I ordered dresses made for you in Chicago, remember? I kept your measurements. These were ordered before we left New York."

"But how did you know I'd be coming with you to Saratoga? We hadn't even discussed it then."

He brushed her cheek with his palm. "I had decided, even then, that I would find a way to persuade you."

Philadelphia felt the familiar thudding of her heart. It took so little, merely his touch to awaken the wanting. "You make me begin to think I came too easily into your trap at Belle Mont."

"Was it a trap?" He trailed the back of his fingers down the side of her neck to tuck them into the collar of her traveling dress. When he had ordered the clothes, he had only hoped to seduce a beautiful woman, but he had done much much more. He had fallen in love. "It is I who feel enslaved."

She stood her ground but it was hard when his other hand came up to cup her breast and pressed so very insistently. "Why are you back? You were going to take the air."

His smiled then and the thudding of her heart rose to a brisk trot. "I prefer to take you, menina."

# 13

Eduardo lifted his eyes from the cards in his hands and surveyed the ring of faces around the table. He'd been playing poker every afternoon for nearly a week, and losing regularly, but he had yet to make an acquaintance who could introduce him to the upstairs salon of Morrissey's Club House, the most fashionable gambling establishment in Saratoga. But today, it seemed his luck might have changed.

To his right sat Mr. Oran Beecham, a broad-chested ruddy-faced horse dealer from Kentucky. They'd met on the block-long veranda of the Grand Union Hotel where half the summer's population sat and watched the other half parade along the avenue in their finest clothing and latest rigs.

A gregarious man with a ready laugh and silver flask in his pocket, Beecham had been the one to invite Eduardo upstairs to his room for a "friendly game" when he learned that the young foreigner was looking for a little diversion. The game, it seemed, was a regular afternoon activity of these men and so he had been pleased to join them. Mr. Beecham's hospitality was as gregarious as his character, and soon the Kentuckian's excellent bourbon, smooth as liquid sunshine, burned brightly in Eduardo's veins.

To Beecham's right sat a college-aged young man named Tom Howells. He had a mop of red curls that he'd tried without much success to tame by parting them in the middle and applying a great deal of hair tonic. Despite this, he looked like an overgrown toddler. Eduardo discounted him immediately as being too naive to indulge in serious excess or, if he did, likely to suffer too greatly from his conscience after the fact.

The third member of the group was Hugh Webster, a dentist from Cleveland. Middle-aged, balding, with a thin face so deeply pockmarked that his skin resembled a nutmeg grater, he seldom spoke but played each hand as though he were transacting business. Nothing reckless in this man.

The fourth man, the newest member of the game, called himself Reginald Spaulding. He was dressed in the latest style, wore a diamond stickpin, and even waxed his mustache with scented oil. Handsome in a brittle sort of way with crisp brown hair, slate-gray eyes, and hands as smooth as a lady's, he wore a continual smirk. Eduardo recognized the pearly lustre of his skin and indolent air as the trademarks of the professional gambler. This was a man who might help him gain entry into Morrissey's casino.

Eduardo scotched a twinge of conscience where Philadelphia was concerned. He had left her almost completely alone every day since they had arrived in Saratoga while he set about creating rumors about himself. He had even spent the last three evenings in the company of men of wealth and women who were fond of that wealth. He had drunk more than was wise and gambled at faro, giving the impression to casual observers that he lost more than he actually had. Free with his money and his charm, he had quickly become a favorite among the women. He had even discovered within himself the capacity to be as coquettish as any woman, promising much and delivering less. Philadelphia's was the only bed he sought. Still he should have expected the inevitable result.

He and Philadelphia had quarreled the evening before. What he did, he did for them, he had told her. But he did not blame her for being angered by the scent of another woman's perfume on his clothing. Only after she'd ordered him out of her bedroom did he realize the full extent of his mistake. It was time for them to move on. His heart wasn't in the game. He was stalling for time, and he knew it.

"Phew!" Mr. Beecham swabbed his moist brow with his handkerchief. "The wife keeps these rooms too close for a man's comfort. I'll just throw open the shutters. Man's gotta breathe."

"An excellent idea," Eduardo seconded. "Women are forever closing in about a man, curbing his least inclination toward masculine pleasure."

Mr. Beecham guffawed. "Steady on, son. You've just shackled yourself. Your criticism should be tempered by the pleasures of your new bride."

Eduardo shrugged. "In my country men marry for alliance, position, prospect. The rest is of no moment, providing there's eventually an heir."

"Come, son," Beecham answered with a wise wiggling of his brows. "I met your bride once, at luncheon. She's very lovely, if you don't mind my saying so."

"Lovely like a hothouse flower," Eduardo said with just a touch of impatience. "Her health is delicate. She suffers from the heat and the cold and the damp. Traveling destroys her nerves. It is most regrettable."

Beecham surveyed the other men about the table and when it seemed apparent that they had nothing to contribute to the conversation, he plowed in once again. "My Mae was delicate as a girl. But after the eldest, Joshua, was born, she perked right up. We have five children now, and Mae's never been more sound. Give your bride time, son. You may find Saratoga is just what she needs. I'll speak to Mae and have her invite your wife to take the waters with her. Mae swears by their restorative powers."

"I suppose there is no harm in this." Eduardo shrugged. "In any case, there are other delightful diversions about."

At his words an uneasy silence settled over the table, and Eduardo silently begged Philadelphia's pardon.

When the hand was finished and he'd deliberately lost again, he threw down his cards in disgust. "Is there no more interesting sport in town? I'm weary of so small a distraction."

"There's Morrissey's Club House," Howells suggested and then reddened like a beet.

"I have heard of this place," Eduardo answered. "Why do we not adjourn there?"

Beecham grinned a little foolishly. "With the wife and all along, well, it's not the sort of place Mae would approve of."

Eduardo's arched brows winged upward. "Why should your wife have a say in your habits?"

"The main floor is open to the public, with faro and roulette as well as cards and dice," Spaulding offered with a curious look at Eduardo.

"The rooms above?" Eduardo questioned.

"They are private, open only to a few."

Eduardo's peevish expression brightened. "That is where the real gaming goes on? Where a man may bet a sum that sets his blood pounding? I must go there."

"I'd be careful if I was you, Mr. Milazzo," Beecham said. "There's a rakish element that hangs out there, undesirable types. A man can have his pockets fleeced before he knows what it's all about."

Eduardo smiled. "I thrive in this element, Mr. Beecham. This"—he indicated the table—"is a tea party for me."

"Well now," Beecham began, uncertain whether or not

he should be insulted, "if we're too tame for your tastes, I think we might excuse you."

Eduardo regretted insulting the genuinely nice man but, he thought philosophically, it was all a part of the game. He rose from his seat and reached for the money he'd laid out to bet with. "I regret I must leave you fine gentlemen. It has been a most engaging afternoon."

To everyone's surprise, Spaulding also rose to his feet. "If you would like, Mr. Milazzo, I should be pleased to recommend you to Mr. Morrissey myself."

Eduardo turned to him. "This is possible? Now?"

Spaulding nodded. "Would you care to accompany me to the Club House?"

"But certainly!" Exultant, Eduardo picked up his glass and drained it before turning to Beecham. "This Kentucky bourbon, sir, is the finest thing about America. My felicitations to your distiller. I shall buy a quantity of it to take home with me."

Beecham disliked the young aristocrat's brass and his distinctly un-American attitude about wives. But, a man who complimented Bluegrass whiskey couldn't be all bad, he decided, and rose to his feet to offer his hand.

"It's been a pleasure, sir, having you at our—little tea party. Come back if it suits you. Otherwise, Mae and I hope to see you at the opera tonight."

"Ah yes. It is expected, is it not? My wife has spoken most insistently to me on the matter. I suppose I will allow her this, if she is up to it. Good day to you, gentlemen."

"I don't envy his wife the trouble of him," Beecham said later to his wife. "Pretty little thing, as I recall, but much too meek to tame a young buck like that. Wonder why she married him? Couldn't have been a love match. He doesn't seem to remember he's married half the time. I'd be obliged if you'd take her under your wing a bit, Mae. Left on her own day after day, and so far from home, she must be lonesome."

Beecham's suspicions weren't far from the truth. Philadelphia paced the rectangle of carpeting in her bedroom, feeling lonely and dejected. When she'd agreed to the idea of playing the part of an invalid bride she hadn't expected to be left so completely on her own. She better understood Eduardo's complaints about the role of Akbar, in which he spent a great deal of time waiting to be called on. She hadn't made a single acquaintance, had no one to talk to during the day, not even Eduardo.

He left early, came in late, and smelled often of the brewery. Last night he'd smelled suspiciously of a woman's floral scent. She'd been so angry and hurt that she'd pretended to be ill, and when he offered to sleep in the adjacent bedroom, she agreed. But now that she had had a chance to think it over, she sensed that this tactic was the wrong one to pursue.

She made a sharp militarylike ninety-degree turn at the rug's edge and paused, facing the picture of misery she made in the mirror hanging on the wall in front of her. She had come to Saratoga with the hope that it would draw them even closer together but the experience was driving them apart. While he went abroad in the world, she remained shut in. He was handsome and spending money freely; she shouldn't be surprised that women were interested in him, especially if his wife were nowhere to be seen.

"I can change that at least!" she said to her reflection. Why should she sit around and languish while he helped himself to any and all of the delights of Saratoga? The resort was filled with invalids seeking the curative powers of the natural spring waters. She wasn't his lackey. She was free to go about as she wished. She would go out.

She marched over to her closet and withdrew one of the prettiest dresses. It was a promenade costume of cream faille with an overdress of white striped India silk, trimmed in white lace and red ribbons. It was cheery and cool and would do wonders for her mood. She stripped off her dressing gown and stepped into the dress, thankful that it buttoned up the front so that she wouldn't have to waste time calling in a maid. When it was fastened she pinned the white fichu about her neck with a sprig of artificial red roses and then went to the mirror to rearrange her hair.

She peered first at the temples to be certain that the roots were not beginning to show. Each morning Eduardo applied lemon juice to her hair before she went to sit in the morning light that angled across the little private balcony of their suite. Satisfied with the color, she brushed and arranged her golden curls, pinning them back from her face. She needed a hat.

She found the perfect one in the third box she opened. It was a only a bit of fluff, a chip hat with a turned-up brim filled in with red roses and with two creme feathers curling forward in front. Her spirits rose tenfold as she pinned it in place before the mirror. She looked quite pretty, she decided. Eduardo Tavares would have to notice her now. In fact, she intended for all of Saratoga to know that Signor Milazzo had a wife, a very pretty and young wife. In afterthought, she clipped on the diamond pendant earrings and a narrow bracelet of diamonds and emeralds that Eduardo had given her to wear. Red foulard parasol in hand, she marched out the door.

Her pulse beat a little quickly as she crossed the famous interior garden flanked by three sides of the large U-shaped hotel. The grounds were impeccably kept, the neat borders of pinks and geraniums and hydrangeas in colorful contrast to the deep green lawn. She smiled as she passed guests sitting in the shade of the trees and knew their eyes followed her. She was a stranger in a place where strangers always elicited comment.

When she reached the grand lobby with its red-and-white checkered marble floor she realized that she didn't know exactly where she should go. She paused a moment, looking to the right where she saw four walnut staircases leading to the other wings and floors of the vast hotel. Behind them, she glimpsed what appeared to be small private dining rooms. To the right she saw the world-famous Great Public Dining Hall where she had yet to eat a meal with Eduardo, but it wasn't time to eat. She didn't particularly want to, in any case. She wanted fresh air and sunshine, activity.

"May I be of service, madame?"

Philadelphia turned to the man who addressed her. Her first impression was one of looking up into the frigid eyes of death. His deep-set eyes were like crystal, nearly colorless but emitting bright shards of refracted light as a broken mirror might. The next impression was one of danger. Those pale hooded eyes surrounded by black lashes were set in a face that was both brutal in its strength of brow and jaw, and arresting in the frank sensuality of his thin-lipped mouth.

He smiled, and she knew he'd read her thoughts as clearly as if she had spoken them. He offered her his arm. "Allow me."

"No!" She backed away. "I—I'm waiting for someone. My husband."

Those crystalline eyes swept over her, and she felt every inch of her weighed, assessed, and discarded as unimportant. "Your husband has my admiration and envy."

She knew he didn't mean it, there was too much mockery in his tone for sincerity, yet she couldn't fathom any reason for his open hostility toward her. "If you will excuse me." She began to turn away but he caught her elbow in a grip so hard and unyielding that she stopped herself before she was forced to resist him.

"You don't look like a whore. Who are you?" The question was spoken so quietly that she knew no one else heard it though a few of those passing by gave them curious looks.

"I am Signora Milazzo," she answered, truly frightened now. "Oh! Here comes my husband," she improvised out of fear. Turning away, she lifted a hand in greeting to the phantom just created. "Over here!" she called and felt herself released from the vicious grasp. When she turned back to elaborate on her lie she saw to her astonishment that the man had completely disappeared. Warily, she scanned the room but she didn't see him anywhere, which was a feat she thought, considering that he was quite tall and dressed all in black. Gone. Vanished.

Though the foyer was warm and sunlit and packed with people, she felt a shiver consume her. He'd been like a nightmare visitation in the midst of a bright afternoon. She walked briskly through the entrance onto the famed veranda of the hotel. The afternoon sunshine struck sharply upon her chilled face and her hands were shaking so badly that she laced them tightly and held them to her middle.

The man had suggested that she was a whore. Why on earth would he think she was that sort of woman? She was dressed very properly and strictly in the best of taste. He must be mad. Yes, that was it. Only a madman would accost a lady in the middle of a hotel lobby and question her decency.

Yet she couldn't shake the impression that he had known whom he addressed. The look in his eyes, so chillingly contemptuous and with no more consideration than he'd give a passing dog on the street, had distantly judged her with something less than curiosity but with more venom. Irritation, yes that was it! He'd looked at her as though she were some minor annoyance to be gotten rid of. If she'd been an insect, she knew he would have flattened her with the palm of his hand.

She looked about for an empty wicker chair among the dozens that lined the veranda and took the nearest one. Her knees were shaking now and she felt nearly as ill as the character she was portraying. As soon as she had steadied her nerves, she would go back to her rooms.

"Mrs. Milazzo! Yoo-hoo! Mrs. Milazzo!"

Philadelphia whipped her head about at the sound of her name to find a middle-age couple approaching. She saw their friendly looks falter and realized that she must have turned on them a look of trepidation. She stood up abruptly. "Mrs. Beecham, yes? And Mr. Beecham." She extended her hand to the older woman. "I am most sorry. I'm afraid you startled me."

"I can see that, dear," Mrs. Beecham answered and gave her husband a speaking glance. "Is your husband not with you?"

Philadelphia smiled. "No. But I was so weary of lying about in my room that I decided to take a little walk myself." She looked out at the line of carriages parading down the tree-lined avenue. "Alas, I didn't know where to go once I came this far. So much noise. So many people."

"It is a crush if you're not used to it," Mr. Beecham agreed and indicated her chair. "Sit down, my dear. Your husband is most anxious for your health. Can't have him finding us taxing you beyond your strength."

"I feel fine," Philadelphia answered, "but I will sit if you will join me."

"We'd be delighted, wouldn't we, Mae?"

"Of course, Mr. Beecham. Delighted." While Mr. Beecham went in search of another chair, the two ladies sat down and began to chat. When he returned a few minutes later, followed by a young black boy carrying a wicker rocking chair, he found the ladies deep in conversation. For the next three-quarters of an hour he sat and smoked one of his favorite cigars and rocked and watched the world go by.

Occasionally something the young Mrs. Milazzo said caught his attention. For instance, he learned that she had attended an English girls' boarding school and that explained why her accent was slight compared to her husband's. She also said that her mother was Italian and her father English and that she'd met her husband in Italy where her father was in the foreign service. He frowned as he listened to her speak with obvious love of her young husband. Married less than three months, she hadn't yet begun to find fault with the young rascal.

"Well, she will," he muttered under his breath. She was so pretty that he found himself wondering if she were a "little thick in the head," as the expression went. Why else would she think that there was nothing wrong with being left alone day after day while her spouse cut a swath through Saratoga that most bachelors would envy? He'd heard the rumors. If one wanted to know what was going on in the resort, one had only to sit on the veranda a while. Thick or not, it was a damned shame the girl was not being seen in the right places. The more he looked at her, the more he became convinced that she was just about the prettiest thing he'd ever seen.

"You and your husband are attending the opera this evening, I hope," he said when both ladies took a breath at the same moment.

Philadelphia favored him with a smile that he wished his eldest daughter possessed. "I do most thoroughly hope so, Signor Beecham, but my husband has not yet given his permission."

He made a sound that was a reasonable facsimile of a snort and said, "Why, we spoke of it not two hours ago. I said to him the both of you, and Mae and me would make a foursome of it." He nodded at his wife.

"Oh yes, let's," Mae Beecham seconded. "We'll dine in the public hall. Have you done so before?"

Philadelphia shook her head. "No, but it sounds very nice. If Vittorio agrees, I would love to accept."

Mr. Beecham rose to his feet, an old warrior but a cunning one. If the little bride wanted to attend the opera, the least he could do was make certain that her errant husband escorted her. "I just remembered an appointment."

Mae frowned up at her husband. "What sort of appointment, Oran?"

"Business," he answered with a meaningful frown at his wife. "You might like to stay with Mrs. Milazzo and talk about what to wear, that sort of thing. I'll be back in half an hour and I wouldn't be surprised, Mrs. Milazzo, if your husband doesn't return soon after."

Philadelphia smiled at him but said nothing. Eduardo hadn't returned before midnight since the first evening. "Thank you, both, but I think I am a little weary and should go in now. I'll send you a message if we are able to join you at, say, seven o'clock?"

"Seven it is," Mr. Beecham rejoined heartily. When Philadelphia had disappeared into the lobby he turned to his wife. "What did I tell you, Mae?"

Mae Beecham nodded sagely. "The girl's in love, all right, and it's equally obvious that the young scalawag doesn't appreciate her. Poor dear. I hope none of our girls is foolish enough to fall in love until *after* she's married."

Oran Beecham pinched his wife's arm. "Are you telling me something I didn't know?"

She looked up at him and blushed like a schoolgirl. "Don't go trying to get around me, Oran. You weren't an extravagantly handsome young foreigner with more money than sense. You worked for a living, that settles a man. I had a sharp eye out for what I was getting, even if I was in love."

"Just so you were," Oran answered, and squeezed his wife's arm more gently. "Now I've an errand to run."

"You're going to fetch Mr. Milazzo?"

"I am."

Philadelphia stared at the small French mantel clock as it chimed a quarter past the hour of seven. Eduardo hadn't returned. She should have known he wouldn't. She had dressed for nothing.

She took a sweeping turn about the parlor room of her suite in an evening gown of rich corded green silk. The bustle, accented by a huge flat green bow with ends trailing to the floor swayed gently in time to her step while the flounces of her train swished softly over the carpet. She had had to pay a maid to dress her and the expense annoyed her. Had Eduardo arrived in time, he might have laced and fastened her up. But here she stood, in an off-the-shoulder gown whose deep neckline was wreathed in fake jasmine flowers and rose leaves with no place to go.

The sound of the door latch made her forget for a moment just how angry she was when she turned and saw Eduardo enter the room. Without a word, he crossed the room and embraced her, one arm sliding about her waist to draw her in while the other reached up and slid fingers into her hair at her nape. He kissed her ear gently, murmuring apologies in Portuguese.

For a moment, Philadelphia allowed herself only the feeling of unexpected pleasure that came each time he touched her. It wasn't that the pleasure was unexpected, it was the intensity of the moment, the unchecked recklessness that she'd not yet come to accept as normal. And then she felt his hand at her waist beginning to work the fastenings. "What are you doing?"

"I want you naked," he said with just a hint of thickness.

She sprang back from him, the unexpected joy replaced by her former annoyance. "You're drunk!"

He smiled at her, his dimple seductively tucked into the side of his cheek. "Just a little, menina. I've found something else American I like, besides you. Kentucky bourbon. You must try it."

She shook her head in disapproval. "I thought you were without at least one masculine fault."

Eduardo grinned, then frowned as he rethought the matter. "What masculine faults? I don't have any faults."

"Besides the fact that you're staggering about this parlor in inebriation?" she asked sternly, but struggled against a smile.

He shrugged but the elegant gesture went a little lopsided this time. "A man may drink on occasion."

"You must have found a dozen of them today," she returned tartly. "I can see I made a mistake in dressing for the opera. You're good for nothing more than bed."

His black eyes kindled as he reached out and hooked her about the waist once more. "Yes, I'm good for bed, menina. Come along with me and I'll show you just how good for bed I am."

"I didn't mean that," she answered, bracing both hands flat against his chest.

"But I did. I want to make you naked, menina, and then I want to kiss every naked inch. It will take me a good long time, I think, to kiss every inch. I am most thorough about many things, as you well know."

"I've changed my mind. I'll go to the opera alone. You may stay here and reel about for the remainder of the evening."

She waited until he was steady on his feet and then shoved him. She was amazed that he wasn't thrown off balance. He caught her by the wrist and smiled cockily at her.

"I'm not that drunk, menina. I am enjoying a certain glow that comes from pouring good liquor into my veins but you'll not find me so addled that I can't serve in the capacity which you desire. Shall we retire like civilized people to the bedroom or would you prefer to make love on the carpet? I prefer the carpet. To see you lying there naked and sated, yes, I would like that."

Annoyance vying with amusement, she took his face in her hands and kissed him hard. "Now," she said breaking it off before he could pull her in against him. "Pay attention, senhor. We're invited to the opera tonight. It is a chance for me to be seen in your jewels. That's what we are here for."

Eduardo watched her with tender eyes. "Do you want to go so badly? Has it been such a lonely miserable time for you in this room alone?"

"Yes and yes."

"And later, when we come back, will you lie naked on the rug for me?"

Philadelphia blushed hotly. "I will consider it."

He smiled and lay his cheek alongside hers. "She will consider it, and I will think of nothing else."

"Will you dress for dinner? We are late as it is."

He lifted his head to look at her. "We could be later. I would like that very much."

"Oh no!" She danced back out of reach. "I spent good money on a maid to help me dress. I will be seen as I am, unruffled and untouched."

He nodded. "But later, menina, there will be much touching later. And kissing and licking and—"

"Senhor!"

Eduardo shrugged. "Very well, but I am disappointed in you. After all, it is our last night. We are leaving Saratoga tomorrow."

Philadelphia frowned. "Why? Did you lose sufficient money that we must sell the jewels?"

Eduardo shook his head in annoyance. "I was too drunk. I won! More than the jewels are worth." He smiled at her in a way that made her skin burn. "Have you no kiss for the victor?"

Philadelphia primly gathered her skirts together closer. "I don't dare. I should be singed!"

Opera was not Eduardo's favorite form of entertainment, Philadelphia discovered. By the beginning of the second act, she could hear the gentle soughing of his breath as he dozed quietly in his chair just behind her. She smiled regretfully at the Beechams, whose box they shared, and turned her attention back to the stage. She wasn't surprised to find that the Saratoga audience treated the opera with no more respect than did New Yorkers. They were continually milling about between the boxes, and a low but steady hum of voices accompanied peoples' comments to one another.

Nor was she surprised to find that a great deal of attention was being paid to their box. Somehow she knew that whatever Eduardo had been up to these last days was done solely to draw attention to her when she finally appeared. The occasional flash of light reflected on glass alerted her to the fact that lorgnettes and opera glasses were frequently trained on her. The only moment of unease she knew was when the thought crossed her mind that out there in the darkened theater, the man who had accosted her might now be sitting and watching her.

She shivered, thinking of those light, near-colorless eyes observing her when she did not know it. Unconsciously, she put a hand to her throat and touched the heavy collar of emeralds Eduardo had given her to wear. She closed her eyes and willed herself to remember his touch as he'd latched them about her neck. He had laid his fingers along her neck for a moment, just holding her with this most fragile caress. When he touched her she could forget everything else, could will the world far away.

Later in the lobby of the opera house during intermission, she found herself able to smile at her fanciful thoughts.

"What makes you happy, *cara minha*?" Eduardo asked as he slipped his arm about her shoulders.

She smiled up at him. "Everything. Nothing. It takes so little to make me happy when I'm with you."

She saw his gaze deepen and the shiny black became as soft as velvet. "Let's go home."

"The Beechams," she said without protest.

"We are newlyweds. Do you think it's necessary to tell

them anything?" He laughed softly at her expression. "I will tell them you are ill, if you prefer."

"No," she answered, thinking about the impression the Beechams had of them as distant and unhappy. "We will say nothing. Only hurry, I'm—"

"Cold?" he suggested sweetly.

"No, not cold," she answered, holding his gaze with a great deal of effort. Flirting in public, she was discovering, was a totally new and exhilarating and somewhat daunting experience.

"I seem to remember a promise involving the parlor rug," he said softly as he steered her toward the door. "Such things give a man reason to live, *menina.*"

The Beechams appeared just as the Milazzos exited the lobby.

"Look there," Oran said in alarm as the handsome young couple disappeared into the night. "They're leaving. Must have been a bust for them."

"Oh, I don't think so," Mae Beecham answered, her gaze softening from having seen the tender way the young man had embraced his wife's shoulders. "I think, perhaps, we've done them good after all, Oran."

The click of the door was nearly silent but Eduardo came alert at once. A dozen different thoughts raced through his mind as the door to their suite swung open, from the possibility that it was thieves who had seen the emeralds Philadelphia had worn earlier, to the chambermaid who'd forgotten the room was occupied, to guests seeking the wrong room.

He reached for his shirt and tossed it over Philadelphia, who lay sleeping naked beside him on the parlor rug. The next instant the light switch was thrown, and the drawing room exploded with light.

The man standing in the doorway smirked in response to the scene before him. *"Boa noite,* Eduardo. I wagered

you'd not make the bed. When you're dressed, you'll find
me in room 356."

Eduardo rose to his feet, uncaring that he was naked,
but the man shut the door in his face. "Tyrone!"

# 14

"You bastard!"

Eduardo had dressed and gone to Tyrone's rooms at the opposite wing of the Grand Union with only one thought in his mind, to shield Philadelphia, whatever the cost.

Tyrone regarded his guest without the least recognition for the seven years of their association or the blood vow that held them bound to one another. His fury matched Eduardo's. "If you've come to try to kill me, I advise you against it."

The two men stared at one another across the width of the small parlor room, molten black eyes searing the frigid depths of a wintery ice gaze. The air sizzled as emotions sought grounding. One brilliant flash and violence would erupt.

They were well-matched physically. Tyrone had the advantage of height but Eduardo the heavier cording of muscle. Eduardo knew his only disadvantage came from the fact that incandescent rage scalded him while stone-cold calculation seemed as usual to dictate his adversary's mood. Then he noticed the faint tic of a muscle work in Tyrone's lean jaw and the betrayal of emotion, however slight, astonished him. And it settled him. Something significant had brought Tyrone to Saratoga. There would be no fight, at least not until they talked.

Eduardo turned slowly and quietly shut the door he had entered. Patience! *Mãe de Deus!* Give him that! When he turned back, he saw that Tyrone had seated himself but that his right hand lay casually over the sleeve of his left, where he kept a derringer tucked under the cuff.

"You're surprised to see me," Tyrone said in a flinty voice that didn't quite mask his slight New Orleans drawl. "I thought that was the point. For me to find you."

"You thought wrong," Eduardo answered without heat as he crossed the room to sit down opposite him. "The letter I sent you from Chicago explained that."

Tyrone watched him with all the warmth of a cornered rattlesnake. "I don't like letters. You forgot to mention certain matters."

"Such as?"

Tyrone smiled, if one could call the sharp unfriendly angle of his mouth a smile. "Your golden-haired bitch. I recognized the handiwork as yours. I suppose you did a thorough job of it? Unfortunately, your shirt spoiled my view. Does she like rutting on the carpet or isn't she housebroken yet?"

Eduardo slipped off the role of protective lover and lounged back in his chair. "None of your damned business, is it?"

Tyrone's pale eyes flickered with some unknown interest. "Did she tell you we met earlier today? No? You shouldn't allow her to stray, amigo. Alley cats aren't that particular."

"She's tame enough." Eduardo's expression reflected nothing, but he was puzzled. Had Philadelphia met Tyrone, or was this only a ploy? Tyrone had always known how to find and sink talons into the chinks in his armor-plated life. This time he was pushing, pushing hard, to anger him. Why?

"Who is she?"

Eduardo let several heartbeats pass before he answered. He didn't know how much Tyrone knew, and decided that the truth was his only recourse. "Philadelphia Hunt."

Tyrone's eyes widened significantly and then he threw back his head with a bark of laughter. "You bastard! It's brilliant. Hunt's brat is your new whore? This deserves a toast." He rose and went to pick up the bottle of brandy on his bedside table and poured a generous amount into the glass standing there. "To your whore!" he said as he brought a glass to Eduardo. "May you ride her long and well."

Tyrone downed his brandy from the bottle. "You aren't drinking, amigo. Don't you like the brand?"

"I don't like the toast."

Tyrone took another long pull on the bottle as though Eduardo had not spoken and then sighed with deep satisfaction. "The thing about women is," he said slowly, staring at the bottle in his hand, "once a man's got one, he tends to getting to feel settled. Now, with a whore a man knows what he's paying for and how much he's going get for it. Mistresses are different. A man can get to feeling possessive about a mistress as well, especially one as pretty as the Hunt bitch. It can become as dangerous a liaison as marriage."

His gaze cut toward Eduardo, the crystal irises forming silver shards as the light passed through them. "You took her for revenge. Don't forget why."

Eduardo leaned forward slightly. "When have I ever needed you to remind me of why I do things?"

Tyrone nodded and dropped back into his chair. "So, you wanted a vacation. You've had it. I'm thinking of returning to South America. You were planning to return to Brazil once Hunt fell. I'll go with you."

"You hunted me down because you wanted a companion for a sea voyage?"

Tyrone shrugged, the gesture restless, as though he needed to throw off some burden. "I need someone I trust at my back." He looked up, his gaze clear and blinding. "You're it."

Eduardo sat back. "I'm flattered."

"But you aren't ready to leave?"

Eduardo smiled. "I'm finding certain pleasures to be had among the *norteamericanos.*"

"Like your whore?"

"I was thinking of Kentucky whiskey. Bourbon."

"A pleasurable pastime," Tyrone agreed mildly. "I prefer your whore. I'll trade you a shipload of bourbon for her."

Eduardo cocked his head to one side. "What is your interest in her? You don't even like women."

"I like women. They've got their uses. I just don't believe in long associations."

"Is Adelle once again on the street?"

Tyrone's eyes narrowed but he said evenly, "That's where I found her. It seemed a fitting end."

Eduardo murmured a Portuguese curse and picked up his glass and drained it. "Do I know her replacement?"

"I think you've found her for me." As Eduardo's gaze swung to him, Tyrone nodded. "I'm patient. I'll wait until you finish with her. She's young. Looks untouched. You haven't been particularly unkind to her. In fact, by the way she looked at you as you left the opera tonight I'd say she thinks she's in love with you. You aren't hard to look at but I am impressed all the same, considering you ruined her father. Yet she wanted you so bad I half expected you'd bend her over the nearest hitching rail and toss up her fancy skirts to get at her."

"That's the longest speech I ever heard you give," Eduardo said softly. "Why this interest in her?"

Tyrone smiled a genuine smile. "Because, amigo, she interests you, and whatever interests you interests me. That's the way of blood brothers. We share everything."

"You didn't share Adelle."

"You didn't ask."

Eduardo felt himself tensing in spite of himself. Tyrone wanted something, would push him until he got a reaction. "She's my exclusive property. I won't give her up to anyone. Not even you. So don't wait. You'll grow old."

Still smiling, Tyrone drew a deck of cards from his pocket. "You always liked cards, though from what I've heard since arriving in town, you're losing your touch." He shuffled the deck with quick expert movements, then shoved them before Eduardo. "I'll cut you for her. High card or low. Your choice."

Eduardo did not even glance at the deck. "She's mine. It stays that way."

"Coward?"

"I have nothing to gain."

"My respect."

Eduardo grinned. "I thought I'd done that seven years ago when the two of us stood off a whole garrison of *jaguncos* on the Argentine border."

Tyrone nodded. "You were young then, a wild jungle boy of nineteen with mud in your hair and blood on your hands. Then you thought nothing of taking what you wanted. We fought our enemies and became wealthy together. But you've changed, amigo. You've washed off the mud and the blood. You've begun to think as other men. I see in your eyes a yearning for what they have, a home, peace, a family. That woman's a danger to you."

"You haven't changed, though you like to play the gentleman," Eduardo answered. "What makes you think I'm different?"

"I play the gentleman," Tyrone answered flatly. "You are a gentle man. Give her to me, amigo. It will do you good to see her in my bed." He smiled. "I'll teach her what you've neglected to. Then, if you still want her back, it will be like bedding a new woman in a familiar frame."

"I'm going to marry her."

Tyrone's face went blank. "Shackle yourself to your enemy? It would drive you mad. She is yours by right of your victory. Use her as one would the spoils of that victory, but then let her go."

"I love her."

*"Merde!"* The rare passage of surprise crossed Tyrone's granite features. "You haven't told her who you are!"

"What happened between her father and me has nothing to do with her."

"Then why haven't you told her? *Peste!* You don't have to say it. You're afraid you will lose her."

The talons of Tyrone's accusation sunk to the quick, but Eduardo didn't even blink. Tyrone would not be moved from this issue unless he replaced it with another. "So, now that that's said, let's move on to another topic. I have news for you. If you'd waited in New Orleans you'd have my second letter by now." Eduardo sat forward, understanding the significance his words would have. "The enemy we thought had escaped us through death? He lives."

Tyrone's face was usually so void of expression that the sudden violent animation that flushed it now made Eduardo inwardly cringe. "MacCloud!"

Eduardo sat back. He had baited his hook well. "You will enjoy this irony. He's been living in New Orleans, right under your nose. At least he was a year ago."

Tyrone leaned forward in his chair. "How do you know this? Tell me!"

"Philadelphia has in her possession a letter MacCloud sent her father a year ago."

Tyrone rose to his feet. "I must talk to her."

Eduardo did not move. He hadn't brought his gun and now he wished he had. "She doesn't know anything. She's carrying several of her father's letters, including the one I wrote him just before the bank failure. I read the others. There's nothing special in them. She would not understand the significance of MacCloud's."

"She knows something. Otherwise she would not carry them."

Eduardo cursed Tyrone's sharp mind. He had all the predatory instincts of a leopard, and its ruthlessness. "She once entertained hopes of restoring her father's good name."

"Before you distracted her," Tyrone said unpleasantly. "And they say men keep their brains between their legs! Why should she think her father was innocent? Where'd she get the letters?"

Eduardo felt a faint blush creeping up his neck and reached for the brandy bottle to cover his discomfort. The truth was, he didn't know Philadelphia's entire thought on the matter nor why she had the letters with her. He hadn't known how to bring up the subject without it leading down avenues he wasn't ready to follow. "We have what we need. We know MacCloud is alive. He may still be in New Orleans. We'll find him."

"We?" Tyrone looked down at his seated friend, words falling like stones in a still pond, and the ripples flowing like liquid ice floes over Eduardo's nerves. "You were planning to return to New Orleans in time to help me corner MacCloud?"

"Yes." His letter had said otherwise but suddenly he realized that it was true. The only trouble was, he did not know what to do with Philadelphia. "The oath I swore over my parents' grave won't be fulfilled until we have MacCloud."

"Until we kill MacCloud," Tyrone amended. "We swore a blood oath because of MacCloud. Until he's dead, your part of our bargain won't be met."

"You've never said why you want him, and you want him more than I do."

Icy terrain, Tyrone's face. "I never asked you what they did to you or your mother and father. You volunteered."

Eduardo had learned a long time ago that there was a dead place in Tyrone, a place that was cold and black and

empty. If he had ever had normal human feelings, they'd
been driven out by pain and depravity far harsher than
that he had known. For, despite the rage and pain and
suffering, Eduardo had always wanted to be happy.
Tyrone seemed a man who could not even conceive happiness, let alone desire it. That made being in alliance
with him like living in a hole with a python. One never let
him too close, or let him sense a weakness, or an unready
moment. He had no doubt that, in spite of what they'd
been through together, Tyrone would try to kill him if it
came to a fight between them.

He rose slowly, his weight balanced lightly on the balls
of his feet. "I am tired, Tyrone. We'll talk again in the
morning."

"You'll bring the bit—the girl?"

"No. This has nothing to do with her. Nothing."

"I wonder if she'd say the same if I asked her?" Tyrone
mused aloud as Eduardo walked to the door.

Eduardo turned around and for first time Tyrone saw
the raw power and flat opaque savagery of the young man
he had met in the Amazon jungles seven years earlier. It
glared out at him now from those black eyes. "Leave her
alone, Tyrone. We'll get MacCloud."

"I know we will," Tyrone said when the door had shut
behind Tavares. "You and I, with, perhaps, the girl as
bait."

Philadelphia sat up tensely in the middle of the bed as
Eduardo paced the room. "What kind of friend breaks
into a hotel room? I don't think I'll ever be able to face
him again!"

Eduardo paused to send her a lovely protective smile.
"Tyrone has an unusual sense of humor. He didn't expect
to find me occupied," he lied. "I doubt he saw enough to
remember you."

She shook her head. "I only saw a glimpse of him but I
know who he is. He's the man who stopped me in the

lobby yesterday afternoon. He has the coldest eyes I've ever seen."

He sat down on the edge of the bed, noting that she drew herself in as he did so, pulling her legs up under her dressing gown and wrapping her arms about her knees. "What is wrong, menina? What did he say to you?"

She rested her head on her knees, making her hair slide forward to shield her stinging face. "He thought I was a whore. And now, after what he's seen . . ."

Her muffled voice tugged at his heart but he didn't try to comfort her. "He wouldn't have seen a thing had he knocked."

She lifted her head. "What does he want?"

For the first time since they'd met, Eduardo found he couldn't look her in the eye. "He came to see me. It has nothing to do with you." He rose from the bed and went to stand near the window. "I've been meaning to ask you something. You carry letters with you, why?"

Philadelphia started. "I—How do you know that?"

He turned back to her. "You left them open on your dresser at Belle Mont. I confess, I looked at them. I thought you were writing Wharton."

He was glad to see that his little confession took away the indignation that was forming on her face. "You thought I'd written Henry? Why?"

"Because I was jealous. But you haven't answered my question. Why do you carry those letters? What do they mean to you?"

Philadelphia looked away first this time. It was the moment she'd been waiting for and yet dreading ever since they'd left Belle Mont. No, even before that, she had known that she might have to tell him the truth, but now, at least, she no longer suspected him of having some part in the mystery. "You know I think my father was deliberately ruined. I believe those letters contain clues to the identities of the men who did it. My lawyer said Father had secret partners in the business deals that led to the scandal. There are three letters. One was from a New York banker named Lancaster."

She looked up expectantly and he nodded, saying, "We spoke of him on our way to Belle Mont. He is dead."

"Yes," she said carefully. "The second one is from a man named MacCloud. He lives in New Orleans. I think the letter he wrote my father was in reference to Lancaster's death. I can't prove it, of course, it's just a feeling, the tone of the letter. It talks of present misfortune and spading over old graves." She glanced at him. "It even mentions Brazil."

"I read it." His tone was neutral. "You seem to know a great deal."

"I know nearly nothing. If the letters hadn't been in my father's hand the night he—he died, I would never have known about them."

Eduardo frowned. "He was reading the letters just before he died?"

Philadelphia shook her head, trying to hold at bay the horrible memory of her father's death. "He held them in one hand. In the other he held a pistol."

"Did the pistol belong to your father?"

"The police said it did and our housekeeper confirmed it. I never knew that he had a gun, though I wasn't very surprised. Being a banker he sometimes carried sums of money or important papers with him. I suppose it was for protection."

"How did you get the letters?"

"I found him." Philadelphia winced against the memory, resisting it. So much pain! The acrid smell of smoke. The stillness of her father's body lying at an unnatural angle on the Turkish carpet. And the ugly bluish hole in his temple. She inhaled suddenly, shuddered, and gave a low moan.

Eduardo embraced her quickly as she swayed forward over her knees, and he held her tightly. She cried hard and long. He didn't try to stop her for he suspected that she had not cried this way since her father's death. He remembered the scene she had created about her hair, and wondered if it had been an excuse tricked up by her mind to relieve the tension she had held inside her so long.

Finally, feeling her relax within his arms, he bent and kissed her, then lifted her up into his lap. As her arms slid about his neck he wondered how they would weather the next few days. He had told Tyrone as much of the truth as he knew, but he couldn't trust Tyrone not to question Philadelphia himself. And if Tyrone did, what things might he tell her in order to pull some kind of confession from her?

Philadelphia pressed herself to him, welcoming his warmth and strength. "I have thought at times I would go mad with this secret I've kept," she whispered into his ear. "I am glad at last to be able to tell it to someone, to you. You said you would help me unravel this mystery. I need that help now. This man MacCloud knows something, I'm sure of it! I want to go to New Orleans to see him."

Eduardo stroked her soothingly from the nape of her neck down along the indentation of her spine to the fullness of her hips. "Menina, what do you hope to accomplish? Even if you are right, and this man MacCloud does know of some plot against your father, what can you do? You'll never have the proof to bring the guilty to justice in the courts."

She leaned back from him to see his face. "I want to know the truth. Don't you understand how important that is?"

He tenderly brushed her hair back from her face, his voice patient. "What of this business of old graves? Is there no doubt in your mind that you may find answers you would rather not hear? Perhaps there is something in your father's past which he would rather you never learned about."

The truth was she did fear such a thing and because it frightened her so, she shoved him away. "Why do you keep saying that? Do you think I would believe anyone who spoke evil of my father? No, I won't believe it!"

Eduardo sat back and grew very still. He could hear his grandmother's voice very clearly in his mind but his own temper was routing it. "You're wrong if you think wishing can make it so. Let it be, menina. You can't change anything now."

Resentment replaced despair and it felt good to have a direction for her agitated feelings, even if the target were Eduardo. "You didn't know my father. I have thought until this minute that he would like you, that you would deal well together but I think now I was wrong. He wouldn't approve of you."

He grew very still, thinking back more than fourteen years to when he was twelve, and still believed in guardian angels, and how to satisfy her father's greed, *bandeirantes* had robbed him of everything but his life. "Approve of me for what?"

She blushed, refusing to say the words, that she was thinking of her father's reaction to him as a son-in-law. Eduardo had never mentioned marriage and the reminder augmented her resentment. She was furious that he was calm. "He wouldn't approve of you keeping me as your mistress," she flung at him.

"Yet you do not mind," he countered.

She acted before she thought. Her arm snaked out, delivering a stinging slap that reverberated in the silence. Horrified, she reached out instinctively for him but he recoiled from her.

"Once is quite enough," he said between his teeth and she jerked back her hand. "It has been a long and exhausted evening for you. Go to sleep, menina, before I throttle you."

"Eduardo, I—" Philadelphia faltered before his obsidian stare. She'd never seen that look in his eyes before. It was rabid fury held in check but on so thin a tether that she could feel the sulfurous heat of it along her skin. "I am sorry."

"Of course you are. Whenever we are at odds, you resort to formalities, Senhorita Hunt. If your precious virtue concerns you, you may turn the lock in the door tonight . . . and every night hereafter. I've never taken an unwilling woman. I prefer those who would lie naked on carpets for my pleasure. Good night."

She did not stop him, she did not have the nerve. Instead, she flung herself upon her bed and cried long and hard, and though it was small compensation, it at least gave her emotional release.

"I'm certain that the waters from this spring will perk you right up, Mrs. Milazzo," Mae Beecham said encouragingly as she entered the Congress Spring pavilion with her little party. They joined the throng of early-risers partaking of the daily ritual of "taking the waters." "We positively dote on them, don't we, Cassandra?"

"Yes, ma'am, we do," Mrs. Beecham's eldest daughter replied. "Sarah Ames says her megrims have disappeared since coming to Saratoga. You do look a bit piqued, if you don't mind my saying so, Mrs. Milazzo. Two glasses will do wonders."

Philadelphia smiled wanly at the mother and daughter. She did have an insistent pain in her temples. If they hadn't arrived at her door at eight A.M., she would still be asleep, having completely forgotten the assignation. Four hours of sleep had done little to improve her mood. In fact, she was angrier now with Eduardo than she had been in the middle of the night.

"Here we are," Mrs. Beecham said triumphantly as they reached the bar in turn. "Three glasses," she said to one of the pump boys dressed in the regulation smock and matching beret. She watched him dip his ladle into the basin where the spring waters flowed fresh from the ground and fill each of three glasses. When he had set the glasses on the bar before her, she offered him a few coins and picked up the first and handed it expectantly to her guest.

Philadelphia accepted the glass and took a tentative sip. As the sulfurous-tinged water slipped down her throat, the violent urge to spit it out made her choke, and she sputtered, gasping for air.

"It takes a bit of getting used to," Mrs. Beecham said calmly. "It is medicinal, after all. A little bit of sugar wouldn't go amiss, I sometimes think, but we are all adults and know how to do what's good for us. It's best when swallowed straight down."

Philadelphia balked at the motherly advice as she stared doubtfully at the clear liquid. The water was slightly effervescent and smelled faintly of rotten eggs. Who could possibly down the contents of a glass in one swallow?

As she looked up to express those doubts she was amazed to see mother and daughter swallowing the noxious water with relish. In fact, as she gazed about, the inhabitants of the pavilion seemed to actually be enjoying imbibing the famous water. Under the ornate roof with its fretted and arabesqued ceiling, inlaid floors, and tall stained-glass windows of rainbow hue, the entire company was pleasantly jovial and good-spirited. No thanks to the water, she was certain.

"Signora Milazzo."

She turned too quickly, before she had a chance to brace herself, and met unprepared the glacial gaze of the man called Tyrone.

"Good morning, signora." His gaze swept insolently over her. "I trust you slept well, after your strenuous evening." The greeting was conventional, but a malicious amusement glinted in his eyes, and she knew he was remembering how he'd seen her lying naked on the carpet beside Eduardo.

A black wave of mortification rolled over her. The glass slipped from her nerveless fingers, splashed the contents down her front, then shattered on the floor.

"Oh my! You've had an accident," she heard Mrs. Beecham exclaim from what seemed a great distance. From farther away she heard Cassandra's cry of alarm, and then a hard merciless hand was gripping her arm, the pain a counterbalance to her acute embarrassment.

"Allow me," Tyrone said, and he brushed the moisture from her bodice with a handkerchief. It was an insulting, shockingly intimate thing for him to do and she heard the Beechams' indrawn breaths of surprise, but she was helpless to defend herself.

"That's better," he said and whipped the handkerchief back into his breast pocket. "A little accident. Nothing of value was damaged." He glanced at Mrs. Beecham for the first time. "The waters don't seem to agree with my cousin. If you'll excuse us, I'll just see her back to her rooms."

"Cousin? Well in that case . . . I'm sure . . . if you think that's best, Mr. . . ." Mrs. Beecham's voice trailed off as she sent Philadelphia a questioning glance. "Are you certain you're quite all right, my dear?"

"Yes," Philadelphia said in a fear-parched voice. "I'm fine. It's the water." She tried to pull away from Tyrone but his grip was so strong that her attempt made no impression on it.

"Don't be embarrassed, Cousin, for your weakness," Tyrone said in a steely tone. "I'm certain they'll understand if you need to lean on me. Take my arm."

It was a command but with it he also offered her a modicum of pride. Besides, she suspected that if she did not walk out on his arm he would drag her out by her own. She set a nerveless hand on his arm, shivering at the coiled strength she felt beneath his coat sleeve. She tried to find some comfort in the fact that he was Eduardo's friend, but she didn't know how much he knew about them or if he knew the truth, that they weren't married.

"Morning, ladies," she heard him say as he began to lead her away. She did not know exactly what she said to them, only that she mumbled some courtesy. The thing uppermost in her mind was to escape them before he insulted her in front of them.

She walked out into the morning air, and the fresh breeze blew away a little of the choking fear. At least she knew she was not going to further embarrass herself, but the presence of the tall forbidding man beside her kept every muscle locked in tense anxiety, waiting for his next words. When he finally spoke they had walked nearly two blocks away from the Congress Spring pavilion.

"We'll stop here." He indicated a nearby park bench.

She balked. "I don't wish to sit. I want to go back to my rooms."

The austere lines of his face altered. "I thought you'd prefer a public conversation, *Miss* Hunt, but I never turn down a lady's invitation to her rooms." His laughter was dry as dust when she quickly turned toward the bench.

Her knees trembling, Philadelphia crossed the dewy grass in near panic. He knew who she was! Had Eduardo told him? Even so, what could this man possibly want with her?

She sank down onto the bench and watched warily as he leisurely strolled over to her. He was tall with long bones strapped by whipcord muscle. There was a rangy edginess to him, as though he was accustomed to watching his back or wearing a gun belt like a cowboy. Chicago had its fair share of them in town during each cattle-drive season. She'd seen daguerreotypes of them in the papers, gun belts slung low over hard narrow hips. Yet this man was much more predatory. The realization struck her; Tyrone looked like a gunslinger.

He did not sit but propped a booted foot on the bench seat beside her and rested his folded arms on his bent

knee so that he leaned over her. He did not need this
attitude of intimidation. His blinding stare, throwing into
relief his weathered bronzed skin and dark hair, was
enough. Under other circumstances, she might have
thought him attractive but at the moment she felt like a
prisoner before sentencing, and every compelling thing
about him drew only the response of fear.

"I've always admired Eduardo's taste in women. You
are an amazingly beautiful exception."

Staring straight ahead, Philadelphia swallowed the
double-edged insult. Knife thrusts. She had been wrong
to think he would merely sit in judgment. It was to be an
execution.

"I've come a long way to help Eduardo see the error of
his ways."

"Meaning me?" she said stiffly. Why was she giving
him this chance to maul her? Because, she thought
bleakly, she had no choice. He knew who she was. She
would be thrown out of the hotel and asked to leave Saratoga if it became public knowledge that she was not
Eduardo's wife but his mistress.

"Meaning that a man sometimes confuses pity with
whatever it is he thinks ought to be love."

"Pity?" The word surprised her into looking up at him.
"Why should Ed—Mr. Tavares pity me?"

"What else could he feel for a young pretty lady in your
position? Your father is dead. You've been turned out of
your home. Eduardo fancies himself something of a gallant. He felt honor-bound to save you from your fate."

Courage jellied in the pit of her stomach. How did he
know so much, unless Eduardo had told him? "Is that
what he told you?"

"Did you expect different?" he drawled with a smirk,
"Like he'd confessed his undying love for you?"

Of course that was what she had hoped. It was like
needles edging under her nails to realize that he had not.
When had Eduardo said these things, before or after

their fight? "I have no idea what Mr. Tavares said to you. Why don't you enlighten me?"

He looked as pleased as if she had offered him her neck for his guillotine. "He told me he hasn't asked you to marry him, and considering what I happened onto last night, I'd say that should give a woman in your position something to think about."

She resisted the shame that ran like stinging nettles over her skin. "I know you think me shameless—"

"Actually, I find you mighty appealing, considering," he replied but his sensual appraisal didn't thaw his wintery gaze. "Or maybe I'm wrong about you, maybe you have considered your situation and you like it just fine. I saw the emeralds you were sporting last night. That's not a bad trade for a lady's virtue, to my way of thinking. Eduardo's wealthy and generous to a fault. Emeralds and gowns and fine company, you'd be hard-pressed to find a husband to equal him."

She felt like she had slipped backward into Hell without any possible reprieve. She stood up, her face within inches of his because he did not yield. "Why don't you make yourself perfectly clear, Mr. Tyrone. What exactly is it you want of me?"

He smiled and she saw with a shock that it was colder than his eyes. "I want you to leave Eduardo. Oh, he wants you but he doesn't need you, and he certainly doesn't intend to keep you. If money's a problem, I'll make it worth your while."

The man despised her, loathed her, held her in contempt. Those things she recognized. "Why?"

He gave her another long slow contemptuous look, as though he would as soon strike her as answer her, and Philadelphia trembled though dozens of people strolled past them as they stood in the open. "Do you know what a *caboclo* is?" At the shake of her head, he said, "It's a mongrel Brazilian whose ancestors are Indian and Portuguese, or Spanish, with a tarring of African thrown in for good measure. Some women aren't too particular about what they whelp, but in New Orleans a woman of your obvious quality wouldn't soil her skirts by walking on the same side of the street as a mulatto buck. Yet you've taken one as your lover, Miss Hunt. I'm doing you a favor. Choose as your next lover any man in Saratoga and you'll be trading up."

She was too shocked by what he said to be insulted. "You call yourself his friend? What kind of man are you?"

He caught her chin in a brutal pinch and lowered his face to within an inch of hers. "I'm a dangerous man to cross, Miss Hunt. That's what I am!"

She knocked his hand away and, lifting her skirts, fled down the sidewalk to the accompanying stares of passersby.

Tyrone watched her go, a grudging admiration for her tugging at him despite his anger over her refusal to be browbeaten into submission. He thought he had gotten to her with that last thrust but she had turned it on him so neatly he had not guessed it was coming.

*"Peste!"* If she told Eduardo what he had said just now, he might be looking down the barrel of his friend's gun before sunset.

Unease made his stomach jump. Ever since he left Chicago several months ago, he had been troubled by a sense of danger just out of range. Now he knew his mortal enemy, MacCloud, lived. Lancaster and Hunt had meant little to him. But news of MacCloud's continued existence gave his disquiet a focus. It was no mistake that Eduardo had brought him the news. They were bound by the mystic bond of a blood oath.

A funny unfamiliar feeling shot through his gut. He felt as though he suddenly stood to lose something precious, that this fancy piece of femininity was threatening to take away from him something as important as his life's breath. But, of course, that could not be true. He had never needed anything or anyone that much. He admired Eduardo, respected him as he did no other man. But need him?

Tyrone turned and walked slowly toward the park. For seven long years he had counted on Eduardo, known he would come to his aid without question, and the reverse was true. But an oath sworn in blood was only as good as the men who'd sworn it. If Eduardo came looking for him, choosing to side with the girl over their friendship, then he would be ready. Nor would he apologize for what he had said. He had not spoken his own prejudice and if Eduardo did not understand that by now, then damn him!

Jesus, but the Hunt bitch was a beauty! He understood why Eduardo could not think of anything else but loving her. He would not mind the opportunity to make love to her himself.

Tyrone paused on the sidewalk as an unholy smile suddenly lifted his features. He had tried using the stick to run her off. Maybe he should have used a carrot. The trouble was, if he succeeded in winning her, even for a night, Eduardo would want his hide. He would just have to make certain Eduardo believed that it was her doing and not his. No one was going to come permanently between them. They had business to finish and he was not about to allow any madonna-faced whore to interfere.

# 15

Philadelphia stared at the dinner menu of the public dining room at the Grand Union. Reputed to be the largest dining hall in the world, the public room seated twelve hundred diners, served by two hundred and fifty Negro waiters. There were twelve courses, including Consommé Sago Soup, Boiled Keenebee Salmon, Boeuf à la Mode, Calf's Brains en Cassises Au Gratin, Lobster Mayonnaise, Cold Ham, assorted vegetable dishes, and to finish there were tarts, fresh fruit, vanilla ice cream, and nuts. It was a menu fit for kings served at a table of snowy linen set with burnished silver and crystal goblets. It should have been an impressive dining experience. Instead, she found herself unable to think of food or to enjoy the setting or even to simply read the menu, while Eduardo glared at her across the table.

When she had returned to their rooms after her disastrous outing with the Beecham ladies, she found that he had left her a message asking her to meet him in the dining room at one o'clock. She had dressed very carefully in a high-necked dress of cream India lawn with matching straw bonnet but he had looked at her with such indifference that she was immediately sorry that she had spent a minute's worry over the matter. He was still angry about the night before and her own guilt made her think she could still detect the faintest impression of her hand on his cheek.

"What will you have?" Eduardo asked impatiently, for she had been hiding behind the menu for a full five minutes.

She lowered the menu. "I told you before, I'm not hungry."

He muttered an expletive and reached over to snatch the menu from her hands. "Then I'll order for both of us. The least you could do is look pleased. We are supposed to be on our honeymoon."

Still smarting from her meeting with Tyrone a few hours earlier, her glance was scorching. "Oh, are we still playing games? I thought we'd abandoned our ruse for the present."

He glared back at her. "What the devil is the matter with you? Is it last night? I apologized for that. What more do you want?"

She met his furious black gaze with sudden wariness. "I want the truth. Who are you, really?"

His black brows shot up. "Is this some new game, menina? Because if it is, I don't like it."

She changed tactics, sorry she'd even allowed Tyrone's insinuations to spark her curiosity. "I want to go to New Orleans. Will you take me there?"

He did not even bat a lash. "No."

"Then I will go without you."

"So you said last night." He looked down at the menu. "It's a mad scheme. You will only needlessly hurt yourself."

"Why do you object so very much to my pursuit of justice for my father's memory? I almost believe you hope I will find out something terrible."

Eduardo looked up slowly until his eyes met hers and made her hold his gaze by sheer force of will. "You are like a spoiled child, menina. You must have what you want, no matter the cost. If you are denied, you throw a tantrum. I'm not a patient man by nature, yet I have given you months of my life in the hope that you would come to realize that what has past is best left alone. I know you loved your father but you cannot bring him back. You should be looking toward the future, but you are willful and stubborn and will not listen to any needs but your own."

He sounded hurt, and she was incredulous. Something important was being said but she couldn't quite grasp the full meaning of it. "What do you need of me?" she asked softly.

"Well now, if it isn't the Milazzos. Mind if I join you?"

Philadelphia looked up into the translucent gaze of Tyrone, who had walked up behind her. Too furious by his intrusion to be frightened this once, she whispered, "Go away!"

"Your lady friend doesn't seem to like me much, Eduardo," Tyrone said, his New Orleans drawl more pronounced than usual. Eduardo shot him a warning glance. "Oh that's right, it's 'Vittorio' and 'wife,'" he amended with a smirk and pulled out an empty chair and sat down. "Tell me, how's married life treating you?"

Eduardo shrugged, annoyed also by the interruption but glad that Tyrone was openly acknowledging them. It was when Tyrone disappeared that his prey had need to worry. "For myself, well enough. You should ask my wife if you want her opinion."

Tyrone shifted his gaze to Philadelphia. "We've already talked." At Eduardo's expression of surprise he said, "Didn't she tell you?"

Eduardo frowned as he looked at Philadelphia. "No, she didn't tell me." In fact, she had not said two unprovoked sentences to him since he'd left her bed at three o'clock in the morning.

"We met at the Congress Spring pavilion this morning," Philadelphia supplied with a hostile glance at Tyrone.

"I didn't know that you were taking the waters." Eduardo watched a telltale blush infuse her complexion and knew that it had not been a pleasant meeting, but she had not confided in him so his sympathy was muted by that fact.

"The Beechams invited me," she answered stiffly, wishing that she were anywhere but here, sharing a table with these two men.

"It would appear that there are many things you don't know about one another." Tyrone's crystal gaze ranged back and forth between them. "Yet you have so much in common. For instance, signora, did you know that your husband and I have been searching for years for a man by the name of MacCloud?"

"He—what?" Startled, Philadelphia looked at Eduardo but he did not even spare her a glance. He was staring at Tyrone.

"Don't."

"Then you tell her," Tyrone answered, making no effort to conceal his malicious glee.

"Yes, tell me." Philadelphia reached out to touch Eduardo's sleeve. "What does he mean?"

"He means to make trouble for you, menina. And if you don't shut your beautiful mouth you will get it."

She snatched back her hand. "I don't like this new attitude of yours. You needn't address me like I'm some sort of—"

"Bought goods?" Tyrone suggested with knife-edge humor. "But we were discussing MacCloud. I understand that you, too, have an interest in this man."

"Yes, I—"

"Don't be a fool!" Eduardo hissed. He turned to Tyrone, his expression deepening into a rage hot enough to provoke his friend into something that only one of

them might live to regret. "Even you can push me too
far."

Tyrone nodded, his eyes silvering behind lowered lids.
"Anytime, amigo. You'll find me most accommodating."
He deliberately slanted his gaze toward Philadelphia. "I
can help you find MacCloud. Eduardo's told me that you
know he's living in New Orleans. I'll even take you there,
if you like."

Eduardo stood up, nearly knocking over his chair, and
took Philadelphia by the arm. "Come with me. Now."

Willfully, Philadelphia resisted the insistent pressure of
his touch. The expression she turned on him was defiant.
"Will you take me to New Orleans?"

He shook his head sharply. "No."

She looked again at Tyrone, seeing that he was enjoying every moment of Eduardo's discomfort but feeling
impelled by a vow that she had made over a not-yet cold
grave. "Will you take me to New Orleans? Will you swear
it?"

Tyrone nodded.

"I'll be ready by nightfall."

She felt Eduardo's grip fall away, but when she looked
up into his face she was not prepared for his expression.
There was anger, hurt pride, and pity in his face, but
there was also something completely new. Fear, startling
and stark, was etched on his handsome face. For an instant he allowed her a glimpse of himself that she had
never before seen. She drank in the moment, memorizing
without understanding every line of his face, his graceful
powerful body, and the arrogant lift of his head. And
then it was gone, replaced by hard cold contempt. "Not
all men are the fool I am!"

He turned and walked away, and she knew then what
she did not understand the instant before. He had said
good-bye.

She started to rise but Tyrone's hard fingers gripped
her wrist, preventing her from moving. "I wouldn't do

that. I've seen him in that mood before. You'd do well to leave him to his own thoughts awhile."

He was mildly amazed by the intensity of the hatred in the look she turned on him, but he was learning quickly about the passionate nature she hid so well under that veneer of propriety. In fact, the more he looked the more intrigued he became, and the better he understood Tavares's beguilement. She was no momentary diversion for him. She had sunk her claws into the Brazilian for good and all. It was just his luck that she was too naive to realize the full extent of her advantage. And so, that gave him the advantage.

He released her wrist slowly, his lean fingers staying to tease the back of her hand. "I meant what I said about taking you to New Orleans. I'll match whatever Tavares has offered you."

Philadelphia removed her hand from his touch and placed it in her lap. "I can pay my own way. I require your protection, Mr. Tyrone. That is all."

"There's just one tiny problem." He leaned back and smiled. "Sounds like you're hiring me. You haven't asked my price."

She knew better now than to ask him to name one. Thinking more quickly than she ever had in her life, she said recklessly, "You said you are looking for MacCloud, yet you didn't know that he was living in New Orleans until Eduardo told you. That makes no sense, unless he has changed his name and you don't know what he looks like. I think you will take me to New Orleans because I have something you want."

"What would you have that I want?"

"An identification. I know what MacCloud looks like!"

Her words so astonished him that he allowed her to rise and leave without even moving a muscle in protest. He stared transfixed as she crossed the enormous dining room, her bustle moving in a graceful tantalizing sway that made him turgid with pure lust. While he had been

taking her measure he had not realized that she might be
sizing him up as well. There was only one thing she had
missed, and that was that he intended to separate her
from his friend permanently. She had agreed to go with
him to New Orleans. Eduardo had heard her say so of
her own free will. Once he had seduced her—and
Eduardo had time to cool off—he was certain that
Eduardo would come to realize what he already knew
about women; the worst of them were less faithful than
alley cats and the rest were too fickle to be trusted with a
man's heart.

He threw back his head in laughter that startled the
nearby tables and sent the head waiter scurrying across
the room to find out the cause of the commotion.

*New Orleans, August 1875*

    *"Allez-vous-en! Allez-vous-en!"*
Philadelphia awakened instantly at the cry, her heart
thumping uncertainly inside her chest. Had someone
called her? Was it Eduardo? For a moment she didn't
know where she was. She lay in a four-poster canopied
bed that was draped in mosquito netting that obscured
her vision. Then she remembered, and a familiar pang of
regret began to pulse through her. This wasn't Saratoga
or Belle Mont. Eduardo's black head didn't lie on the
pillow beside her. She was in New Orleans, with Tyrone.

They had arrived in the city the night before, having
traveled in the last week by train from New York to St.
Louis and then down the Mississippi river by paddleboat.
Without asking her permission, he had brought her here
to his home. Too weary to protest, she had come straight
to this room and gone to bed.

It had been more than a week since Eduardo had
packed and left the Grand Union during the night, without so much as a word or note to her. Caught between
fury and anguish, she had simply sat and stared at the

four walls of her bedroom until midday when Tyrone had come to find her. He had taken the news of Eduardo's departure calmly, but she had suspected from the questions he had asked that he, too, wondered where Eduardo had gone and what he planned to do next.

*"Allez-vous-en! Ventre à terre!"*

She sat up with a jerk, realizing that the shrill cry came from just outside her room, and drew back the netting. The simplicity of the room was in stark contrast to the rich polished-wood furnishings. In the morning light, the whitewashed walls were as spotless as the crisply starched sheets on which she'd slept. The cry came again.

*"Allez-vous-en! Chien mechant! Merde!"* The strange inflection of French veered off into an unintelligible garble.

Who was being shooed away and by whom? Quickly, she slipped her feet into satin slippers and pulled her peignoir over her thin cotton nightgown as she crossed the highly polished hardwood floor. Opening the floor-to-ceiling doors of her bedroom, she stepped out onto the rear gallery and into a world she had never before known.

Below her she saw a brick patio with a tiered cast-iron fountain at its center. The strong morning sunshine poured into the open space. Even in the shadows where she stood, she felt the warm moist breath of the Mississippi upon her skin and the prickling promise of the heavy heat of midday. Along the edges of the patio, deep green shades of tropical foliage cast long leafy shadows onto the pavement and climbed the high brick walls that sheltered the yard. Thick turgid vines snaked up and around the trunks of slender flowering trees. Other plants dipped low under their burdens of scarlet and golden-yellow blossoms. Still others lifted fanwork fronds, like sentinels set about the grounds to fan the breeze. Through the tangle of shrubs and vines and leaves at the back of the garden she could dimly make out the angular walls of other buildings. The sounds of distant chatter and the unmistakable aromas of a kitchen came wafting back across the brilliantly lit patio toward her.

*"Allez-vous-en!"*

Startled by the cry at her back, she swung about to face the intruder only to be startled into laughter.

A large green and yellow parrot in a cage stared out at her from one corner of the gallery. As she approached, he eyed her suspiciously, screwing his head around at an impossible human angle. Gazing at her with one glossy eye he said, *"Grosse bête, va-t'en!"*

She smiled but said quite censoriously, "Who are you calling a great fool, you overgrown sparrow?" She peered in at him, cocking her head to one side and closing one eye to mimic him. "I've a nice straw bonnet that your tail feathers would complement admirably."

The parrot seemed to understand that he had been threatened, for he backed up three steps on the perch and gave an ungodly screech.

"Welcome to the heart of the Vieux Carré, Miss Hunt. I trust you slept well."

Startled yet again, at least this time Philadelphia recognized the voice and knew who she would face. She made herself turn around slowly. Tyrone stood at the other end of the gallery. She glanced at her doors and then behind him to realize that he had entered the gallery from a set of matching doors farther along. Had he been there all along, unnoticed by her, or had her voice drawn him to the gallery?

"Good morning," she said in a carefully neutral tone.

He lounged against the railing, a cigarette held between the thumb and forefinger of his left hand. He wore black trousers and boots but he was in his shirtsleeves. When he turned to face her she saw that the shirt was unbuttoned. Before she could stop herself, she glanced at the hard sun-baked planes of his chest and the mat of red-brown hair curving across his upper chest, and found herself automatically comparing it to Eduardo's darker smooth heavy-silk skin.

She knew the exact moment when she had looked too long, for he reached up to stop a small sweat bead from continuing its passage down his chest and rubbed it into his skin with a slow massage that made her lower her eyes in embarrassment.

He made a sound halfway between a grunt and a hum, a short masculine sound of amusement for something not worth laughter, and stood up. "You'll become accustomed to our unconventional ways, Miss Hunt. New Orleans is an old city." The sound of his footsteps accompanied the rise in volume of his voice as he neared her. "Things happen here that the rest of the country wouldn't even dare dream of. There's the soul of an ancient city here, for those who value pleasure in all its forms."

He stood before her now, and he reached out with the hand that held the cigarette and lifted her chin with his free fingers. "We believe in saints and sinners with equal fervor."

She backed away from his touch but she kept her expression deliberately cool. "I prefer saints, myself, Mr. Tyrone. Now if you will excuse me . . ."

He did not touch her, he simply braced a hand against the wall, effectively blocking her path. "You wouldn't be afraid of me?"

"I might, given sufficient cause," she answered promptly.

He let his eyes roam down the front of her open peignoir to where her breasts were prominently silhouetted by her sheer gown. "You might have cause at that."

She resisted the urge to jerk her robe closed or to try to push past him though she thought he must be able to hear her frantic heart. "You told me the morning we left Saratoga that you would keep your distance. I believed you and you have. If that's changed, then I must leave here now."

He did not lift his eyes from her breasts, more intrigued than he had been in some time by the outline of puckered nipples. Perhaps it was fear, but perhaps it wasn't. He flicked his cigarette over the rail.

She did not expect him to reach for her when he did. For the rest of her life, she would wonder why she did not simply scream. She told herself that it would be foolish, embarrassing, unnecessary. But when his hands closed over her shoulders, forcing her up against the stuccoed wall, she did not even resist.

*"Querida,"* he said in a guttural whisper. He touched her hair softly. There was no softening in the passion that came into the harsh lean face hovering above hers. His savage-bright crystal eyes demanded surrender.

He ran a finger down her cheek to the corner of her mouth where a muscle had begun to tremble. "Soft," he said, watching the color flow into her cheeks. He had not seen a woman blush in her passion in a long time. Whores and married women dissembled but they seldom blushed. He moved the hand on her shoulder down to her waist, and splaying his fingers palm-flat down across the top of her buttocks, he drew her hard against his loins.

"No! Don't!" She began to struggle, but he cut it short by moving his hand from her cheek to her throat and squeezing ever so gently.

"I only want a kiss. Only a kiss."

Too frightened to resist now, Philadelphia stood still as he bent his head to her. Yet a whimper of fear escaped her as he brushed his mouth over hers, and the trembling moved down inside her into her bones. And then his mouth was on hers, hard and demanding, his breath forcing the heat of his kiss inside her mouth.

She kept her teeth clenched against the assault of his tongue but he would not be denied. He caught her chin tightly in his grip, lifted her head back, and sank his teeth into her lower lip. The sharp nip made her gasp and then his tongue snaked inside, filled her mouth, plunging in again and again as he held her tightly against his arousal.

Her hands moved frantically over his chest, pressing, pushing, begging release, but he did not seem to notice. He lifted her up in his arms, bracing her back against the wall as he nuzzled her breasts through the thin fabric of her gown. He found one nipple and drew it into his mouth, moaning in pleasure.

She fought against the torment of his assault, afraid of him and of her own sense of helplessness. Finally, he lowered her and she slipped down his body as his open mouth left a wet trail of passion on her skin until he once more found her lips.

This time his kiss did not demand or punish, it coaxed and praised, persuasively sought to erase the earlier pain and offer only pleasure. He felt her surrender to the moment in the sigh she offered into his mouth and then he simply held her and kissed her until he, not she, needed to be free.

Tyrone raised his head and stared at her as though she were a stranger. Her face was blotched with feverish emotion, her eyes struck wide with fear. There were tear-tracks on her cheeks and a single bead of blood on the full curve of her lower lip. He bent his head and licked it away. Then almost angrily, he levered himself away from her, the weight of his body rising off of hers so that cooling air once more flowed between them.

*Merde!* He had not meant to get caught up in the passion. He was the seducer, she the prey. He never let his emotions rule him, especially not lust. Yet she had kissed him with more honest curiosity than was wise for either of them. Oh, but she was soft, and warm, and tasted of springtime. It had been a long time since he had tasted innocence. He wanted more.

Philadelphia had been too afraid to speak but when he raised a hand to her cheek she flinched away. "Please don't!"

Tyrone jerked as if she had struck him. She seemed terrified, as if she expected him to beat her. Or was she thinking, as he was, of how Tavares would react if he learned of this moment? He reminded himself that she was the reason he and Eduardo were at odds. She was the interfering little whore who threatened their partnership. Seducing her might cost him more than an hour between her thighs was worth. She was here because he had a use for her, but once MacCloud was found, he would cast her off as Tavares should have.

He glared at her, wanting now to hurt her, force her back outside the dangerous emotional zone which she had entered unwittingly. He reached down and shoved a hand between the junction of her thighs and smiled as she gasped at the insult. "The next time you tease me, *querida,* you will pay the full price!" He removed his hand slowly, more reluctant than he wanted to admit.

He moved away, then looked back. "I sleep just there, only six steps from your door." He pointed to his room. "Don't be too proud to come and get what you want." He smiled, the sharp edges of it like ice. And then he walked into his room and closed the shutters.

Both hands shielding her face, Philadelphia stumbled back into the cool room in which she had awakened. The world was suddenly a nightmare. The man she had entrusted herself to was not to be trusted. She had known that. Eduardo had tried to tell her that in his own way, and yet she had chosen Tyrone over him because he suited her purpose better than Eduardo.

She went over to her basin and poured water which she splashed over her face and neck, hoping to wash away the taste and feel of Tyrone. She took a towel and began rubbing her skin, wanting the impression to be erased yet unable to think of anything else. Finally, when her skin was stinging from the rubbing, she sat down on the bed and stared unseeingly at the slats of sunlight measured out on the floor before her.

*She had wanted him!* For a moment, when her reasoning powers had been overwhelmed in some secret, dark, betraying corner of her soul, she had felt an avid curiosity to know what it would be like to lie with Tyrone. And he knew it. She had seen it in his eyes, and he had rubbed her face in her own weakness. He had said that he was a very dangerous man. Now she believed him.

She raised her hands to her face again, hiding her eyes. She told herself that it was only that she missed Eduardo. Her body cried out in bitterness and loneliness for him. Tyrone had known how to tap into the emotions she held in check for Eduardo, and had used her need to his advantage. Yet the desire was slow to recede. It had taken on a life of its own and it was quite beyond her power to completely control it.

She was learning something new about herself as a woman. There was a willful reckless nature inside her that could sometimes get the better of her. It had encouraged her to leave Saratoga in Tyrone's company when what she really wanted to do was wait for Eduardo to return so she could apologize to him. She would not have willingly bedded Tyrone, he would have had to make it rape, and she knew that. But the disquieting thought was there, inescapable, that she had wanted to experience his kiss. Never again would she look on passion with the wholesome eyes of total innocence.

She loved Eduardo. That was the difference. She knew that now. That was why she had said yes to him and would have said no to Tyrone. She loved Eduardo Tavares, and she did not know where he was or even if she would ever see him again.

"You're a fool, Philadelphia Hunt! A damned fool!"

The late-summer sun had set on the bayou city but its heavy, fetid breath hung low and stiflingly on the back streets of the Vieux Carré. Men stood in clusters around open doorways, talking of old times and new days, but mostly waiting for the heat to leave so that they might once again enter their own homes. A few of them smiled and waved at the coterie of musicians walking up the street, their instruments in hand or under their arms. It was Friday night and there was not a single weekend evening in the city when music did not flow from the dance halls of the poor as well as the rich.

"Where's the shivoo?" one of the men called to the passing musicians.

"Up on Canal Street," one of them called in answer.

"It's an American shivoo!" muttered the man who had questioned them, and spat in the dirt by his foot. Since the war, all the big money and houses belonged to the Americans.

Five of the musicians had been formally hired. The sixth had offered his services for free. Because he was new, down the river from Baton Rouge, the others decided to allow him to join them. In the decade following the war, jobs had been hard to come by but things were beginning to prosper again, and common wisdom held that one always shared his luck to make it grow. The American whose home they would play in this night would allow them to fill their bellies at the kitchen table, as well as pay them fifty cents each for six hours of indoor work in a clean shirt.

They believed it was a good omen, having a sixth man, especially one who played the Spanish guitar. Not many *gens de couleur* had been to Europe to learn from the masters, as these five had. Because of that fact, they jealously guarded their professional status in the city; but this man, this Manuel, he had proved by audition that he was fit to play with them. It was too bad about his bad eye, the one he wore the patch over. Still, he was handsome enough not to offend the ladies.

They caught the trolley at the edge of the French Quarter and rode uptown. There was laughter and many jokes swapped back and forth. Only the new man, Manuel, seemed preoccupied by thoughts, but they forgave him that. He was not yet one of them. They agreed among themselves to give him time to adjust.

Only when they reached their destination did they grow unusually somber, their bright smiles dimming and their flashing eyes suddenly dulled. They went straight up the drive and around the back, to enter by the servants' door.

Philadelphia touched one of the gold ringlets by her ear as she stared at herself in the mirror. She frowned, unable to remember exactly what she looked like in her own natural coloring. Brunette, blond, would she ever again be herself?

"M'sieu' gon' like," Poulette said with a broad smile. "He say blond woman make fire in 'Nawlins genmen's trousers."

Philadelphia ignored the comment. She wondered fleetingly when she had become accustomed to being thought a whore. It must be Tyrone's influence, she decided with a bitter smile. The only reason she had decided to answer his note left by her luncheon plate, inviting her to accompany him to the soiree, was because it would give her a chance to meet people and ask questions about MacCloud. "Please get my black evening dress for me. Monsieur Tyrone says it's to be a formal affair."

Poulette shook her head. "M'sieu' done picked de dress, mam'zelle." She went over to the tiny cabinet room and opened it and withdrew a gown of robin's egg blue trimmed in rows and rows of blue silk cabbage roses. It was beautiful but Philadelphia shook her head. "I will wear only my own clothes."

Poulette said nothing, only shrugged and continued to hold the dress.

"Very well," Philadelphia said, "I will inform him myself." She stepped out onto the gallery, crossed to

Tyrone's bedroom before she had time to change her mind, and knocked firmly on the shutters.

He came to the shutters at once and opened them. "What do you want?" His eyes were like disks of silver in the twilight but she saw that he was dressed for the evening in a swallowtail coat and white cravat with pearl studs. His eyes raked her once. "Why aren't you ready? We leave in ten minutes."

"The dress," she said as coldly as she knew how. "I prefer to wear my own."

He smirked. "Wear the blue, damn you!" and he slammed the shutters in her face.

Philadelphia stood a moment in the dark, anger vying with the common sense of using caution where this man was concerned. "I refuse to go."

She waited for the explosion, wondering if he would simply tip her backward over the gallery railing or would seize and rape her where she stood. Two seconds passed. Four. Six. Ten. "Did you hear me?"

She took a backward step as the shutters opened a second time, deciding that she might prefer to throw herself over the railing rather than suffer his violence.

He stood backlit by the lamp in his room, tall, spare, every masculine line rigid. "You asked me to find a man for you. I'm trying to do that. Even you have guessed that MacCloud has assumed an alias. The party tonight is given by wealthy Americans. He may be among the guests. I thought you might want a chance to talk to him before I kill him."

"You found MacCloud!" Philadelphia burst out, regaining her step. "But I don't—I mean, I don't want you to kill him."

He was silent a moment but the air about him vibrated. "I won't kill him for you. I'm going to kill him for my own reasons."

"I don't understand."

"I know. Now get dressed or I'll leave you behind."

Philadelphia hurried back to the room and motioned to Poulette. "Hurry! Help me dress! He mustn't leave me!"

Twenty minutes later Tyrone's carriage turned off Canal Street onto a private lane lined with carriages waiting their turn to deliver their occupants before a large two-story brick home from which lights blazed in every window.

"See if you can remember two things, Miss Hunt," Tyrone said as he sat in the dark beside her. "I am known to these people as Monsieur Telfour. It is my business name."

"What is your business?"

"Cotton. American and Italian. Now shut your beautiful mouth and listen to me. You are to be yourself, Philadelphia Hunt, orphan and my new ward."

"Ward? I'm too old to be your ward."

He leaned forward and grabbed her bodice at the nadir of her low décolletage. "Then I will introduce you as my new mistress. Does that suit you better?"

"It would suit me best if you didn't attach my name to yours in any manner," she answered and lifted her chin. "Why must we play games?"

"I thought you liked games." He ran a finger lightly down between the cleft of her breasts and smiled as she struggled against the touch. "Eduardo does. MacCloud does. For more than a year he's been right under my nose and until you came along, I thought he was dead." He released her and sat back. "It's not often that one gets to kill a man twice."

Philadelphia refused to let him know how frightened she was of him. "Why didn't you recognize him?"

Tyrone looked at her. "I've never seen his face. Tonight will be a first."

"I don't understand."

"You said that before. You're beginning to bore me. No wonder Eduardo kept you on your back."

She breathed a sigh of relief as their carriage rolled to a halt before the house. A black doorman in tails and white gloves opened the carriage door and helped her down. She felt Tyrone's hand on her elbow. "Don't forget who I am or you'll regret it!" she heard him mutter under his breath.

"Oh, I know you," she murmured back. "You're the reason children say their prayers at night."

He squeezed her elbow. "You're closer to the truth than you know. Now let's go find our prey."

# 16

The Garden District house was filled to capacity. The sweltering heat did not keep the guests from wearing their finest. As she entered the residence on Tyrone's arm, Philadelphia noticed that everywhere she looked she saw dresses of satin and silk and lace fashioned into the latest Parisian styles. The ladies were gorgeous but plied their fans with uncommon vigor. Her own dress felt like a hair shirt next to her skin. She remembered her boarding school etiquette that said a lady never perspired. If pressed, she glowed. At the moment, she thought, she must be as shiny as an electric bulb. All the doors leading to the front and rear galleries of the house had been thrown open to give entry to whatever breeze drifted in off the river but it did little good. New Orleans in August was not amenable to style or fashion.

"Come here," Tyrone said as they entered the first drawing room. He pulled her none-too-gently with him toward the marble fireplace that dominated one wall. With fleeting interest, Philadelphia saw that the hearth screen had been removed and the interior filled with pots of flowering geraniums. In fact, the entire room was filled with bowers of flowers and miniature fruit trees fresh from the hothouse.

When Tyrone stopped before a middle-age couple she
was surprised to see him bow slightly but gracefully as he
addressed the man. "Good evening, Colonel de Carlos."

"Telfour! Didn't know you were back," the colonel
greeted. With a broad smile on his face which was permanently reddened by the sun, he shook Tyrone's hand.

"Just returned," Tyrone answered smoothly and turned
to the colonel's wife, a petite woman with flawless skin
and heavy dark hair piled becomingly on her head in a
style more than a decade old. "Mrs. de Carlos." He
reached for the woman's hand and brought it briefly to
his lips in salute. "You are charming, as ever."

The woman's dark eyes shone brightly as they moved
from Tyrone's lean face to Philadelphia. "And you, I see,
have been as busy as ever. Won't you introduce us?"

Tyrone nodded. "But, of course." He reached back to
pull Philadelphia forward. "I would like to present to you
Miss Philadelphia Hunt, lately of Chicago. My new
ward."

The de Carlos's faces registered amazement. The first
to recover, Mrs. de Carlos said incredulously, *"You* have
been awarded guardianship of a young lady?"

"Felise!" the colonel said under his breath with a
dampening look at his wife. He smiled paternally at Philadelphia. "What my wife means is we're surprised that
Monsieur Telfour has taken on an additional responsibility. He's a most busy man, seldom in the city for more
than a few weeks at a time." He glanced up uncertainly at
Tyrone. "I suppose things will change now, with a ward to
be looked after. A niece, is she?"

Tyrone's manner was bland. "The daughter of a recently deceased associate. Of course, I don't take every
charity case." He smiled suddenly with the unholy amusement of one who has made a joke which no one under-
stands but himself. Philadelphia felt it and a glance at the
de Carlos confirmed her suspicion that they felt it, too.
He was toying with them and none of them knew why.

Feeling sorry for the bewildered young woman, Felise de Carlos reached out and laid a small soft hand on Philadelphia's arm. "Would you like to come with me? If you are to reside in the city you may as well begin by being formally introduced."

"That won't be necessary," Tyrone said peremptorily. "Miss Hunt and I are only beginning to be acquainted ourselves. Later, perhaps, she will want to form other associations. You will excuse us?" With a rudeness that brooked no obstacle, he pushed Philadelphia firmly ahead of him as he moved away.

"Well! What do you make of that?"

Colonel de Carlos glanced at his wife. "I'd say that's putting the fox in the henhouse, all right. Unless Telfour is on the road to reforming, that young woman may soon wish she were in an orphanage. Pretty thing, isn't she? I don't think I've seen hair that bright in twenty years."

Felise de Carlos's eyes narrowed. "Neither have I. You don't suppose . . . ?"

The colonel looked askance at his wife. "Telfour's a devil and rogue but he wouldn't bring *that* sort of woman into a respectable home." Still, the skeptical look on his wife's face made him turn to look toward the couple who had reached the entrance to the second parlor where the refreshment tables had been set up. No, he thought. The girl was perfectly poised and obviously well-bred. The trouble would begin later.

Echoing his thoughts his wife said, "With Telfour's reputation with women, he'd better hire a chaperon immediately or soon the girl won't be received anywhere."

Not unaware of the slant of the conversation he had left in his wake but completely unconcerned about it, Tyrone steered Philadelphia toward the first table. "What will you have? You look flushed and I'll be damned if you faint at my feet."

"That's a lovely speech to buck up one's spirit," she answered, resentment of his manhandling overcoming her wariness of him. The ebb and flow of her fear was determined solely by circumstance. "I suppose they assume I am your new mistress. Ward, indeed! You might have done better to tell them the truth."

His gaze struck her but through the filter of amusement. "Choose a drink, *querida,* before I change my mind about how to steady your nerve."

She glanced at the contents of the first table, behind which stood a formally dressed young black waiter. The refreshments were geared toward comfort for the ladies with a rich variety of cool tropical syrups, orangeades, lemonades, orgeats, and barley-waters served from crystal pitchers. For the gentlemen there were several wines, fine West Indian rums and, for the American palate, silver cups of mint julep with shaved ice.

"Lemonade," she ordered. The memory came so swiftly she had no chance to buttress herself against it. It was of Eduardo's handsome face bright with laughter as he helped her with the daily applications of lemon juice they had used to keep her hair bright while in Saratoga. Eduardo! Just the thought of him made her ache deep inside. Where was he? How would she find him again? Did he want to be found?

"Here you are."

She stared stupidly at the frosted glass Tyrone offered her, then looked up. "I don't want it."

For an instant, gazing up into his inscrutable expression, she thought he might pour it down the front of her bodice. Instead, he switched hands, offering her a silver tumbler. "You need this more than I. But drink it slowly."

"What is it?"

"It's whiskey, damn you," he muttered in a low voice. "Drink!"

She raised the tumbler to her lips and took a small sip. The zest of mint leaves mingled with the sweetness of sugar made a favorable impression on her tongue. It was only after she swallowed that the full strength of the liquor bit into the back of her throat, making her gasp.

Tyrone held the tumbler to her lips. "Drink again! Better," he said brusquely when she had obeyed. "That color in your cheeks is what will attract MacCloud."

The color drained out of her face at once. "He's here?"

Tyrone grunted. "He is or soon will be. Make yourself useful by looking for him. Circulate, but don't talk to the de Carloses. You don't lie well enough." He didn't look down at her or suggest where she might go or what she might do, just left her standing alone.

Insulted yet relieved to have him out of her way for a few minutes, she picked up the lemonade that had been poured for her and strolled toward the veranda where she heard music playing. Once she reached the railing she looked out onto the enormous gardens of the de Carlos home. Unlike the Vieux Carré where the inner court-yards of Creole homes were designed in exquisite miniature, she saw that the yards of the Garden District were aptly named. Wide and deep, the verdant grounds contained ancient oaks and bright borders of flowers surrounding walkways and rose arbors. Just below her was the patio where the musicians played. Farther out a huge striped awning had been set up on the lawn, and the steady stream of servants carrying silver-covered dishes toward it indicated that this was where the meal would be served. Paper lanterns had been hung in the limbs of the trees to shed their colorful light on the couples who were dancing on the flagstone walks.

She set her glass aside and leaned her elbows on the railing to listen as the Spanish tune played on. The lively tempo was made for dancing and laughter drifted up to her from the dancing couples trying to keep pace. As her eyes became accustomed to the dark, she saw shimmering shadows reflected by silk skirts among the deeper shades of the foliage at the edge of the garden and knew that some couples had sought seclusion in the privacy provided by the veiling Spanish moss trailing from the tree limbs. Envy thrust its fangs into her. In Eduardo's arms she had known moments like those being shared just outside her view.

The lively music came to an end followed by a scattering of applause and then the tempo changed as a solo guitarist plucked the first chords of a plaintive melody. The notes came softly at first, then deepened with passionate intensity. As she listened, longing swept through Philadelphia as her love for Eduardo, now an indescribable sadness, was lured forth by the fingers caressing the strings. She felt sorrow tug strongly at her as the guitarist strummed it to life with his music, stroking the pain and sorrow into revealing itself. She felt a tear slip down her cheek but she did not brush it away. She was alone at her end of the veranda, alone in the whole world but for the guitarist's splendid and terrible melody of love and loss and isolation.

It came all at once, the revelation so clear and absolute that she didn't even question it. She stood up, turning her head frantically from side to side as she looked for a pathway to the patio below. When she spied the stairwell at one end she moved toward it, oblivious to all else. She lifted her skirts, flying down the wooden steps as quickly as humanly possible.

When she reached the ground floor, her breath came in hard swift gulps but not from exertion. She saw six young men sitting under the overhang of the gallery, their faces shrouded in shadow. Two held violins in their laps, another had a cello, the fourth was seated at a small upright piano, and the fifth embraced a banjo. But it was the sixth man's face she sought as he sat behind the others. But the shadows were deepest there and his was only a vague silhouette of a man in a white shirt. Yet she knew the melody he played, had heard it played before in just such a cadence, and were she to hear it a thousand times, she knew no other man would ever play it in just this way.

She waited until he finished, her heart pounding so hard that she pressed her hands over it to ease the ache. She didn't join in the applause, didn't move from the shadow of the stairwell for fear that she was wrong. Yet she knew she wasn't. He didn't say a word but she heard the other musicians praise him as they twisted about in their chairs to shake his hand.

Finally, the men rose from their chairs to take a break and moved into the lantern light. Disappointment sharp as a blade plunged into her. They were men of color! From rich caramel to the palest shade of honey. She vaguely recalled Poulette clucking with positive excitement as she helped her dress, saying that she would hear the best mulatto orchestra in New Orleans at the soiree. She caught only a glimpse of the guitarist's face with its black patch slanted across a ruined eye before she turned, blinded suddenly by tears, and hurried away.

She walked past the dancers, grateful that she was a stranger and so did not draw their attention. She walked toward the striped awning as if she meant to enter it, only to swerve around past it at the last moment. The garden on the back side of the awning was darker and quieter, the sheeting having eclipsed the lights from the house. She walked more quickly past smooth-leafed banana trees and a tangle of wild roses until the gray-green lace of drifting moss brushed her face, and she entered the azure shadows of a giant oak. Exhausted, despairing, she braced her hands against the rough bark of the tree and rested her face on them to weep.

At first there was nothing but the metallic chirp of cicadas, the distant hum of life, and her own sobs. But then she heard footsteps, muffled by the grass but coming toward her. She did not move, hoping that she was shielded from passersby by the drapery of moss. The snap of a twig made her jump and she pressed herself against the tree trunk, struck with dread by the thought that Tyrone had followed her. She had been impetuous and

foolhardy in coming to New Orleans but he had traded
on her needs and weaknesses to lure her here. For two
days he had seemed only a gesture away from rape. Yet,
after the first scorching kiss, he had not touched her. He
simply threatened and watched with satisfaction when she
cowered. Suddenly, she hated him. If not for him, she
would not be crying because some stranger played as
beautifully the violent passionate music Eduardo had
once played for her.

The footsteps came closer, paused, then resumed as
the soft swish of leaf on leaf sounded at her back. The
hand that grasped her arm was strong and insistent, and
she turned to face the intruder into her sorrow with tight-
faced anger.

"Menina?"

She could not see him clearly but she did not need to.
She knew that voice! "Eduardo!" She flung her arms
about his neck, her tears dampening his shirtfront. She
felt his arms embrace her and something burst inside her.
The pain flowed out, becoming less than nothing as joy
rushed in to fill the void.

"It was you!" she whispered. "I knew . . . and didn't
know!"

Eduardo reached up to touch her face, to feel what he
couldn't clearly see. He had not quite believed his eyes
when he looked up and saw a blond young lady watching
him with forbidden intensity. It was the look on her face
that made him recognize her, the look of passion only he
had ever aroused. And then she'd turned and fled.

Philadelphia lifted her head to look up at his face, but
his features were lost in the darkness. "Why are you
here?"

"I might ask the same, menina. How did you come to
be at the de Carloses tonight?"

"Tyrone brought me." The moment the name was said,
she felt a stiffening in him but then she felt him shrug.

"I should have guessed as much. He didn't recognize me, too, did he?"

"No. I don't think he's been on the patio."

He touched her hair. "We must talk, but not here. Where are you staying?"

Philadelphia hesitated, knowing before she said it that his reaction would be very different from his resignation over the fact that Tyrone had brought her to New Orleans. "I—we have only been in the city two days."

"You're staying with Tyrone." His voice had lost all it's animation. His hands moved down to encircle her waist. "This is a new gown, menina. Does he give you gifts as well?"

The insinuation was clear. She drew back a little, and he did not stop her. "If you had agreed to bring me to New Orleans we wouldn't need to discuss this."

His hands dropped, freeing her. "Are there things we should discuss? I don't think I like the sound of that."

She threw up her hands in defense against his anger. "Don't! Don't make this moment ugly. Please!"

"Very well."

His voice was so cool she shivered as conflicting emotions assailed her. There was joy in seeing him again. There was the need to apologize for having ever doubted him. Yet, there was also a backwater of anger and humiliation that he had walked out on her in Saratoga. The last impulse became the sustaining emotion. "You walked out on me, if you recall. Why should I need to explain to you what the last week and a half have been for me?"

"You've said more than enough. Unlike you, I know Tyrone."

"You—You—bastard!"

She did not see him move but suddenly she was in his arms. His kiss was cool, voluptuous, and brief but devastatingly effective. When he released her just as abruptly, she staggered back against the tree. She heard the soft but cutting edge of his laughter and then the gentle shift of shrubbery as he left her. She took two steps after him, calling his name softly but he did not break his stride.

When Tyrone saw her coming across the grounds a few minutes later, he scanned the shrubbery behind her for any sign of a mysterious escort. Seeing nothing, he came forward to meet her. "Where have you been?"

She looked at his furious expression and took a certain satisfaction in possessing a secret, however bitter, which she would not share with him. "Why, I've been flirting outrageously with everything in trousers. It's no more than what you'd expect, is it?"

He took her by the arm and drew her in so close that she felt his breath upon her face. "Don't push me, *querida*. You may flirt until there's not a limp man on the premises but you go home with me. Understood?"

"If that is your idea of lovemaking, Monsieur Telfour, then I suggest you try another tactic. I am completely unmoved."

His grip tightened but she set her teeth against the moan that came to her lips. "When I make love to you, *querida*, there won't be any doubt in your mind about my ability to move you."

She thought he might kiss her and she recoiled, not in fear but out of an unwillingness to have his lips replace Eduardo's kiss. "Don't," she said softly.

Her defiance annoyed Tyrone. After the kiss they shared, she had expressed only frigid dislike for him. Oh, she was careful not to tread too often on his temper but it was clear that nothing short of brute force would again bring her into his arms. He had never raped a woman in his life. He did not need to. But he was not accustomed to being denied.

His kiss was hard and punishing and, to Philadelphia's mind, mercifully brief before he shoved her away. "Now go inside, stand by the doorway, trip every man who crosses your path if you must to get a look at his face. Do your part, damn you, before I decide to use you for other sport this night."

She understood his threat and hurried across the lawn with a confused sense of elation and dread. Eduardo was nearby. The knowledge made her feel safer. She would do nothing else to provoke Tyrone, but neither would she help him.

She was surprised by how calm she felt as she made her decision. If she recognized MacCloud among the guests this night, she would tell no one, not Tyrone or even Eduardo, until she had had a chance to talk with Mac-Cloud in private. She did not wish to mark another for death, and she believed Tyrone when he said he would kill MacCloud. Perhaps she would tell Eduardo, if first he told her why he, too, sought the man.

She reentered the house by climbing the stairs near the patio, but she did not look down at where the musicians were reassembling themselves after a short break. It was enough to know Eduardo was nearby. He had said that they would talk again, and she believed that he would find her.

Nearly an hour passed before she gave up trying to keep track of the many guests entering and leaving the de Carlos's home and retired to a corner to sit. Her head ached from the heat and her dress clung to her wherever it touched, making her skin itch from perspiration. She sank down on a stool and hoped that Tyrone would soon be ready to leave.

From the corner of her eye she saw a passing gentleman pause when he spied her behind the curtain of palm fronds, but she was too tired to even smile at him. Instead, she pretended not to see him. But he wasn't deterred by the snub. He came straight over to her and lifted back a fern leaf, the better to see her.

"My dear young lady, you shouldn't be hiding your beauty behind a fern."

Philadelphia looked up at the man who addressed her

and froze. Looking at him was like staring down a long corridor into the past. He had the same red hair, though it was now hoary in places from age. She recognized the red cheeks that had made her think of Santa Claus that wintery night so long ago. The same spider-veined nose centered his face, broken so often it looked more like a knob than anything else. She had wondered until this moment if she would recognize him. Now she knew she could not have failed to do so.

"Did I startle you?" he asked as the pretty girl continued to stare mutely at him. "I apologize, I assure you. My name's Angus MacHugh, a resident of this fair city. And who might you be?"

"Philadelphia Hunt," she answered, unable to say more.

He cocked his head to one side and thumbed his ear. "Hunt? You wouldn't be one of the Charleston Hunts, by any chance?"

"I'm a Chicago Hunt."

"That so?" he said mildly. "Don't know as I know any Chicago Hunts."

"My father was a banker."

His pale eyes remained blankly polite as he said, "Well, by all means, I should become acquainted with a Chicago banker. In my business, one can never know too many bankers."

"What is your business, sir?"

"Futures, trading, the stock market, and such. If it rains or it doesn't, if it floods or if there's drought, it's my job to profit from it."

"I see." Philadelphia rose from the stool, wanting nothing so much as to run away, but she did not. It was the moment to confess that she knew who he really was, to make him acknowledge her, and to insist upon learning his part in her father's misfortune, yet she held back, inexplicably afraid. "It's been most entertaining to talk with you, Mr. MacHugh. Perhaps we'll meet again."

"Perhaps," he said with a nod and smile. "Will you be long in our fair city?"

"That depends on my host," she answered evasively.

"Really, and who is your host? It may be that I know him."

"Ty—Telfour, Monsieur Telfour. He deals in cotton."

"Do tell? Then I should know him, shouldn't I? Evening, ma'am. Delighted. Purely delighted to make your acquaintance."

Philadelphia watched him move away, too stunned to do or say anything more. When Tyrone suddenly appeared at her side, she was relieved.

Tyrone had noticed her distracted look from across the room and had come over to determine the cause. "What the devil's wrong with you now?"

"I feel sick," she said in a husky voice. "Take me home, at once."

"It's the heat," he said in exasperation. "It takes some that way. You'll get used to it."

"No." Philadelphia shook her head as he steered her toward the door. "I don't intend to be here long enough for that."

Tyrone glanced down at her but did not say anything for she was clutching his arm so tightly he was afraid she would swoon if he did not get her out of the house immediately.

"I don't suppose you recognized MacCloud?" he said when he had handed her up into his carriage.

She turned a blank gaze on him. "Who?"

Tyrone sat back with a muttered curse. She looked close to hysteria. No point in pushing her. "We'll try again. There are always parties in New Orleans. We'll find him."

Philadelphia stared out into the darkness as the carriage rolled away. She didn't need to look for MacCloud. She had found him.

* * *

She heard the clock chime three A.M. She had lain awake to hear it chime one and then two. Her mind was made up. Tomorrow she would pack her bags and leave Tyrone's house. She had just enough money for a ticket back up the Mississippi to St. Louis, where her cousins lived. But first, she would go to see Angus MacHugh— MacCloud. Tyrone could not stop her. He could not force her to be a prisoner in his home. She would wait until he went out, leave her things behind if forced to. She was afraid of him, but she was more afraid of missing the opportunity to speak with MacCloud.

She heard footsteps on the balcony and held her breath. Tyrone had paced the balcony until after one. Each time he paused before her closed shutters, she held her breath and prayed. But she thought he was asleep now. She had listened in quiet fear as he moved about in his room next to hers, and then she had heard his bed-springs creak a little after two A.M. and knew he had gone to bed. But now he must have awakened.

Footsteps traversed the balcony, no more than whispers, sounds she would not have heard had she been asleep. But she was wide awake, her heart thumping, and her hands clenched into fists. A shadow leaped up on the shutters, and she knew he stood just outside her room. She swallowed a cry of fright, hoping that he would move away if he believed that she slept.

The opening shutter was nearly silent, and then she saw him, through the mosquito netting, silhouetted against the moonlight. This time there was no betraying desire in her for his kiss, or his embrace. Terror choked her while her mind conjured up nearly unbearable images of what the next moments might bring.

He came forward slowly, feeling his way through the darkness. She heard him curse as he stubbed his toe and then he reached out for the netting surrounding her bed. The anxiety was too much. She bolted upright. "Don't touch me, Tyrone! I have a gun!"

She heard his low laughter in wretched surprise. He did not believe her!

"Don't shoot, menina," he said quietly. "I should have trusted you."

Philadelphia leaped forward to tear open the netting. "Eduardo!"

He put a finger to his lips and whispered, "We mustn't wake the master of the house. Move over, menina, so that I may join you."

Incredibly she felt him slide into bed beside her and then embrace her. A dozen questions sprang to mind but he answered them all with his kiss. As she wrapped her arms about him, she felt him pushing up her gown and knew that the words could wait. It seemed far longer than two weeks since they had last made love, and she was as eager as he to make up the loss. Their hands were everywhere at once, working buttons, unclasping a belt, pulling arms and legs free of fabric until they both lay naked in one another's arms.

She had forgotten so much in that short time. She had forgotten just how much pleasure there was to be found in his kiss. It made her smile inside to think that she had been afraid of Tyrone's lust-inspired passion. It was nothing compared to this all-consuming joy, this soul-searing passion that made her body arch in need and her heart beat in perfect time to Eduardo's. He did not say a word to her, nor did he need to. She was with him, as eager as he, needed no coaxing to meet his desire with a fervor equal to his own. Then he finally entered her and she gasped out, "Oh yes! Yes!"

And then the world was encompassed within the space of their embrace. She forgot every thing other than his body surging high and hard on hers, and the perfect pleasure of it.

Long after he spilled his seed into her, Philadelphia held him tight, refusing to give up his weight or the part of him still within her. Nothing could ever hurt her again, she thought, nothing would ever again make her afraid. Eduardo had come for her. She would go away with him, leaving every other consideration behind.

The sudden flare of light in the room surprised both of them but Eduardo recovered first, shifting his body to conceal Philadelphia's as he turned to the intruder.

"I assume my timing's correct," Tyrone said from where he stood by the lamp. He held a pistol negligently in his right hand but that did not make it seem any less menacing. "My door's always been open to you, Eduardo, but you've exceeded my hospitality tonight." He glanced at Philadelphia, his pale eyes like bits of shattered glass reflecting his icy wrath. "I thought you preferred to sleep alone."

"Her sleeping arrangements are no longer any concern of yours," Eduardo answered levelly. "She's leaving with me."

"I don't think so."

Tyrone nodded as he saw Philadelphia's gaze dart from his face to his gun and back. "I might have killed you sooner but I was curious to see if the Brazilian could truly melt your ice." The corners of his mouth lifted without mirth. "Your love cries are most charming, *querida.*"

Tyrone glanced at Eduardo, the thin leash of his anger slipping. Jealousy was a new emotion for him and it stung like a scorpion. For more than two hours after their return, he had lain awake on his bed wrestling with lust for Philadelphia. Then he had heard the footfalls. The audacity of them making love beneath his roof! Only pride had kept him from breaking in to stop them. "You think because she spread herself for you that it proves she loves you? I can prove different."

He shifted his attention to Philadelphia and the chilling amusement in his gaze made her shrink back into the bedding. "You say you love him? You don't even know him. Ask him who ruined your father."

"Tyrone!" Eduardo lunged up from the bed but Tyrone brought his gun up, forcing him to a standstill.

"Don't make me kill you, Tavares. She's not worth it." He glanced back at Philadelphia. "Ask your lover why we've been looking for MacCloud. Ask him who ruined Lancaster. Ask him who wrote that third letter to your father. Ask him if he was your father's enemy."

Philadelphia smiled at Eduardo. "I won't listen to him. I know he'd say anything to hurt us."

Tyrone's voice was a sneer. "Ask him, damn you! He won't lie."

When she looked back at Eduardo, her courage faltered. He was watching her but his gaze was guarded. She looked wildly from one to the other. It must not be possible. Yet the clues were falling into place. Little by little her confidence began to shred. The mention of Brazil, the connection in two letters that she refused to credit because she had fallen in love, came back to haunt her. Her mouth was dry. Her heart felt like a stone in her chest. "Was it you?"

Eduardo flinched as though she had struck him. "Menina, you ask the wrong question. You do not ask me why."

She felt numb, embedded in an iciness to match Tyrone's stare. "The reasons don't matter." She heard her voice as if from afar. Could it be possible that Eduardo was one of her father's enemies? "Tell me the truth. Did you ruin my father?"

A sad smile eased into Eduardo's expression. "How fragile are dreams, menina. I tried to warn you, told you to give up the search, that it would only wound you."

"Hurt you, you mean!" she cried, her anger breaking free of its moorings of love. "You lied to me! You let me believe that you were good and honorable, and it was all a lie!"

"Was it? Even my love for you?"

"Don't!" She raised her hands as if to shield her face.

"Don't—you dare speak that word to me! You betrayed me! And you let me betray everything that matters to me!"

"I will excuse myself," Tyrone said in a voice as dry as sand.

"No!" Philadelphia came to her knees on the bed, uncaring that the action bared her to both men's gazes. "Senhor Tavares is leaving, and never coming back. Never!"

Eduardo did not protest. He bent and picked up his clothes to begin dressing. When he was done he turned to her, and was glad to see that she had gathered the covers about herself once more. "You've worse ahead of you if you don't give up this nonsense. I never meant to hurt you. But I realize now what I should have known all along. I can't save you from yourself. I've tried. *Até logo*, menina."

When he was gone, Philadelphia turned a dull gaze on Tyrone, wondering what he would do but no longer afraid of him.

Tyrone just looked at her. "You're more of a fool than I thought," he said finally. "Tavares was right. You didn't ask the right question. He ruined your father, and I helped him do it. Yet you don't ask why. He's too proud to say it but I will. Your father was a greedy man, and that greed got people killed. He deserved what he got. And, being the sorry yellow coward he was, he killed himself rather than face disaster. Hasn't it occurred to you that if he really loved you, he would've stayed alive to protect you?"

Every word was a slingshot of stone against the fragile shell of silence into which she had retreated. She began to moan, rocking herself in time to the sounds as she clasped her arms tightly about her body.

Tyrone cursed under his breath and walked out of the room. She would be of little use to him if she drove herself mad. As for Tavares, now that he had pushed him into facing the truth, he would have to be on guard.

He lifted his pistol and stared at it a moment as he stood on the balcony in the moonlight. Tavares was the closest thing to a friend he had ever had. It would be a waste if he were forced to kill him, and he hated waste.

He should be satisfied. He had severed Philadelphia's relationship with Tavares for good. But he felt no elation in the victory. In winning he had violated his own peculiar code of honor. He had stabbed a friend in the back.

He holstered his weapon and leaned upon his elbows on the balustrade. For the first time in a long, long while, the gut-sickening suspicion gnawed at him that he just might be every bit the lowlife, son-of-a-bitch people believed he was.

# 17

Philadelphia slipped into the last pew of the dim interior of St. Louis Cathedral just as the six thirty A.M. services began. Because she was not Catholic and did not know what else to do, she knelt and bowed her head as the voices of the choir, singing in Latin, filled the vaulted ceiling.

She had run away from Tyrone's house, waiting only until it was light enough for her to make her way along the unfamiliar streets of the city. She had no clear hiding place in mind but the tall spire of the cathedral had caught her eye, and she had used it as a landmark as she had walked through the narrow streets of the Vieux Carré toward it. It seemed fitting to seek shelter from the devil in a church. And Tyrone was a devil.

She clasped her hands together and shut her eyes. If she lived to be a hundred, she would never forget the ruthless, inhuman delight he had taken in shattering her trust in Eduardo. He had known the full truth all along and yet waited to use it against her when it suited his purpose. She hated him, despised him, and most of all feared him. A tremor shook her, and she clenched her teeth against it. After a moment, she took a deep breath to quiet the residual trembling but it had moved down deep inside her and would not be stilled.

Every moment of the past four months was a lie. From the moment Eduardo Tavares entered her life until now, his reasons for being with her had all been lies, all deception, every moment a masquerade of false emotion and calculated mummery designed to keep her from learning the truth.

*Truth.* The word tolled in her head. What was the truth? She no longer knew which of her feelings and thoughts to trust. How much of what Tyrone had told her could be believed? He was a cold hard man, capable of any deception. He had called her father a greedy man— no, more—the man responsible for the deaths of others. That was absurd. Her father had no violence in him. He was a kind quiet man whose only absorbing interest was the beautiful things he brought home to share with her. The fact that he could afford to amass a great fortune in beauty did not make him avaricious.

Yet deep inside she knew that Tyrone had not lied about Eduardo's part in her father's destruction. Eduardo was guilty, she had seen his confession in his eyes, that same deep black gaze that had seemed to reflect his love for her. Perhaps the greatest lie of all had been Eduardo's. He said he loved her, but how could he? He had hated her father enough to destroy him. Then he had turned his powers of persuasion on her, had made her fall in love with him. Had that been his purpose all along, to make her betray her father's memory in the arms of his enemy?

No, she could not quite believe that. Eduardo had been too generous, too concerned with her welfare these last months. Those first days in New York when she had been terrified, he had been there for her, as Akbar, a quiet ever-present comfort. And then those weeks along the Hudson when he had made her aware of herself as a woman and of the power of erotic love, surely Eduardo could not have faked his desire. Yet, if he did love her, his actions became even more inexplicable. Why would he allow himself to fall in love with the child of a man he despised?

Why? It was the question both Eduardo and Tyrone had chastised her for not asking. What would make a man hate another with such rage that he would deliberately set out to destroy him? Tyrone had called her father a coward, said his suicide was proof of his lack of love for her.

Philadelphia shied from that thought. It was the one suspicion she had not dared. Her father had been a man hounded, besieged, not thinking clearly. He would not have abandoned her, otherwise. Or had he?

The niggling suspicion that there was something she did not know would not be silenced. It clamored about in her mind demanding her full attention. An old memory pushed in on her thoughts, drowning out the cherubic voices of the choir. Christmas of 1862. The year of Mac-Cloud's visit. The glimpse of the beautiful blue Brazilian stone before she was sent fleeing from the library by her father's order. Never before or since had he raised his voice in anger to her.

She took a deep breath, shaken by the depth of the emotion the remembrance roused within her. Yet this time she forced herself to look back on the memory with an adult's awareness. What had caused her father's sudden rage? The sight of the blue stone, she suddenly realized. It was a precious jewel. Even as a child she realized the value of something so large and brightly colored. Was it possible that the stone had caused a rift between Mac-Cloud and her father? But what connection could that have with Eduardo?

She lifted her head in alarm as a gentleman knelt down beside her. Tyrone! No, it was a stranger who had joined her in the pew. He smiled and nodded but she turned away, shaken by the encounter.

She was beginning to understand the power of hatred. She hated Tyrone, would do him injury if it was within her power. Perhaps it *was* within her power! Tyrone was seeking MacCloud. What if she told MacCloud about Tyrone, so that he might escape?

She gazed up to where the sacred ceremony of unselfish love was being performed on the altar, and wondered if God would strike her dead for her thoughts. Certainly it would be an unholy revenge, but it might just cast a devil back into Hell.

She waited until the service was complete before slipping out of the pew and exiting the church. She was surprised to find the street before the church damp from a brief morning shower. Yet even as the clouds scudded past to reveal the sun, the heat of summer eased into the air. With two thoughts in mind, she skirted the puddles on the cobblestones and traversed the street to Jackson Square. First, she must hide from Tyrone, who would no doubt set out to look for her when he realized that she had disappeared. Second, she must find MacCloud.

She wandered down toward the bank of the river, stopping at a street vendor's to buy corn fritters with honey and coffee in a tin cup. The sight of the river had a calming effect on her. No one would think to look for her here, among the mercantile trade along the wharves. Even the rough seamen and riverboat men kept a respectful distance from her. When she stopped at a merchant's storefront to inquire about a cotton merchant named MacHugh, as MacCloud was now calling himself, she discovered that he was well known along the waterfront. Within minutes of the friendly conversation, she had his address.

"Come in, come in, young lady," MacHugh greeted as he ushered her into his office on the second floor of the Royal Street Auction Exchange. "It is Miss Hunt, isn't it?"

"Yes. Philadelphia Hunt," she answered as she crossed the room and took the leather chair he indicated before his desk.

"Well, I'm most honored by the unexpected pleasure of your visit," he continued as he rounded the desk which stood before tall open windows. She glanced beyond him and saw that his view included tall magnolias, and in the distance the golden back of the Mississippi.

"Is there anything I can get for you?" He gestured toward the silver service on the nearby tea cart. "A cup of cocoa? Café au lait?"

"Yes, coffee would be nice," she answered. She gazed around the well-appointed room, noting the mahogany-stained cedar paneling, heavy dark plantation furnishings interspersed with delicate Louis XVI tables, and a superb collection of Chinese porcelains. "I see you are something of a collector, Mr. MacHugh," she said when she spied a pair of Meissen statuettes flanking the fireplace opposite his desk.

"I dabble," he said, offering her the cup of coffee he had poured.

"My father was also a collector. It would seem you have much in common."

MacHugh's eyes narrowed as he continued to smile at her. "You said last evening he is a banker, I believe?"

"Was. He is dead."

"My sincere condolences, Miss Hunt."

She stared at him, feeling as calm and cold as a frozen fjord. "I know who you are. You came to Chicago when I was a little girl. You brought me hard candies, and peppermints, and a doll dressed in a Scottish tartan. Were they the colors of the MacCloud clan?"

She saw him falter. He set his coffee cup down so hard that the contents splashed over the side and wet his hand. Then he recovered, smiling as he patted his hand dry with a linen napkin. "I should have remembered you. It's been some time, Miss Philadelphia. Nearly ten years?"

"Thirteen. Christmas, 1862."

He nodded, seemingly recovered from his surprise. "A fateful time for all of us. The South was aflame with war, its industries in shambles." He favored her with a sentimental smile. "I'm a Southern gentleman by birth and persuasion. Charleston is my real home. A man does what he must in times of conflagration. Your father and I were friends long before the war. We were men of commerce first and last."

He was evading a direct answer to her question but she did not stop him. Sooner or later he would say something that would give her a clue as to how to proceed.

"I suppose you're wondering why I changed my name, just as I'm wondering why you've come here today." He looked away and picked up his cup. "Frankly, there are those who would pay well for the information you possess."

"Because I know your real name? Why would that be of value?"

He glanced at her with dislike that he masked almost at once. "Why? Because the South lost the war, my dear. Victors often brand as criminal that which would have been considered an act of valor had it been performed for the winning side. So, I changed my name and my place of residence. I had a family to think of. My daughter's about your age. I'd lost two sons in the war and every cent I sunk in the cause. I was destitute and heartsore. I'd given up enough without tendering my life, don't you think?"

"You wrote my father a year ago."

He looked puzzled by her abrupt change of topic but his tone was polite. "Did I? Perhaps I did. What of it?"

"I think it was in reference to the death of Mr. Lancaster in New York."

MacCloud began to thumb his earlobe. "So, Wendell told you about that, did he? I wouldn't have thought he had it in him." He looked up sharply. "What exactly did he say?"

She did not answer directly. There were other things she might learn from him before she revealed how little she really knew. "My father committed suicide four months ago with your letter clutched in his hand."

"Damned fool!" he muttered, thinking of his letter. He lifted his hands in apology. "Forgive my rough language, little daughter. But a man must learn to live with his mistakes as well as his triumphs, or the grief will kill him. I was sorry to hear your father sought that method to end his troubles."

"Why would someone want to ruin my father?"

He frowned. "What do you mean?"

"My father was deliberately ruined. He was lured into a scheme to discredit him and destroy his bank."

MacCloud looked genuinely surprised. "Are you certain? Many a bank has gone under when its officers overspeculate. I should know. Speculating is my business."

"Did you take part in the speculation that ruined him?"

His thick orange brows rose three-quarters of the way up his forehead. "I should say not! Had he asked my advice, and he didn't, I might have warned him away from the sort of scheme that could bring ruin. Your father and I were longtime friends and associates. Been together since the late forties. He struck it rich before me but then I struck it bigger than he."

His ruddy face split with a grin. "We were a pair of young scalawags in those days, I can tell you. Into everything and afraid of nothing. Fortunes aren't made by the fainthearted, Miss Hunt. Your father was a regular tiger in his day."

"He must have made enemies," she said quietly.

"Well now, every man worth his salt has an enemy or two." An arrested look came into his expression. "You don't mean to say you think he was ruined for the purpose of revenge?"

Philadelphia removed a letter from her purse and offered it to him. When he had read it with a guarded expression he looked across at her. "Sounds like tomfoolery to me."

She took back the letter. "My father died holding three letters: this one, an hysterical note from Mr. Lancaster just before his death, and yours. Your letter mentions Brazilians and a warning about spading over old graves. Mr. Lancaster's letter mentions retribution for old wrongs. This letter speaks of graves and judgment. What is the connection between them, Mr. MacCloud? What had my father done?"

The man rose to his feet, swearing under his breath as though she were not there, and turned his back on her to gaze out of the window.

Forcing herself to sit perfectly still, Philadelphia waited, dreading yet almost unable to bear waiting for the moment he would turn back to her. He knew something! The hair lifted on her arms and nape. And, suddenly, she knew that what he would say wasn't what she wanted to hear.

He turned slowly from the window, a slight frown on his face. Then he moved from behind the desk and approached a painting on the far wall. The frame was hinged and swung away from the wall like a shutter. Behind it was a vault. He worked the tumbler with the speed of familiarity and then opened it. When he had reached in and withdrawn a velvet pouch with gold cording ties, he turned and came back toward her, opening the bag.

"Hold out your hand, young lady. And be very careful, for it's heavier than you'd expect."

Reluctantly, she complied. He withdrew an object and placed it in her hand. The huge sky-blue crystalline stone could scarcely be accommodated within the cradle of her fingers and palm.

"It's called the Blue Madonna," MacCloud pronounced. "Can you guess why?" When she shook her head, he took her gently by the elbow to help her rise.

"Come toward the window. You need strong light. Yes, stand here. Now hold it up so that it faces you at eye level. What do you see?"

For a moment she saw nothing, only the polished uneven surface of an uncut gem. Then the light refracted beneath the surface of the jewel merged into the ghostly configuration of a woman's face. It was more an impression of features rather than a clearly delineated image. The delicate outline of a woman's high rounded forehead, narrow nose, and gentle curve of chin were radiated back from the depths of the gem, as was a faint aura surrounding the head.

Philadelphia looked up at the man standing beside her with wide eyes. "It's amazing. I see a woman's image."

He nodded, pleased that she was impressed. "That's the madonna of the blue stone; the Blue Madonna. At least, that's what the Brazilian villagers who discovered it call her. Not only is a blue topaz of that size rare, the fact that it's a religious relic makes it nearly priceless."

Philadelphia looked down at the stone. "I remember that you offered it to my father the Christmas you came to see us."

"I offered to sell it to him," he corrected. His frown returned. "I was wiped out, the war on. I was moving my family west and needed money. But Wendell wouldn't touch it. He gave me a few dollars and told me to get out."

"Why?"

He lifted the topaz from her hand and placed it back in the velvet bag before turning a lazy-lidded stare on her. "Don't know as I ought to tell you, without your father here to defend his side. Still, it was a long time ago. It was back in '60. We were in Brazil, in Manaus where the Amazon and the Rio Negro converge. The three of us, Lancaster, your father, and I were there to cut a deal for rubber."

"My father traveled often when I was a child," Philadelphia prompted.

MacCloud looked away a moment, as though wondering if he had said too much. "Well, that's where we heard the story of the Blue Madonna. It was said to be in the possession of savages who lived deep in the rain forest. The idea of possessing the gem just took us over. The three of us maintained a friendly rivalry when it came to collecting rare objects. Even so, we couldn't very well search for it ourselves so we went in together to offer a reward to whoever would bring us the Blue Madonna."

"You hired men to steal the gem?" she asked incredulously, trying to understand that her father had been party to the theft.

MacCloud grinned. "Have you been in a museum lately? They're full of the booty people have carted back from their adventures. *Humph!* What good was the Blue Madonna doing lying in the jungle being worshiped by half-naked savages? A man makes his chances by seizing opportunities, and don't make the mistake of thinking your father was any different than I. Your father owned more than one item I know personally was stolen at his instigation. Why, we had bought and sold our way around the world before you were born. Rubber, gold, silks, copper, tea; we made and lost more fortunes than I care to remember. The Blue Madonna was a mere bagatelle."

"Then why wouldn't my father buy it from you?"

His gaze wandered away from hers. "Sometimes a man loses his nerve. It took two years for the stone to surface in New Orleans. By then everything had changed. The war was on. Men suddenly began to value life differently. Lancaster and your father were Yankees while I was the Reb. Maybe that made a difference. All I know is after looking into it once, your father wouldn't touch it again. Do you know what he said? He said it was cursed. Had he been a religious man, I'd have thought he'd had a vision.

Anyway, he and Lancaster up and sold out their shares in it to me."

"That doesn't explain why someone would have wanted to ruin him."

"There's no proof he was ruined. You're dodging shadows."

"I know the name of the man who ruined him."

MacCloud's indifference evaporated, his pale eyes narrowing. "Who?"

She hesitated, though she did not quite understand why. Tyrone had destroyed her dreams of a life with Eduardo and nothing she had heard here had changed her feelings about that. He deserved no consideration. "Do you know a man called Tyrone?"

She had never seen a man's face alter so radically, the guarded alertness became amazed fury, distorting his mouth and bulging his eyes. "Tyrone?" He thrust his face into hers. "What do you know about Tyrone?"

She took an involuntary step back. "I know that he searches for you, and that he wants to kill you."

He caught her by the wrist. "How do you know that? Damn you! Answer me!"

She winced at the pain his fingers inflicted but she did not back down. "I thought you'd know the answer to that, Mr. MacCloud."

He looked like he might strike her. Instead, he released her with a shove that sent her staggering back against the drapes. "You don't know a damned thing, do you? Oh, you know something, but not much. Did Tyrone send you?" Even as she shook her head, he reached into his desk drawer. "I advise you to tell me everything, Miss Hunt, if that's your real name."

"I am Wendell Hunt's daughter," Philadelphia said with as much dignity as she could summon. "I'm sorry I disturbed you. I'll leave now."

"Oh no." He withdrew a pistol from his desk drawer. "You can't walk out of here, knowing what you do about me. If Tyrone sent you, he'll be waiting for you. Once you've confirmed who I am, my life won't be worth warm spit."

"Mr. Tyrone is no friend of mine," she said with the force of truth.

MacCloud smiled as he saw the flush of genuine anger enter her face. "Well now. You, too, have a grievance against the man. You say you won't further Tyrone's interests. But you wouldn't mind poking a stick in his spokes, would you?"

Philadelphia hesitated. MacCloud was a far different man from the one she had expected. His rages were very much like Tyrone's. "How?"

He waved the pistol menacingly. "The less you know the better. You just take me to Tyrone and I'll do the rest. I've been waiting a long time for this accounting."

She eyed him with great dislike. "And if I won't help you?"

His smile turned ugly. "I didn't tell you everything about the Blue Madonna. From the beginning, your father wanted it more than the rest of us. He doubled the reward when no one would take our first offer. It wasn't until he learned that the men he had hired had killed several Indians in order to obtain the gem that he changed his mind about owning it. He said he saw a death mask, not the Madonna, in it."

Philadelphia felt her world slip sideways. He had spoken the same accusation that Tyrone had used to condemn her father, that he had hired murderers. Why would they both say this . . . unless it was true? "How can you expect me to believe you?" she whispered.

MacCloud looked surprised. "You want to know more? Seven years ago, we learned that the bandits we had hired had been tracked down and murdered, but not before they had been tortured into revealing the names of the Blue Madonna's buyers. Of course, we thought we were safe in the U.S. Seven years had passed since the incident. I'd even changed my name after the war. But then last year Lancaster received a series of threatening letters. When his bank collapsed, he died of a seizure on the spot, so we thought no more about it. But then your father cabled me the day before his bank collapsed, and we knew they had found us. The letter you showed me confirms it."

Philadelphia recoiled but MacCloud pressed her with his words. "Tyrone is the man who destroyed your father. He's after me and maybe he'll be after you, too, when he learns who you are."

"He knows," she said dully.

"God in heaven! Then tell me where to find him before he murders us both."

She was no longer listening. She had gotten the information she had come for, but the answer was bitter, so very bitter. Her father had caused needless deaths and desecrated a holy shrine out of greed. And when he was found out, he had killed himself out of shame and guilt, leaving her to face the world utterly alone. Eduardo had warned her against seeking the truth, had told her she might not want to learn the reason for her father's suicide. Why hadn't she listened to him? Dear God! Why hadn't she listened?

She turned and walked out through the door, heedless of MacCloud's shouts and threats. He held a gun. Would he shoot her, here in his offices, over the exchange? And if he did, would it matter? She couldn't think of a single reason to be alive at the moment.

Yet, she did pass through MacCloud's door. She descended the stairs without being accosted by him, and then walked out into the brilliant sunshine of the Louisiana day.

Tyrone strode through the courtyard of his house and climbed the back stairs with his riding crop still in hand. For hours he had been combing the city looking for Philadelphia only to learn from Poulette upon his return that she was up in her room quietly and calmly packing. He struck his boot top with the whip to relieve a little of his frustration, and then tossed it over the railing. In his present mood, it would take blessed little in the way of provocation for him to use it on her.

He had awakened with a headful of plans for leaving New Orleans immediately, and taking Philadelphia with him. They would go up the Mississippi, to Memphis, or St. Louis. Start over. He had money, plenty of it. He would buy her a house, hell!—a mansion. And then he had discovered she was gone.

He paused on the landing and took a deep breath. Perhaps he had been more angry in his life, certainly with better cause, but he could not remember ever being so moved by his anger. She was more trouble than she was worth. Yet, her disappearance had only made him want her more. If this irrational desire for her was not love, it was as close as he had ever come to it.

He was shocked by the admission. After enduring the torture of listening to Eduardo making love to her, he had lain awake the entire night, aching with desire for her but holding that wanting in check. He was still amazed he had not killed them both.

Somehow she had gotten under his skin. Maybe the turning point had been that moment last night after he had called her father a coward. Appalled disbelief had drained her face of its beauty. She had never been more vulnerable, and he had never been more moved by tenderness toward another.

She was turning his world upside down, forcing unwanted feelings from him, and that made her more dangerous than any bullet. He was beginning to think of a future he had never before desired. For a man who wanted to live was likely to become cautious, to hesitate, and in his experience more likely to die. He had to get rid of this fever, and there was only one way to do it.

He kicked open the shutters to her room without knocking, and they snapped back against the wall with a loud crash. She hardly moved, only looked up without surprise.

The fact that she was not frightened annoyed him. "Where the hell have you been?"

She looked at him a moment in silence as she folded the petticoat she held. "I know about the Blue Madonna."

Her answer surprised him but he did not show it. He did not care who the messenger was. Whoever it was, even Eduardo himself, the news had not prevented her from returning to him, and that was all that was important at the moment. "What do you know?"

Her voice sounded tired, strained, weak. "I know that my father hired men to steal the blue topaz and that they killed innocent people and desecrated a holy place to obtain it."

"And Tavares? What did you learn about him?"

Philadelphia shook her head. "Nothing."

Tyrone frowned. "Did your informant not tell you that Tavares's parents were the people the bandits killed?" At her stricken look, he cursed under his breath. What woman could resist pathos? So then, he would give it all to her. Perhaps the complete truth would rout her remaining feelings for Tavares.

"You should ask him about his scars the next time you see him. Your father's responsible for them." His voice was a sneer. "The bandits raped and killed his mother, then tortured him to make his father produce the Blue Madonna. When his father finally broke and gave it to them, they slit his throat. So there you have it, the story he might have told you, if he dared."

"Dear Lord!" Philadelphia closed her eyes against this new blow.

"You didn't know him at all, did you?"

"I don't think I know anyone, not even myself." She

looked at him without really seeing him. "I went to see MacCloud."

*"Dios mio!"* He caught her by the shoulders. "What did you tell him?"

"That you were looking for him."

He shook her brutally. "Who is he! Tell me or I'll beat it out of you!"

She looked up into his merciless crystalline eyes. "I believe you, but I won't tell you. So kill me."

He released her, afraid once more of his temper. "I hate martyrs! I don't want your miserable life." His eyes turned suddenly strangely dark. "But I do want you."

She did not even struggle against him when he swept her up in a brutal embrace. She did not feel anything as his mouth engulfed hers. Dimly she was aware of her bodice being ripped open, of hard hands seeking her body. There was no fight left in her as he half-dragged, half-carried her to the bed and fell upon it with her under him. She tasted blood on her lips and then his hot mouth was on the skin of her throat, moving lower as he cupped a breast through the thin fabric of her chemise. From far away she heard an urgent voice telling her to fight him, to deny him this easy victory but she was too tired, too weak and sick at heart to heed it. She did not even realize when his heavy body suddenly stilled on hers. She knew nothing until the moment when he gripped her face in his broad hand and shook it.

She opened her eyes to meet his forbidding stare. "Fight me, damn you!" he growled. "Kick and scream, but don't retreat from me!"

"Why?" she whispered wearily. "So you can hurt me more and feel justified?"

He recoiled from her like she had suddenly grown fangs. *It was true.* He did want to punish her for her love of Tavares. He sat up, facing away from her, and pushed both hands through his hair, then wiped the back of his hand across his mouth, all the time swearing methodically and viciously in a mixture of Creole French and Spanish.

With face averted, Philadelphia lay listening to her pounding heart, aware that any movement, any distraction at all might provoke him into finishing the rape he had begun.

"Who is MacCloud?"

She heard the chill in his voice and wondered if he had mastered his lust. "Why?"

He swung around as she turned her head toward him. "Haven't you asked enough questions for one day? You know now why Eduardo did what he did. You know why he wants MacCloud. Don't you think that's reason enough to tell me where to find him?"

"Eduardo wanted to ruin the men responsible for his parents' death. You, too, want to kill MacCloud. Why?"

"If you're expecting me to confide in you a story similar to Eduardo's you're going to be disappointed!"

"Are you a hired gun?"

He smirked and rose off the bed. "What if I am?"

"You kill for money?"

His was the coldest smile she had ever seen. "Sometimes I kill for the pure pleasure of it!"

He saw the horror in her eyes and was glad for it. Her response to his lie made it easier to move away from her, to pull his gaze away from the lovely breasts he had exposed, to leave her as he must. Yet he could not resist asking the question whose answer he was certain he did not want to hear. "You still love him, don't you?"

Philadelphia did not pretend to misunderstand. She looked up into his savage yet strangely compelling face. "I do. Not that it matters now. Eduardo won't be back."

Tyrone felt a burning sting cross his cheeks and wondered at its origin. What was this? Rage? Chagrin? No, no, as alien as it was to his nature, he recognized it. Guilt. Her answer had been no more than he expected. Yet it contained an accusation, a suggestion that he was at fault.

He had known Tavares's feelings from the first moment he had seen them together. Tavares was ready to walk away from their blood oath because of her. He had been furious and jealous; hard admissions for a man of his pride. So he had driven them apart, once in Saratoga and again here in New Orleans. What he had not counted on was falling in love with her himself. If he had left them alone, they might have found a way to overcome the impossible. Though, from his experience, he doubted it.

But she was not meant for him. He suspected love seldom made its bed permanently in the hearts of men like himself. This anguished pain he felt would pass, like a gallstone. Soon he would not remember it at all. At least, he hoped to hell not! Until then, he would cauterize it with the one emotion he had always counted on to keep him alive; hate.

He stared down at her, making his own expression as pitiless as humanly possible. "I'm not going to ask you again, and I don't particularly want to hurt you, but I'm not leaving this room until you tell me MacCloud's new name."

He did not have to reach for her. Philadelphia knew this time that he meant it. "MacHugh."

As he turned to leave she sat up abruptly, trying to gather the pieces of her bodice together. "What are you going to do?"

He turned at the door. "You know, If I were you, I'd misplace that conscience of mine for the time being. It'll make things so much easier for you." He turned and walked out.

The sun was bloodred as it slid below the horizon. Was the color an omen, Philadelphia wondered. She sat by her door, listening as Tyrone moved about his room. She had expected him to go after MacCloud immediately. When he did not, she finally realized why he waited. Murder, even cold-blooded murder, was a deed best accomplished

under the shade of night. Moments before she had heard
him give an order for his horse to be saddled. He would
soon be leaving and, when he did, she would leave, too.

When he stepped out onto the balcony she saw that he
had strapped a gun belt low on his hips. His face was
expressionless, cold, void of human warmth or frailty. She
shivered and hugged her arms though her room was stiflingly hot, drawing back as he moved past her doorway.
But he did not enter or even say a word. He simply
moved on to the stairs and descended.

She heard him whistle for his horse. Moments later,
the sounds of horseshoes rang sharply on the flagstones
as he rode out through the *porte cochère*.

# 18

She waited nearly ten minutes after Tyrone rode out before acting. She put on the hat she had laid out on her bed, tied the ribbons under her chin, then reached for her portmanteau. She had packed only what she could carry and even that seemed too much at the moment. She was exhausted and feeling ill. She had sent one man off to kill another.

"No! I mustn't think that way," she whispered to herself as she lifted her case and walked to the doorway. Escape must be the thing uppermost in her mind.

The courtyard was curiously deserted, and for that she was thankful as she reached the patio level. It had occurred to her that Tyrone might station one of his servants to keep guard over her, but then, why should he? He had gotten what he wanted from her, MacCloud's new identity. She was free to go because he no longer needed her.

She crossed to the narrow door in the gate and opened it. The bell atop it suddenly hopped to life with a merry tinkle. Appalled, she shoved herself through the opening and then ran down the narrow dark alley.

She heard footsteps behind her almost at once but she did not turn to see who might be following her. She ran

past dark gateways and past a private carriage coming up
the alley. She would be safe, she told herself, as soon as
she reached the main street and the protection of other
people. But just as she stepped up on the wooden ban-
quette that provided a raised walkway over the muddy
street, she was caught from behind and hauled back into
the alley.

She screamed once before a hand was clapped over her
mouth, and she was pulled back against the hard wall of a
man's chest.

*"Deus!* But you can run, menina." Eduardo removed
his hand from her mouth, laughing as he did so. "I've
been waiting all afternoon for you to—"

Philadelphia heard the sickening blow that cut short
Eduardo's speech, and then darkness descended as she
was enveloped from behind in a thick brown cloth that
dampened her cries. She fought the arms that gripped
her but she was lifted off her feet, her ankles caught and
quickly bound by a second pair of hands, and then she
was being carried between the pair. They traveled only a
few steps before she heard the snort of a horse and then
she was lifted up. Her elbow caught against the corner of
a hard surface as she began to struggle again, and the
pain was like an electric shock.

"Git her in quick!" she heard a man say close by her
ear, and remembered the carriage she had run past in the
alley. A moment later she was dumped onto a hard surface.

"To the river!" she heard the same voice say and then
she felt the jolt as the vehicle was set in motion.

She was being kidnapped. And what of Eduardo? The
blow she had heard seemed to reverberate in her mind
with ten times its original impact. She tried to sit up as
hysteria shot new strength into her bound limbs. Dear
Lord! Had he been brought along also, or was he lying in
the alley bleeding to death?

A booted foot found the small of her back and pressed down hard.

"Lie still," a gruff voice said. "Won't nobody hurt you."

Too frightened to think properly, she tried to scream but the cloth was thick and the air inside it in short supply. Was this Tyrone's revenge against her? He had threatened to dispose of her if she did not cooperate with him. Now that she had provided the information he needed, only she would be able to name MacCloud's murderer. Perhaps he had left her behind because he had arranged for her death. Gasping for breath, she remembered hearing tales of people who had been bound in sacks and tossed in the river to drown.

Reason pitched over into mindless terror as she released scream after scream. Very soon she felt a dizzying darkness and then nothing.

"She's all but smothered to death, you stupid fool! What good will a dead hostage be to me?"

Philadelphia tried to swallow but her tongue was stuck to the roof of her mouth and every breath she took moved painfully in and out of her lungs. She struggled to open her eyes but her lashes were matted and seemed glued together. She jerked instinctively away from the hand that touched her but when she realized that it held a cool cloth, she held tensely still as it was gently applied to her face. Finally, her lashes parted over eyes that seemed to be filled with sand.

"Good evening, Miss—ah, Hunt? I regret the inconvenience of your journey but I'm in a bit of a hurry."

Philadelphia found herself gazing up into the face of MacCloud. He held out a glass to her. "You'll want a drink. I apologize for the rough handling. Reliable help is hard come by since the war. I trust there are no serious injuries."

Only then did she realize that she had been untied and was free to move. She had been placed on a bed in a tiny

dark-paneled room and covered by a light blanket. She
sat up slowly, not looking directly at him. Her head felt
like an explosion had been set off inside it but she fought
the disorienting pain. "Where am I?" she asked, gasping
against the ache in her throat.

MacCloud thrust the glass at her. "Drink first. You
need it."

They shook so badly, it took both of her hands and the
additional help of one of his to steady the glass enough
for her to take a swallow of water. When she found that it
would go down, despite the rawness of her throat, she
drank a little more and then more until she had emptied
the glass. Only then did she look directly at him. "Why
am I here?"

"You're a guest aboard my steamboat, little lady."

Philadelphia realized the truth of his words in the fact
that the bed beneath her trembled ever so slightly with
the vibrations from the engine room. Hard on that first
understanding came the awareness that MacCloud, not
Tyrone, was her captor. The thought made her no more
safe but it heartened her all the same. Tyrone did not
hate her enough to have her murdered. She turned on
MacCloud a look of disdain. "You've abducted me."

He smiled and shrugged, setting the glass aside. "I regret the necessity, but you gave me little choice. Your visit
to my office this morning came as quite a shock. I
couldn't risk Tyrone finding me before I'd taken out some
insurance."

"I don't know what you mean?"

"Why, I mean yourself. You live under his roof. Oh yes,
I had you followed. Telfour. Tyrone. It struck me as ironic
that we've actually done business together, each in ignorance of the other's true identity. I must say that I admire
his taste in mistresses. He'll want you back unharmed,
and I surely intend to do just that, as soon as I'm safely
out of his reach."

"Abducting me won't protect you from him."

"I certainly hope you're wrong." He sounded genial, almost jovial. "I've sent him a note informing him that you'll be returned when I'm satisfied that he hasn't followed me. I—"

A cry from the deck interrupted him, signaling readiness to cast off. "Ah, we're ready. Excellent. It's quite an enjoyable trip upriver this time of year."

When she did not respond to this, he turned and walked over to the cabin door. "You'll be locked in. Otherwise, you may enjoy the freedom of the cabin. I suggest you rest. You've had an unpleasant shock."

She was a prisoner. Was Eduardo, also? "What about the other man, the one who accosted me first?"

MacCloud's brows rose. "Was there someone else? I didn't hear about that. My, you have had a trying evening. I'll be back to chat once we've left port. You must tell me how you learned so much about Wendell Hunt and his family. You had me going for a while, until I remembered that Wendell's daughter has brown hair. Yours is blond. A tiny mistake but a telling one. Still, I do admire a good performance. When you've rested you may find it to your advantage to provide me with the same degree of hospitality you've shown Tyrone. Until later."

She heard the key turn in the lock but she still rose to check it after his footsteps died away. She had to steady herself as the paddle-wheel boat drifted sideways until the current caught it and the motion smoothed out. Fully alert now in the face of danger, she looked about the cabin for a means of escape. She had lost a shoe in the struggle and when she did not see it anywhere about she kicked off the remaining one.

As she did so, she felt a sharp jab under her ribs on the right side. Exploring the area with her fingers, she found she had broken a stay in her corset. There were also tears in her sleeves and something that looked suspiciously like dried blood beneath her fingernails. With revulsion and satisfaction she realized she had offered her captors quite a fight.

She went to a porthole and looked out but could not see anything on the riverside. The porthole on the dockside had been covered from the outside, and would not open. One thing was certain, she would not sit and wait patiently for MacCloud to return. She needed protection, a weapon of some kind.

Ignoring her aching head, she went through the cupboards of the small cabin one by one, pulling out every item. The clothes belonged to a man. The implication of his last words suddenly came clear to her. They were MacCloud's clothes. The hospitality he spoke of meant sharing his bed.

Angrily, she tossed them about the room, emptying every space. She scattered papers as well, even the charts she found. It was a small defiance in the face of what lay ahead, but it bolstered her courage to be active. When she came at last to a locked drawer in the desk, she found a galley spoon and pried it open without a thought for what the consequences of her actions might be. With a jerk, she pulled the drawer open to reveal a velvet pouch.

Even before she touched it, she knew the Blue Madonna was inside. After lifting it out very carefully, she balanced the weight in her palm as she carried it back to the bed where she sat down. Without opening the bag, she simply held it while wondering how something so lovely could be the cause of so much hatred and death.

Because of the way light refracted through a piece of crystalline mineral many people had died, how many she would never know. Some had given their lives in hopes of protecting it, others had forfeited their lives in attempts to possess it. Her father was one of them.

Philadelphia closed her eyes to bring in close the most painful revelations of her life. Had her father knowingly made an offer that would lead to bloodshed? How could she believe that? He had admired beauty in all its forms.

Nothing delighted him more than a new object of exquisite design; be it a piece of jewelry, or a painting, or a chandelier. Things of legend drew his interest most. He had told her again and again how it had taken him ten years to track down the necklace containing Mei Ling's pearls. He had boasted to her of how on each of his many trips to San Francisco he had offered a reward for even the tiniest scrap of information until, finally, that trail led him to a merchant in Chinatown who owned the pearls.

"Greed is a powerful lure," Philadelphia said softly, repeating part of the legend her father had taught her. "The pearl fisher saw the greed shining in the warlord's eyes, and knew that he had chosen the right lure."

She opened the pouch and slid the Blue Madonna into her lap. The stone lay dark and still upon her skirt, shades of rich blue color undulating beneath its surface as the cabin light played upon it. Those dark depths hid the mysterious face but could not mute the beauty of the perfect gem. This had been the lure, the forbidden prize her father could not resist owning.

*Pride was the warlord's greatest sin. And so, the monster of the deep took him, a treacherous riptide that not even the warlord could defeat.*

In his selfish determination to own this jewel, her father had set in motion the riptide of events that had overtaken him in the end. His weakness had been the compulsive need to possess beautiful things, and he had traded on the weakness of greed in other men to obtain his goal. He could not have known the thieves would commit murder for his reward, but if MacCloud were to be believed, he had seen his own guilt when he first looked upon the gem. No wonder he could not keep it. Like the pearl fisher's catch, the Blue Madonna had brought some men their hearts' desire while others found destruction.

She put the stone away, no longer able to bear the sight of it. She would never be persuaded that her father was an evil man. He had been too gentle in his life and too joyous in his sharing of his love of beauty with her. Yet she could accept that he had become reckless in his methods and that the crosscurrents of events had swamped his judgment in the end. Perhaps he had thought that by dying he was putting an end to it. Yet he could not have known that the final cost would be hers, that his legacy would cost her the loss of the only other man she had ever loved, Eduardo Tavares.

She did not know how long she sat lost in that contemplation, perhaps she even dozed with her eyes open, but suddenly there came a series of cries, followed by gunfire. Booted footsteps pounded past her door as she heard MacCloud's voice from above crying orders. The boat lurched, as though shoved by a giant hand, and then began to move again but more slowly, sluggishly.

She leaped across the room to the door which she pounded with fists and stockinged feet as she added her cries to those of the men on board the steamboat. She was ignored for so long that she was shocked when, suddenly, she heard an answering shout from the other side of the door.

"Stand back!" she heard a man cry, and jumped away just in time for the lock exploded as a bullet ripped into it. And then the door swung open and Tyrone stood framed there. "Come on!" he roared. "Eduardo's waiting for us."

Clutching the velvet pouch, Philadelphia ran to him. He caught her in a hard embrace for an instant but then he pushed her out of the cabin ahead of him. "Go to the railing!" he shouted.

As she headed for the rail, she saw that the boat was far from shore, and gaining more speed with every second.

"Hurry up!" he urged as he came up behind her. "Eduardo's going to blow the boiler." He pushed her against the rail. "Climb over and jump!"

She swung around on him, horrified. "I can't swim!"

The announcement distracted Tyrone long enough for her to take a backward step along the deck away from him. And then he saw a man move from the shadows behind her.

Tyrone's reflexes were slowed by the knowledge that Philadelphia stood between him and the man. He reached out to shove her out of harm's way but the action put him at a disadvantage. The boatman fired on them even as she cleared his line of vision.

Tyrone felt the bullet go into his left shoulder like a tongue of fire even as his own shot brought the man down. He heard Philadelphia scream as he staggered forward, then the first explosion shook the deck.

"Over the side!" he roared and again pushed her up against the rail. "Jump, damn it!"

Philadelphia clung to him as he threw a leg over the top of the railing but when he leaned forward to tumble headfirst into the river, she jerked free of his embrace, panicked beyond reason by the thought of that dark water closing over her head.

A second explosion buckled the deck under her, and she fell to her knees, still clutching the pouch. Then she saw MacCloud coming toward her. He was shouting at her and pointing a gun. Behind him the world seemed to have caught fire. From the hole in the deck caused by the explosion in the boiler room below, flares of flame shot high into the nighttime sky.

MacCloud was on her in an instant, grabbing her by the hair to drag her to her feet. "Give me that pouch!"

She twisted away from him, kicking and swinging the heavy stone at him like a weapon. He yelped as the stone struck a painful blow to his temple but he did not let her go. He pulled viciously at her hair until she thought it would come out by the roots.

"Damn bitch! Give it to me!" he growled close to her ear.

Philadelphia gasped in pain and swung the pouch a

second time, this time high over her head. "Let go or I'll
toss it overboard, I swear!" she cried.

Suddenly cold metal pressed into her left temple. "Do
that and I'll kill you."

"MacCloud!"

Philadelphia felt MacCloud stiffen, and she did as well
for that voice was well known to her. Ignoring the threat
of the barrel, she twisted around to see Eduardo standing
on the deck ten feet from them.

MacCloud released her hair to grab her about the
neck, pulling her before him like a shield as he shoved his
pistol into her already sore ribs. "Let me pass, or I'll kill
her!"

Eduardo stared at him. "Then you'd give me no alternative but to kill you. Let her go, MacCloud, and I might
just let you live!"

MacCloud dragged Philadelphia back against the railing, calculating his chances if he were to jump overboard
with her.

Realizing what he meant to do, Philadelphia began to
fight him, heedless of the danger presented by his pistol.
"Don't! I can't swim! Don't push me!"

MacCloud smiled. "You hear that? The girl can't swim!
If I toss her in, she'll drown. Back off."

"Go to hell!" came the answer.

The third and biggest explosion knocked Philadelphia
off her feet. For an instant she was airborne, pelted by
the shattered bits of wood tossed up by the blast, and
then she was falling through the flame and darkness. Finally the warm flood of the Mississippi closed over her
head.

She did not scream. She could not. The wet grip of the
river was pulling her down and down and down into its
oily blackness. Something snagged her skirt and she
stopped sinking. With clawing hands she sought the surface, and air. The river water rushed past her face as the
need to breathe became of overriding importance. She

fought the urge until her lungs ached and her diaphragm began to convulse, and then she lost the battle.

The first mouthful of water made her choke and then, miraculously, her head popped through the surface and the night air struck her face. She gulped it in, greedy for what she knew would likely be her last breath.

Frantic not to be submerged again, she scrambled wildly to grab hold of something that bumped her shoulder in the darkness.

"Easy, menina! You're going to drown us both!"

The warm friendly voice close by her ear had never been more welcome. She turned instinctively in the dark water to embrace Eduardo.

She had not drowned! It seemed a miracle.

Eduardo had saved her, dragging her from the muddy river. She did not remember much after that, only the sight of the conflagration of the steamboat that burned like a lantern on the black waters. And, a little later, the voices of those on shore who had come to aid in the rescue.

It was now after dawn. She had awakened moments before and found herself once again in the bedroom she had slept in as Tyrone's guest. Tyrone must be dead. She had seen the blood spreading across his shirtfront in those brief moments before he had plunged headfirst into the river. Her fault. She shut her eyes in anguish.

"Menina?"

Philadelphia turned her head to find Eduardo bending over her. Her joy was pure and bone deep, but it did not last. Looking up into his handsome face she remembered every moment of the past twenty-four hours, and how wrong she had been about him, about her father, about everything. Ashamed, she looked away.

Eduardo reached out and gently slid a finger along her jawline. "What is this? Are you still angry with me?"

"Oh no." Philadelphia turned back to him, trying not

to react to the mere brush of his fingertips along the upper swell of her breast. "I know the truth, Eduardo. Tyrone told me everything."

"Everything?" She heard no condemnation in his voice as he said, "What is that, I wonder?"

"I know about the Blue Madonna. And your parents." She nearly touched his hand when it stilled on her shoulder but refrained. She felt unworthy. "And about your scars. I—I am sorry, so so—" She could not finish for the constriction of emotion that suddenly swelled closed her throat.

His dark eyes seemed to draw her in, to offer deepest comfort. "You have nothing to be sorry for, menina."

How kind he was, she thought, and strong and good. How would she ever be able to live without him? "I know my father was responsible for what happened to your family. You—" Her voice broke once more but she continued when she saw pity enter his expression. "You were right to hate him."

He touched her face again but she flinched. He dropped his hand. "Menina, it never had anything to do with us. You must believe me."

She shook her head miserably. "You can't mean that. I know how I feel. I think I hate him a little myself." She tried not to cry but the tears seemed to have a will of their own, freeing themselves one by one to slide over the curves of her cheeks. "I want to go back to Chicago. Alone."

"Would you have me follow you as I followed you around the city yesterday? I don't think so."

She looked up at him again. "You followed me?"

"You didn't think I'd leave you unprotected with Tyrone, did you? After I left your bed I waited in the alley until daybreak, when I saw you coming down the stairs. I wondered where you were going at dawn so I followed you." He smiled. "Mass, menina? And, later, why did you go the exchange?"

"I went to see MacCloud."

"Mac—? *Deus!* How did you find him?"

"He goes by the name Angus MacHugh. But how did you know where to find me? I thought the blow to your head might have killed you."

Eduardo ran a hand roughly through his black curls. "This head has suffered worse. Tyrone found me staggering in the alley soon after you were taken." He smiled a dimple into being. "We weren't very polite to the messenger who brought the ransom note. He told us enough for us to guess MacCloud's strategy. A riverboat is not hard to catch when two men are rowing with a purpose."

His expression sobered. "The note did not say you were with MacCloud. Tyrone went to kill MacCloud while I scuttled the boat. *Deus!* We might have killed you as well."

"It doesn't matter now. Did he—drown?"

"We aren't certain, a fact that has done nothing for Tyrone's present mood, let me tell you."

She sat up in surprise. "Tyrone's alive?"

He reached out for her but she again recoiled. Frowning, he deliberately placed his hands on her shoulders and held her firmly. "Gently, menina. It would take more than one bullet to bring Tyrone down. He's in pain and half-drunk on whiskey, but then he's never been one to revel in his pleasures. I had to threaten to tie him to his bed to keep him from riding north along the river, just in case MacCloud survived to crawl away in the darkness."

"I told MacCloud about Tyrone," Philadelphia said dully. "I would have been responsible if he had died."

He cursed and shook her none-too-gently. *"Deus!* You are more burdened by your conscience than any saint." And then he pulled her close, folding her within his hard embrace so that she was forced to rest her head against his chest.

She heard his heartbeat beneath her ear and inhaled the unique masculine scent of his skin. Every ounce of her body reacted to his touch, to the safety and security presented by his physical reality. In this moment, there was nothing else she would ever have asked of life. Why then could she not hang on to it, she thought in quiet desperation.

Eduardo sensed her despair, understood her pain better than she realized. But he was also jubilant because he knew that pain passes, and behind it there is always the possibility for joy.

After a few moments longer, he pushed her a little away so that she could see his smile. "You performed a miracle last night, menina. I could not believe my eyes when I opened the muddy sack you'd been clutching when I pulled you from the river." His dark eyes were jewel bright. "You found the Blue Madonna!"

Philadelphia absorbed the delight in his expression with gratitude. "It is the piece my father had stolen from your village."

"Absolutely. I have not seen it since I was twelve years old but no one who has seen it once could forget it. Since there had been no word about it in the last fourteen years, I assumed it had been lost or broken into smaller stones. I had given up hope of ever seeing it again."

She tried to shrug off his hands, wanting to find a way to retreat from him but he merely slid them down her arms to rest them in the bends of her elbows. Seeking refuge from his gaze, she looked down at the strong brown fingers curved over her paler skin. "MacCloud had it all those years. I'm glad I could save it for you. It is little enough recompense for all you have suffered."

Eduardo urged himself to remain patient but her distant voice and manner were beginning to annoy him. "I don't want your gratitude." He reached up and snagged her chin in his fingers to lift her face to meet his gaze. "Don't you see? Without you, without your fearless search for the truth, it would have been lost to my people forever. You have done what you set out to do. In finding the stolen Blue Madonna, you have cleared your father's debt. May he now rest in peace, menina."

Philadelphia gazed at those dark eyes, so full of promise, and denied what she saw there. "If only it were that simple."

"But it is." He nodded slowly. "It is."

I will never forget this moment, Philadelphia thought as she marveled at the happiness on his face. He could and had absolved her of every grievance he had once held against her father. But even if he could accept what had happened, she could not. When she looked at him in love, her feelings were tainted by thoughts of the scars on his back and wrists, and she felt again her father's guilt as strongly as though it were her own.

"What will you do now?"

"Once you are well enough to travel, I want you to come with me to Brazil. I must return the Blue Madonna to its rightful place. After that . . ." He shrugged, the wicked gleam of dazzling sensuality replacing the joy in his eyes. "I am *yours.*"

"No, you must make that journey alone. I have no place in what you must do. Surely you can understand that."

Eduardo could not pinpoint the cause of the reluctance he heard in her voice but he sympathized with the sentiment. "Perhaps you are right. You can stay at my *estância* while I journey inland. You will like it there."

Philadelphia shook her head. "I do not want to travel to Brazil or anywhere else. I want to go home. And soon."

"Then I will wait, until you are ready to go with me."

"No, you mustn't." She reached out to touch him for the first time, her hand settling on the warm skin of his neck left exposed by his open shirt. "You must take the Blue Madonna home. This will never be finished until it is back where it belongs."

Eduardo searched her face, plumbed the depths of her

eyes for an understanding of her real thoughts. "Very well. I am anxious to do this."

"Then leave at once. Today." She smiled to take away the suspiciously anxious tone of her words. "Think of it. There will be great rejoicing. You will be a hero."

Though she could not know it, she had touched on a truth Eduardo had been thinking of himself. "It will exonerate my father's name, as well. The curse will be lifted."

Philadelphia did not ask him what he meant for the resolution in his face could carry him to Brazil, and far away from her.

When he kissed her she clung to him with every bit of her strength. His heat and passion were like embracing the sun, and she knew she would bear the scars of his love upon her soul for the rest of her life.

When he lay her back against the sheets, a groan of pain escaped her. "Oh, love, I mustn't hurt you," he said regretfully. He framed her face in his hands, his thumbs propping up her chin so that he could more easily kiss her. "You are too bruised for me to make love to properly. But when I return, menina, I will make a most thorough job of it. I promise." And then he was gone, his final kiss still tingling upon her lips.

"Why didn't you go with him?"

Tyrone was standing by her bedside, naked to the waist but for the expanse of linen strapping the left side of his chest. He had just waved good-bye to Eduardo, who had ridden out at first light, and he was now in her room for an explanation.

"I couldn't." Philadelphia met his hostile gaze with equal enmity. She had gone as far as the balcony to watch Eduardo leave, afraid that if she went down to his horse, he would see her tears and remain. "How can he look at me and not think of his dead parents?"

"Can you look at him and not think of your father?"

"Yes, of course, but it's—"

"That you are a woman and therefore a fool!" Tyrone finished without a speck of consolation.

His voice sounded strained. Beneath his heavy tan his complexion was gray from the loss of blood but Philadelphia thought she would still rather take her chances with a rabid dog than Tyrone if it came to a fight. He was alive, no thanks to her.

He lowered himself onto a nearby chair with an appropriate expletive and then caught her again in his crystal-bright stare. *"Dios!* Women. You are all alike. He is better off without you. I said so at our first meeting."

"You did," Philadelphia agreed, more wounded than she cared to admit by his words. Eduardo was gone. She had let him go. She was a fool.

Tyrone put a hand to the wound over his heart and grunted. "And you told me to mind my own business." What might have been the beginning of a rare smile tugged at his mouth. "You had more courage then than now, and with far less reason. So, you are a fool."

"Yes, of course," she answered, her gaze sliding away from his.

Tyrone watched her a moment, more in tune with her feelings than she would ever know. Her face revealed every nuance of her emotions, as he had cause to know. Each time he had approached her, he had been able to gauge the exact degrees of fear, distaste, and sexual excitement he inspired. She would never have admitted to the last, and to be honest he knew it was less than the other two emotions. But it had registered with him, and it remained a tantalizing marker of what might have been. Just the reminder tightened the knob of desire at the base of his belly but he clamped down on his lust for her this once. Jesus! This was hard. Ha! *He* was hard.

He began to rhythmically massage the burning pain lodged in his shoulder. What he did not understand was why she had let Tavares leave without her. The suggestion that he could not separate his feelings between father and daughter was unreasonable, considering he had fallen in love with her *knowing* who she was. That left her own feelings to be explored.

"Most women have a fairly high opinion of their powers of persuasion. What's wrong with yours?"

Philadelphia blinked. "I beg your pardon?"

"I said most women who have snared a man of Tavares's worth would not have let him go."

Philadelphia pinkened under his razor-sharp regard. "I was not attracted by his wealth."

"Then it must have been his pretty face. Of course, the women I've seen him with were more impressed by his hidden assets. What's the matter? Weren't you satisfied with his skill in bed? Or was it the equipment? You need something to compare it to, you just say the word."

"You're a rude and crude man, Tyrone."

He nodded. "Only I don't ever lie to anybody, especially myself. You're lying to yourself right now. Hell, if I know what this is about. But if you lose Eduardo, you'll have nobody to blame but yourself." He rose to his feet with another, louder grunt of pain.

Philadelphia noticed he was wearing his pistol slung low on his hips. "Where are you going?"

"To kill a varmint." Once more his voice had lost its animation, his clear gaze again fathomless.

"MacCloud?" she whispered, as if invoking a spell.

He nodded. "He didn't wash up dead on the riverbank. I won't again make the mistake of believing he's dead until I've kicked dust in his face myself."

"Why?"

She thought, then, he would revert to type. His eyes turned icy, his face a study in granite. She braced for ugly words, but they did not come. The ice began to melt, the granite softening into almost tender emotion. "Come with me, Philadelphia Hunt, and I just might tell you."

"I—" She never finished the syllable. He turned and

walked out. Was it something in her expression, she wondered even after his boot steps on the stairs had faded.

Yes, he could have told her. It was fear.

She left Tyrone's residence the next day. While Eduardo sailed into the Caribbean and Tyrone rode north along the Mississippi to look for clues to MacCloud's continued existence, Philadelphia took a steamboat to Natchez where she caught a train heading east toward New York.

# 19

*New York City, November 1875*

"I distinctly remember telling you not to wear that dress again in my presence," Hedda Ormstead said in her most censorious voice. "You look like a dying bat in all that black."

Philadelphia bowed her head. "I'm sorry, Mrs. Ormstead. I will go up and change."

"Change into what, I'd like to know? It's too much to hope, I suppose, that you would change into a cheerful companion. No doubt, you'll come floating down in another gothic horror."

She picked up the bell by her plate and shook it like she hoped to dislodge its clapper. When a footman scurried in a bit belatedly, she pinned him with a hawk-eyed stare. "You took your time, didn't you? Were you sparking behind the cupboard door with my new parlormaid?"

"Oh no, ma'am!" The poor young man turned red as a beet but did not know how to defend himself. The call of nature had come at a most inconvenient moment but he could not very well tell her that.

"If it occurs once more, you're out of a job. I demand

promptness. Oh, how I miss Akbar. Now there was a servant worth his weight in gold!"

She did not miss Philadelphia's wince at the mention of the name but she was determined, once and for all, to exorcise that ghost. The girl had been back with her nearly two months. During the first week she had done nothing but talk about her father, and Senhor Tavares, and a highly suspicious individual named Tyrone. Now Philadelphia could not even bear for the Brazilian's name to be mentioned in her presence without going pale.

After careful consideration, she had decided to take matters into her own hands. Today, for instance, the girl's mourning for her father would be dispensed with. The man might not have been a thief, but from what she gathered from Philadelphia's sketchy explanation, he still had much to answer for in Purgatory. Yet the present was for the living, and it was high time Philadelphia got on with it!

She addressed the footman. "I want you to go up to Miss Hunt's room with the parlormaid and help her remove every bit of mourning drapery in Miss Hunt's closets. Understand me. If she is left with even one black-bordered handkerchief to weep in, I'll sack the pair of you!"

"Very good, ma'am." The footman bowed and hurried away.

"An excellent young man," Hedda pronounced with a sly smile. "You've always had an eye for men in household service, Miss Hunt. Wouldn't you say my new footman is worth a glance?"

"You're being very provoking this morning, Mrs. Ormstead," Philadelphia said quietly.

"And you're spoiling my breakfast. Just look! You've curdled the cream in my coffee with your sour face." She dropped her cup back into its saucer and rose. "That does it! Either you must change, or you must go."

She bent an unkind gaze on Philadelphia's startled expression. "You heard me. One week! I thought when I agreed to take you back that I was hiring a companion to enliven my last days. What I did not expect was a preview of the silence of the grave. Your expression is fit only for the mortuary. Perhaps one of them will give you a job."

Hedda ignored the younger woman's stricken expression. "In the meanwhile, I've set a task for you. Nephew Henry is coming round at eleven. He's back in one piece, thank heavens, after that interminable European tour his mother insisted he embark upon soon after you left New York. Why she thought a series of views from musty castles and strolls through dim museums to squint at ancient art would rid him of his infatuation with you, I can't imagine. But then his mother always was one to connect pain with learning. Recall his riding lessons. Ah well. I've explained a few things to Henry about the reasons for your return, but he's hopelessly confused. Don't attempt to set him straight. Just smile at him and he'll be too besotted to think of questions." Without another word, she left the room.

Philadelphia rose from her dining room chair to go up to her room on the third floor of the Ormstead's Fifth Avenue mansion, but her mind and heart were, as always, thousands of miles away. In the peace and quiet of the Ormstead library, she had read a great deal about the country called Brazil. She now knew the names of the major rivers, cities, and mountain peaks. She could even put her finger on the spot where the Rio Negro and the Amazon converged and knew that somewhere nearby Eduardo had once lived. What she did not know was where he was now.

When she reached her bedroom she waited patiently while the parlor maid and footman collected and removed her mourning attire. The chill of an early winter had found entrance through the solidly built walls of the house. As she changed out of her last black gown, while the maid waited in the hallway to take it away, she found herself beginning to shiver uncontrollably.

She had come to Mrs. Ormstead because she could not think of any other place where she would be welcomed. She could not go back to Chicago, as she told Eduardo she would, because she could not in truth clear her father's name of bank fraud without pointing a finger at Eduardo, and that she would not do. But now she realized that she was a burden even here. She had failed to be the companion Mrs. Ormstead so generously paid her to be. She had tried, but joy was not something to be demanded of oneself. Yet, in recent weeks, even contentment escaped her. She would try harder, she owed Mrs. Ormstead that much. And if trying to please meant entertaining Henry Wharton in the parlor, she would do even that.

She glanced at herself in the mirror. She had not cared about the sudden demarcation of dark roots as her blond hair grew out though it would be more than a year before the new hair would be long enough to permit her to cut off the blond. But, at Mrs. Ormstead's insistence so that she could go about in public, she had resorted to henna to blend the two shades. The reddish highlights were particularly attractive when she wore lavender, as she did now, and the fact lifted her spirits a little.

At the appointed time she heard the jangle of the doorbell below. Henry was certainly punctual. She hoped, with a sinking heart, that he had gotten over his infatuation with her. It would make the next hour so much easier.

She waited for the maid to announce her visitor and then she descended the stairs at a leisurely pace. What would she say to Henry? What should she say? Now that she thought of it, Mrs. Ormstead had not given her a single clue as to what she had told the dear young man. Did he know that she was not Felise de Ronsard? Did he know that her disguise had been part of a scheme to sell jewelry at inflated prices? Did he know who she really was?

She entered the drawing room, as the footman opened the door for her, with a smile of greeting. "Good morning, Hen—" But the man standing with his back to the door was not Henry Wharton. His hair was black and his shoulders . . .

He turned to her slowly with a smile full of brilliant sunshine and seductive shadow. "Hello, menina."

She stared at him as though he were an apparition. *He is no different,* she thought wildly. He had not changed a hair in the months since she had last seen him. He looked as fit and heartbreakingly beautiful as ever. The eyes still held black fire, his mouth designed for kisses. The dimple, that shameless flirtation of nature, lay tucked in his cheek as before. She thought her heart would burst. Blood roared in her ears. She had not allowed herself to think of ever seeing him again. It would have driven her mad.

"Have you no greeting for me, menina?"

"I thought—I thought Henry Wharton . . . was here."

She saw quick humor alter his expression. "And I thought I had driven that man from your mind once and for all. I see I must work harder in future."

As he came toward her she nearly turned and fled, and then he touched her, a hand to her cheek, and she knew that nothing less than death would ever again part them.

"Did you miss me, menina?" She nearly wept at the sound of his voice. "I'm sorry I have been away so long. But there were things I had to do before I was free to come back to you. For instance, you'll be glad to know that the Blue Madonna has been safely returned to her rightful place."

Philadelphia shook her head in bewilderment. He had not left her. She had run away from him, and had been hiding ever since.

Eduardo saw her confusion but he did not try to relieve it. There would be the rest of their lives to sort out the details of the last months. He had found her at last, and that was all that was important.

"Did I say that Tyrone sends you his regards? No, and it's just as well. He is still very angry that MacCloud escaped. *Sim.* But that need no longer concern us. Tyrone has had to leave New Orleans. MacCloud was smart enough to alert the city to his alias, and it seems Tyrone is wanted by the authorities in half a dozen places. Don't frown, menina. Tyrone thrives on opposition. He said he thought he would go west, perhaps to Colorado."

He brushed a thumb lightly across her trembling lips. "Let's talk about us. I brought you a gift."

He reached inside his waistcoat and withdrew a long slender jeweler's box. "Open it."

Philadelphia took the box but her eyes never left his face. "I don't need gifts."

"And because it's true, I'll take great pleasure in giving you many of them," he answered. "Pleasure me, now. Open the box."

Because it was no longer so easy to look into his eyes full of erotic promise, she looked down at the box and opened it.

Three strands of perfectly matched pearls lay inside the satin-lined box; the treasure of Mei Ling.

"For your wedding day, menina."

Philadelphia glanced up and saw what she dared not hope for. He still loved her, after everything, in spite of everything. "How did you come to possess them?"

"I will admit that I didn't know until you told me that they were to be your wedding dowry. But I knew as I listened to you tell the tale of Mei Ling that they meant a great deal to you." He brought both hands up to frame her face with his warm fingertips. "As you mean a great deal to me, menina."

Philadelphia was incredulous. *"You* bought them at the auction?"

"I thought you knew that."

She shook her head, looking down at the pearls once more. "I couldn't abide knowing which of my father's detractors bought them so I didn't watch the bidding. I'm glad it was you."

He lifted her face with his fingers. "You are making me do all the work, *menina.* Have you nothing to say?"

She met his black gaze and felt again the fire, and the love, and the joy that she had thought she would never feel again. "You are wondering why I ran away."

"I know why you ran away." He brushed the tip of one thumb over the fullness of her lower lip. "But you are done with running. *Sim?"*

"How—how did you find me?" Why was he watching her mouth like that, like he would like to take a bite out of it?

"You may thank your employer, though she did not choose the most direct route to locate me. She sent private investigators to find me and I, suspecting them to be agents of MacCloud, avoided them quite well. If I had not happened to surprise one of them as he was going through my luggage in Chicago last week, I might not be here even yet."

He slid his little finger under the curl covering her ear and began rimming its shell. The thrill of his touch made her softly gasp. "Three months is a long time to be without you. I have not slept well at all. How could I, when I can remember how perfectly you fit against me in bed, how your lovely spine curves so sweetly against my belly, and the pressure of your shapely buttocks against my loins makes me eager to awaken?"

He stepped up so close to her so that his lapels touched the rounded curves of her bodice. The fingers beneath her jaw turned her face up so that his breath brushed her lips with his next words. "Tell me what you remember, menina."

"You. All of you."

He kissed her then and she thought her heart would stop from the joy of it. He tasted of exotic music and tropical sunshine, of jungle darkness and lush wild fruits bursting with ripened nectar. Dark rich rivers began to flow within her. Deep and life-filled and urgent currents flooded her.

Finally, the gentle hands that had drawn her to him held her a little away. His bittersweet chocolate gaze was so penetrating that her world ceased spinning. "Have you nothing to say to me even now, menina?"

"I love you."

He played his words against her mouth. "I know that."

"I will marry you."

*"That* is what I came to hear."

He took the pearls from her hands and set the case on a nearby table. "Now come here, menina."

She went with him to the sofa without a thought for their circumstances or for propriety, or the chances of being caught. She was astonished at his ability to rid himself of the essentials, and even more surprised that she let him free her of her gown. And then she was in his arms, his glorious warm copper-skinned embrace, and she forgot that she was in the Ormstead mansion parlor, on Fifth Avenue, and even that it was eleven fifteen on a Monday morning in November. There was nothing but the pulse of Brazilian music in the exquisite power of his love to fill her senses.

He took her to dark and passionate places, showed her jewel-filled midnight skies, brushed trade winds over her skin, and dressed her in his earthy scent.

Hedda Ormstead was not a gambling woman. She had known exactly what she would see when she opened the drawing room door. Still, it came as something of a shock to find her best camel-hair sofa being so freely abused. If she had not already been making wedding arrangements for the past week, she would have been thoroughly outdone.

She shut the door discreetly and set herself before it as guardian. It would not do at all for the footman or parlormaid to know that she was permitting such goings-on beneath her roof. She had trouble enough keeping her staff in order.

Age had its privileges, and one of them was the right to be improper, and imprudent, and to revel in it. And to think, she was actually playing cupid at her age!